Ann Granger has lived in cities all over the world, since for many years she worked for the Foreign Office and received postings to British embassies as far apart as Munich and Lusaka. She is married, with two sons, and she and her husband, who also worked for the Foreign Office, are now permanently based in Oxfordshire.

Bricks and Mortality is the third novel in the brilliant new Cotswold crime series, featuring Superintendent Ian Carter and Inspector Jess Campbell. Ann Granger is also the author of three other hugely popular crime series: the Mitchell and Markby novels; the Fran Varady series and the Victorian mysteries featuring Scotland Yard's Inspector Benjamin Ross and his wife Lizzie.

Ann Granger's previous novels have all been highly praised:

'A good feel for understated humour, a nice ear for dialogue'
The Times

'This engrossing story looks like the start of a highly enjoyable series'
Scotsman

'An intriguing tale, with period detail interwoven in a satisfying way'
Oxford Times

'Enjoyable crime featuring credible characters in a recognisably real world'
Belfast Telegraph

ANN GRANGER

BRICKS and MORTALITY

headline

First published in 2013 by
HEADLINE PUBLISHING GROUP

First published in paperback in 2013 by
HEADLINE PUBLISHING GROUP

1

Cataloguing in Publication Data is available from the British Library

ISBN 978 0 7553 4915 9

Typeset in AGaramond by Palimpsest Book Production Ltd, Falkirk, Stirlingshire

Printed and bound in Great Britain by Clays Ltd, St Ives plc

Headline's policy is to use papers that are natural, renewable and
recyclable products and made from wood grown in sustainable
forests. The logging and manufacturing processes are expected
to conform to the environmental regulations of the country of origin.

HEADLINE PUBLISHING GROUP
An Hachette UK Company
338 Euston Road
London NW1 3BH

www.headline.co.uk
www.hachette.co.uk

To John and Diane Boland
The New Zealand Connection

'Begin at the beginning,' the King said, gravely, 'and go on until you come to the end: then stop.'

Lewis Carroll, *Alice's Adventures in Wonderland*

Chapter 1

Sooner than the fire-raiser might have wished, a crimson haze seeping across the night sky gave warning of flames below. Glowing cinders dusted the rosy cloud with sparkling points of gold like a tiny firework display. Woken by the wail of the fire engines, people living up to a mile away hung out of their upper windows and told each other, 'That'll be Key House.'

'You mark my words,' declared Roger Trenton, 'this will turn out to be the work of squatters. Haven't I said it, time after time? That place was a regular tinderbox, just sitting there, empty, not properly secure, waiting for something like this to happen! I blame the council.'

'Not the council's fault,' muttered his wife, climbing back into bed. 'They didn't go up there and put a match to the place.'

Her husband turned his head in her direction. 'They might just as well have done!' Against the pink sky his wispy hair stuck up in a disordered halo above his glistening, balding brow. 'A high forehead, that's what I've got,' he was wont to say. 'I've still got plenty of hair, but I've inherited a high forehead from my father.'

He was bald, too, thought Poppy Trenton, burrowing down among the pillows. High forehead be blowed! I remember his father being bald when Roger first took me home to meet his family. I should have studied my future father-in-law more closely. If I'd realised that Roger would turn out just like the old blighter, I might've broken off the engagement, there and then. Look at him! He even wears the same sort of pyjamas as his father, striped flannel with a draw cord at the waist, and corduroy slippers.

'Ho, ho, ho!' cried Roger. He raised a hand and shook a triumphant finger at the distant fire. 'Told you so!'

His wife peered over the duvet towards the window where her husband stuck to his station. It was a wonder he didn't start capering with glee. Aloud, she said crossly, 'Even if squatters are responsible for the fire, I hope no one is trapped.'

'Plenty of windows – they'll have got out if they needed to,' retorted Roger. 'Got out the way they got in. None of the windows properly boarded up, you know. Door with a lock a child could probably pick. I've written to the council about Key House, if you remember, several times. You can read my letters yourself. The copies are all in my file of correspondence with the council. It's blighted the landscape, that's what it's done. No need for it, no need at all. A fine old house just left to decay. I told that young fellow at the council, they should get in touch with the present owner and make the fellow do something about it.'

'Gervase Crown,' mumbled his wife. 'He went to live in Portugal.'

'I know that!' snapped Roger. 'Ruddy playboy, I suppose it was never any use expecting him to do anything. Pain in the backside.'

'His father was very handsome,' murmured Poppy unguardedly.

That caused Roger to spin round from his observation post. 'Whose father?'

'Gervase's father, Sebastian Crown.'

'No he wasn't. I went to school with him. There was nothing

handsome about the fellow at all. You do talk some nonsense, Poppy. But he was a good chap, Sebastian, very sound. Never had any luck, though, not with his wife and not with that useless wretched boy. Good thing young Crown left here and took himself well away.'

'Funnily enough,' Poppy began, 'the other day I—'

Roger had already turned back to the window and Poppy let her sentence remain unfinished. Roger would only say it was nonsense. But at the time she really had believed it. And now the fire . . . It was worrying. Perhaps I should ring Serena, she thought.

'Aha!' crowed Roger from the window where, with his comb of pink-glowing hair, he did resemble some demented overlarge cockerel. 'Do you know what wouldn't surprise me a bit? They might find a body in the ashes when the fire's burned itself out.'

'Oh, no!' Poppy, shocked into wakefulness, gave a convulsive twitch and sat upright. 'Don't say that, Roger!'

'Oh, go to sleep, Poppy,' said her husband.

The fire had done its utmost, but Key House was not easily destroyed. It was a stone-built construction dating from the early 1700s. Its first residents moved in while Queen Anne still ruled. The Hanoverians were poised to take the throne on her death, and exiled Stuarts plotted to deny them the prize. Key House saw them and future generations come and go, weathering all storms until now. Its walls were nearly three feet thick at the base, tapering as they rose to less than a foot in width beneath the eaves. It had been roofed with some of the twenty-six sizes of traditional Cotswold roofing slate, each with its own name and allotted position on the roof. They had cascaded into the interior and now lay, higgledy-piggledy, below: long and short bachelors, becks and wivutts. They would be salvaged eventually because they were of value and, if not used to re-roof this building, be used for another.

The rest, oak staircase with turned banisters and ornately carved newel post, floorboards, joists, beams and age-darkened panelling in the entrance hall, study and dining room, was all gone. The remains of the beams were still recognisable; they had been fashioned from ancient tree trunks. They smouldered, badly charred and blackened, broken into irregular lengths. But they still showed the knotholes and the occasional gouge where the carpenters, fashioning them by hand, had scored too deeply.

It was mid-afternoon before it was realised that a body lay beneath the rubble in the area that had been the kitchen, where the remains of modern fitted cupboards hung blackened from the walls. Roger Trenton would soon learn he had been right.

Inspector Jessica Campbell was a late arrival on the scene, in the wake of the grim discovery. She watched the steam and smoke billowing from the defiant shell and felt on her cheeks the heat being given off in palpable waves from the once-mellow blocks of Cotswold stone. Now soot-blackened and still too hot to touch, they, too, were survivors. She put her cold fingers to her face and felt them absorb the warmth and the tips tingle.

It had been a mild month until recently. But over the last couple of weeks winter had announced itself in uncompromising fashion with the strengthening winds and first frosts. The mechanical hedge-trimmer did not venture down this lonely road so the trees and bushes around offered up a dishevelled display of skeletal arms. The fallen leaves piled in drifts and filled the ditches. Any trees still sporting growth did so with an air of defiant apology. It was as if they knew the few shabby scraps of foliage clinging on were no substitute for the reds and yellows of their autumnal glory days, even less the verdant shades of spring to come.

Dry leaves had floated across the neglected lawns of Key House, forming mulch between the tangled blackberry bushes that had escaped from the hedgerows around and invaded the garden. Over years they had colonised it, creeping almost up to the building. The activity of the firefighters had flattened some of the spiny tentacles and the water from their hoses made the leafy blanket glisten. When the human presence had left again, the blackberry bushes would shake off the temporary rebuff and resume making their remorseless inroads. The leaf mulch would moulder down to crumbling brown tilth. If no one rebuilt Key House, the undergrowth and bushes would enter through the gaping holes left in the stonework by broken windows and burned-out doors.

Now the wrecked house seemed of a piece with the withered nature around it. Jess entertained a moment's fancy in which the whole thing disappeared in a riot of tentacles and thorns, like Sleeping Beauty's castle. Her reverie was broken by the voice of the doctor, standing beside her.

'Druggies,' he opined laconically. His name was Layton and he was a tall, stooped, middle-aged man, perhaps not far off retirement. His greenish tweed suit was well cut and made, but old fashioned in style and hung on his frame in a way that suggested he'd once had a more burly figure. As he spoke he was attempting, with little success, to brush a powdering of soot from his sleeve. Finding that he'd created a black smear in its place, he gave a grunt of annoyance. 'You wouldn't believe the number of times they render themselves unconscious and then something like this happens. Oh, well, perhaps *you* would, Inspector! You'll have seen this sort of thing before, I dare say.'

Layton gave her an apologetic nod. His grey hair, worn a little long, became more disarrayed.

For all the loneliness of this minor road, they were not the only spectators. It never ceased to puzzle Jess how people turned up to watch a disaster or its aftermath, even in such a spot. The audience was admittedly few in number. There was a tall, lean elderly man in a waxed jacket, a fringe of grey hair standing up around his balding pate like a halo. Where on earth had he come from? Further away were a pair of younger men of weather-tanned complexion and slightly furtive attitude who were surveying the scene from a discreet distance. Jess put them down as travellers, probably speculating whether it would be worth returning later when all had left the scene, to see if there was anything to scavenge in the metal line.

Nearest to Jess stood a bespectacled elderly woman clad in a woolly hat pulled down over her ears and a bright yellow canvas coat and trousers designed to make her visible on this footpath-less road as she walked her dog. The dog in question looked disgruntled. Its walk had been interrupted. It had no interest in the fire. It was of pug type, stocky in build with bandy front legs, but larger than the breed usually is, hinting at an intruder from another breed in its ancestry. But it had inherited the standard squashed features. Jess speculated that its pop eyes probably always had that resentful expression. Or perhaps it was just an example of people looking like their pets. Certainly the pug's owner looked on fiercely, as if the blaze had been a personal affront.

Layton was speaking again. 'You'll find the fellow who was dossing in there shot up some vile substance, passed out and a candle fell over and started the fire, or something like that. Electricity to the house was disconnected, I know that much. Gas sealed off, too. It's been empty since Sebastian Crown died. His son probably still owns it but he never comes near the place. Shame, really, because it was an attractive old building. There will be needles lying about in the ashes. You'll have to watch out!' he called suddenly, turning away from Jess.

His advice was addressed to the fire inspection officers who stood nearby and those smoke- and soot-stained firefighters who were still at the scene, damping down. They would be coming back for several days on the same task. A fire may appear to be out; but it can spring to life without warning in some hot spot, Jess knew.

'Go right through your boots, those bloody needles,' called the nearest fireman. Everyone nodded.

The charred body still nestled unmolested in its bed of cinders and ash, huddled in a foetal position, face twisted towards the floor. The fallen beams had formed a kind of tent over it and it was uncrushed. The arms were raised and crooked in the attitude typical of bodies found at the scenes of fire, fists clenched in a grotesque parody of boxing stance, as if taunting the crackling flames with, 'Come on, then!' A figure dressed in a protective suit was making a filmed record of the scene from a prudent distance.

'No doubt about that,' Layton summed up. 'He's dead, all right. No need to mess about examining him now, even if it were possible to get close enough. Besides, the remains are probably brittle, likely to snap apart like a biscuit. I wouldn't want to be responsible for that before the body is autopsied.'

He had been anxious not to make himself even filthier, rolling a blackened corpse over and prodding it, burning his hands in the task. Besides, he might encounter one of the discarded needles he'd warned of. Jess sympathised. Layton was not a regular police surgeon called in for such tasks. He was in private practice, but had been the nearest available at the time and they'd turned to him occasionally before. Give the man his due, he had come without demur and had done his job, certifying death.

Perhaps because this was a little outside his usual medical experience, he could not resist speculating a little. 'It'll be up to your pathologist, of course, to decide the exact cause of death and whether he'd been taking drugs. The contraction of the muscles suggests to me he was alive when the fire broke out. But he was probably too deeply unconscious to help himself. There will also be smoke deposit in the lungs, if he was alive. But he wouldn't have known anything about it. He'd have been unaware, mark my words, and the smoke probably killed him, not the fire.' Layton grew brisk. 'I should be on my round. I've got housebound patients to visit.' He put a hand to his untidy grey locks and smoothed them back.

She accompanied him to his car and asked, 'You say you know the family who owns the place?'

The question seemed to surprise him and he stared at her for a moment as if she'd made some social gaffe. Then, perhaps recollecting she was a police officer and this was the beginning of an investigation into a fatal incident, he began a cautious reply.

'I knew Sebastian – the previous owner – as a private patient. Oh, years ago. He's been dead a good while. He was one of my first patients when I came here to practise, that's why I remember him. There are still people who prefer alternatives to the NHS. I was his doctor for twenty years. I can hardly say I knew Gervase, his son. Not as an adult, that is. I knew *of* him. He was away at school much of the time and giving his father the usual headaches. Perhaps the school's doctor treated him for any illness. I never did when he was a teenager as I recall, and certainly never saw him professionally when he was adult. His mother brought him to see me a few times when he was an infant, usual preventive jabs and baby problems. After that, don't ask me what he did for medical advice. He may have registered as an NHS patient with another practice. I don't think I saw Gervase once in my surgery. His father used to grouse about him as people do about their teenage kids.'

Jess studied the smouldering remains of the house again. 'So presumably Sebastian Crown was a rich man.'

'Pretty well off, I'd say. We have a few wealthy residents hereabouts. I understand he made his money out of shampoo for dogs.'

'What?' Jess was startled.

'Not just shampoo, canine beauty products and treatments,' Layton qualified his statement. 'People spend a lot of money on their pets. Believe me, as a doctor, I've known cases where people lavish more care on a dog or cat than on a child.'

'Did Sebastian Crown lavish care on his child?' Jess asked as casually as she could.

Layton paused and began again in a circumspect manner, 'I'm speaking generally now, not about the Crown family specifically, you understand. But everyone accepts that there are problems bringing up a family if you're poor. Fewer people realise how many problems there are bringing up a family if you're rich. No money shortage, of course. But a son, particularly, may feel he's living in the shadow of a very successful father. If the father is a self-made man, then he may, perhaps unintentionally, keep reminding the son that his hard work has provided the lavish lifestyle the family now enjoys. He may be surprisingly stingy when it comes to handing out money because he wants his son to realise that it needs to be earned. I'm not saying this was the case with Sebastian and Gervase.'

'No, of course not,' Jess assured him.

'It's natural for there to be an element of rivalry in the relationship between a maturing young male and his father. In animal terms, you'd call it a challenge to the established leader of the herd or pack, that sort of thing. You probably watch some of the nature programmes on television. The younger man feels he has to prove himself. Sometimes he relishes the challenge and, well, sometimes he resents it. You know, just drops out and refuses to try, a sort of proving himself in a different way – by *not* doing what's expected of him. After he left school Gervase disappeared for about a year, backpacking as they do. I understand he got as far as Australia and discovered surfing. When he reappeared round here, well, he'd got used to doing as he pleased, I suppose. He started getting into trouble, but it's not my business to tell you about that. It wasn't a good situation. Sebastian stopped mentioning him.' Layton frowned.

'What about Mrs Crown?' Jess prompted, anxious this unexpected source of information should not dry up.

'Mrs Crown? Oh, you mean Sebastian's wife. She left them – husband and child – when the boy was very young, about ten or eleven years old. Ran off with another fellow, some people said.' Perhaps to change the subject he added, 'I'll be retiring next year. Times flies.'

Jess thought this over. 'How old would Gervase Crown be now?'

The doctor considered. 'Mid-thirties? He lives abroad somewhere. I don't know why he didn't just sell this place if he didn't want to live in it. Open invitation to dropouts of all kinds to move in.'

'Was it furnished? It's hard to tell at the moment.' Jess smiled encouragingly.

Layton was fidgeting again. The general drift of the conversation worried him. He hadn't meant to linger and chat, certainly not about even an ex-patient, Sebastian Crown. He'd been keen to stress that Gervase Crown had not been a patient, but he was treading very near the thin divide between professional discretion and 'helping the police'. There was a dead body in the wreckage, that couldn't be overlooked. How it got there would be the subject of an extensive inquiry. He'd come here to certify death, nothing more. He was being drawn in more deeply than suited him.

'Oh, no idea! Shouldn't have thought so. If any furniture were left in it, someone would have stolen it by now! I believe young Gervase moved the furniture out or sold it. He probably sold the antiques at auction. I dimly remember some kind of sale taking place. But I've never heard that he sold the family home as well. I think I'd have found out if he ever had. That sort of thing soon gets round. It matters hereabouts if you're going to have new neighbours.'

He'd opened the car door in a purposeful manner. Her source of information had been stemmed. Jess thanked him for coming.

'All part of the job,' the doctor said, cheerful now that he was getting away. 'Pity it's not a murder, I could increase my fee.'

Jess watched him drive off. Like Layton, she wouldn't normally be at the scene, not at this stage and not in the absence, so far, of foul play. But the uniformed officers first to arrive had been called away to a traffic incident on the main road. When the call came in about a body being found, she had been free and she had jumped in her car and come. Now she turned to the spectators. Anticipating her actions, the two travellers had already melted away and she was left with the tall man and the woman with the pug.

She approached the tall man first because he seemed to be

expecting it, and introduced herself. He treated her to careful assessment before he informed her that his name was Roger Trenton. He lived a little under half a mile away at Ivy Lodge. He had seen the red glow in the night sky from his bedroom window at around midnight. 'Lit up the room, like a candle.' He had known straight away it would be Key House.

'Why?' asked Jess.

Trenton grew indignant at her question. 'Because the place has been left to go to rack and ruin and it was only a matter of time before squatters moved in. That, or some yobbo bent on mischief. I have written myself, numerous times, to the council and twice to the owner, Gervase Crown.'

'You have an address for Mr Crown?' Jess asked hopefully.

'No. I've got an address for his solicitors, and I can give you that. I wrote to Crown care of them. I supposed they sent the letter on. I got no reply. I asked Crown what he intended to do and when. That was an excellent property in good order when he inherited it. He lived in it less than six months, then sold off the contents in a house sale – half the county turned up for that! Crown pocketed the cash and took off into the blue, leaving the place abandoned. Man's a lunatic.'

'You spoke of squatters,' Jess said. 'Had you seen anyone around recently?'

'No,' Trenton told her reluctantly. 'I don't see it my job to look after the property if Crown can't – or won't.'

This statement was at odds with his earlier claim to have written twice to the owner about the state of Key House and to have bombarded the council with his grievance.

'Don't think . . .' added Trenton, drawing himself up to his full height. 'Don't take it into your head that I'm here because I'm some sort of ghoulish sightseer! I always take a good brisk walk every morning. Often come this way.'

At this the woman with the dog turned and directed what could only be described as a sneer at the speaker.

'Someone will come to speak to you later, Mr Trenton, if that's all right,' said Jess. 'Ivy Lodge, you say?'

'Straight on that way.' Trenton pointed down the road away from the scene. 'Can't miss it. It's got a splendid old oak tree just behind it.'

Trenton departed and Jess turned to the dog walker.

'Gasbag!' said the dog walker pithily, watching as Trenton's figure disappeared at a quick march.

'You are?'

'Muriel Pickering – and I *do* walk by here every day, with Hamlet.' She pointed at the pug, which turned a baleful stare on Jess.

'You live nearby, then, or have you driven out here?'

'I walk!' repeated Ms Pickering. 'I've just told you so. I'm not afraid to use my legs. I live at Mullions, that's the name of my house. It's down that lane there.' She pointed at a narrow turning just visible some yards behind them. She then directed another scowl towards the vanished Mr Trenton. 'I *never* see Roger Trenton walking this way. Load of rubbish. The only place Trenton does any walking is on a golf course. He was out here rubbernecking. And no, I didn't see any suspicious person or persons, creeping about the place. Yes, there have been tramps using the place occasionally in the past. Not recently. It probably wasn't difficult to get in. I dare say, if you were to take the trouble to go round the back of the house, you'd find a window smashed or a catch broken. Only,' added Ms Pickering, 'no use you trying to check that *now*. Everything will be broken now.'

This was true. Jess made a note of her address and said, as she had told Trenton, someone would be round to speak to her.

As for the travellers, wherever they were camped, it was unlikely they had been responsible for the blaze. They'd have left the area immediately if so. Having sighted Jess, they were probably packing up and leaving even now. If tracked down and questioned they would have seen and heard nothing.

There were people who wanted to talk to the police but didn't know anything. Roger Trenton would probably prove one of those. There were those who, if they did know anything, wouldn't tell you out of sheer contrariness and Muriel Pickering might well fall into that category. Then there were the people such as the travellers who didn't want to talk to the police, whether they knew anything or not. Occasionally, one pearl in a whole bed of oysters, there was someone who actually knew something and was prepared to come forward. Jess crossed her fingers and hoped they found such a witness soon.

One other person had been present, but unnoticed, and had left shortly before Jess's arrival on the scene. Alfie Darrow had set out at first light to check his snares. Alfie was not a countryman, although he'd lived most of his life in Weston St Ambrose. But his grandfather had been skilled in country ways and it was he who had shown his grandson how to make a simple snare. Alfie's grandfather had been the male presence in the family when Alfie was a child. His father had run off when Alfie was in the cradle. There was an ancient rabbit warren extending over a large area in a field on the edge of a copse of tangled native woodland, which formed a border between the single-track lane called Long Lane and the 'rabbit field' as Alfie knew it. Over the years the rabbits had made little paths all over the copse and through the undergrowth, each one leading back to their warren. They were creatures of habit. As they scurried back along these narrow tracks to their burrows, they had to pass under a wire fence half buried in nettles, thistles and dock, and it was to this fence Alfie fixed his most successful snares, just where the rabbits emerged.

Today, when he'd set out, he'd soon become aware of the activity around Key House. The smell of burning hung in the air. From time to time a flame would shoot upward into the lightening sky as some still-remaining beam or upper floorboards of the house fell victim to the remorseless progress of the fire. Alfie concealed himself behind the untidy hedgerow by the road and watched it all, spending the most entertaining and exciting couple of hours he could remember. The fire crew were the real-life action heroes of the computer games that were Alfie's favoured amusement. Uniformed and helmeted, they bellowed instructions and warnings to one another as they played the hoses over the fire, and sent great jets of water into the air. When the burning remains of the upper floor crashed down into the interior, filling the air with a meteor shower of golden sparks, Alfie had to press both hands to his mouth to stop himself whooping aloud with joy. The water fell on to the crackling timbers below and they cracked and spat like cornered wild beasts. It struck the hot stones of the building with a great hiss, and sent up clouds of steam to mingle with the smoke. Alfie's mouth now hung open in wonder. Burning embers flew across the road like rockets. It smelled like Bonfire Night. Alfie continued to watch it all entranced, heedless of his cramped hiding place and the awkward way his limbs were bent to squeeze into it.

Then the first police car had arrived, with two uniformed officers, and put an end to the fun. With the arrival of the law on the scene, Alfie decided it was time for him to go. He was not unknown to the local police and he thought he recognised one of the coppers. The plod would recognise him, if he spotted him, and the next thing Alfie knew, he'd be accused of starting the fire. The police were like that, in Alfie's view, they grabbed the first familiar face and pinned whatever they could on its owner. He could come back the next day to check the snares. He crept out of his den, stretched his stiffened limbs, and set off over the field home. What a story he had to tell. If he'd waited a little longer until the body had been discovered, he'd have had an even more dramatic tale.

Chapter 2

The best laid plans of mice and men seldom work out. Had they been contemporaries, Ian Carter thought, the Scottish bard who penned the words might have had him in mind.

Sitting in his one and only armchair with a mug of instant coffee in his hand, he felt a moment of reflection creep over him. It was very early, only just light enough to see without electricity, and the house was quiet. It was that hour when, for a brief interlude, events weren't rushing by while he laboured to keep up. He had time to think.

He sipped his coffee, which managed to be hot, bitter and tasteless all at once, and considered his life. To start at the top, a really big plan to have gone astray had been that in which he'd envisaged Sophie and himself growing old together, peacefully. Arm in arm, they'd have watched their daughter mature into a poised, graceful and charming young woman. The sort of young woman Sophie had appeared to him, when all was going well at the beginning of their relationship.

That plan had gone out of the window when Sophie met Rodney Marsham. Rodney! I ask you! Not for the first time, Carter asked himself how his then wife could have been swept off her feet by someone so pale, podgy and thoroughly dull; a man whose permanent air of bonhomie Carter found intensely irritating. A man, moreover, whose business interests, undeniably profitable, appeared to Carter elusive, if not dodgy.

'That's the copper in you, Ian,' Sophie had retorted when he'd made this last objection to her, at the time of their break-up. 'You suspect everyone!'

To be fair, she'd accused him of that many times during their marriage and not just at the end of it. He supposed she was probably right. He had not been the husband for Sophie. Things had been going wrong between them long before Rodney appeared on the scene, smiling and looking satisfied with life. Who wouldn't give up a cantankerous policeman who spent his working days contemplating all that made man vile, and came home at night tired and disinclined to party? Why not change him for a cheery, sociable fellow with a golden touch in business matters? Rodney and Sophie were probably made for each other. He should not begrudge them their contentedness. But Millie, that was another matter altogether.

There was a faint clatter and then the sound of small footsteps padding towards the living-room door. It creaked open and Millie's face peered through the crack. Seeing her father sitting there with his coffee, she pushed open the door and came in, hopping across the floor in bare feet and nestling into the beanbag opposite him. She'd put on her dressing gown over her pyjamas, even if she'd forgotten her slippers, and clutched MacTavish to her.

MacTavish was a disconcertingly humanoid bear, acquired on a visit to Scotland in their days as a family. He wore a tartan beret sewn between his ears and a tartan shawl slung rakishly across his furry tummy. He had originally had a plastic buckler and claymore, but Sophie, in one of her anti-war phases, had detached his weapons and disposed of them. It was typical of Sophie, thought Carter, that her contribution to world peace consisted largely of symbolic gestures of that sort. On the other hand, she would organise the occasional coffee morning to raise funds for a charity to help those whose lives were disrupted by conflicts; and he had to admit that probably did more good than waving home-made placards and hanging effigies of politicians. In any case, MacTavish's smile, embroidered on his plush countenance, was hardly warlike. He had a smirk that reminded Carter of Rodney Marsham's.

His daughter had fixed him with a direct accusing stare that reminded him of Sophie. What had happened to the daydream of graceful, charming . . .

'Why have you got up so early?' demanded Millie.

'I didn't mean to disturb you,' Carter apologised. 'I tried to be quiet.'

'I heard the tap running in the kitchen. It sort of groans when you switch it off. You ought to get it mended.'

Yes, that was Sophie's voice all right.

'I'll get round to it,' he said defensively. He had the horrible feeling he'd had this conversation many times in the past with her mother.

'MacTavish heard it too.'

He opened his mouth to argue that MacTavish had, literally, cloth ears. But there was something about her relationship with the toy that both touched him and made him feel guilty. MacTavish had never let her down.

'Sorry, MacTavish,' he said. 'Did you sleep all right, both of you, before I made a racket in the kitchen?'

'Mmn . . .' murmured Millie, her gaze travelling critically around the room. 'Mummy and Rodney are calling in an interior designer.' She spoke the last words with respect. 'An interior designer,' she explained kindly, 'picks out your furniture for you.'

Stung, Carter retorted, 'I can pick out my own furniture.'

'Why did you pick this?' asked Millie with that innocent candidness that renders any question unanswerable.

'I was in a rush. I just needed some furniture. By the next time you come, I hope I'll have got the place fixed up.'

Her visit had not been planned. Sophie had rung up and told him that it was an emergency.

'My school has asbestos in the roof,' said Millie now, obviously expert at picking up thought waves.

'Yes, your mum told me. I'm surprised. I thought all the asbestos had been taken out of buildings.'

'They didn't know about it,' Millie explained. 'They'd got a false ceiling in the hall and it was discovered when the decorators came to paint it. You have to do special things when you remove asbestos. So we can't use the school because we might get ill. They're taking the asbestos away this week. Then we can go back.'

'So I understand.'

'Mummy and Rodney couldn't put off the trip to New York—'

'Millie,' Carter interrupted. 'I'm very happy that you're here. I'd like to see you more often . . . It's a bit of luck, your school finding the asbestos and Rodney having a business trip to New York and – and all the rest of it. It gives you a chance to visit me here.'

MacTavish's black, shiny eyes were fixed on him. His embroidered smirk suddenly appeared more a snarl. *Can't you do better than that?* he seemed to be asking.

'Am I going to Auntie Monica's again today?' Millie homed in on the weak point of his defence.

'Yes. I have to go to work, I'm afraid. We have investigations underway. I could've arranged some leave if I'd had more notice—'

He broke off. 'You like staying with Auntie Monica for the day, don't you?'

'Oh, yes, she's got two cats. You ought to get a cat.'

'I wouldn't be here all day to look after it.'

'Auntie Monica's back door has a cat flap in it, so her cats can go in and out by themselves. So if it's sunny and they want to sit in the garden, they can. And if it rains and they want to go inside, they can do that, too. She's my great-aunt, you know. She's Mummy's aunt, so that makes her my great-aunt. But she doesn't like to be called that because she says it makes her feel old. She is old, isn't she?'

'Oldish. I'll go and make us some porridge; it's just about breakfast-time. Why don't you and MacTavish lay the table?'

'What are you investigating?' asked Millie moments later as she rattled the cutlery in his untidy knife drawer. Ten year olds are not deflected from a topic that interests them, however unsuitable. He was finding that out.

'There was a big fire yesterday, at an old house in the country, an old empty house,' Carter emphasised quickly from his place at the porridge pan. No need to trouble her young mind with thoughts of a dead body.

MacTavish had been propped up on the draining board alongside the stove and was watching him in the way a Scottish bear could be expected to watch an Englishman make porridge. *Listen, MacTavish, I'm not putting salt in it, just to satisfy you!*

'Did someone start it on purpose? Will you find out who it was?'

'I hope we shall.'

'How?'

'I don't know yet.'

MacTavish's smirk mocked him. *Watch it, MacTavish, or I might drop porridge on that tartan pancake on your head . . . and then you'll have to go in the washing machine again!*

'They might have been playing with matches,' said Millie censoriously. 'You shouldn't do that. You shouldn't play with fire.'

'You're absolutely right,' said her father.

After breakfast he drove her, with MacTavish, to Weston St Ambrose where his former wife's Aunt Monica lived. She was a retired primary school headmistress and pleased at having a child around the place again, if only for a few hours.

'Don't worry about us, Ian,' she assured him. 'I have plenty of things planned for us to do. I'll give her lunch and her tea, and then you can come and pick her up tonight when it suits you.'

Carter glanced to where Millie was introducing MacTavish to a pair of suspicious cats. Millie was wearing a white fake fur gilet. It struck him the cats were a tad suspicious of that, too.

'I really appreciate it, Monica. I'd have taken some time off if I'd known.'

'It's fine, Ian, really. Off you go.'

So he kissed Millie and left. MacTavish, manipulated by his owner, waved him goodbye.

I can't communicate with my child, he thought sadly. She probably finds it difficult to communicate with me. That's why MacTavish has been brought along. He's our intermediary.

The reason he had to go in to work today was because Tom Palmer, the pathologist, had conducted his examination into the body found at Key House and was ready to come up with his conclusions. The luckless Sergeant Phil Morton had attended the procedure, but it was Carter and Jess Campbell who later found themselves in Tom's tiny office, down at the morgue.

The pathologist rustled papers and eventually, giving up finding what he sought, scratched his mop of black hair and announced, 'This one was a challenge.'

'Too badly damaged?' Carter asked.

'Badly damaged, certainly. But I like a challenge. Let's see . . . Deceased is male and about thirty years of age. I've got it on my tape recorder but it's not all up on the computer yet. You'll have it all nicely printed out for you eventually but we're short handed here.' Tom gazed at them as if they were somehow responsible.

'We're all of us operating short handed!' said Carter, riled.

'Just tell us,' Jess invited hastily, 'what the cause of death was and whether it's suspicious.'

'Oh, that,' said Tom, 'cause of death was suffocation from inhaling the smoke. That's straightforward enough. Lungs clogged up with soot.'

'Would he have been unconscious at the time? Asleep? Drugged?' Carter asked.

Tom's manner changed and grew suddenly cautious. 'Tests couldn't trace any drugs in him so no, not drugged. The arms were raised in a defensive attitude. I suggest that's almost certainly due to the effect of the heat, not because he was in a fight. Perhaps confusingly, however, in my opinion he *was* attacked shortly before the fire started. The back of his skull is fractured and that *is* suspicious. I don't think that happened in the fire. I think someone walloped him, laid him out flat, unconscious. I believe he was struck at least twice. The first blow might have knocked him to the floor, perhaps stunned him. The second blow would have rendered him completely unconscious.'

'But it didn't kill him,' Carter murmured, more to himself than to the other two. 'Did the assailant think he'd killed him? Is that why he started a fire?'

Jess replied anyway, 'The fire was started at night. The electricity, I was told, was disconnected. If all the attacker had to examine his victim was a torch, he could have believed he'd killed him.'

'Or, having laid out his victim, he could have counted on the smoke and the fire finishing the job,' Carter said.

A moment's silence followed. All three of them were acquainted with the aftermath of violent death. But it was always chilling to face the calculated cruelty lying dormant in the most civilised of men.

'Other injuries?' Jess asked briskly, breaking the moment's introspection.

Tom seized on her question and began to talk quickly. 'Other than the head wounds, there's no sign of trauma from injuries inflicted before the fire that I can find. The body . . .'

The corpse was no longer 'the victim'; it had become 'the body', an object. Tom hesitated as if he realised this before continuing. 'It was shielded, I understand, by the way the beams burned on the outside but remained solid enough not to disintegrate. When they fell they cracked apart, but in chunks, some pieces landing propped on others, making a sort of wigwam over him. So I repeat that in my opinion falling debris did not cause the skull fractures. The wounds are just not consistent with that sort of accidental damage. Both wounds are pretty well textbook examples of a powerful blow with a blunt object, concentrated in a small area, causing a dent in the skull. Some other damage is consistent with fire. The skin has split in places on the body, for example –' he spread a hand dismissively – 'the fire would do that. There are no traces of any substances, legal or illegal, that would have caused him to pass out. He was knocked out deliberately. One thing may help you in confirming his identity. The arm muscles contracted due to the heat of the fire, as I said. But when they did, the fists clenched, protecting the inner surface of the hands to a certain extent. The backs of the hands are badly damaged. The palms, though scorched by hot ash, are less so. The underlying area of skin might still yield a print or two.' He looked up at them. 'Have you had a report from the fire investigators yet?'

Jess shook her head and said, 'From what you say, and from we both think –' She glanced at Carter, who nodded his agreement – 'this fire was almost certainly started deliberately in an attempt to destroy the body and/or other evidence. If the fire inspectors find an accelerant was used that would confirm it. Even without that, we're looking at unlawful killing.' She turned to the superintendent, still silent beside her. 'You agree, sir?'

Carter, too, had become brisk in manner. 'Yes, that's pretty well what the coroner will rule. Then it will be up to us to find the how and why. Thank you, Tom. We'll leave you in peace to write up your findings. Thanks for doing such a quick and efficient job.'

Tom opened his mouth to reply but at that moment his mobile phone rang. He gave them an apologetic glance instead and took the phone from his pocket. Jess and Carter indicated they were leaving.

As they went out of the door, they heard Tom's voice, speaking to the caller. 'Oh, hi, Madison! Sorry I didn't call you earlier as I promised, darling, but I've been rather busy . . .'

Outside the building, Carter said awkwardly, 'Sorry if you and Palmer have broken up.'

She stopped in her tracks and spun round to glare at him, a small, red-headed, truculent figure. 'We haven't broken up because we were never an item. Tom and I have been – we still are – friends! Friends only, right?'

'Sorry again, I mean, sorry for putting my foot in it!' Carter hastened to recover from the obvious gaffe.

She subsided like a boiling pot that someone has removed from the stove. 'I should be the one apologising, sir. I didn't mean to fly off the handle. It's just that, well, Tom and I used to eat out occasionally or go for a drink when both of us were at a loose end. Only Tom isn't free, not any more, not now he's met Madison.'

'That's her first name?' Carter asked incredulously.

'That's it. Tom's a keen rambler and Madison joined his club, or group, or whatever. I know some people got the impression that he and I had a thing going, but we didn't, never did, never likely to.' Jess managed a grin. 'It's been my nightmare that my mother might find out and get the wrong idea. My mother . . . Oh well,' she shrugged, 'families, you know.'

'I've got my daughter staying with me for a few days,' he heard himself say.

Her initial surprise quickly turned to interest. 'That's nice for you, sir.'

'It would be better if we hadn't just found out we've got a murder on our hands. I was hoping to take a couple of days . . . Her school has asbestos in the roof. I don't know how they didn't find out about it before now. So the place has closed until the stuff's removed. Her mother and—' He stopped and began again. 'Sophie and Rodney, her now husband, had arranged to fly to New York. Difficult to change. Yes, it is nice to have Millie here but I don't feel I'm making the most of it.'

'We could probably manage.'

'It's all right. Millie is spending the day with Monica Farrell. You remember Monica?'

'Yes, of course I do.'

Carter heard himself say, 'I'd like you to meet Millie, and I know Monica would like to see you again. Perhaps you could come with me when I go to pick Millie up, either today or tomorrow.'

Jess concealed a moment of pure panic. She liked children well enough, but had had little to do with them. Moreover this wasn't any child: it was Carter's daughter. She was still struggling with the idea of him as a doting dad. Besides, her arrival at the cottage with him might be misinterpreted by Monica, or worse, by the little girl. But she couldn't refuse. She sensed his vulnerability on the subject. That wasn't her problem, she told herself. It was his! She ought to tell him frankly that it wasn't a good idea. But to refuse would at the very least be uncivil.

So what she said was, 'Yes, I'd like to meet Millie and see Monica again. Tomorrow, then, to give you a chance to warn Monica that I'll be turning up with you.' She tried to put a decent amount of enthusiasm into her voice.

'Great!' Carter said.

They'd reached his car and both got in. 'Well, let's go and set up a murder investigation!' Carter said, turning the ignition key. He spoke much more cheerfully than the occasion warranted. But he was feeling suddenly more cheerful, murder or no murder.

Earlier in the morning, about the time Ian Carter had been cooking up the breakfast porridge under MacTavish's disapproving eye, Alfie Darrow had returned to check his snares. He first surveyed the scene of devastation that was all now left of Key House. Blue and white police tape cordoned it off. There were notices warning visitors to keep away as it was a crime scene, and also requesting them to give any information they might have about the fire to the police. Alfie would have liked to forage in the blackened ruins for souvenirs. But even now the latent heat from the fabric of the building made it too hot to go poking around in there. Besides, as the debris settled, it echoed with sound, crackling and rustling in sinister fashion. It was as if the wreckage was talking to itself, or unearthly beings whispered terrifying truths. Alfie had heard by now – they all had in Weston St Ambrose – that a dead body had been recovered from the scene. An atavistic dread of spooks and spirits, encouraged by his other favourite type of entertainment, films featuring haunted houses and bandaged mummies staggering out of their tombs, overcame him. He scurried off across the fields to the rabbit warren, out in the open where you weren't likely to encounter a spectral form or risk a skeletal hand laid on your shoulder.

There were rabbits everywhere, nibbling at the scarce tough winter grasses and wild plants. Most scattered as Alfie approached but some ignored him, if they thought him far enough from them to be no danger. He was out of luck. His prey had eluded him. Moreover, one of the snares was missing. This happened from time to time. Something, perhaps a fox, had passed by and dislodged it. It would not be far away. Alfie climbed over the fence into the copse, not a difficult thing to do as it was partly collapsed anyway, and began to poke about in the undergrowth seeking to retrieve it.

He didn't find the snare, but he did come across something else. At first he thought the discovery meant he was not alone in the copse. He first looked around and, seeing nothing, stood listening.

He had a sharp ear for the small sounds of the countryside that told you so much if you knew how to interpret them. The tree branches creaked softly in the breeze but he caught no snap of a twig or sudden rustle of disturbed undergrowth. To make sure, he called out, 'Hello?' No one replied. Alfie gave a little smile. He approached the unexpected discovery still cautiously and prowled round it, examining it.

'Well,' he murmured to himself at last. 'I'm not leaving that here.'

Jess had barely returned to her desk. She had just told Sergeant Phil Morton, 'It's a murder.' Morton had just replied, 'All the evidence has gone up in flames, I suppose.' Then the phone rang. Jess picked it up.

'A call for you, ma'am. A Mr Foscott who says he's a solicitor. It's about the fire where the body was found. Shall I put him through?'

'Yes, go ahead,' she replied, thinking, *Well, well, Reggie Foscott, who'd have thought it?*

An image of the man formed in her head, gangling, pale, formal, and wily. What on earth did Key House have to do with him? But Roger Trenton had spoken of writing to Crown's solicitors. Morton had interviewed both Roger Trenton and Muriel Pickering in the early evening of the previous day following the discovery of the body. Somewhere in his notes must be Foscott's name.

'Inspector Campbell? Forgive the intrusion . . .' Foscott's voice echoed in her ear.

'Not at all, Mr Foscott. I understand you have rung about the recent fire at Key House?'

'Ah . . .' Foscott never approached anything directly and didn't now, even though he was the caller. 'Yes, indeed, a most unfortunate occurrence. I understand the building is very badly damaged.'

'Yes.' Jess spoke curtly. Get to the point, Reggie.

'I also understand, although perhaps this is rumour, that a body was found in the – um – wreckage.'

'Yes, it was.'

'Do you perhaps . . .' Reggie was growing even more cautious. 'Do you have an identity for the unfortunate victim?' Hurriedly he added, 'If you do, then of course I understand that you would have to inform next of kin first, before releasing any name.'

'We've not identified the body yet, Mr Foscott.'

'Oh dear,' said Foscott dolefully. 'Have you any reason to believe the – ah – deceased may be the owner of the property, Mr Gervase Crown? My firm represents his interests in this country, hence my enquiry.'

'Not as yet. Anyway, I understand,' said Jess, 'that Mr Crown lives abroad.'

'Indeed he does. Mr Crown has a home in Portugal near Cascais, on the coast about half an hour's drive from Lisbon. He is a keen surfer, when conditions are right. I must stress that I'm not aware that Mr Crown is visiting this country. When he does, he usually calls by my office to, ah, touch base, as they say. Naturally, when we heard of the fire, we thought we ought to get in touch with him. Damage to his property, insurance and so on.'

This time Jess waited and didn't prompt him. Foscott was obliged to continue.

'We have emailed him but so far not received a reply. Again, I should mention that Mr Crown does not always reply to emails at once. He does generally reply eventually. We – ah – also tried to phone him, but the answerphone picks up at his house. His mobile number is also switched off. I have left a message on his voicemail.'

'Is it usual for Mr Crown to be unreachable?' Jess was making notes on a pad with her free hand. Foscott was concerned and apparently had some reason to be. Morton wandered over and read what she'd written. He pulled a face.

'Well, not usual, but on occasions he, ah, isolates himself from contact,' the solicitor's voice said in her ear. 'In addition to the surfing, and other sporting activities, he also plays a lot of golf. Nothing worse on a golf course than a mobile phone ringing just when someone is about to make a shot . . .'

'So? Is the dead man Gervase Crown?' Sergeant Phil Morton asked later. The question was rhetorical. It was what was in all their minds.

He and Jess were in Carter's office. The heating system had lumbered into action but so far seemed to have raised a lot of year-old dust and not much heat. Morton, over by the window, was looking glum. That didn't mean Phil thought they had no hope of solving the case. It was just that he tended to approach all investigations as likely to be strewn with unforeseen pitfalls. His attitude was born of experience. Right now, he was working out what the snags might be in this one. As he remarked to Jess earlier, a mystery corpse and a scene of crime destroyed by fire was a good enough start.

As for the rest of the team today, Sergeant Dave Nugent was in his favourite place, before a computer, trawling Missing Persons in the hope of finding a possible lead to the identity of their corpse. Detective constables Bennison and Stubbs had divided between them the area within a five-mile radius of the murder scene, and were driving round the countryside calling at all dwellings, including farms, hoping someone might have noticed something suspicious on the day of the fire or during the previous days. In particular they were asking about strangers. Someone had died, but someone else had set the fire.

'This fellow . . .' Carter glanced at Jess's notepad. If she had realised everyone would be queuing up to read her scrawled summary of the conversation with Foscott, she would have written it out more carefully. 'Even if he's resident abroad, we still have to start with him. He could be over here on a visit. Gervase Crown. You seem to have found out quite a bit about his family already, Jess. Also, his solicitor is concerned enough to call us when he can't contact the man over there in Portugal by phone or email.'

'Crown doesn't have to be at home in Portugal to read and answer his emails,' Morton put in, 'or to answer his mobile.'

Jess reminded them, 'Apparently Crown does disconnect from the outside world when he doesn't want to be interrupted. He often goes surfing in suitable conditions and plays a lot of golf and other sports the rest of the time. It's in my notes, sir.'

Carter gave her a look. 'That didn't stop the solicitor grabbing the phone. He's covering his back. He doesn't want his client annoyed by a set of Portuguese police officers turning up, sent at our request to check him out. But he's desperate to know if the dead chap is Crown.'

'Some people have all the luck,' muttered Morton. 'What does Crown do to finance his lifestyle?'

'Private income.'

Morton's expression said clearly that there was no end to this world's injustices.

'When was he last in this country for certain?' Carter asked her.

'We don't know yet,' she admitted. 'Nor, I fancy, do his solicitors. He generally calls on them but that's not to say he might not, if it suited him. He'll have to be careful how often he comes here on a visit, won't he? Because of the tax situation? I mean it'll be a question of where he's resident for tax purposes. If he's paying his taxes in Portugal, then there's a limit how long he can spend in this country before the Inland Revenue here queries his genuine residence abroad.'

'On the other hand, if he pays his taxes here, he'll be able to come back as often as he likes,' Carter pointed out. 'We can find out if he's officially resident for tax purposes here or in Portugal easily enough. Those solicitors should know. Does this firm represent all his interests here, while he's sunning himself on some beach or knocking a golf ball around? Which firm is it? You say it's local.'

'Yes, and we've dealt with them before,' Jess told them, 'not all that long ago, in the case where the girl's body was found at that farm . . .'

'You had this conversation with *Reggie Foscott*!' Carter exclaimed, tapping her notepad. 'Why didn't one of you say so?'

'The one with the horsy wife,' Morton confirmed, adding a little defensively, 'it's in my notes, sir. I spoke to a guy called Trenton who has been writing to them, or rather, writing to Crown care of Foscott's. Trenton's never had a reply to any of his letters.'

'Yes, Trenton told me that, too, at the scene, but he didn't mention the name of the solicitors at the time,' Jess said. She should have got the name of the solicitors from Trenton at the scene, or at the very least from Morton first thing this morning, before Foscott rang. She hoped Carter hadn't noticed the slip and categorised it as screwing up. But he was the sort who wouldn't miss it. 'As Foscott rang me, I could follow it up, go and interview him again,' she offered. 'See if he can come up with anything else of interest about the house.'

'No, I'll go,' said Carter. 'He might not expect me.'

Is that, wondered Jess, telling me I did get it wrong and I'm not to be allowed to speak to Reggie Foscott? Or am I being paranoid?

'The thing that bugs me about the house,' muttered Morton, 'is that this fellow Crown didn't live in it and hasn't sold it. That makes no sense at all to me. Look at the money those big old places round here fetch! OK, he's rolling in dough and doesn't need the cash. But leaving it empty was asking for trouble and, well, trouble is what we've all got now because of it.'

Carter stood up. 'Whatever his reasons, the first thing we have to do is establish whether the body is or isn't that of Gervase Crown. We agree that, because he hasn't told his solicitor he's in this country, it doesn't mean he isn't here – alive or dead. Or he may still be on the golf course in the sunshine. I'll get on to the Portuguese police to check it out for us, at the risk of putting Mr Crown off his golf stroke. If Crown is out of the country, then we have to start looking for another name for our dead man.'

Jess offered, 'Pete Nichols at Fingerprints is still hopeful. He says he's got prints from worse cases. He tells me fingerprints are readable below the surface skin. If the body is that of a vagrant, drug addict or squatter, then we may well have his prints on record.'

Carter was looking thoughtful. 'Didn't Dr Layton tell you Gervase Crown got into some sort of trouble here, before his father died and he left to take up residence abroad?'

'Yes, Layton said it wasn't his business to tell me about that. I put his unwillingness down to his professional scruples,' Jess said. 'I got the impression the doctor felt he'd already been too chatty.'

'How about if Layton was so coy because Gervase Crown's spot of trouble involved the police? Has anyone checked to see whether we have *his* fingerprints on record?'

Chapter 3

'Ah, Superintendent Carter,' Reginald Foscott greeted his visitor. He rose from his chair and extended a long, bony hand.

Carter shook it briefly. He took the chair Foscott indicated to him with a slightly jerky sweep of his freed hand. As on the previous occasions, the man made Carter think of a marionette dangling from strings; its thin, stiff, though jointed, arms moving at the bidding of some unseen puppeteer.

Foscott retook his own seat, and leaned back with his long fingers steepled and a half smile on his pale face. His manner was outwardly benign, but there was caution in his eyes. Fair enough. The last time they'd met the occasion had concluded with Carter charging Foscott's then client with murder, among other crimes. Now Foscott didn't sit in an interview room on a client's business, Carter sat in Foscott's office and the balance of power had subtly shifted. Tables turned? Not exactly, Carter thought, although we seemed destined to be linked by murder inquiries, Reggie and I.

There was a framed photograph on the solicitor's desk, showing a little girl, not much older than Millie, sitting atop a sturdy pony. So they were linked in another way, too. They both had daughters. He wondered briefly what sort of a family man Foscott was – probably an ideal husband and father.

'Very sad affair,' said Foscott, by way of introducing the subject of the visit. He waited.

'A death is always a sad investigation to be making,' agreed Carter.

'No doubt about it being suspicious, I take it?' Foscott raised eyebrows so nearly hairless that the puckering of the skin was the chief sign of the expression.

'No doubt at all.'

'Ah . . .' murmured Foscott again, and looked disapproving.

'You telephoned Inspector Campbell,' Carter continued, slightly irritated, 'because you were concerned the dead man might be the house owner, Mr Gervase Crown. You told her you'd not been able to reach him by email or phone. May I ask whether you've yet heard from him?'

'Yes, we have, only minutes ago, as it happens.' Foscott reached out a hand and picked up a sheet of paper. 'By email. I have a printout, you may like to see it.' He handed it to Carter. 'I must say, I am relieved. I also apologise for troubling Inspector Campbell. But one's first thought, you understand, when hearing of a body . . .' His voice trailed away.

'"Hi, Reggie!"' read Carter aloud. '"Alarming news about the old home burning down. Some bloody tramp, I suppose, or a loony with a box of matches. Do we know who the stiff is/was? I suppose I need to come to the UK. Will book a flight today. Be in touch as soon as I arrive, with a bit of luck tomorrow, or if I'm really lucky, late tonight."'

'As soon as he arrives,' Carter said, 'ask him to contact the police at once, asking either for me personally or Inspector Jessica Campbell. If neither of us is available, he can speak to someone else, but we do need to speak to him urgently.' He held up the printout. 'Do you mind if I keep this?'

Foscott hesitated briefly. 'No, no, I don't see why not.'

'How long has Mr Crown been living in Portugal?'

Reggie Foscott pursed his thin lips and looked up at the ceiling as if the answer might be written there. 'Five or six years. He lives on the coast in an area where there are a number of excellent golf courses. He's a keen golfer. He also keeps a horse at some livery stables there and does a little competition showjumping. But chiefly, I understand, the attraction of the area is that it's near a beach called Guincho. It's a spot for surfers. Mr Crown is very keen on the pastime – or the sport. I don't know quite what you call it.'

'At his age, I'd call a lifestyle like that immature!' Carter said sourly, getting to his feet. 'Has he ever done any kind of work? He's what, thirty?'

'Mr Crown is, ah, thirty-five,' Foscott said in a prim way. 'He did inherit a considerable fortune from his father.'

'Even though we've been given to understand he and his father had fallen out?'

Foscott raised his eyebrows disapprovingly. 'I have no such knowledge, Superintendent. I don't know who told you that. Even if it were so, I don't think Sebastian Crown was the sort of chap who would cut his only heir out of his will, and leave everything to the cats' home. Gervase can afford to avoid the nine to five daily grind, Superintendent, and has taken advantage of it. Which of us, given the opportunity, would not do the same?' Foscott smiled benignly at his visitor.

'That's the obvious explanation, certainly,' Carter returned as blandly. He did not add, *but is it the only one*?

Even so, Foscott looked mildly discomfited.

'Is he resident in Portugal for tax purposes, do you happen to know?'

'I do know.' Foscott's confidence returned. Direct questions and answers were his forte. 'He is resident for tax purposes in Portugal. The firm of canine products that was the source of the family wealth was sold some time ago. Mr Crown's other financial interests are dealt with through a firm in London. I only deal with his private affairs.'

'And he usually gives you – and one assumes this firm in London – warning when he's likely to make a visit to the UK?'

Foscott looked cautious. 'I am not privy to his communications with the London firm. He would normally let me know if he's coming to this part of the world on the very rare occasions that he does. We keep an eye on Key House for him, so it is rather unfortunate that it's burned down. Although perhaps "burned down" is an exaggeration. I understand the walls are still standing but the interior is pretty well gutted. I have not yet been out to the scene myself. I am hoping to drive over there before it gets too dark, so that I can make a report to Mr Crown when he arrives. He will want to view the damage himself, naturally, and no doubt arrange for a survey as soon as the fire investigation is complete. He may decide to restore the property, or it may be beyond that.'

Struck by a thought, Carter asked, 'Was it a listed building?'

'Yes, a Grade Two listed building, constructed just a little after 1700, and although it isn't, or now wasn't, the finest in the area, it did have a few features of particular interest. Some late Stuart oak panelling, I recall. It was a farmhouse originally. It became a family home around 1880 and all the outlying farm buildings were knocked down except for some stables and a barn used as a coach-house. The former coach-house was later converted to a garage for motor vehicles. The stables were unused and what remained of them pulled down in the late 1960s after being extensively damaged.'

'How were they damaged?'

It was Foscott's turn to look bland. 'I understand there was a fire. They burned down and it was not thought necessary to rebuild them.'

Outside again, and sitting in his car, Carter contacted Jess on his mobile.

'Gervase Crown has been in touch with Foscott by email to tell him he's on his way back to the UK. I suppose we can assume, in the absence of evidence to the contrary, he did send the email and the dead body isn't that of Crown himself.'

'It's not,' Jess's voice echoed in his ear. 'Pete Nichols has just got back to me. He managed to lift a fair set of prints from the fingers on one hand. The other hand was a bit too badly damaged. Gervase Crown's prints are on record, as it turned out, so we were able to compare them and eliminate Crown as the corpse.'

'The dickens they are!' interrupted Carter. 'Why do we have his prints? What's he done?'

'He was in a little trouble being caught in possession of banned substances, when he was a teenager.'

'Wealthy public schoolboy,' Carter interrupted. 'Natural target for dealers.'

'He also managed to write off two cars before he was twenty-two. Both instances put down to driving while under the influence of alcohol. He caused a three-car pile up the first time. His car and one of the other vehicles were a write-off. By some miracle, none of the drivers or passengers was seriously injured or killed. Paramedics did attend the scene, and treated some of those involved and a passer-by for cuts and bruises. One person went to hospital with whiplash injury to the neck. Young Crown was breathalysed at the scene and the reading was well over the limit. The second crash, however, resulted in a far more serious injury. A passenger in his car, a girl, suffered spinal injuries. She was left in a wheel-chair for life and later awarded considerable damages in a civil case. Young Crown got a year and served six months.' She paused. 'Dr Layton told me Gervase had "got into a bit of trouble" when young. I can understand now why he didn't want to give me any details.'

Carter gave a growl. '"Bit of trouble" sounds the understatement of the week! I'm not surprised his father was fed up with him. It was probably the last straw. Did Gervase Crown, on leaving school, volunteer to go backpacking round the world, I wonder, or did his father send him? When he eventually turned up again and started writing off cars and earning himself a prison record, his father must have been furious.'

'But he made no move to reduce his considerable inheritance,' Jess commented.

'Only heir of his body? People put up with a lot of aggravation before they start thinking of leaving their money outside of the blood. I did try to draw Foscott on that one, but he said Sebastian wasn't the sort of man to leave his fortune to an animal sanctuary. A little odd, that, considering he'd made that fortune out of canine health products. Still, it can't have been a happy situation.'

Carter drove slowly away from the solicitor's offices, aware the solicitor watched him discreetly through a Venetian blind. After a few minutes, he drew into the car park of a supermarket, where he sat in the car reviewing his conversation with Reginald Foscott. Around him harassed housewives wielded heavily laden trolleys, some with a baby crammed in a wire seat aloft above the soap powder and cornflakes. More than one trolley had recalcitrant wheels, plotting a course of its own. Some of the infants were loath to cooperate, too, one or two quite purple with rage. He didn't blame them, poor little tykes.

That's how it goes, he thought. It starts, when you're a teenager, with having fun, eyeing up the talent. Then you meet one person in particular. It progresses to candlelit dinners and wedding bells, and the next stage is this, parenthood, home life . . . Then, in his case, the wheel had come off their wedding trolley and it had all fallen off a cliff and into the divorce court. Somewhere I went wrong, he thought; not Sophie, me.

Gervase Crown had been a young tearaway, driving fast, smashing up cars, causing serious injury to a girl passenger. In a few years' time, Millie would be a teenager, going to parties, meeting young fellows with more money than brains. He hoped Millie herself would have the good sense not to get into a car with any of them. But wasn't it every father's nightmare? It was certainly his.

He supposed that, eventually, Gervase Crown would deign to return to the land of his birth and see what had happened to the family home he'd abandoned. He'd declared that to be his intention in his email. But how reliable Crown might prove in any intention he expressed, they had yet to find out. Carter had never met Crown, but already felt he disliked the man and that would never do. Keep an open mind! he told himself as he turned the key in the ignition. Perhaps Crown is a changed character now. Grown-up, grown sensible . . . And living by the sea in Portugal so he can surf.

Carter said aloud, 'I'd put my last penny on his not having changed a jot!'

* * *

43

Jess went to find Phil Morton. 'Phil? What did Roger Trenton have to say when you spoke to him yesterday evening? I know you've written it all up in your notes, but I'd like to hear your impression of him.'

'I'd put him down as a local busybody,' said Morton. He pushed his chair back from his desk, stretching his arms above his head. 'I'm sure he'd take a keen interest in anything going on, but as the house stood empty, all that was going on there was that squatters broke in from time to time. Trenton ranted about the council. He reckons some official somewhere should have done something about it. When it came down to exactly what the council was supposed to have done, he rambled on about making the place secure. But that would have been the job of the absent owner. Trenton grumbled about him, Crown, in general terms, as well. But he hadn't seen him in some years so was short on specifics. Pompous old buffer didn't have information of any interest, when it comes down to it, apart from Foscott's Solicitors being the firm handling the owner's legal business. Trenton hadn't seen any strangers about apart from the elusive squatters. He'd got them on the brain. But he can't describe any of them, or say exactly when they occupied the house. He makes a lot of noise and it's difficult to stop him talking, but he doesn't actually tell you anything.'

'I might talk to him again, even so,' Jess said thoughtfully. 'He might not have any information himself but he might give a lead to someone who does. Gervase Crown is on his way back to this country, by the way.'

'So he is in Portugal?' Morton sighed. 'Not him in the ashes, then. Well, who is he, our victim?'

'That's our priority, Phil. No news from the fire service investigation?'

'Yes, there is.' Morton picked up a notebook with a scribbled message on it. 'They've been in touch. The fire was started deliberately, they believe, in the area of the kitchen where the body was found. An accelerant was used, probably petrol. I suppose that doesn't tell us much we didn't already suspect.'

Jess had not telephoned ahead to Ivy Lodge to forewarn Roger Trenton she was on her way. In her experience, it was better to catch people unawares before they had time to start imagining what they saw or knew. But it did sometimes mean a wasted journey.

'He's not here,' said a plump but attractive middle-aged woman with thick, bobbed, iron-grey hair. 'He's driven into Cheltenham. Can I help? I'm Poppy Trenton, his wife.' She had been sweeping up leaves when Jess arrived, and now leaned on her broom.

'Perhaps you can, Mrs Trenton. Did you know the Crown family when they lived here?'

'I knew Sebastian when I was in my teens,' said Poppy. 'We used to go to the same parties, as youngsters do. Gervase, on the other hand . . .' She hesitated. 'I can't say I really knew Gervase very well. I used to see him around when he was a little boy. Then he had to go off to school at a very young age.'

'I understand Mrs Crown left the family home,' Jess prompted.

'Yes.' Poppy's voice was suddenly bleak. 'It didn't work out.' She saw Jess had raised her eyebrows enquiringly. 'Their marriage,' she said crisply. 'Sebastian's marriage. His wife's name was Amanda.'

'Do you know where Mrs Crown went, after leaving the family home?'

'No idea. No one knew. I can't be sure Sebastian knew, although they must have been in touch, I suppose, through lawyers, to get a divorce. But I really don't know anything about it.' Poppy spoke firmly.

They gossip around here, thought Jess, but only up to a point.

'What about Gervase Crown when he grew older? He went through a wild patch, I believe.'

Poppy was beginning to look unhappy and fidget with the broom, making brisk brushing motions.

That question has upset her, thought Jess. She waited.

At last, Poppy said, 'I don't think Sebastian understood his son. Gervase probably felt his father ignored him and his mother, well, she abandoned him. Even before that, he was packed off when such a little boy to spend all that time away at school. I doubt Sebastian realised how lonely the child was. He must have had school friends, of course, but he was isolated at home. During the school holidays he wandered around the place like a little lost soul. I tried to bring up the subject once with Sebastian, but got rebuffed in double-quick time! I don't suppose his father ever gave a sympathetic ear to anything Gervase said. Sebastian was a businessman. He understood profit and loss. Perhaps the desertion by Amanda had damaged him, too. He believed he'd done his bit in educating the boy. One can't blame Gervase for – being a little foolish as a youngster. There was no one to guide him . . .'

Her voice had become sad. She gave herself a little shake and added, 'I can't be of much help to you, I'm afraid.' She hesitated. 'Although, it was a funny thing . . .'

'Yes?' Jess encouraged her.

'No, no, it's nothing!' Poppy obviously regretted her last remark.

'If it's nothing, I'll disregard it,' Jess told her gently. 'But I'd like to hear it.'

Poppy was turning a colour that reflected her name. 'It's such a silly thing and it happened about two weeks before the fire, so really of no interest to you. It's just that I thought I saw Gervase.'

'Saw him? Here?' Whatever Jess had expected, it wasn't this.

'Yes, that is to say, at Key House. I'd gone for a walk. It was a little late in the day for it and I'd already decided I should turn back. It was starting to get dark early. The road is little used, but that means motorists tend to roar down it as if it were a racing track. I was passing by Key House when I saw a light, moving about in the garden. I was suspicious, because I knew the house was empty and no one should be there. On the other hand, I didn't want to face a gathering of drug addicts all on my own! Roger's seen people of that sort there. He told the sergeant who called here yesterday evening, Sergeant Morton. But I was curious and I thought I ought, as a local resident, to take a look. So I crept up very cautiously and peeped over the wall. As I did, a young man came round the corner. He was holding a torch – it had really got that dark. He was playing the beam all over the outside of the house and, as I watched, he stopped and shone the light through a window, trying to light up inside. I was really worried and wondered if I ought to call the police on my mobile. But just then, he moved and the torch jerked in his hand and the beam played over his face. It gave me such a shock. I thought it was Gervase. He must be on a visit to England and checking out the condition of the exterior of the house. I knew he couldn't be staying there because the power had been cut off and there wasn't a stick of furniture in the place.'

'Did you call out?'

Poppy hesitated. 'I was going to. It would have been nice just to say hello to him. But then the man switched off the torch. He turned and left, striding off quickly across the garden and out of the front gate. I saw then that there was a car parked up under the hedges. I hadn't noticed it. He opened the door and got in and the light inside the car showed me his face again. It looked very like Gervase . . . that is to say, like Gervase as I remember him. I could have been wrong, because we haven't seen him around here for quite a while. He didn't see me behind my wall. He drove off and I lost my opportunity. I felt quite sorry about it. But then I thought perhaps it wasn't him. But if it wasn't, who could it be? I worried about it for a while. If it *had* been Gervase I saw that evening, I thought he'd come back again, so for a few days I kept an eye open. Only whoever it was didn't come back again to my knowledge.'

Poppy fell silent and stared down at the little heap of leaves she'd amassed.

'Did you mention this to your husband?' asked Jess, thinking that if Poppy had, then Roger hadn't seen fit to mention it to the police. Nor had Poppy spoken of it when Phil Morton had called to see them.

Poppy looked up in surprise. 'To Roger? Of course not! He'd have said I was being silly. Or worse, he'd have started phoning the council again, or the solicitor who acts for Gervase. Roger has a bee in his bonnet about Key House standing empty, you understand. It would never have done to encourage him.'

That was why Poppy hadn't mentioned it to Morton in her husband's presence, Jess decided, and it was understandable.

Poppy had also realised she perhaps ought to have spoken out before. 'I wasn't really sure it was Gervase,' she said earnestly. 'The more I thought about it, I felt it couldn't have been. So, in the end I decided it was probably just someone interested in the house. It's a very desirable property. Or it *was*. It's not now, of course.'

She sighed. 'Goodness knows what Gervase will do with it now. Anyway, when the house caught fire, I started worrying about Gervase again, in case it *had* been him I saw that night a week or two earlier. He might have gone back and been there when the fire broke out. So, in the morning, while the fire engines were still at the house, and Roger was up there watching it all, I rang Serena Foscott.'

'Serena Foscott, the solicitor's wife?' Jess asked in surprise.

'Yes, and she told me Gervase was still in Portugal. So that put my mind at rest – and it was a big relief because the man I'd seen had looked so like him. It doesn't explain whom it was I saw, if it wasn't Gervase. That's a mystery.'

'Mrs Trenton,' Jess asked, 'may I ask why you rang Serena Foscott to find out where Mr Crown was?'

Poppy appeared mildly surprised at the question. 'I asked Serena because her husband, Reggie, handles Gervase's business in this country. He'd have known if Gervase had come over. But Serena told me Reggie hadn't said anything about it and she thought he'd have told her.'

'Forgive me keeping on about this,' Jess continued, 'but why would Mr Foscott tell his wife about a client's movements and she pass it on to you?'

Poppy looked dismayed. 'You make it sound so suspicious! Reggie wasn't – or wouldn't have been – breaking any confidences. He wouldn't talk about Gervase's business details, I'm sure! He'd never do anything so unprofessional. But he would have told his wife if he'd *seen* Gervase, or Gervase was in the country, because Serena Foscott is his cousin.'

'Mrs Foscott is *Gervase Crown's cousin*?' Now Jess was startled.

'Oh, yes, old local families, you know; they are all connected.'

Ian Carter will be interested to know that! thought Jess. I don't think Reggie mentioned the relationship to him when they had their chat.

But Poppy was looking a little alarmed again, but this time staring past Jess. 'Here's Muriel,' she said.

Jess turned and saw Muriel Pickering walking towards them in her yellow coat and trousers, this time with a matching yellow plastic hat jammed on her head. The pug plodded along beside her.

'Ho!' said Muriel, coming to a halt at Poppy's front gate. 'Got a visitor, have you?' The words were addressed to Poppy but the speaker fixed Jess with her truculent gaze. 'You're the policewoman, the inspector. I saw you at the scene of the fire.'

'You did, Mrs Pickering.'

'Snooping around, are you?' Muriel demanded ungraciously. 'I suppose it's what you're paid to do. Asking questions and wanting to know everyone's business.'

'Yes,' agreed Jess cheerfully. 'That's a fair description of a detective's job.'

Her equanimity appeared to disconcert Muriel who sniffed loudly and squinted at Jess as if to see her better. Hamlet gave a little yelp of impatience.

'Snooping,' Muriel repeated eventually. 'One of your chaps came to talk to me at home about Key House. Not that I could tell him anything. Hamlet didn't take to him. He was very restless all the time the fellow was there. Hamlet is usually pretty good with visitors but he didn't like your Sergeant Morton at all. He was being protective of me, you see. Dogs are very protective of their owners.'

Jess took another look at Hamlet, who returned her gaze with a low growl.

'See?' said his owner triumphantly. 'Hamlet knows you're a copper, not a friend or a normal visitor.'

'Can I do anything else for you, Inspector Campbell?' Poppy asked politely.

'No, no, not at the moment. Thank you for giving me your time, Mrs Trenton. Good bye, Mrs Pickering.'

As she drove away, Jess found herself thinking: Hamlet didn't like me, I don't think Muriel Pickering likes me much and I'm pretty sure Poppy Trenton wasn't delighted by my visit. Is there something, I wonder, they don't want me to know?

Chapter 4

Carter drove out to Weston St Ambrose that evening to collect Millie. He found her ensconced, with the cats and MacTavish, on a battered sofa before a crackling log fire. His child was sorting, magpie-like, through a cardboard box containing old buttons and colourful glass beads from broken necklaces, a treasure trove of shiny objects.

'Ah, there you are, Ian,' said Monica Farrow comfortably. 'Right on time. Millie and I made a quiche this afternoon. We have been waiting for you to come to sample it. I thought we could make it our supper.'

After they'd eaten, Carter carried a pile of dirty dishes into the kitchen and, carefully closing the door, turned to Monica. She raised her eyebrows and waited.

'Monica, I know I've picked your brains before, your local knowledge,' he began apologetically. 'I hope you won't mind if I do it again. Did you know a family called Crown?'

'The only Crowns around here lived at Key House, the place that's just gone up in flames. We all heard about a body being found there.' Monica paused, then asked with a worried note in her voice, 'The dead man – it's not young Gervase, is it?'

'We believe not. Gervase Crown has been living abroad and is, as we speak, preparing to return to this country to deal with the situation regarding his property here. I haven't met the fellow, but of course we hope to interview him – even if he was in another country when the house caught fire.' He paused and added, knowing he sounded censorious, 'He's thirty-five now.'

Monica pursed her lips and looked reflective. 'Yes, I suppose he must be. Time flies. Poor little boy – I mean, he was when I knew him. His mother left them, bunked off and never looked back. He was sent off to boarding school even before that, at a very young age. I felt very sorry for him. It couldn't have been a happy home.'

'Sebastian Crown, the father, didn't remarry?'

'No, never. Threw himself into his business and made a fortune, I believe.'

'Oh, he did that all right,' said Carter.

'Has Gervase married?' asked Monica suddenly.

Carter realised that he'd never asked Foscott whether Gervase Crown had a girlfriend of any sort, let alone a wife.

'I don't know, Monica. All I know is that he plays golf, surfs and rides horses.'

'Horses?' Monica sounded surprised. 'It used to be cars when he was young.'

Carter felt his mental antennae twitch. 'Smashed up a couple, I'm told.'

'Oh, yes . . .' Monica turned aside, suddenly unwilling to talk.

'A young girl was badly injured, do you remember that?'

'Petra Stapleton, she still lives locally.' Monica pressed her lips tightly. This was not up for discussion.

The kitchen door creaked open and Millie, clutching MacTavish, appeared framed in it, suspicion writ large on her face.

'What are you talking about?' She looked from one to the other of them accusingly.

'Nothing of interest to you, young lady!' Monica told her. 'Have you put the lid back on the box?' Millie nodded. 'And got all your belongings? Because Daddy wants to be off.'

Millie disappeared to collect her other baggage. Even going somewhere just for the day, Carter had discovered, involved packing a rucksack of necessities for his daughter, just as if she were going on a journey.

'When I come tomorrow night for her,' he said to Monica. 'I might have Jess Campbell with me. You remember Jess?'

'Indeed I do! I'd like to see her again.' Monica could not hide a note of curiosity.

'I'd like her to meet Millie,' Carter said, wondering if he'd done the wrong thing and started some speculation.

'Good idea!' said Monica cheerfully, which didn't allay his fears at all.

As he was checking that her seatbelt was properly fastened, Millie leaned forward and said in his ear, her voice holding a kind of contained ferocity, 'I'm interested in *everything*!'

So am I, thought Carter, if it has anything to do with Gervase Crown. Then he thought, do I tell her now about Jess coming with me tomorrow? No, I'll wait.

'Petra?' Kit Stapleton called loudly from the middle of the paved area that was in lieu of a front garden. A neat wooden board at the gate announced that the property was called The Barn although the name accounted jointly for two buildings on the site.

This gave Kit a choice. Either her sister would be in the cottage, over on the right, or she would be in the actual former barn directly ahead of Kit, where Petra had her studio. She knew her sister was around the place somewhere because her invalid-driver adapted car stood in its usual parking spot.

'In here . . .' called a faint voice.

Kit made her way towards it and peered through the door. Most barns are shadowy places, but this one had a whole section of roof replaced with glass to give her sister the necessary light for her work. She was an accomplished painter of animal subjects and made a fair living out of painting portraits of people's pets and, when lucky, won a commission to illustrate children's books on animal themes or occasionally a jacket for an adult book. Not surprisingly the barn was cluttered not only with stacks of canvas and general artist's necessities, but with a variety of 'props'. Her sister was currently working on the jacket of a new edition of the Victorian classic, *Black Beauty*. There was reference material in a side-saddle hanging on a peg and an antique dressmaker's model clothed in a red velvet lady's riding habit, itself almost a hundred years old. Kit paused by the door, as she always did, to pat the head of the venerable rocking horse. This noble steed had once amused Kit and Petra as children, and various other family members before that. Now, in his old age, he had cantered his way across a variety of infant tales. Petra sat with her back to her visitor, before an easel. She didn't turn her head. She was concentrating.

Kit walked slowly across to stand beside her and waited until Petra set down her brush and swivelled round to face her. She was wearing one of her painting smocks. It wasn't a flattering garment but Kit thought sadly that Petra was still a lovely woman. Lovely, yes, that was the word. Her dark blond hair was thick, long and held in place by an Alice band. Her skin was unblemished and relatively unlined. Considering the pain she had known, the several operations, and the grinding discipline of the physiotherapy designed to force limited response back into her muscles, Kit thought that amazing. Only her sister's eyes held the legacy of suffering. But she smiled now in welcome.

'I wasn't expecting you this morning.'

'Not a good time to disturb you?' Kit asked.

'Absolutely the right time. I need coffee in large quantities.' Petra set the wheelchair in motion and sped off towards the barn door, Kit hastening behind.

The cottage towards which they were heading had not started life as a dwelling for humans but for horses. As such it had large door openings. This made it ideal to be converted for her sister's use as a dwelling, giving her the independence she so much valued. The traditional cottages locally all had tiny doorways and windows and so many preservation orders attached to them that permission to alter them would never have been obtained.

Indoors, Petra's home was open-plan in design, kitchen and living area united in one large, sparsely furnished whole. Only the bedroom and bathroom were separated. All had been designed with Petra's needs in mind. 'I'm lucky,' she would often say, and she meant it.

It had not been easy, Kit remembered, to persuade their mother that Petra could live independently. Even though Petra had proved it, Mary Stapleton still fretted constantly. It was understandable up to a point. Following the accident, there had been a terrible period of doubt that Petra would even be able to do much for herself at all. But the doctors who expressed the doubt didn't know Petra. She had never given up and use of her upper body had returned; but not that of her legs to any significant degree. When out of her wheelchair, she could only propel herself along using the two crutches propped just inside the front door. Kit watched her sister struggle out of the chair. She handed her the crutches and Petra grunted thanks. The family knew that one had to be very careful about offering physical help in any way. 'If I need it, I'll ask!' Petra would say tartly.

Nevertheless, Kit said firmly now, 'You've been slaving away painting that nag, I'll make the coffee.'

'I can do it,' Petra responded, as she'd known she would.

'Of course you can. I recognise that! I'm not saying you can't. But let me do it, can't you? I want to.'

'Oh, all right,' the words sounded ungracious but Petra was grinning. They had this conversation every time Kit dropped by.

They settled themselves by a window where a semicircular settle had been built at the right height for Petra to slide on to. Kit sat at the other end and looked down at a sheaf of snapshots scattered on the seat between them.

She picked up the topmost one. 'Yikes! What an ugly pooch. Don't tell me the owner wants you to paint it!'

'Yes, I'm very happy to say, she does.'

'Have you seen the mutt in the flesh?'

'Yep! She brought him to meet me. I told her, quite truthfully, that he has lots of character. Animals are like people. Beauty and personality don't always go together. Nice when they do, of course. I admit Hamlet got a bit short-changed on the looks. But he does have the personality.'

'I believe you,' said Kit, returning Hamlet's photo to the pile.

'So, what's new?' asked Petra, cupping her hands round the coffee mug. She'd decorated the mugs so that each one in the set of six showed a different breed of cat. Petra had the Siamese, because she always did, and Kit had the blue-grey Persian, because that was hers.

Habit, thought Kit, watching her sister. Habit keeps us going.

Little things like always having the same mug. Silly, but they matter. But it did underline how fragile our personal world can be. Petra had built one for herself in which she could declare herself happy. Kit had news for her sister that might shatter her confidence. She wasn't sure how to broach the subject. She and her mother had had a long conversation, well, argument, about it. There was no question that it would be Kit's job to tell her sibling. But that hadn't avoided heated debate.

'Or have you just dropped by?' prompted Petra, when her visitor remaining silent.

'No, it's not a casual call. I came to tell you something.'

'Aha! Good news or bad?' Petra's grin faded. 'Mother's all right, isn't she?'

'Absolutely fine,' Kit reassured her. 'Nagging away at me as always. But as long as she's got the energy to do that, I know she's all right. I don't know quite how to categorise the news, good or bad. Well, it's not good.'

Petra gave a theatrical groan. 'Just tell me, can't you? I can't stand the suspense.'

'OK, Key House caught fire. It's pretty well burned down. The walls are standing, just, but the roof's gone, fallen in, and all the floors and inside fittings. I thought you might not yet know, if you hadn't seen anyone.'

'Oh, that's awful . . . a shock,' said Petra, what little colour remaining in her face leaching away to leave her alabaster-pale. 'I didn't know. When did this happen?' She added almost, but not quite, at once, 'Anyone in it when it caught fire?'

'The fire was the night before last. Yes, someone was in it; but no, it wasn't Gervase.'

Petra's fingertips, gripping the mug, were white but the pressure on the fingernails had turned them mauve. 'I thought it was empty of furniture. Surely no one was staying there. Is whoever it was safe, get out all right? How did the fire start?'

'I don't think the police know yet or if they do, they haven't made that public. I'm afraid the person didn't get out safely. They found a body in the ruins. They don't know who it is yet. But they do know it's not Gervase. Honestly, Petra, it isn't his body.'

She had known this would be the most difficult bit of the news she'd come to impart. It had been her own first thought, her mother's first thought and, naturally, Petra's first thought as well. The body might have been that of Gervase Crown.

'Is he in Portugal?' Petra's voice was studiously bland.

'Yes, fooling around wasting his time as always. But I understand he'll be coming back to attend to things. Reggie Foscott phoned Ma to tell her, warn her I suppose, that she might find herself bumping into Gervase in the street or somewhere. I hope not. She couldn't handle it. She hates his guts. She'd mow him down with her shopping trolley. So do I loathe the useless blighter.' Kit paused and added sadly, 'But I know you don't. For the life of me, I don't understand why not.'

'We were both young and stupid and drunk,' said Petra evenly. 'He shouldn't have been driving. I shouldn't have got in the car with him. Does Reggie think he'll be staying long?'

'As long as it takes, I suppose. The house is in ruins and some decision will have to be made about its future – and the police have started a murder hunt.'

The Siamese cat mug tilted and coffee splashed down into Petra's lap. She gave a squeal and swore.

'Oh, hell, my fault, sorry!' Kit jumped up and went to fetch a cloth. 'Were you scalded?'

'No, only startled. What murder?'

'I rehearsed all this to myself, you know,' Kit said wretchedly, 'just how I was going to tell you. Then I mess it up! I was putting off telling you how it was murder or trying to lead up to it in a gentle fashion. But it's not gentle news, is it? So I might just as well tell you it all. I told you that when they'd put the fire out they found a body in the ruins of the house; but the really horrid thing, more horrid than someone dying there, is that whoever it is didn't die in the fire accidentally. The cops have decided that guy was murdered. They believe the fire was started deliberately to cover up the evidence.'

'And Gervase is definitely in Portugal?' Petra's whole body seemed frozen.

'Yes! I told you, Reggie has been in touch with him. Gervase is on his way back, may have arrived by now for all I know. *He's not the body in the ruins.*' Kit leaned forward to emphasise her words, but something more than alarm in her sister's face made her ask, 'Or did you think Gervase might have put him there, whoever the victim is?'

That served to unfreeze her sister's attitude. 'No! Of course not! How could you ask that? Why should Gervase murder anyone? He'd be pretty daft to do it in his own house, if he did. But he wouldn't. He didn't!' Petra's face had reddened. Energy suddenly surged through from some hidden source. She waved her hands. 'And if he's in Portugal, just as you keep saying, he couldn't be here doing such an awful thing. Honestly, Kit, I know how you feel but even you can't believe Gervase could be a deliberate murderer?'

'It's been years since you last saw him, Petra, since any of us saw him. You don't know what he might or might not do. You only remember the numbskull show-off that he was. If he's matured to resemble his father in character, he'll be pretty ruthless now. But yes, he was in Portugal at the time of the fire and no one is accusing him of anything.' She tried to smile but it didn't work. 'I don't know why I said that. I'm shocked, I suppose.'

'Of course you are. Mother must be. I am. Reggie and Serena, too. We all are.' Petra looked down at her folded hands.

There was a pause and Kit added ruefully, 'I'm still blaming him for smashing you both up in that car, but that's back then. I can't accuse him of anything more recent.'

There was a long silence. Petra stared out of the window towards the barn. 'I must get back to work, Kit. Sorry to hurry you along. But I have got a delivery date for the picture.'

Kit carried both mugs to the sink where she rinsed them under the tap. Turning, she saw that Petra still sat as she'd left her, staring at the view from the window.

'Petra, if the louse should turn up here . . .'

'He won't,' Petra said curtly. 'Why should he?'

'He *shouldn't*, precisely. No decent man would do that. But Gervase lacks basic decency. He was always thick enough and conceited enough.'

Petra burst into laughter and turned her head towards her sister. 'If he comes, I'll ring you and you can rush over here and beat him up.'

'Just you remember, if he does appear, get on the phone straight away. I'll come immediately. Promise?' Kit's voice was sober.

'Sure, yes, I'll tell you at once. But Kit, he won't. Tell Mother, if that's what she's worrying about, that this is the last place Gervase Crown is going to turn up.'

Chapter 5

'I want to speak to someone. I need to speak to someone now. It's urgent!'

The voice was clear, young and well educated. The desk constable for the day, Abby Lang, looked up from the register of lost and found. She'd been trying to collate the two and decide whether the worn engagement-type ring handed in by a conscientious citizen, as found on the pavement outside the Oxfam shop, was the same one as an engagement ring reported lost by an agitated elderly woman three days before. The problem was that the elderly woman had declared her ring to have four diamonds set in platinum and the ring handed in had three stones. Normally that would mean it wasn't. But the owner of the lost ring had been in a 'real old sweat about it', so the desk officer of the day had remarked, adding, 'She was bit vague, too. You know, dithery, not sure of the time of day if you ask me!'

Abby closed the book and took measure of the young female visitor who stood before her, hands jammed into the pockets of a leather, or leather-look, full-length coat. Dealing with lost and found had made Abby cautious about descriptions.

'Can I help you?' she asked automatically.

The newcomer was about twenty-six or -seven, at Abby's estimation, slim, short, shiny black hair cut short with a fringe from beneath which glared striking green eyes. Her whole manner

63

bristled. Not aggressive in the drunk-on-Saturday-night way: more 'I pay my taxes and I expect something for it!'

'Yes, I certainly hope so. I told you, it's urgent!' Perhaps it was agitation, not aggression. People sometimes sounded belligerent when they were only frightened.

'What seems to be the problem?' Abby asked. She was well aware the phrase was well worn, but it served the purpose. Not everyone who came in here declaring they had an insoluble problem that the police must solve at once turned out to have nothing but a lost cat to report.

'I want to report a missing person.' The words came out in a rush.

Abby drew a notepad towards her. Not a lost pet, then. But sometimes people are 'lost' because they choose to be. 'Can I have your name and a contact phone number?'

'Sarah Gresham, look, here's my business card.' She drew a small white card from one pocket of the leather (or leather-look) coat, and handed it over,

Abby read it. Ms Gresham's card only gave her name, the name of a local bank and a business contact number, but she was pointing at the card and making an irritable circular motion with a finger at the same time. Abby, interpreting the gesture, turned the card over. On the other side an address had been written by hand. 'Chestnut Lodge,' Abby read aloud. 'What sort of building is that?'

'It's an rambling old Edwardian house and you'll see I've written "basement flat",' Sarah said impatiently. 'Look, don't you want to know about the missing person?'

'How long has the person been missing?' asked the unruffled Abby. If it turned out to be a mere twenty-four hours it would be far too early to panic, and this girl was definitely panicking under that demanding exterior.

'Three days. That is, two nights and this is the third day.'

'I see.' That sounded much more serious. 'What is the name of the missing person and can I also ask, what is the relationship?'

'His name is Matthew Pietrangelo . . .' The speaker paused and then carefully spelled the name, watching as Abby wrote it down. 'He's my boyfriend – my partner.'

Oh dear, thought Abby. Has he done a bunk, I wonder? Left her in the lurch? Didn't have the courage to break it off? Time to be tactful. On the other hand, they'd only just been told to pass all reports of missing male adults straight up to CID.

'Does Mr Pietrangelo live at the same address? Can you tell me his age?'

'He's thirty. Yes, he lives there. We've been together two years. He's never done anything like this before. I've phoned his sister and she hasn't heard from him. I didn't want to worry his mother, not yet, anyway, and his sister – her name is Georgia Evans – agrees. But she did ring her mother and ask in a roundabout way if she'd heard from Matt lately and she – Mrs Pietrangelo – hasn't. Matt's mother is beginning to wonder why; because Matt rings her regularly, once a week, and he's missed his usual day.'

'Where do these ladies live?' asked Abby practically. 'Both in the UK?'

'For crying out loud, of course they do! They both live in London, or the London area. Georgia lives in Camden and Mrs Pietrangelo lives in Harrow. I know it's an Italian name, but that's because Matt's grandfather came to Britain in 1950 and opened a café near King's Cross, of all places.'

Abby realised that the speaker was very near to tears. 'Just a moment,' she said.

She picked up the internal phone. 'Sergeant Morton, please.

Oh, it's Abby Lang down at the front desk, Sarge. Someone has come in to report a missing male, aged thirty. I saw the internal memo and I thought you'd— Yes, right away.'

'Come into one of the interview rooms,' she said more kindly to Sarah Gresham. 'I'll organise a cup of tea and someone will come down and talk to you in a few minutes.'

It wasn't Morton, but Jess Campbell who came downstairs to interview the visitor. Now that Sarah Gresham had a sympathetic ear to pour her troubles into, her manner relaxed slightly. But she remained a frightened woman.

'It not like Matt just to drop out of sight like this. Where's he living? He hasn't even got a change of clothes. I checked all that out. Everything is at home where it should be, right down to his toothbrush and electric razor. His collection of DVDs, his sports gear, all of it . . . I know you're going to suggest Matt has left me. I don't believe he has. But even if he had, he wouldn't have vanished off into the blue and left everything behind, not even a change of socks with him.' Sarah began to sound combative again.

'What does he do for a living?' Jess asked. 'If he's not turned up for work . . .'

'He's a freelance website designer and works from home, our home. But his car's gone. It's the one thing he has taken.'

'Had he had been behaving normally recently? Feeling OK? Depressed about anything? Money worries?'

Sarah's face was white. 'He hasn't topped himself somewhere. He wouldn't do that to me. Anyway, he wasn't depressed. Work has been slow recently, from his point of view, perhaps. But he's confident another job will come along. If you're self-employed it's like that. I work for Briskett's bank and so there is regular money coming in. Matt's work is well paid. It's just not a monthly salary like mine.'

Jess changed tack. 'So tell me if there is anything at all that Matt's been doing recently that's a change to the usual pattern?'

Sarah hesitated. 'He's had a bit of time on his hands, as I said. He didn't want to hang round the flat. We're hoping to buy a place of our own. We'd like an old traditional house in the country somewhere round here, near enough for me to drive in to work and with pleasant quiet surroundings for Matt to do his work. The trouble with our flat is that it's noisy. The road outside is busy; it's on a bus route. The other people in the house, other residents, are always coming and going. The flat's not very big and rather dark and we don't have a garden. You can see why we'd like to move somewhere more secluded and roomy.'

'The sort of country house you were describing would be expensive,' Jess commented.

'We realise that. We would like to find a place that needed renovating. It could be really run down. Then we could buy cheaper and take our time fixing the place up. Matt's been driving round the countryside, looking out to see if he can spot anything within a reasonable journey time from Cheltenham.'

A prickle ran along Jess's spine. 'So Matthew has been exploring the back roads recently, looking out for rundown properties?'

'Yes! I just told you so.' Sarah sounded impatient again.

'Had he found any possible property for your purposes?' Jess tried to keep her voice casual.

Sarah's gaze sharpened and she measured Jess with a look. 'He did say there was one place, but he wasn't sure about it. I don't know where it was exactly. I think he was worried there might be a problem with ownership . . . or with the owner. He wanted to clear that up before he took me to see it.'

'The problem wouldn't be that the owner lived abroad, would it?' asked Jess.

Sarah blinked. 'How do you know?'

'Did he tell you the name and address or the house in question?' Jess avoided a direct answer.

'No, he didn't. It was out of the way, he said. He asked about it in a local pub and the landlord told him about the absentee owner and directed him to a solicitor who represents the guy. So Matt talked to the solicitor, who was the one who said he didn't think the owner had any intention of selling.'

'Name of this solicitor?' asked Jess, picking up her pen.

'Began with an F . . . Fawcott? No, something like that.

'Foscott?'

'Yes, that's it!' Sarah's green gaze held suspicion. 'You sound as if you know the property I'm talking about. What's happened?'

Jess again ignored the question. 'It would help if you could let us have a photo of Mr Pietrangelo.'

Sarah dived into her capacious shoulder bag. 'Here, I've brought you three.'

'Thank you. We'll be in touch,' Jess said.

'That's it?' Sarah blinked and looked taken aback.

'We'll be on to it straight away, don't worry about that. There's a procedure in these cases.'

Sarah got reluctantly to her feet. 'I've tried the local hospitals,' she said, 'in case he'd had an accident. But he's not in any of them. They've no record of him turning up at A and E. If he had smashed himself up, somewhere in the countryside, you'd know about it by now, wouldn't you? Where's his car, anyway?'

Where, indeed? 'Do you have the make and registration of the vehicle?'

'It's a Renault Clio. I'll write the registration down for you.' Sarah rummaged in her bag and produced a notebook and pen. She scribbled in the notebook, tore out the page and handed it to Jess, who thanked her.

'That's fine. We'll send out the car's details and someone should spot it pretty soon.'

Sarah wasn't moving towards the door. 'There's something you're not telling me,' she said accusingly. 'And I'm not budging until I know what it is. You do recognise the property from what I told you, don't you? Where is it? Has Matt been there?'

Jess drew a deep breath. 'There is an outside possibility . . .'

'So it seems the body may be that of Matthew Pietrangelo?' Carter said. 'She's not going to be able to identify him for certain from the burned remains.'

'I've explained that,' Jess said. 'It was difficult. She was all for rushing down to the morgue. When I finally managed to convince her that what was there was pretty gruesome and unrecognisable, she broke down. But she's pulled herself together. She's a tough nut, in my view. She worried, of course, and even more worried now. But she won't go to pieces.'

'Mm . . . It does seem a distinct possibility Pietrangelo could be our corpse. We need either to establish that or eliminate him from our enquiries as quickly as possible. But all the signs point in his direction! Mrs Trenton saw a man examining the house by torchlight. We know from the girlfriend that it was just the sort of place she and Pietrangelo were hunting for. It's situated off the beaten track. It was clearly empty. Mrs Trenton says she didn't speak to the man she saw, and so we don't know for sure. But, according to his girlfriend, Pietrangelo spoke to someone in a pub about the house and was told the owner lives abroad and does business through a solicitor named Foscott. He took the next logical step to establish who owned it, hoping to get in touch. Pietrangelo looked up local solicitors and found Foscott. He spoke to him and realised immediately there was a problem. The owner didn't want to sell. A really wealthy expat might well choose to hold on to a property in this country in case he needed to return. Pietrangelo had come up against an obstacle and was working out a way to get over it, not telling his girlfriend too much about the property until such time as purchasing it appeared more realistic.'

Carter's voice hardened. 'I'll certainly be having another word with Reggie Foscott. He's been holding out on us, on me in particular! If Key House features in a case, then anyone asking him questions recently about it and its owner is of interest to the police. Foscott's been around long enough to know that. When we spoke, he should have told me.' Carter's voice was grim. 'Add to that, Mrs Foscott is apparently related to Gervase Crown. I wonder if that's the reason Foscott is being so discreet?'

'In the meantime,' said Jess, 'we'll get out to their flat and bring away some personal items like the DVDs she mentioned, and the electric shaver, to see if we can get Pietrangelo's fingerprints, and hair samples. The damaged prints Pete Nichols lifted from the corpse are only good enough to rule out Crown. It's another thing to identify Pietrangelo from them for certain. It's probably going to come down to DNA, always supposing we can get some usable stuff from the remains. Tom thinks that will be possible. Pietrangelo also has a sister and mother we can ask for samples for comparison, so we'll get on to that straight away.'

'Do the sister and mother know Pietrangelo has gone missing? Someone will have to inform them before we turn up on the doorstep talking about DNA analysis of a corpse.'

'Sarah Gresham has undertaken to inform them, now there's a possibility her boyfriend is dead. She didn't want to alarm them before. She said it would be better if they heard it from her before we contacted them. Luckily, Sarah comes across as a sensible and reliable person, now the first shock is over. She's also given us the name of his dentist. He had some dental work done six months ago, so there should be a good and up-to-date record of his teeth.'

Carter stared down at the photographs Sarah Gresham had left with them. 'He may be third-generation in this country but he's still got a Mediterranean look about him. Handsome chap, would you agree, Jess?'

'Yes, but full of himself. I mean, he looks a bit overconfident to me.' Jess was cautious.

'Overcurious, perhaps,' said Carter with a sudden and totally unexpected grin. Seeing her blank look, he explained, 'Curiosity killed the cat. Pietrangelo was curious about Key House. Did that kill him? Send Bennison and Stubbs around the local pubs with copies of these and find the pub Pietrangelo was in. It couldn't have been so long ago that he was there asking and the landlord should remember. It would be nice to have confirmation we are talking about the same enquirer or if there was someone else asking about the house.'

'The superintendent made *a joke*?' Morton asked Jess disbelievingly, a few minutes later.

'I wouldn't call it a joke, more a witticism.'

'Not his style,' opined Morton. 'What's he got to be so cheerful about?'

Chapter 6

Petra had returned to work after Kit left. She needed to. She had to have something to take her mind off the disturbing news. Gervase was coming back. She ordered herself not to be stupid and let herself get into a state about it. As she'd told Kit and repeated to herself now: the last place he'd turn up was here at The Barn.

It couldn't be the first time Gervase had returned to the area, surely? If so, he'd sneaked in and out without attracting notice. Reggie Foscott would know but might have been discreet about it, probably under instruction.

'And I,' said Petra aloud, as Kit's car roared out of the driveway in a shower of gravel, 'am probably the last person he'd want to see.'

Still, as people occasionally pointed out and Key House began to crumble into decay, Gervase Crown did still own the family home even if he'd not attempted to live in it after his father's death. He had a responsibility. But Gervase had never been strong on taking responsibility. He'd only hung around long enough after his father's funeral to empty out the house like a giant waste bin of things no longer of any use to him. Out had gone the memories, good and bad. Out had gone the books to some second-hand bookshop in Cheltenham, and clothes to Oxfam. Gervase's boyhood train set and box of Lego bricks had pitched up at a local church fête. The nearest saleroom had benefited from the antique furniture and china. A house sale had pretty well taken care of everything else and a house clearance company had come in to remove what little had remained. Everyone had fully expected that, following the clearance, the house would appear on the market and there had been much speculation as to who might buy it. It had not happened. If at long last Gervase was coming to the area now it was only because that neglected family property had burned down.

The news of the house's destruction had shocked her more deeply than she hoped Kit had realised. Petra's earliest memory of Key House dated back to the days when Sebastian had been alive – and still married – and Gervase a little boy living in a then family home. Yet even as a family home it has seemed wanting to young Petra. Her own home had been a noisy, untidy place but full of laughter and squabbles with Kit, various animals adopted as pets, her mother standing over an open recipe book in the kitchen, surrounded by boiling pots, her father bravely eating the exotic but botched result, when all he'd really wanted was straightforward meat and two veg.

The Crown household had been perfect to the eye, not a thing out of place, an image from a glossy magazine of upmarket interiors. But it had been so quiet that Amanda Crown's high heels tapping across the polished parquet echoed noisily as she came to greet her visitors. Amanda had cut a glamorous figure, elegant and restless, usually clad in some floaty garment of rippling silk or other expensive material, and cleverly draped scarves that must have been kept in place by hidden pins, because they never moved. She'd overawed young Petra and Kit and their mother, too. Mrs Stapleton had always 'made an effort' when visiting Key House, digging from her wardrobe a little-worn outfit. Inevitably she had put on a pound or two since the outfit's last appearance, or the skirt length was no longer in fashion. Mrs Stapleton would then sit on Amanda's white leather sofa, tugging unhappily at her hemline, while Amanda poured tea or coffee, depending on the time of day, into bone china cups.

Petra, also forced into a 'best skirt and top', would squirm in sympathy with, and embarrassment at, her mother's awkwardness. She had overheard her own father describe Amanda as a 'clothes horse'. But Petra would have given her eye teeth to grow up looking like that. As a little girl, she'd just gazed at Amanda, fascinated. Kit hadn't cared. She would drum her heels against the white leather of the armchair in which she slumped, despite the increasingly desperate telegraphed messages from her mother.

What Petra had always secretly hoped was that Gervase would be there, home from school. Then Amanda would say carelessly, 'Why don't you two girls go outside and see if Gervase is there? He's around somewhere.'

If he was, and they found him, he and Kit would immediately begin to argue. She, Petra, would follow behind as they roamed over the fields, longing to join in, not to argue but just to talk to him, yet not knowing how.

Curiously, considering that the money paying for all the expensive luxury came from canine care products, the Crowns kept no dogs as pets. It wasn't just the dogs that were missing. There was no love at Key House. Petra had sensed its absence without really understanding it.

She'd met Sebastian several times and not liked him much. He had seemed distant. No one had expressed any surprise that the Crowns had split up, although Petra had been surprised at the lack of reaction on Gervase's part at the time. Her questions, put to him with a childish lack of subtlety, had been received with a brusque, 'Don't ask me about it. No one ever tells me anything!' She'd sensed his hurt and wanted to console him but realised consolation wouldn't be well received.

Later in her teens she'd taken to hanging round Gervase whenever he was home and the opportunity occurred, hoping to gain his attention in another way. I always had a crush on him, she thought now ruefully. When he offered to drive me back from the party that evening, I knew he was drunk, of course I did. I knew he'd already had one accident in which he'd smashed up a car. But I was just so happy that he offered me a lift home, I hopped into the car with nothing in my mind but that I'd have his company all to myself.

And then . . . Petra closed her eyes but couldn't shut out the memory. It must have happened quickly but at the time seemed to happen in slow motion. The car slewing round, the dry stone wall of a field coming ever closer. Gervase swearing, panic in his voice, and twisting the wheel, powerless to avert disaster. She'd thrown up her arms to shield her face, but she couldn't remember the moment of impact or the immediate aftermath. She regained consciousness in a hospital bed.

Petra thrust away the memory. She wheeled herself out to the barn and picked up her paintbrush. She'd nearly finished the commissioned artwork for *Black Beauty*. Another hour at it, perhaps not even that, and it would be ready. She was pleased with it. She'd attempted and dismissed various ideas, and in the end rejected all the assembled period props, too: the riding habit, the side-saddle. She'd settled for the single figure of the horse-hero himself, rearing up, mane tossing, nostrils flaring, glossy black coat gleaming, set against a pale landscape.

When she heard a car stop in the road outside she paid little attention. Tourists, driving round the lanes, did sometimes stop to take a second look at The Barn. Then she heard the creak of the gate and the footsteps. The visitor hesitated, probably wondering whether to go to the cottage or come here to the studio.

He opted for the studio. She knew it was a man from the weight of his tread and also because her senses had sprung into life with an awareness that was almost panic. Not the sort of panic associated with fear, but of facing a moment she had imagined so often over the last few years and which was now about to become reality. Black Beauty, rearing up on the canvas, seemed to express her feelings, his wild eye directed over her shoulder towards the entrance.

She herself didn't turn round, couldn't bear to, but found herself thinking, *Thank God Kit has left.* The newcomer cleared his throat to attract attention.

Petra swivelled the wheelchair at last to face the shadowy outline in the open barn door.

'Gervase,' she said.

Chapter 7

The back-street garage and repair business had a battered sign outside that read: Used Motors. MOTs. All Types of Service. On its forecourt a variety of cars, certainly far from the first flush of youth, awaited potential purchasers. Cards announcing the prices were propped in the windscreens. The cards had yellowed through long exposure to the sun. There was no sense of bustling activity. The business did not appear to be thriving.

The Renault Clio turned into the forecourt and a young man got out. He walked over to the open door of the workshop and peered into the gloom.

'Gaz? You here? Gaz?'

Receiving no reply, he ventured inside and made his way cautiously to an office at the rear. Through its glass panels he could see someone sitting with feet propped up, mug in hand, reading a tabloid newspaper. The visitor tapped on the glass.

The man on the other side turned his head, but didn't lower his feet, put down his mug or his paper.

'What do you want?' His voice was muffled through the glass. He could now be seen to have a long narrow face, made to appear more so by the lack of hair on the top of his head. To compensate for this, hair still growing at the back of his head had been allowed to curl down over his collar.

'I got a bit of business for you, Gaz.' The visitor sounded

positive, even optimistic. He'd rehearsed the words before coming, lest a nervous tremor destroy the confidence of his approach. He brought them out now with an air of achievement.

'What sort of business?' The muffled voice was sceptical.

'Clio. It's in good nick.'

Now the man in the office put down coffee and newspaper and got to his feet. Like his head, the rest of him was long and thin. He came out of his retreat and looked the visitor up and down. 'Where is it, then?'

'Out front.'

The thin man peered past him at the Clio out in the forecourt. 'Stupid sod,' he said. 'What did you leave it out there for? Trying to advertise it to the cops?'

'I didn't steal it, Gaz, honest. I found it.'

Gaz drew in a deep breath. 'Do me a favour and cut out the jokes. The car's hot. It has to be. How would you come by a decent motor? You couldn't afford a pair of roller-skates.'

'I *found* it, Gaz. It was abandoned. In the street, back of the bus station. I saw it there in the morning, real early, about six. That's funny, I said to meself . . .'

'Spare me the long story as well.' Gaz's voice was curt.

'Well, I watched out all day and that evening, it was still there. So I went back early this morning, and it hadn't been moved. So then I went and had a good look and I couldn't believe my eyes – the keys were hanging in the ignition.'

Gaz had been studying the view of the car framed in the open door of the workshop. Now his head snapped round. 'Keys?' he said sharply.

'That's right!' the visitor sounded triumphant. 'I told you I didn't steal it. I didn't hotwire it. No one had. It was abandoned. Like I said, I found it.'

'You really ain't very bright, Alfie,' Gaz told him in a conversational tone. But for all its casualness there was a hint of something dangerous behind it.

The visitor's self-assurance, which had been slipping as they spoke, now slid off his whole person like a discarded garment. He looked frightened.

'You ain't very bright,' repeated Gaz, 'because . . .' He lifted his hand and the visitor flinched and stepped back hastily. However, the hand had not been raised to strike a blow but so that Gaz could number off the points of his argument, working along the fingers with the forefinger of the other hand.

'One, I don't believe that yarn you spun me about it being left in a street back of the bus station. Any motor left there like you told it would've been either clamped or removed or someone else would've nicked it before you said you did. Two, in any case, no one abandons a decent motor with the keys in the ignition. Three, if you didn't steal it in the first place, you've stolen it now, ain'tcha? Four, you drive it here, to me, in broad daylight and you leave it out there, like I said, advertising it.' He paused. In the silence something at floor level, a small dark body with clawed feet, ran past them and scuttled into the darkness. 'Bring it inside.'

Alfie Darrow let out the breath he'd been holding in an audible hiss. He scuttled away much like the little clawed creature. A few moments later and the Clio rolled into the dark interior of the workshop. Gaz walked round it and peered through the windows. He didn't touch it.

'Anything in the boot?'

'Old rug and a road atlas. Nothing else.'

'You mean, you took out anything else there that was worth anything, before you brought it here. You still got whatever it was? And don't get clever and think you can say you haven't when you have, right? Because I'll know.'

Alfie opened his mouth, hesitated, then said, 'Yes. A camera.'

'I'll send someone round to collect it. Where are you dossing now?'

'I'm back home, Weston St Ambrose, where I was before – with me mum,' Alfie whined, adding, 'she don't know nothing about it. She's not seen the car, or the camera. I don't tell her what I do.'

'I bet she wonders what she did to deserve a loser like you for a son, all the same. I'll send someone there for the camera later today. You hand it over like a good boy, right? You can leave the motor here.'

'We've got a deal?' Hope returned to Alfie's voice.

'We might. Don't speak to anyone about it. Come back in a week.'

Alfie shuffled his feet. 'I'm skint, Gaz.'

'I'm not giving you any cash now. You'll go flashing it around and someone will notice. Same as that camera, if I let you keep it. You'd try to sell it.'

'A few quid on account?' asked Alfie without much hope in his voice.

'No. You do exactly as I say. You go home, get the camera and wait for the person I send. Then you wait a week. You don't talk to no one. You don't get chatty in a pub or anywhere else. Not here in town. Not in that village, Weston St Whatever, where your family lives. Don't bother me meantime.'

'Awlright,' muttered Alfie dejectedly.

Gaz watched his visitor depart. 'Thick as two planks,' he murmured. He returned to his office where he picked up the phone. When a voice answered he said, 'Gaz here. I might have what you're looking for.' He replaced the receiver and then, in a sudden movement grabbed a grimy copy of *Yellow Pages* and hurled it into a far corner. 'Got to do something about them rats,' he told himself.

Gervase Crown walked slowly towards the easel and the waiting Petra, his hands thrust into his jeans' pockets. Seeking a way to control her agitation, she began deliberately making a mental note of details of his appearance, as she would have assessed the subject of an animal portrait. She even had a sense of being in the presence of some underlying animal restlessness. Does he affect everyone like this? she wondered. Or am I the only one to feel it? Slung round his neck, over his navy sweater, was a narrow scarf. That would go in the portrait she was already creating in her mind's eye. He'd grown his hair longer so that it was an untidy mop. It was still dark, although the sun had given it a bronze patina and there were streaks of early grey in it. She must include those. Sun and sea breezes had burned his skin to an olive hue. The blue of his eyes seemed a mistake as if, she thought, another artist, less careful that she was, had picked up the wrong brush.

'Hi,' he said.

'Hello to you, too,' returned Petra.

'Want me to go away?'

She should, of course, say 'yes', and say it immediately. Naturally, what she said was, 'No, sit down. There's a chair there.'

He sat down on the paint-splashed wooden chair that awaited

visitors, and stretched out his legs. She could suggest they went over to the cottage, as she'd done with Kit, but here was better. Here was a neutral place. If you invite people into your home, you invite them into your life, she thought. But isn't Gervase part of my life already? Don't I sit here dependent on these wheels because of him? Perhaps Kit's right. Perhaps he does lack normal human sensitivity. But he did look a bit embarrassed, sitting there. Or was he just physically uncomfortable? The wooden chair was small and, because the barn floor wasn't absolutely flat, wobbled under unwary guests.

He didn't begin the conversation so she, perforce, had to. 'Sorry to hear about Key House,' she said. 'A lot of damage, I understand.'

He hunched his shoulders. 'It's gutted, absolute wreck. I've just been to have a look at it. Whoever put a match to it did a good job. I suppose the fire's been a big talking point locally.'

'It still is, although news only reached me this morning. I'm a bit out of touch here. But Kit drove over earlier and she told me about the fire . . . and that you were expected back.'

He gave a rueful grin. 'Ah, Kit. Does she still have such strong opinions? She pushed me into a drainage ditch once, when we were kids, because I annoyed her. I climbed out soaking wet and stinking of goodness knows what. Do you remember? Were you there? I had to sneak into the house through the kitchen where, luckily, I found the au pair we had at the time. She was a Dutch girl. Perhaps she was used to people falling into canals or dykes. I don't know. But she whisked me upstairs to change and stuffed my dirty clothes into the washer, before my mother saw me. How is Kit – and your parents?'

'Dad died two years ago. Kit and my mother are both fine. No,

I wasn't there on the occasion you fell or Kit pushed you, as you claim, into a ditch. I'd remember it.'

'Sorry to hear about your dad. I'm the one who's out of touch, I'm afraid. Glad Kit and your mother are well. Did Kit come to tell you I was coming back – or to warn you?'

He'd looked the picture of nonchalance there, rocking back and forth on the chair, but Gervase was shrewd. He always had been and she should remember it.

'I don't know what's in their minds,' she said.

'Don't you? I do. They hate my guts.' Petra didn't reply to that so he went on, fixing her with a sudden direct stare, 'Do *you*? Do you want me to leave? Just say so and I'll go.'

'You don't have to leave. I don't hate your guts. Kit and Mother aren't keen on you, I admit, but I wouldn't say they hate your guts either.'

'Wouldn't you? I bet Kit would.' Soberly he added, 'I'm sorry, Petra . . .' He gestured briefly at the wheelchair. 'Sorry about everything. It's a pretty weak thing to say, but I don't know what else I *can* say.'

'There isn't anything else. You've said it now and there's no need to keep on about it. We were young and daft.'

'I was young and drunk.'

The last thing she wanted was to rehash the accident. 'Why didn't you sell the house if you didn't want to live in it?'

'I did intend to live in it at first after I inherited it. But, somehow, I couldn't.' He paused and looked away from her towards the far wall. 'I hated my childhood. Whenever I went into the house, I relieved every miserable moment of it. Every stone in the walls, every stick of furniture, the views from each of the windows . . . Everything conspired to wipe away the years and took me back, more effectively than a family album of snapshots would have done. Only we never had an album of family snaps. We were never a family, other than in the biological sense.'

He turned his gaze back to her. 'And I couldn't change a damn thing about it because it's a listed property, you know. Only Grade Two listed, but that's enough. I did make enquiries. I was told I couldn't touch the exterior, of course, but was also given a list as long as my arm of "special features" inside the place that couldn't be altered or removed. About the only things I could have done, if I'd wanted to, was change my mother's stripped pine kitchen, because that was modern, likewise the two existing bathrooms, tinker with the downstairs cloaks and replace the clanking iron radiators of the old central heating system. After that, I'd have been sleeping either in my old or in my parents' bedroom, eating in our family dining room and watching TV in my father's old study. No thanks.'

'So why didn't you sell it?' she asked again.

'It sounds weird . . .' Gervase paused and went on slowly, 'I think I resented the power it had to dictate my feelings. If I sold it, it would be because I couldn't get over my hang-ups about the place. It'd be a sort of admission of weakness on my part. It would be like owning a wild animal I couldn't tame. So I haven't sold. I kept saying, one day I'll go back and I'll put some furniture in it and live there for a while. I'll force out the old memories and make it accept my new ones. Then I'll sell it, because I choose to, and not because it's driven me away. Now the wretched place has burned down and that means it sort of had the last word. I'll never live in it now because it has stopped me, not because I've done anything about it. That makes me sound a nutcase, doesn't it?' He looked up and smiled.

Petra felt her heart lurch and was furious at the treacherous organ. 'No, I understand. Old houses do have personalities.'

'Ah, you're an artist and have a sensitive soul!' Gervase indicated Black Beauty rearing up on the canvas. 'That's great. I own a horse now, you know, in Portugal.'

'Didn't know you were keen on horses.'

'Only fast cars, eh? A chap I was talking to on the beach one day – I surf quite bit – this guy wanted sell the horse. So I bought it. I keep it in stables nearby and pay them to look after it. I did think I would take up showjumping. I entered myself in a few events around Portugal with singular lack of success. I still ride every week, just hacking round. I shall probably sell the horse on when I get back. It's a needless responsibility and all it does is eat and get fat.' Another pause and he added, 'I'm not good at taking responsibility, as you know.'

Petra asked quietly, 'Then why are you here? Isn't it because you feel responsible for this wheelchair I sit in? Don't be. I told you, we were young, stupid and it was just one of those things that happen.'

Gervase leaned forward in a sudden jerk that nearly sent his wooden seat toppling and him with it. 'No, it didn't just happen! Do you know what one of the police officers at the time told me? He said, "There are no accidents. Someone is always responsible." That someone was me.'

'I don't care, shut up about it, will you?' Petra heard herself shout at him.

He sank his head and gripped his tousled hair with both sunburned hands. 'I shouldn't have come. It was a thoroughly bad idea. I just wanted to know you were—'

Petra interrupted him. 'I'm *OK*. I like painting. I like living here. I've got Kit and Mother and other friends who call by and my life is just fine. I'm sorry I yelled at you like that. But I did tell you not to keep on about it. I hope you come to a decision about Key House soon because I think that's preying on your mind, too. But I suppose, as it's a murder scene, you won't be able to do anything soon.'

Gervase recovered his self-control and sat back. 'Yes, it is a murder scene. The cops are sure now. First of all, so Reggie Foscott tells me, they thought it might be me in the ashes. Then they thought the body was that of a tramp or squatter. Now they're keeping their options open, but they are sure someone killed the guy and then set the place afire. Wonder who the poor sod was . . . The cops are keen to talk to me. Much I can tell them.'

'Why do they need to talk to you?' Petra blurted.

His reply came just as quickly. 'I don't think they suspect I did it. But I own the place, so they'll have questions. They will want to know why I left it empty for so long. They'll ask me why I don't live there or haven't sold it. I really don't think I'll be able to explain to them about the house having a personality and my tangled emotions regarding it. Cops don't do that sort of explanation. But it's like my owning a horse and hardly ever riding it, I suppose. Can't make up my mind, that's what I'll have to tell 'em. Always put off until tomorrow what you should do today, that's my motto.'

He grinned and Petra laughed. But the laughter was an outer cloak; inside there was no merriment.

'When are you going to see the police?' she asked.

'I'll do it this afternoon. Reggie thinks I ought to go at once – before they start to think I'm avoiding them. Reggie didn't actually say the last bit, but he meant it.' He held out his hand. 'Part friends?'

She took the outstretched palm. 'We part friends. Good luck, Gervase.'

'God bless,' he said in that sober voice that seemed to come from another, hidden, Gervase; and stooped to kiss her forehead.

Chapter 8

'Gervase Crown is downstairs, ma'am,' said Phil Morton. 'Do you want to interview him or shall I go down and do it?'

'I'd better go,' Jess said. 'Oh, and tell Mr Carter about it, will you, Phil? I think he probably wants to have a look at our beach boy. Have you seen him?'

'I've seen him,' said Morton.

'What's he like?'

'Like someone who's permanently on holiday,' said Morton sourly. 'Arrogant blighter, too. I told him I was sorry his house had burned down, thought I'd better be polite. He just shrugged and said yes, it was a bloody nuisance and were the police going to be crawling all over what was left of it? I told him that any clues there might have been have gone up in smoke so no, we weren't. He just muttered. So I stuck him an interview room to stew while I came up here to tell you.'

'Can't wait to see him,' Jess murmured. 'Where are those photos of Pietrangelo? Let's see if one of them jogs Mr Crown's memory.'

'You'll be interested when you see him,' Morton called after as she started on her way.

Jess didn't stop to ask him what he meant. She thought she heard him chuckle but perhaps that was imagination.

* * *

91

Gervase Crown had clearly been pacing up and down restlessly in the interview room. When Jess opened the door, he'd almost reached the far corner and had his back to her.

'Good afternoon, Mr Crown,' said Jess, entering, 'I'm Inspector Campbell.'

He stopped in mid-stride, spun round and subjected her to close scrutiny.

Jess was taken aback, but not because of his imperious stare. Now she understood what Morton had thought would surprise her. It did. They had never met, but this man didn't appear a stranger. I've seen you, she thought in amazement. I've seen you before . . .

She knew where. *In the photos, in the photos Sarah Gresham had given them of her partner. He looked like the missing web designer!*

The likeness was remarkable, even if on closer study the differences would become apparent. Jess had brought the photographs with her in her pocket to see if they meant anything to Crown. Now an entirely new train of thought had started up in her mind. Hadn't Poppy Trenton thought she'd seen Crown recently? It now seemed more likely she'd seen Pietrangelo. Had the murderer made the same mistake? Had this man turning restlessly round the interview room been the intended target? If so, why?

Crown spoke impatiently, perhaps wondering why she stood there just gazing at him. 'You're in charge of this, I take it? Not that graceless oik who shoved me in here?'

Jess rallied. 'That's right. You met Sergeant Morton. I'm sorry if you found him unfriendly. He's a very efficient officer. Do sit down, Mr Crown.'

Gervase subsided unwillingly on to a chair and glanced round the room. 'This, I suppose, is where you haul in suspects for grilling?'

'It's one of our interview rooms. I dare say it looks a bit Spartan. It's not meant to be a coffee lounge!' Jess heard herself snap. And it's not the first time you've been in an interview room, is it? she also thought. Aloud, she managed ask more civilly, 'Would you like some coffee or tea?'

'No, thanks.' His voice was curt. He hadn't liked the implied criticism. 'Who burned down my house?'

'We don't have any suspects, Mr Crown, not at the moment,' Jess began. 'Originally the fire was put down to tramps or someone squatting in the property. I understand there were several instances of people using it as unauthorised temporary accommodation since it had been left empty. But post-mortem examination of the body found in the ashes showed definite signs of his having been attacked before the fire started.'

'Was he dead?' Gervase Crown asked in his abrupt way. 'I don't mean, dead in the ashes. Of course he was that. I mean, was the guy dead when the fire was started?'

'No. There are signs that he wasn't but he was almost certainly unconscious. He died from smoke inhalation.'

'He didn't know anything about it, then?' Crown's bright blue eyes bored into hers.

He's nervous! thought Jess with sudden insight. He's not insensitive. It does concern him the dead man might have known he was trapped. But Gervase Crown is definitely on edge about something. Or does dealing with the cops dredge up reminders of a part of his life I'm sure he'd rather forget?

'He didn't know anything about it, I think we can say that with certainty,' she told him.

Gervase Crown heaved a sigh. 'Poor blighter, whoever he was. Do you know yet?'

'We believe it's possible the body is that of someone who has been reported missing for a few days. His partner contacted us.' Jess paused. 'We have photographs of him and wonder if you wouldn't mind taking a look.'

'Dead?' asked Crown in alarm.

'No, not dead.' No one would have recognised the unfortunate web designer in death. 'Taken when he was alive. This one, for example.'

She took it from her pocket and couldn't help looking at it quickly again herself. Yes, there was a distinct resemblance. It wasn't so close now, not now she'd been talking to Crown and her first surprise had worn off. But it was there. Would Crown himself see it? She handed it to him. 'Can you tell me if you recognise him?'

Crown hesitated and then took it from her. 'No, don't know him.' He stared down at the little rectangle and frowned. When he looked up, the expression on his face was one of suspicion. 'Am I supposed to say he looks a bit like me?'

'I think he does,' Jess admitted. Whatever else, Crown was quick off the mark.

'And that's it, is it? Someone thought he was me? I was the intended victim and this poor guy got in the way?' Crown was beginning to sound vehement. Anger? Fear? Amazement? Jess couldn't tell.

'We don't know . . . we didn't know of the resemblance until this moment. But now, well, it is a possibility. Can you think of any reason why anyone would want to kill you?'

'I think the entire population around Key House would dance on my grave. That's not quite the same thing, I know. As you continue your enquiries, Inspector Campbell, you'll find I am not a popular man. But you'll know about my motoring convictions.' His tone and look were sarcastic.

'We do. But that was a long time ago now and you have been living abroad. That someone would still want to kill you now, well, it would be a long-held grudge. It's easy to chase after a theory and find out it's a wrong one. Your resemblance to the victim may be coincidental. His name is Matthew Pietrangelo. He was a web designer.'

'Then what was he doing at Key House? He wasn't a tramp.' Crown sounded puzzled as he handed back the snapshot.

Jess returned it to her pocket. 'We think, from information received from his partner, that he had been scouring the countryside looking for a property to buy and restore. Key House seemed to fit the bill. I believe he went to see your solicitor, Reginald Foscott, about purchasing it. Foscott told him you weren't selling.'

'No, I wasn't. You're right, Reggie did tell me someone had been to see him. I might sell what's left of it now. But now, I suppose, no one will want it and the man you say wanted to buy it is dead.'

'Have you had a report on the state of the structure?'

He shook his head. 'Not yet. I've commissioned one from an expert, a structural engineer. With luck I'll be able to knock down what's left. I'll have a better chance of selling the site for a new build.'

The door opened and Carter walked in. Jess and Crown both got to their feet.

'Mr Crown? Superintendent Carter,' Carter thrust out his hand.

Crown shook it briefly. Carter brought forward a chair from the corner of the room and they all sat down again.

'Mr Crown was just saying,' Jess told Carter, 'that he's

commissioned a structural engineer to look at Key House. He's anticipating it may have to be pulled down.'

'Pity,' said Carter. 'Fine old house, I understand, before the fire.'

'I have no regret about it burning down, in case you're wondering,' Crown told him, 'other than the inconvenience to me and you – and the fire services. I have no sentimental attachment to the place. Once the ruins come down and the site is cleared, I'll put it up for sale, as I was just telling Inspector Campbell here. Some developer might want to take it on – or someone looking to build his dream home in the country.' His voice was dry.

'Why didn't you sell it before?' Carter asked him. 'You live abroad. You say you had no sentimental attachment to the house.'

Crown looked away from their enquiring faces. 'Just never got round to it. I kept thinking I might live there again, one day, I suppose.'

'It was a listed building, I understand,' Carter said mildly.

'Oh, yes, but only Grade Two. It wasn't a stately home. It had a lot of hideous old dark oak panelling and a staircase you expected to see Lucia di Lammermoor come plummeting down at any moment.' Crown's voice was careless and he raised his eyebrows as he turned to Carter again, as if to query the superintendent's interest. 'I can't give you a logical explanation as to why I didn't sell and didn't live there or rent the place out. I just didn't. I'm staying at The Royal Oak at Weston St Ambrose, by the way, if you want me again. It's the nearest village to Key House and the postal address for the old house. I'll be here in the UK for a bit. I'll have to sort things out, wait for the report on what's left standing of the house, and take whatever action has to be taken.'

His lips formed a mirthless smile. 'Pushed me into action at last, you see. Perhaps I should be grateful to the arsonist. Although that's a crass thing to say, isn't it? Someone died there. I am truly very sorry about that. Inspector Campbell suspects he may have died because he looked like me, isn't that right, Inspector? That, I assure you, disturbs me very much. I hope you catch your murderer quickly. Then I'll be able to sleep quietly in my bed at The Royal Oak.'

They saw him off the premises. 'We'll be in touch, Mr Crown,' Carter told him.

'Have you got a hope in hell of finding out who killed – what did you say he was called – Pietrangelo?' Crown asked by way of his farewell. 'Or whoever the dead man is, if he's not Pietrangelo?'

'We always have hope,' Carter told him and held his questioning gaze.

Jess, watching the two men, fancied there was a moment when they met and jousted on some mental plane. Then Gervase Crown nodded and turned to run down the steps and stride towards a dark blue BMW that was probably rented for his time in England.

Carter and Campbell made their way back upstairs in silence. She followed him into his office where the silence lengthened until Carter decided to tackle the elephant in the room.

'So, Jess, do you think we have a case of mistaken identity?' he asked. 'I agree there's a passing resemblance between the photograph and our friend Mr Crown.'

Before she replied there was a knock at the door. It opened to reveal Phil Morton. He still had that quizzical look on his face.

'Come in, Sergeant,' Carter invited him. 'We have all now seen Mr Crown and we're comparing impressions.'

Morton sidled into the room. 'Was it just me?' he asked.

'No, Phil,' Jess told him. 'We all saw it. He looks a lot like Pietrangelo.'

'So, did the killer make a mistake and hit the wrong man over the head?' Carter turned back to Jess. 'You think it's on the cards.'

'I think it's a possibility,' she admitted. 'From the photographs we have of Pietrangelo, there is a definite resemblance and we all saw it. I showed one to Crown and even *he* could see it, unprompted. It startled me, I can tell you, when I first saw Crown downstairs. It's really weird, quite spooky. We can't discount it.'

'No, no, of course not.' Campbell sounded thoughtful. 'But is it going to help or mislead us?'

'I think it's the only lead we've got,' said Jess firmly, 'and we have to work on that assumption until we know differently. So, let's say, as a working hypothesis, the dead man is Matthew Pietrangelo. Someone with a grudge of some sort against Mr Crown might have seen Pietrangelo poking round Key House and thought it was Crown. Crown's been abroad most of the time for the last few years. The light fades early at this time of year. In fact, we know that at least one person did see Pietrangelo on an earlier visit he paid the house, when the light was poor, and think at first it was Crown; Poppy Trenton.' She added, 'I can see that Crown might annoy people just by his manner. He admits he's not popular.'

'Not enough in itself to inspire thoughts of murder,' Carter pointed out. 'However, he also caused a lot of trouble as a younger man. There's the car crash that put a young girl in a wheelchair. He served part of a prison sentence for that. Some people might have thought he wasn't punished enough. The young woman's name is Petra Stapleton and Monica Farrell told me she still lives in the area. It might be helpful if you sought her out, Jess. Have a chat to her. We need to interview anyone who'd have a grudge against Crown.'

'Perhaps it's more complicated,' Jess suggested. 'Are we also working on the assumption that the person who attacked Pietrangelo set the fire, to hide his handiwork and destroy evidence? But perhaps the arsonist didn't know Pietrangelo was stretched out unconscious from head wounds in the building. Perhaps he or she came along to set the fire and having done so, got out of the place as fast as possible, still unaware that a man lay unconscious but alive in there.'

Carter had objections to her theory. 'It would mean that the attacker and the arsonist missed encountering one another by minutes.'

'Fire started in the kitchen, the experts think,' Morton spoke up. 'Pietrangelo was in the kitchen, out cold. The arsonist, if we're thinking it was a different person, would have seen him.'

'Perhaps not,' Jess said, playing devil's advocate. 'There was no electricity in the house and no street lighting outside. In the kitchen it would have been as black as pitch. The arsonist wouldn't have wanted to call attention to his presence by making much light when he arrived. He might just not have seen Pietrangelo's body. He was intent on lighting his fire. He didn't look around the place. The body was in shadows. Once the fire took hold, the arsonist would have hurried out of the place, for fear of being trapped.'

They all considered this in silence. 'So you think we're looking for two different people?' Morton asked with the air of man already burdened with enough cares, and whose life had just been made more difficult. 'Leaving aside who killed Pietrangelo, who would have wanted to burn the place down? If it wasn't just mischief.'

'Crown himself might have wanted to,' Carter said slowly. 'It was a listed building. From the way Crown spoke about it he clearly didn't appreciate its finer points. He also didn't want to discuss his reasons for leaving it standing empty for so long. Possibly he didn't want to live in it because he couldn't make the changes to it he might have wished. Foscott told me that years ago some old stables on the site burned down. It might have given Crown the idea to burn down Key House itself. Then he could build whatever he liked there to replace it. Perhaps he's tired of living abroad and wants to come back here. I'm thinking that Foscott found it difficult to contact him with the news at first. Then he received an email from his client, which, as Phil pointed out, Crown could have sent from anywhere. I'd be surprised if he's not got a smartphone. We could check flights into the country and find out just when he arrived. Or, if he wanted to be cautious, he could have paid a fire-raiser. Someone would have been willing to do it for cash. Then he could turn up here after the event with nothing to link him to it.'

'He did seem genuinely sorry to hear someone had died in the fire,' Jess said. 'But if he did pay some crook to set the fire, letting him believe that it was insurance fraud, well, it will very difficult to find our arsonist. He could be miles away.'

'I'll ask around our usual informants,' Morton said. 'But if the hired firebug has discovered now that he killed a man when he set his fire, he'll definitely have put distance between himself and the scene of the crime; and be busy fabricating a cast-iron alibi.' He paused. 'I'll ask Dave Nugent to check out the passenger lists on flights from Lisbon over the last few days. It's the sort of job he likes.'

'I'll find out where Petra Stapleton lives now and go and talk to her,' Jess said. 'Also to find out if she's still in a wheelchair. She'd be the obvious suspect, wouldn't she, or one of her family or a close friend?'

'Are we working on the attacker and the fire-raiser being one and the same – or are we now assuming we are looking for two people?' Morton asked. 'I'm getting confused.'

'Keep an open mind, Phil,' advised Carter kindly.

Morton looked at him.

When the car drew up before Monica Farrell's cottage at the end of the working day, Millie came bouncing out of the door in greeting. She stopped short when she saw that her father wasn't alone. For the brief moment her mouth opened in astonishment and then snapped shut. Jess found herself subjected to an intense and critical scrutiny.

On the way there, Jessica had remembered to ask Carter if Millie knew her father was bringing someone with him.

'I left it to Monica,' he'd said evasively.

Monica, obviously, had left it to Fate.

'This is a friend, a colleague from work, Millie,' Carter was explaining now, none too happily.

Jess felt a spark of annoyance. She felt she had been dropped in it. Either Carter or Monica should have prepared the ground before a newcomer burst on the scene.

'Her name is Jessica Campbell – and she knows Monica,' he added lamely.

'Yes,' said Millie in acknowledgement of the information.

'Hi, Millie,' said Jess. 'Nice to meet you.'

Millie made no reply but subjected Jess to close scrutiny head to toe. She opened her mouth but, to Jess's relief, Monica appeared in the doorway at that moment and called out, 'Do come on in! The place gets cold so quickly when the front door is left open. The heat just flies out.'

Millie disappeared indoors behind Monica. Jess caught at Carter's sleeve and held him back long enough to mutter, 'You should have warned her!'

'I did work out something to say, but it went out of my head,' he defended himself.

Then they hurried after the other two and Jess found herself in the remembered comfortable, old-fashioned, rather cluttered sitting room. Neither of the cats was to be seen.

'I'll put the kettle on,' said Monica. 'Millie and I made sausage rolls today. I hope you're hungry because we made rather a lot, and I seldom eat in the evening, and never after six, so will probably only nibble at one or two.'

'Have you found the murderer?' asked Millie, not bothering with domestic trivia. She had clambered into a chintz-covered armchair where she sat, cross legged, clutching some sort of toy bear with beady black eyes. Jess noticed it wore a tartan beret on its head. Millie held the toy in front of her as though a barrier against the stranger's intrusion.

Monica gave her the sort of look teachers give a child speaking out of turn. But Millie was proof against looks.

Monica said apologetically to Carter and Jess, 'It's been reported on the local news. They said the death was being treated as murder now.'

'Well?' urged Millie impatiently. 'Have you caught him?' The bear echoed her mood, giving a little jump in her hands.

'Not yet,' Carter admitted. 'It takes a little time, you know.

'He might murder someone else,' said Millie with relish. The bear nodded its tartan beret as if giving sinister agreement.

'That's enough of that!' Monica said firmly. 'Come and carry in the tea-tray for me, would you, Ian?'

That was blatantly getting him out of the room so that Jess and

Millie could strike up an acquaintance. Carter wasn't sure the strategy would work. He muttered his excuses to Jess and followed Monica, knowing Jess watched him go with a gleam in her eyes MacTavish would have envied.

In the kitchen, Monica said, 'Don't worry about her asking about the murder. It's not real to her, you see. It's the same as some detective series she's seen on the television. She'll expect it all to be tidied up in an hour.'

'If only . . .' Carter grimaced. 'I hope it wasn't a bad idea to bring Jessica Campbell along. I don't think Millie quite understands. I should have prepared the ground better.'

'You have your friends, Millie should understand that.' Monica was apparently intent on stacking the tray with plates and cups.

Somehow her indifference made Carter feel even more unsure about the wisdom of turning up here with Jess.

Back in the sitting room, Jess, sure of the mistake, wondered how to begin a conversation now Carter had departed.

She needn't have worried. Millie began it.

'Are you my father's girlfriend?'

'No,' said Jess honestly. 'He's my boss. I'm a police inspector. I have met Monica before when we were – your father and I – working on a different case.'

'Was that a murder?' There was note of hope in Millie's voice. The bear perked up, too, or seemed to.

'Yes, it was.' The kid seemed obsessed with murders.

'Did you catch that murderer?' Millie leaned forward.

'Yes, we did.'

Millie seemed suddenly to lose interest in the progress of the investigation. She flopped back against the chair cushions and held up the bear. 'This is MacTavish. He comes from Scotland. That's

103

why he's wearing tartan. He used to have a shield and a sword but Mummy took them away. She doesn't believe that toys should mimic the violence of the real world.'

Mimic the violence of the real world . . . That was surely a direct quote from her mother. Perhaps that was why Millie was so interested to hear about the murder. It was a novel and forbidden subject. As such, it held a special fascination.

'I had a stuffed cat who was a special friend, when I was young,' said Jess. 'He was called Stripes.' Millie said nothing so Jess added lamely, 'He was striped.'

'What colours?' asked Millie in the nit-picking tradition of examiners worldwide.

'Brown and white.' Thanks goodness the toy hadn't been striped blue or pink. That would not have gone down well, Jess suspected. 'I took him everywhere with me.' So she had, she remembered now. Whatever had happened to Stripes? She must ask her mother next time they spoke on the phone. It was possible Stripes lurked in a box in the attic in her old home. But her mother would ask why on earth Jess wanted to know.

'*Have* you got a boyfriend?' asked Millie now in a complete change of subject.

Thrown off-balance, Jess spluttered, 'I, no, I haven't at the moment.'

'Why not?'

Jess's wish, that she'd declined the invitation to accompany Ian Carter here this evening, was strengthening by leaps and bounds. The child had all the tact of the Spanish Inquisition. It was time to make a stand. Millie would run rings round her, if allowed to.

'That's not really something you need to know,' she said in as kindly a tone as she could.

'I'll find out,' warned Millie. Her tone and the look in her eyes sharpened. She had inherited her father's eye colour, hazel, sometimes appearing more brown and sometimes more green.

'Go ahead.' Jess knew all about dealing with threats, whether they came from crooks or from Millie.

'I knew about Mummy and Rodney long before Dad did.' There was satisfaction in Millie's voice.

'Did you? Well, that would be none of *my* business. That's private to your father and family.'

'Things can't be private,' objected Millie, 'if everybody knows about them.'

Jess had a moment of insight. The divorce of her parents must have shattered Millie's secure world and with it one aspect of her innocence. If she really had known that her mother had found another man, long before her father found out, that had put a burden on shoulders too young to bear it. You couldn't say the child had become cynical, that was too adult and too strong a term. But she had suddenly acquired a brittle veneer to protect herself against any further shocks. MacTavish, still clutched to her chest, was that veneer made visible.

'It doesn't mean everyone talks about it,' explained Jess. 'Some people can be embarrassed at having something private talked about with strangers.'

'That's just pretending,' argued Millie. 'It's not like a secret. If nobody knows, it's a secret. If everybody does know, it isn't.'

Luckily Carter and Monica were back, bearing between them the makings of a snack tea. Besides the sausage rolls there was a plate of assorted cupcakes iced in somewhat lurid colours.

'We didn't make *those*,' said Millie disparagingly.

'No,' agreed Monica. 'We have a lady in the village who runs coffee mornings, with bring and buy, to raise funds for our church. There are always a lot of cakes on sale. These cupcakes are very nice to eat. The baker got rather carried away with the food dye.'

Over tea, the atmosphere relaxed and became quite jolly. Even the two cats returned, one at a time, and sat at a safe distance, watching.

As they got ready to leave, Carter drew Monica aside. 'Thanks for taking care of her,' he said quietly.

'A pleasure. She's a splendid little girl.'

In the narrow hallway, Jess had stooped to stroke the nearer cat, the black one. 'Nice to meet you, Millie,' she said cheerfully as she did, looking up at the child.

Millie was casting a shrewd eye over her. 'I've told Dad to get a cat. He needs company. He hasn't got a girlfriend, you know. You could—'

Jess interrupted. 'Millie,' she said, 'a word of advice. Don't try and fix your father up with a girlfriend! These things happen naturally or they don't happen at all.'

'All right,' said Millie placidly. 'Would you like to say goodbye to MacTavish?'

Jess shook MacTavish's paw solemnly. She was rewarded with a sudden brilliant smile from his owner.

Chapter 9

The following morning Jess crunched across the gravel forecourt of the property called The Barn and made for the cottage. The barn itself still existed but, she saw, had not been turned into a fashionable country home, as had so many other old barns. She wondered about its use now.

She wasn't the first visitor. There were two cars parked before the cottage already, one with a blue badge in the windscreen. That could be Petra's, and the other belonged to someone else, which was a pity. She'd hoped to find Petra alone. She rapped at the brass horseshoe-shaped knocker.

The door was opened almost at once by a very fit-looking woman in her mid to late thirties. She wore her thick dark-blond hair bobbed; and was dressed seasonably and country-fashion in a quilted navy body-warmer, peacock blue sweater and jeans.

'Petra Stapleton?' asked Jess cautiously. If so, this was not what she'd been expecting.

'No, I'm Petra's sister, Katherine, usually called Kit. Who are you?' Kit Stapleton assessed Jess rapidly. 'Journalist?'

'No, I'm a police officer, Inspector Jessica Campbell. I'm leading the enquiries into the death and fire at Key House.' Jess produced her warrant card.

Kit glanced at it and then stood to one side. 'You'd better come in, then. I don't know what you think we can tell you about it. I suppose this has to do with Gervase Crown, somehow or other?'

'You've seen Mr Crown recently?'

'No,' Kit replied in a brusque voice. 'And don't want to.'

'I've seen him,' a quieter voice said from the window.

Kit spun round, horror printed on her face. 'You have? He came here, Petra? Why didn't you say? I told you to ring me—' She broke off to glance at Jess.

It was time to take charge of this conversation. Jess walked towards the window where another woman sat on a padded semi-circular settle.

There was a likeness between the sisters, but it wasn't close. Katherine, apparently known in the family as Kit, burst with energy and good health. Beneath it bubbled something else. Anger for Crown's temerity in calling on his victim? That the family was to be dragged into a police inquiry? No one liked that. Or could it be sorrow for what had happened to her sister? Even fear?

In contrast, there was an inner stillness about Petra Stapleton. Perhaps it was the years of suffering that had taken the bloom from her, but she was still a very attractive woman. She had the sort of pale, delicate features the Victorians liked so much. Certainly her long hair and the calm oval of her face would have inspired the Pre-Raphaelites to paint her. Jess noticed that two crutches were propped against the settle. She had passed by the wheelchair as she came in.

'Please sit down, Inspector,' Petra invited, indicating the settle. 'Kit, love, could you pop the kettle back on? Then we can all sit round with a brew, like the three witches.' She smiled at Jess and then threw another smile towards her sister.

There was something both placating and warning about that

second smile. Kit had already struck Jess as impetuous. The news that Crown had been here had come as an unwelcome shock. Was Petra already warning her sister to be careful what she said?

'We'll speak about it later!' Kit promised her sister grimly, marching towards an area set up as a kitchenette.

'Kit's my bodyguard,' said Petra quietly to Jess. 'She gets upset at mention of Gervase. He came here yesterday, late morning, just after checking out what was left of Key House. I think he was horrified at the amount of damage and wanted to talk to someone. He didn't actually come in here . . .' She waved at the spacious living area around them. 'He came into the barn where I was working. I'm an artist, you know. The barn is my studio.'

'I didn't know,' said Jess. 'Were you surprised to see him?'

'I was astonished. Kit had only just left. She'd come to warn me he was around so I knew he was somewhere nearby. I hadn't expected he'd want to see me.'

And she must have been relieved that Kit had left, thought Jess. Had that been good luck? she wondered. Or had Gervase realised Kit was visiting her sister and had hung about somewhere out of sight until he was sure Kit had left?

'How did you feel about seeing him? Other than surprise?' Jess was aware that her question might be deemed tactless and fancied that Kit, over by the kettle, threw her a look. But that was being a police officer. You had to charge right in there where angels feared to tread.

'Relieved,' said Petra unexpectedly. 'Because, although Kit had assured me the dead man – so awful to think of it – wasn't Gervase, it was still good actually to see him alive and well.'

Kit was approaching with a tray on which three mugs, painted with cats, were balanced. 'I don't do teapots,' she said brusquely to Jess. 'I make the tea straight in the mug with a tea bag, so I hope you weren't expecting something more elegant. I'm the Persian, Petra has the Siamese. Yours is the tabby.'

'It's the way I make it at home. At work it comes from a dispenser. That looks very nice, thanks.' Jess took the mug illustrated with a truculent tabby cat of the sort usually called a mouser. That's me, she thought ruefully. The sisters each have an elegant pet on their mugs. I've got the everyday, working model.

'I was explaining to Inspector Campbell that I didn't expect Gervase would come here,' Petra told her sister, although Kit had clearly overheard. 'But that I was relieved, not upset, at seeing him. He didn't stay long; so don't get hot under the collar, Kit. I would have told you when the moment was right. Probably about now when we'd got our coffee!' Petra gave another of her placating smiles. 'But Inspector Campbell arrived before I did.'

'I hope he's not going to come anywhere near me or Mother,' snapped Kit. 'He'll get a dusty reception if so. He is amazingly thick skinned, but we'd make it clear to him just what we feel.'

'Kit . . .' Petra murmured warningly.

'It's all right,' said Kit. 'I'm not going to threaten him before a witness. Nor, Inspector Campbell, did I decide to burn down his house. I've had years in which I could have done that and haven't. What do you want to ask Petra? Just if she'd seen him? Have *you* seen him, by the way?'

'Yes,' said Jess briefly. 'But I didn't realise he'd been here. You would have known him when he lived at Key House. We are, of course, investigating the fire and the discovery of a body in the ruins. That has brought Mr Crown back to England from his present home in Portugal. He doesn't appear to have visited much over the years. Have you, either of you, been in any other contact with him during that time?'

'No!' chimed both sisters indignantly.

'I understand he was responsible for the car crash in which you were injured.' Jess gestured apologetically at the crutches. 'Forgive me mentioning it.'

'He was and remains responsible for everything,' declared Kit.

'I carry my share of blame,' Petra objected unexpectedly. 'I got into a car with a young man I could see was drunk. I suppose I was a bit tipsy myself. Stupidity's not blameless, Inspector. I should have known better. I was very young, but I wasn't a child. Also, I knew Gervase had already been involved in one smash. No one was killed or seriously injured that time, but, well, it was a sort of signpost to the possibility of another one some day. So please don't apologise for mentioning my sticks!'

Had Petra confessed to a moment's teenage foolishness in getting into a car with a drunken Gervase, wondered Jess, to defuse any suspicion she harboured a desire for revenge? More likely because she's had time to think it over and she's honest. What's more, Petra Stapleton isn't stupid, far from it. She has more insight than her sister.

Aloud she asked, 'Does either of you know, or can you guess, why he didn't sell Key House before now? Apparently he didn't want to live in it.'

'To sell it would have made sense,' agreed Kit, 'but Gervase isn't strong on common sense.'

'I think it was a complicated thing,' Petra said slowly. 'It had been his childhood home. He didn't need to sell. I don't think we can criticise him for not selling if he didn't have to. In the end, it's none of our business, is it?'

The words were spoken pleasantly, but there was steel behind them. Jess glimpsed the determined young woman who had fought back against her injuries to make a new life.

Kit sniffed loudly but said nothing.

'Does either of you know if he ever applied for planning permission to alter it, turn it into something he might want to live in?' asked Jess of both of them.

They stared back at her in a united front. 'Why on earth should he tell us, if he did?' Kit asked. 'We haven't been in contact with him, Inspector. We've told you that. From the time of the accident and what followed, until he walked into my sister's studio yesterday, we've had nothing to do with him.'

She paused. 'As for the planning permission, if he'd ever asked for it, that would depend on what he wanted to do. Certainly he'd have been told there were limits to any changes or additions he might want to make and they'd have insisted he didn't overstep the rules. Even my sister's cottage here . . .' Kit waved a hand to indicate their surroundings. 'We had to draw up very careful plans for this place. It was a stable before. Admittedly the planning people are often more concerned about the outside of a building than the inside. They're keen to preserve the look. But in the case of Key House, the inside mattered. It was historic, you know. All the staircase and panelling were original to the house, and they'd have wanted to preserve that. I agree it was gloomy, lots of dark wood, and I wouldn't have wanted to live in it. But generations had. There was even a local tradition about a ghost, a child who stood by visitors' beds and pulled the bedcovers off them. I've never met anyone who saw it.' Kit smiled unexpectedly and it lit up her face. Suddenly she was an attractive woman, but one under strain.

'What happens to a ghost when the building it haunts has gone?' asked Petra thoughtfully.

'It gets pretty frustrated, I imagine,' Kit told her sister. She turned back to Jess. 'Amanda, that's Gervase's mother, did her best when she lived there. We were only kids at the time, but I remember a lot of white leather furniture and table-lamps everywhere. There were polished parquet floors. Probably the original flagstones were underneath, but the Crowns had laid parquet over it.' Unkindly she added, 'They were that type of people. You know, buy a period property for the upmarket look and then tinker with the inside because it's old fashioned. Amanda would have wanted something that resembled a picture in *Homes and Gardens*.'

'I expect the old flagstones were cold,' Petra said and Kit had the grace to look as if she regretted her last remark.

However, she rallied quickly. 'I suppose there's irony in their putting down the wooden floors, because the parquet would have burned in the recent fire and the old stone flags wouldn't have done.'

'The parquet did burn,' Jess said quietly. 'We have wondered whether the arsonist knew that, was familiar with the house.'

Both sisters looked upset.

'How do you remember it?' Jess asked now of Petra. 'Your sister remembers it as dark and gloomy.'

'The panelled hallway was quite dark. But I don't remember the rest of it as gloomy. As Kit said, the interior was a bit like a picture in a magazine. But one wouldn't have expected anything less. Amanda was very elegant herself,' said Petra a little wistfully. 'I thought, when I was a kid, that she looked like a film star.'

Kit's assessment was more robust. 'Did you? I thought she was a freak, all that warpaint and silly high heels.'

'Does either of you know why she left her husband?'

'Because she couldn't stand him, I suppose,' said Kit. 'Neither could I.'

'But she didn't take her child with her,' Jess pointed out.

The sisters looked at one another. Kit spoke for them both. 'We all felt sorry for Gervase then, when he was a kid. But it doesn't excuse how he turned out.'

'We were children, too,' Petra added. 'We didn't know the circumstances of Amanda's leaving. It wasn't the sort of thing discussed before us.'

Jess recognised she wasn't going to get any further with that line of questioning. A door had been closed, just as it had been closed over the matter of the sale or non-sale of Key House. Both times Petra Stapleton had closed it. Kit was free with her opinions, but Petra got her own quiet last word. She changed the subject. 'Does the name Matthew Pietrangelo mean anything to either of you?'

They shook their heads. 'Who's he?' asked Kit.

Jess produced one of the photos given to them by Sarah Gresham. She held it out. The sisters stared it.

'Never seen him!' declared Kit, taking it from Jess and then handing it to Petra.

Petra said quietly, 'He looks a bit like Gervase.' She raised her eyes from the photo to Jess's face. 'Is he the one who died in the fire?' she asked. 'Did he die because someone thought he was Gervase?'

No, Petra wasn't stupid. She was very smart! 'We think it's possible that is the dead man,' Jess began. 'We're awaiting the result of tests and dental checks—' She was cut short by the sound of yet another car drawing up outside.

Kit went to the window and peered out. 'Bother, it's the woman with a funny-looking dog. I think it's that dog you've agreed to do a portrait of, Petra.'

Petra put a hand to her mouth. 'I forgot! I arranged that Muriel Pickering would come today with Hamlet, so that I could do some preliminary sketches!'

Jess cursed mentally.

A heavy hand bashed the brass horseshoe against the door. Kit went to open it. Petra smiled at Jess and whispered, 'I don't suppose you've met Muriel Pickering? She lives locally.'

'I have, as it happens,' Jess replied in a similar low voice.

'I don't have to prepare you, then! I hope you like Muriel because she really is very good hearted . . . Come in, Muriel!' Petra raised her voice. 'Good dog, Hamlet! Let's have a good look at you!'

The pug dog came in first, grunting to itself. Its slightly bandy legs gave it a rolling, nautical walk. It gave Jess a suspicious look, ignored Kit and went to Petra. It sat down in front of her and looked expectant.

'He's waiting for a biscuit,' said Muriel's voice from the door. 'You gave him one last time and Hamlet never forgets.'

She appeared in the room. It was the first time Jess had seen her not dressed in her yellow oilskins. She wore corduroy trousers and a hand-knitted sweater with holes in both elbows. Without her yellow hat, her hair could be seen to be iron-grey and irregularly chopped into a sort of pageboy, probably by her own hand. A thick fringe reached down to the rims of her glinting spectacles, through which she fixed a belligerent gaze on Jess.

'Hello,' she said, 'you again. You pop up everywhere.'

'I might say the same thing of you, Mrs Pickering,' said Jess.

Muriel blinked at that and retorted ungraciously, 'I suppose you're still investigating, but you certainly leave no stone unturned, do you?'

'That's the idea,' Jess told her. From the corner of her eye she thought she saw Kit Stapleton exchange a wry look with her sister. 'I might even come and visit you at Mullions, Mrs Pickering.'

'Welcome, I'm sure,' said Muriel carelessly.

Now, thought Jess, is that the first lie that's been told to me during my visit here? Or have I been comprehensively led up the garden path from the start?

Kit followed Jess out into the gravelled forecourt, leaving Muriel to expound on Hamlet's finer points to Petra.

'I hope you can sort this out quickly,' she said, 'because until you do, Gervase Crown is going to hang around. Nobody hereabouts wants that and certainly my family doesn't.'

'He seems to be aware of his unpopularity, or that's the impression I got when I spoke to him,' Jess told her.

Kit pulled a face. 'He'd be even thicker skinned than I thought him if he wasn't. I'm not surprised he didn't stay here to live in Key House. He wouldn't have been made welcome in the community.'

'But he didn't sell it,' Jess returned to the matter of the non-sale of Key House. 'I still find that hard to understand.'

Kit shrugged. 'So he didn't sell it. Perhaps he's just hung on to it to annoy us all. I don't know. Who knows what does go on in Gervase's mind? Anyway, I'm not his greatest fan so don't listen to me . . .' She put her head on one side and smiled at Jess. 'I didn't attack that unfortunate guy with the Italian name because I thought he was Gervase. I didn't burn the house down.'

'I haven't accused you of either crime,' Jess told her mildly.

'No, but you must be compiling your list of suspects. I noticed, when you showed us that photo of the victim back there, that the poor chap looked a little bit like Gervase. I wasn't going to say so in front of my sister, in case I was the only one who thought it.

116

I didn't want to worry her. But Petra noticed it too anyway. You've seen Gervase. Do you think it? Does he look like the victim?'

'It did strike us that there is a similarity,' Jess had to admit. 'But we're not reading anything into that yet.'

'Really?' asked Kit disbelievingly. 'Well, good luck with your enquiries.' She gave a laconic wave and turned to go back into the cottage.

Jess got into her car and drove away slowly. Since she was so close to the murder scene, it would be a good idea to go and take another look at it, if only to check that sightseers hadn't been trampling across it.

But Key House was as she'd last seen it, standing desolate and in ruins. The smell of charred wood still hung in the air. Puddles spotted the scene where the fire brigade had returned to dampen down the site as a precaution against a hotspot breaking out again in flames. Gervase Crown would not be rebuilding this, she thought, and no one could reasonably expect him to.

Her mobile phone jangled as she climbed back into her car. She put it to her ear. 'Phil?'

'Just to let you know,' came Morton's voice, 'that Gervase Crown flew in to Heathrow late on the day immediately following the fire, on an Air Portugal flight. The ashes of his house would still have been hot, so he didn't waste time. He picked up a hire car, a BMW, at the airport and drove straight down here and took a room at The Royal Oak that night.'

'So he didn't set the fire himself,' Jess murmured.

'What's that, ma'am? Oh, that's right. He didn't start the fire. He could still have hired someone to do it. He might even have hired Pietrangelo. Didn't Pietrangelo's girlfriend tell you that he had no work in hand at the moment and new commissions were slow coming in for him? They wanted to buy a house. He needed to earn a few quid.'

'We'd have to establish that Crown knew Pietrangelo. When I showed him the photograph of the victim he denied it. If he hired him to set the fire, then of course he would deny it. But his reaction struck me as genuine at the time. However, it's a thought, Phil. We'll add it to the list of possibilities. Oh, and we now know that on the morning following his arrival, Crown's first action was to go early to what was left of Key House and check it out. After that he paid a call on Petra Stapleton, the young woman so badly injured in the car crash that resulted in his being given a prison sentence. It left Petra in a wheelchair. In the afternoon he came to see us.'

'What did he go and see her for?' came Morton's voice, incredulous, in her ear. 'I'd have thought he'd be, well, ashamed.'

'Petra says she thought he was in shock and wanted someone to talk to. The opinion of Petra's sister, Kit, is that he is thick skinned and quite possibly bone headed as well. That's quite interesting because I got the impression from the brief conversation I had with him that he's neither. Certainly not the second. As to the first? Well, possibly he's thick skinned to some extent. But not to the degree Kit Stapleton would have us believe. Nor do I buy that she thinks he's stupid. Both sisters, incidentally, remarked unprompted on a physical similarity between Gervase Crown and Pietrangelo. Can you find out something about Kit Stapleton, Phil? Just background. There's something going on there, but I don't know what.'

'Will do,' promised Morton.

'And even if Crown is just lacking in normal sensitivities, it still doesn't explain why he went to see Petra Stapleton. There's something in that set-up, something private to the people concerned.

Whether it has to do with the burning of the house is another matter. I'd like to know what it is, even so, because at least we can then discount it.'

She clicked the phone off and sat with it silent in her hand at the wheel of her stationary car. She was still thinking about Kit Stapleton. Kit was so insistent that she disliked Gervase and she certainly had good reason. But she did keep repeating it. 'Yes, I think the roots of all this go back a long way,' Jess confirmed to herself aloud. 'Kit wants me to accept an edited version of events as she gives them to me. But I've got to keep talking to people. Someone must know something.'

She started up the engine and, as she did, her eye fell on the narrow turning a little further down the road. Muriel Pickering's house, Mullions, was down there. Phil had already interviewed Muriel and Jess had had a couple of chats with her. But she was a long-time local resident and it might be worth talking to her again. To be sure, Muriel wasn't the chatty sort, but if Jess kept up the pressure she might eventually come up with something.

Muriel would still be at The Barn, anxious to direct the artist's attention to Hamlet's squashed features. It would be a good moment to take a look at Mullions in its owner's absence. Jess drove slowly forward and turned off where Muriel had indicated. A battered road sign, suggesting past collision with some large vehicle attempting to turn, told her this was Long Lane. The lane was narrow and twisted in a serpentine progress indicating its origins as a path between fields. Jess wondered just how far it ran and where it came out. There was woodland another half a mile or so ahead. Perhaps it stopped there? One more twist and she was obliged to brake. She'd come upon Muriel's home.

It was not only its sudden appearance that was surprising about

Mullions. Jess had been imagining a cottage, once belonging to a shepherd or gamekeeper. But Mullions was an imposing old house, tall and narrow, with attic windows gazing out over the countryside around. At the very top, in the middle of the roof, it had a funny little turret that might once have been a dovecote. It suggested a former rectory or a local landowner's dwelling more than a labourer's home. The whole place had a neglected look. The garden was overgrown, the house unpainted. Jess pulled up on to the verge in the unlikely eventuality that any other vehicle came down this way and wanted to pass, and got out.

The entry to the property was barred by an unlovely construction consisting of a wooden frame filled in with chicken wire. It hung on rusting hinges between posts and bore a notice. PLEASE SHUT GATE. LIVESTOCK. Jess looked over it. There was no sign of any animal life. She lifted the rope loop that fell over a post and cautiously opened the gate.

'Hello!' she called, just in case. She was presuming that Muriel lived alone but perhaps she didn't. No one showed him or herself in reply. She dropped the rope loop back over the post, keeping the gate closed as desired by the property owner, and walked up to the house. Shielding her eyes, she peered through the window of what must be a sitting room.

'Phew!' she said aloud. 'What a dump!'

The room was cluttered with dark, battered furniture. Some dingy oil paintings, indiscernible in subject, hung on the tobacco-coloured walls. Crumpled sheets of newspaper, books, what looked like used crockery left from a meal, lay scattered like fallen leaves across the surfaces of various small tables and seats, and the carpet. The interior of Mullions, all this suggested, was as poorly maintained as the exterior. Jess thought she could make out a zinc bucket by the hearth, containing wood chunks for the open fire.

She left the window and walked slowly round to the back of the house. A corrugated-iron garage stood ahead of her, doors open and empty. Suddenly she came upon the livestock. A gaggle of hens set up a cackling and fled before her down the length of the back garden. They were soon lost from sight among the undergrowth. Only a belligerent and scruffy cockerel remained. It flew up on to a wooden sawhorse and perched there, from time to time giving her a malicious squawk, accompanied by a flap of the wings.

'OK, buster,' said Jess to him. 'I'm not after your wives.'

Someone had been sawing firewood on the horse. Chippings and sawdust covered the surrounding area. A couple of fallen tree branches lay nearby, suggesting they were next for dismemberment. Beyond, to the left, stood a large wooden shed once painted green, but with only peeling flakes of colour remaining. It had one grimy window and a rain-barrel stood outside the door. Jess went to inspect the shed further. It wasn't locked. She pulled the door open and took a look inside. It was no tidier than the house, filled with every sort of implement and rubbish. There were fishing rods in their canvas jackets stacked in one corner, thick with dust and obviously never used by Ms Pickering. Jess wondered who had been the fisherman. There was a wooden bench piled high with tools, some appearing old enough to be donated to a local museum, and empty flowerpots. Others hung on the wall beyond, together with a net on a pole presumably designed to scoop out the catch from the river. All suggested a lifestyle long gone.

She closed the door and walked back to her car, carefully closing the gate. The brief tour had depressed her. No wonder Muriel was so ungracious, waking up to this every morning. No wonder, too, that she thought so highly of Hamlet who shared this desolation. Jess drove away.

Carter, too, was paying a visit. In his case it was on Serena Foscott. The Foscotts lived in a large house in the architectural style known as Mock Tudor. The outer walls were pebble dashed and a dirty brown. The wooden fretwork applied to the exterior and meant to suggest the sixteenth century now needed a lick of paint. It was a style of house he'd never cared for, although in its heyday – which Carter guessed had been in the 1920s or thirties – it probably had looked very smart and the latest thing. It sat in the middle of a garden laid almost entirely to lawn surrounded by trees, and was approached by a weed-strewn gravel drive. Other houses strung out along one side of the same road were of much the same type, if slightly better kept. It was difficult to tell. Most owners had chosen to put tall trees between themselves and the highway. All the properties were, he was sure, worth a lot of money. The other side of the road was still occupied by fields. 'Secluded' was what estate agents usually called that sort of situation and it put the price up.

'I don't think we've met,' said Mrs Foscott, eyeing him up and down as if he might have had a 'For Sale' tag hung round his neck. She was a small, wiry, weather-beaten woman who gave the impression of reserves of unspent energy fizzing for release. But not in order to do housework, it seemed. As she spoke, she removed a pile of unironed washing from the depths of an armchair and stood with it in her arms, looking vaguely round the room for somewhere to deposit it. Eventually she solved the problem by lobbing the load towards another chair in a far corner. Most landed on the target, some on the floor where Mrs Foscott ignored it. She indicated the freed chair to Carter who sat down in it cautiously. It twanged under him.

'Springs going,' said Serena casually. 'My husband knows you. You went to see him.' In contrast to her tone, her body language was wary.

'Indeed, he does, Mrs Foscott.' Carter looked round the room, seeking an opening that would lead to Serena Foscott letting down her guard. As on Reggie's desk at work, there was a photograph of a child on a pony near at hand. 'Your daughter?'

Serena glanced at it. 'Yes, that's Charlie. We got rid of that animal. It was useless. It never would have made it in competition. It couldn't step over a pole on the ground without tripping, let alone jump a fence. Charlie kept falling off it. We've bought a better animal now. Charlie's doing much better. Blue rosette last time out.'

'Oh, I'm pleased to hear that. My daughter is staying with me at the moment.' Carter registered the common interest. 'Normally she lives with her mother and stepfather. But they've got asbestos in her school. She looks about the same age as – Charlie.'

Serena Foscott assessed him. 'Divorced?'

'Er, yes.'

'Bad luck,' said Serena kindly. 'You're looking into the business of the fire, I suppose, and the stiff. Rum business, that. You never know what's round the corner, do you?'

'You don't indeed,' Carter agreed with her. 'The police are investigating and that means we ask a lot of questions, some of which turn out irrelevant. Occasionally we hit the mark. We make nuisances of ourselves to a lot of people. I'm sorry to trouble you, Mrs Foscott, as I'm sure you're busy.'

'Always,' confirmed the lady of the house. 'Never get a moment to myself. Would you like some tea?'

Carter hurriedly held up a hand. 'Oh, please, no. I won't stay long. I came to call because I understand you are Gervase Crown's cousin.'

'That's right. Haven't seen much of him over the years. But we weren't close as kids. He was a few years younger than me; and Amanda, that was his mother, she was a cold fish. So was his father, Sebastian. So there wasn't much visiting back and forth between our families.'

'Let's see,' said Carter, 'are you related on his mother's side or on his father's?'

'Sebastian Crown was my mother's brother. They were never close, either.' Serena paused and added, as if to underline the connection, 'That means *she* was a Crown. She married my father, whose surname was Mayhew, and so I was a Mayhew before I became a Foscott.'

Carter filed this scrap of ancestral tree in the back of his memory but did not allow it to distract him. 'So you would have known Key House, even if you didn't visit it very often.'

'Certainly. Are you sure about the tea? Won't take a jiff.'

The repeated offer to make tea suggested to Carter that his visit wasn't altogether unwelcome. Perhaps Serena was glad of a chance to sit and talk, instead of doing the ironing. He said, well, if she insisted . . .

Serena strode out of the room in a purposeful manner and could be heard rattling and clanging things in the kitchen with what seemed unnecessary zeal. Carter took another look round the room. The furniture was good, even if old and in need of a polish and some repair here and there. He fancied there was a faint smell of horses about the place, or perhaps only about Serena. The television set looked new. A note propped against a vase on the mantelshelf above the tiled Art Deco fireplace read: Dentist!!! Carter smiled. It was untidy but it was a family home. Suddenly he found himself envying Reggie Foscott.

Serena was back, carrying a mug in either hand. She put one down on an occasional table by his chair and retook her own seat on a large chesterfield that seemed to have strayed into the room from some London club or a stately home. 'I haven't got any biscuits. I did buy some but Charlie must have filched them to feed that pony. Is that what you want to talk about, Key House? Or about my cousin?'

'I wondered if you could suggest why Mr Crown didn't sell Key House, before now. He seems unclear himself about it.'

'Blowed if I know,' said Serena. 'It was his decision to make, I suppose. He's the one you should ask and you say you have. I only know he refused to sell, even to us when we asked him.'

'*You* thought of buying it?' Carter sipped cautiously at the dark brown brew in his mug.

'I did, although Reggie wasn't keen on the idea. I thought it seemed a shame to let a good house already in the family just slip away into the ownership of strangers. So I put the suggestion to Gerry. But Gerry was so adamant he wouldn't sell, we let the matter drop.'

'Gerry? That's what people call Gervase Crown?'

'It's what I've always called him. His mother didn't like to hear it. Both his parents always called him Gervase. Most other people do as well, I fancy. I don't know why I've stuck to calling him Gerry. I suppose, in the beginning, I did it to annoy his mother.'

'And your cousin didn't give you any reason for his refusal to sell the house to you?'

She shook her head. 'Nope. He dug in his heels, laid back his ears and refused the fence. As I was telling you, we weren't close, never went in for confidential chats. If he didn't want to tell us, or me, his reasons, then he wouldn't. And he didn't.'

'But you are otherwise on good terms? I know your husband does his legal work. I would have thought he might stay with you, in your home, while in England, to give you a chance to catch up,' Carter remarked with his most disingenuous smile.

'We offered!' Serena said sharply. 'I wouldn't have minded having him here, especially now he has a horse.'

Did she imagine Gervase had brought the horse with him?

'Something to talk about other than Key House,' explained his hostess, seeing his puzzlement. 'It surprised me to learn that Gerry had bought a horse. In fact, I was flabbergasted. It was always cars with him. But you'll know all about that. Gerry asked Reggie to book him a room at The Royal Oak. Not a bad place, I understand. He'll probably be warmer there than here. Our central heating is on the blink again.'

'You say Mr Foscott wasn't keen on buying Key House, even before your cousin refused to sell. Did he have any particular objection to the idea?'

The question threw her for a moment, but only a moment. 'Cost of keeping the place up, largely. Five bedrooms, you know. Or it did have, before someone burned it down. Not to mention three downstairs' reception, huge kitchen and a butler's pantry. Reggie said, "Look here, it's buy Key House or keep Charlie's pony. We can't afford both, not with livery costs being what they are. Make your choice." Well, naturally, we'd have kept the pony. But we hadn't to make the choice as things turned out, because, as I said, Gerry didn't want to sell.'

'Have you any idea who might have wanted it destroyed? Set fire to it?'

'None. I can only suggest that it did attract a rather rough bunch of wanderers who broke in and slept in it from time to time. One of *them*? I believe they did light fires in there. I can easily imagine one got out of control. It's probably a wonder it didn't go up in flames long before now. Reggie did worry about it, what with Gerry being abroad. But I told him, "Let Gerry worry, if he wants to, and if he doesn't want to, there's no need for you to do it in his stead." There's a fellow called . . .' Serena's brow furrowed in thought. 'Trenton, Roger Trenton. He was always bugging poor Reggie about it, as if Reggie could do anything. That's the guy you want to talk to, Roger Trenton.'

'I think an officer has already spoken to Mr Trenton.'

'No joy there, then?' Serena commiserated. 'Bad luck. He'd have been your best bet.'

'So you think really it was a tramp who lit a fire and it then got out of control?'

'Pretty well something like that.' Serena beamed at him. 'These things do happen. There was a case a few years ago when some hippies broke into a holiday cottage not far from here. They caused no end of damage before they were persuaded to move on. Amongst other things, they'd burned a large hole in the sitting-room carpet. A log must have rolled out of the hearth. Well, why not something similar at Key House?'

'What about the dead man?' Carter asked mildly.

'Oh, I don't know about *him*,' returned Serena. 'Perhaps he lit the fire?'

'He wasn't a tramp. We believe we know who he was, although we're awaiting confirmation. He lived in Cheltenham and has been missing from home.'

'Really? What was he doing out there?' Serena gazed at him with such innocence that it riled Carter. He did not like being treated like a fool.

'We don't know for sure, do we?' He was provoked into retorting. More formally he added, 'We are following a line of enquiry. He may have been interested in purchasing the house.'

'Ah . . .' said Serena, leaning back on the chesterfield. 'Could he have been the chap who went to see Reggie, oh, several weeks ago? If he was, Reggie told him the house wasn't on the market. We – Reggie – thought that was the end of that.'

You know he must have been the fellow who went to see your husband, the inner Carter snarled.

'He seems not to have taken it as final,' he said aloud, adding with a touch of sarcasm, 'nor can we think of any reason why he might have lit a fire. Or any reason why someone hit him over the head.'

'Bit of a mystery, then. But that's your line of business, I suppose, mysteries. Well, my bright ideas are exhausted,' said Serena cheerfully. 'You've heard 'em all. Sorry I can't help you.'

There was a sound of a car drawing up outside. 'Oh, here's Reggie,' said Serena with no attempt at faking surprise.

What are the odds, wondered Carter, that all the banging around in the kitchen was to cover the sound of her phoning her husband to let him know I was here? Well-matched pair, the Foscotts. At any rate, the visit was over.

'I mustn't detain you any longer,' he said, rising from the chair. It gave a triumphant farewell twang. 'Thank you for the tea.'

'Nice to meet you,' said Serena. 'I've met an Inspector Campbell once or twice, one of your lot. It was another case of murder. She struck me as a very bright sort.'

'She is, indeed.'

'Ah, Superintendent Carter!' Foscott appeared in the room, smiling benevolently. 'How are things going?'

'As well as can be expected at this stage,' Carter told him.

'Excellent,' murmured Foscott.

They both beamed at him.

Chapter 10

It was about three o'clock that afternoon when Kit Stapleton walked into the lounge of The Royal Oak, and stopped to peer into the recesses of the narrow L-shaped room. The low ceiling, with its blackened beams, and small windows set in thick stone walls encouraged the gloom and made it a place of secret corners. As usual in such public lounges, sofas and armchairs were grouped in defensive clusters like wagons drawn up in a circle on the prairie, giving an illusion of privacy to guests. It was too early for the management to entertain the expense of switching on the wall lights and any additional light came from the real fire of spluttering logs in the hearth. It made shadows jump about, playing across walls and furniture in disorienting fashion.

Gervase, settled in a far corner, saw her before she located him, and called out, 'Over here, Kit!' He followed his words with a raised arm and beckoning hand.

Kit drew in a deep breath, mentally girding herself for an encounter that was likely to prove a battle, and walked towards him. At her approach, he rose from his armchair to greet her. The shadow thrown on the wall behind him was of a giant distorted figure in the dancing firelight, both cartoonish and sinister. He himself was leaner and tougher looking than she remembered him. With his long hair he really did appear a spectre from the inn's historic past. A highwayman perhaps? Or one of Prince Rupert of the Rhine's cavalrymen, part loyalist, part marauder? Certainly capable of anything, for good or evil. She thought, *Oh, damn you, Gervase Crown! Why couldn't you stay in your Portuguese hideaway?*

Aloud she said, 'Hello, Gervase.'

'Hi!' He gestured at the comfortable leather chair opposite his. 'Take a pew. I've been expecting you.'

'The barman said you were in here.' Kit sat down awkwardly. The light glinted on the tumbler on the low table between them. 'You've started early, I see.' She didn't try to disguise the sarcasm in her voice.

'As a matter of fact,' Gervase said mildly, 'I don't drink much these days except for bottled beer: Sagres, the Portuguese sort. I no longer indulge in the hard stuff. I did allow myself a small whisky while waiting for you.'

'You were so sure I'd turn up here looking for you?' She tried to keep her voice steady.

'Of course. I knew you'd be round here like a shot as soon as you found out I'd been to see Petra. You've come to bite my head off.'

'Of course I have! That was unspeakably bad behaviour on your part, Gervase.'

'I specialise in bad behaviour,' he retorted. 'You know that. I'm not a completely changed character. I may have given up the booze – largely – but there are limits to my capacity for reform.'

A waiter came in to ask if they'd like anything.

'Two black coffees,' said Kit firmly.

Gervase chuckled and returned the waiter's enquiring look with a wry grin and a nod.

Kit took up the subject again. 'You shouldn't have gone to see her.'

'I needed to,' Gervase replied with a sudden obstinate note in his voice.

She glared at him. 'You are a real pig, you know. It's not about what *you* need. It's about what my sister needs; and it's not visits from you!'

He gestured at the room around them. 'No ditch for you to push me into here!'

'Don't joke! There's nothing amusing about disturbing Petra. Her well-being is fragile. I don't just mean her physical health. She's found a sort of balance, made a life for herself, is – or was until you showed up – happy.'

'She's stronger than you think she is,' Gervase told her. 'She can cope with a visit from me.'

'What makes you so sure? You hadn't seen her or been in touch in years. How do you know? You are so damn selfish!' Kit leaned forward and hissed the last words at him. 'Leave her alone!'

There was a silence. The coffee arrived to occupy them. When they were alone again, Gervase took a sip from his cup, winced and set it down. 'Dishwater.'

Without looking at Kit, he went on, 'It is years, as you say. I've paid the odd flying visit to home turf, to chat things over with Reggie Foscott. Usually I've stopped by their place to say hello to Serena. My dear cousin never changes, except to get more leathery. I've always aimed get the whole thing over and done in a day or two and then get away again. So I ought to feel a stranger. Yet, funnily enough, when I came back here the other day, to Weston St Ambrose, I felt I'd never been away. Of course, the old homestead wasn't a couple of miles down the road any longer, just a heap of blackened stones and some flapping plastic tape with "police" written on it. And this place . . .' Gervase indicated the lounge of The Royal Oak. 'This has gone up in the world a bit. Done out to impress the tourists, I suspect. It's got reproduction four-poster beds in the rooms upstairs and the restaurant offers the sort of menu you get in fashionable restaurants. I can remember when it offered nothing but baked spuds or sausage and chips. But it's a superficial sort of change. Otherwise, the years have just slipped past.'

'Life goes on,' Kit told him in a clipped tone. 'We simply have to get on with it. It's not what we imagined it would be, that picture is shattered. We try to make something out of the pieces.'

'It goes on but in some ways it doesn't change at all, that's my point,' Gervase argued. 'The same people are still around. I even bumped into old Doc Layton the evening I arrived, just outside this place. It had all been a rush, managing to get a seat on a late flight, landing at Heathrow after dark, picking up a car and driving down here . . . I was all in and don't mind admitting it. I checked in and slung my bag in the room, and then I nipped out for a smoke before getting my head down. Lo and behold, there was old Layton, rolling up the road wearing, if my memory doesn't deceive me, the same suit he used to wear when he was my dad's doctor. I used to keep away from him then. But I hailed him, anyway. I had to remind him who I was. He didn't look delighted to see me, but he said he was sorry about Key House. He'd attended the scene to certify death. It's amazing, isn't it? There was the poor sod, whoever he was, burned to a crisp, and someone medically qualified had to go and pronounce him well and truly dead.

'I reminded Layton that the last time we'd met had been at my dad's funeral. They let me out of quod for the day to attend. All the mourners had scowled at me as if Dad's death had been my fault, and were hardly able to mutter condolences. Layton didn't like being reminded. He thought my mentioning it was in poor taste, I could see. He harrumphed at me and scurried away. Before he learned I was staying here, he had probably intended to come in for a nightcap in the bar. But he didn't fancy sitting over a drink in my company.'

'Your talking about your father's funeral was in poor taste,' said Kit. 'Dr Layton probably thought it showed a lack of respect for your father and a lack of contrition on your part, after all the trouble you'd caused.'

Gervase leaned forward with a grin. 'I like bad taste. It's a pity my father died while I was in quod, and I do feel I probably hastened his end by being a jailbird at the time. But I wasn't going to admit any guilty feelings to an old hypocrite like Layton. Besides, I like putting people's backs up. They stop pretending when that happens. You get the genuine reaction.'

'I don't pretend,' Kit said crossly.

'No, my love, you don't. You are the same Kit with the sharp eye and sharper tongue.'

He leaned back again right into the depths of the chair and propped one ankle on the other knee. 'So, what about you, Kit? What have you been doing all this time? What kind of life have you made for yourself? Are you in a steady relationship, as they like to call it?'

'No. Are you?' Kit drank cautiously of her coffee.

'Nothing permanent. I think women are wary of me, find me unreliable.'

'You are unreliable.'

'Whereas you, Kit, were and remain utterly reliable,' Gervase retorted. 'You have never pretended, as you say. I always knew exactly what you were going to do and you haven't changed. I knew you'd come charging in here to savage me.'

'Shut up!' snapped Kit, feeling her face burn and not from the heat of crackling logs.

Gervase had managed to turn the tables. She'd come in here, exactly as he'd suggested, full of righteous anger, determined to pulverise him. Now she was on the defensive.

He pressed home his advantage. 'So, do you have anyone in your life? Never found Mr Right?'

'I was married briefly,' Kit told him with reluctance. 'For a couple of years, that's all.'

'Wow!' he said in mock admiration. 'You've achieved more than I have in that line, then. What went wrong?'

'With my marriage? Nothing, really. It was a mistake and, after a couple of years, we were both bored stiff with one another's company and had to admit it. We decided to split amicably while still friends; rather than wait until we loathed one another and started flinging the crockery at each other's heads. We're still on good terms: exchange Christmas cards, that sort of thing . . . occasional phone call to catch up. But we have no plans, and won't ever have any, to try again. Quit while you're ahead, they say. And we had no kids to complicate things.'

'Yes, children do complicate things, don't they?' Gervase said soberly.

He's done it again! raged Kit inwardly. And this time I set it up and walked right into it.

'I shouldn't have said that,' she said stiffly aloud. 'Your parents split up, of course, and you were a casualty.'

'A casualty?' Gervase rolled the word round his mouth as if it had been some sort of strangely flavoured canapé. 'No, I don't think I ever thought of myself as that. They didn't ever get along, my parents. I was well aware of that. It didn't really surprise me when my mother left. Their break-up wasn't a civilised affair, like yours. No one exchanged Christmas cards or phoned. My father seethed about it in that rumbling volcano way he had, always threatening to erupt. I kept out of his way.'

'You must have been very unhappy,' Kit heard herself say.

'Of course I was bloody unhappy!' There was an edge to his voice. 'But when you're a child you accept situations as they are. My father couldn't bring himself to speak about my mother, so neither did I. We cut her out of our lives, as she'd cut us out of hers. Of course, there was no end of gossip in the neighbourhood. No one knew where she'd gone or what was happening. And no one told me. There were the usual stories about a mystery lover she'd run off to join. There was even a theory in some folk's minds that Dad had murdered her and buried her body in the garden, or in a field back of the house.'

'I never heard that!' Kit was shocked.

'Of course not, you were a kid. I knew about it because I heard my father raging down the telephone to his lawyers, threatening to take people to court. He didn't, of course, because that would have meant going public and no doubt his legal people pointed that out to him. He could have stopped the malicious gossip at a stroke if he'd spoken to anyone about what was going on. But that wasn't his style. Never apologise, never explain, was his motto. He was the most private man I've ever come across. He let no one into his life; not my mother, not me. There's no point in whinging about it now.' Gervase spoke the last words crisply, putting an end to the subject. After a short silence, he continued in a different tone, 'So, what do you do with yourself now, Kit?'

'I work shifts as a doctors' receptionist in Cheltenham. That's where I own a little house. I spend a lot of time driving out here to check either on Petra or on my mother. You aren't thinking of pestering her as well, are you?'

'Your mum? I wouldn't dare.'

'Good.'

They both finished their coffee in silence. Gervase pushed his empty cup away from him disdainfully.

'Do you know, Kit?' he began, but then broke off and snorted. 'What a stupid expression that is. Of course you don't know or I wouldn't be telling you now. Last year I met my mother again for the first time since she walked out on me when I was twelve.'

'*You've seen Amanda?*' Kit gaped, made an effort to regain her poise, but found it beyond her. 'In the flesh?'

'Of course in the flesh, you noodle,' said Gervase. 'I didn't mean she appeared, swathed in white muslin and floating in the air, while I was having a particularly bad trip.'

'I meant,' Kit said swiftly, recovering, 'not on a social website or something like that.'

'Do me a favour. I'm practically a recluse in Portugal. I go out of my way to avoid people. I hardly know my neighbours. Why on earth should I want to sit in front of a computer and inform the world about my innermost thoughts and what I had for breakfast? No, she turned up, in the flesh as you put it . . . well, not a lot of flesh admittedly. She was as thin as a rake.'

'She always was,' said Kit unkindly, and knowing it.

'Miaow, Kit! Charity, if you please! Slim and elegant, I think she'd have called it. Anyway, she's been living in California all these years. She was amazingly well preserved: gym-toned muscles, perfect suntan, not a hair out of place, chunky jewellery, painted finger and toenails. She'd remarried – twice. Husband number three had recently died. (Dad being husband number one!) He'd left her pretty well off. She'd decided to come to Europe on holiday, travel round a bit. She'd had her lawyers track me down and found out I was living in Portugal. So, when she got as far as Lisbon, she got in touch. We had a very civilised lunch in a fish restaurant on the coast. We didn't rehash the past. She told me about her home in Sacramento and her European tour plans. I told her about my house and my horse. After lunch I drove her out to see my house. Afterwards, we walked on the beach at Guincho, though not for long. The sand got in her shoes and the sea breeze ruffled her coiffure. We were running out of conversation by then, anyway. I drove her back into Lisbon to her hotel and that was that. We haven't made contact again, still no Christmas cards or phone calls. I think she was satisfied and has expunged me from her life – again. She's probably back in California, busy hunting down husband number four.'

'And how did you feel on seeing her again?' asked Kit.

Gervase thought about it. 'I don't think I felt – or feel now – anything much at all really. I was slightly puzzled, if anything. Now I'm relieved she's lost interest again. I don't think I could be bothered to keep in touch with her. Like you and your "ex", we'd have nothing left to say to one another.'

He looked at her with a sudden, wicked glint in his eyes. 'Unlike you and me, Kit! We never did, and haven't now, run out of things to say to one another. Generally we did it by way of squabbling or you upbraiding me on my ungentlemanly behaviour. You're still able to do that.'

'I won't forgive you for going to see Petra,' Kit told him. 'But I've said my piece now. I hope you've taken it to heart and will stay away from her in future. The cops have been to see her too, by the way, one woman officer, plain-clothes and quite senior, an Inspector Campbell. I was there at the time.'

'Campbell? I met her,' said Gervase briefly. 'Plain-clothes but not plain faced. Red hair, small, neat features, a bit fierce but very attractive, even so.'

'Glad your distress at losing the family house didn't prevent you appreciating her looks.'

'I met her at the copshop, where I also met a grouchy sergeant and a dour bloke with the rank of superintendent. They don't understand why I didn't sell Key House while it was intact.'

'They asked us about that,' she told him. 'Inspector Campbell was very interested in the house. I told her about the ghost.'

'What ghost?' asked Gervase, raising his eyebrows.

'The one you told me about, the child who appeared at visitors' bedsides and pulled off the blankets.'

Gervase gave a shout of laughter. 'That? I made that up to tease you when we were kids. I wanted to scare you. Some hope, you were always scare-proof. I'd forgotten about that.'

'You made it up?' Kit burst out in renewed anger. 'Honestly, you are the absolute limit, Gervase! I thought it was true.'

'You believe in ghosts? You?' he asked incredulously.

'No, I don't believe in actual ghosts! But I believed that there was a real ghost story attached to Key House. Now I've told the police about it, and it's *not true*. It was some dopey idea of yours. I should have guessed. If the cops ever find out they'll think I'm potty.'

'Why should they ever find out? They're not interested in ghosts. They're interested in murderers and arsonists.' Casually, he added, 'Who put a match to Key House, Kit?'

'How on earth should I know?' she railed at him.

Gervase leaned back in his armchair and the leather covering creaked. He stretched out his legs. 'The cops think I had something to do with it, you know.'

'Why? Did you?'

'I was in Portugal when it went up like a Roman candle, as they'll find out when they check. They will check. I know how their nasty suspicious minds work.'

There was a movement by the door into the lounge. The attentive waiter was back. Kit wondered if he'd been listening just outside. Gervase raised an arm to summon him.

'I don't know about you, Kit, but I do need a proper drink right now.'

Chapter 11

Both Carter and Jess returned to base to be informed that dental records and early DNA results confirmed the theory they had been working on. The dead man was indeed Matthew Pietrangelo. Now it was a matter of confirming the sad fact to the dead man's partner and relatives.

Sarah Gresham received the news stoically. 'I knew it must be Matthew. If he were alive he would have contacted me by now.' She had hesitated. 'I feel as though he does want to contact me, but he can't. That must sound foolish. It's as if he's not quite gone away. But he has, hasn't he?'

Later in the day Key House had a visitor. The light was poor, one of those winter days when it never really brightens before the night draws in again. Sarah felt it reflected her mood. She picked her way carefully over ashes, chunks of burned beam and little cairns made of roof tiles; and negotiated what had once been a doorway to enter the house itself. The atmosphere inside was stifling, as if the fire had sucked out all the oxygen. She couldn't stay in here for long, but she would do what she had come to do. She reached the spot she sought, stooped and laid down the flowers she'd brought with her. It was even gloomier in here, so that the flowers seemed to sink into the ground. The odour of the fire, still impregnating everything, obliterated the scent of the blooms.

For her, it was the stench of death. She wrapped her arms round herself, pressing her fingertips into the rough wool cloth of her winter coat, not because she was cold, but because she was comfortless. The bright petals on the blackened ground seemed a mockery, rather than a mark of affection and respect. She felt as though the fire had reached inside her and burned out everything that made her a normal sentient human being. Matt had been a dead husk on this floor: but she was a living husk. She went through the motions of day-to-day existence but felt nothing, only emptiness.

Above her head something creaked and she looked up. A dusting of grit pattered down on her face and she coughed and moved aside. The small incident caused her to look around again and take stock of the extent of the damage. Even Matt wouldn't have hoped to restore the place from the present ruin. There was that creak again, slightly above her and to one side. She looked up again, more carefully this time and shielding her eyes with her hand. She could see right up through the charred joists that had supported the rooms above to the blackened remains of the rafters, sticking up like a carcass from which all the meat had been picked. It was the wood settling she'd heard. The whole place was a death trap. 'Yes, death trap,' she whispered to herself. It had lured Matt here and taken him from her. Even in its former undamaged state, Key House had been a danger because it had been a temptation.

'Oh, Matt,' she whispered. 'Oh, Matt . . .'

'*Watch out!*' It was man's voice, near at hand, so unexpected it made her almost jump out of her skin. But before she could spin round to see who was there, hands gripped her shoulders and pulled her to one side. Sarah lost her balance and fell, bringing down the stranger with her. They finished sprawled together in the dirt a short distance from where she'd been standing before.

It was just in time. One of the former fitted pine cupboards, charred but still intact, fell down and outward from the wall where it had been hanging insecurely, and crashed to the floor just where she'd been standing. It split apart, revealing the sharp points of screws sticking up out of the panels.

Her rescuer released her and scrambled to his feet. He reached down a grimy hand to help her up. 'Sorry,' said a male voice above her head, 'but there wasn't time to ask you nicely to stand aside. I didn't mean you to fall. I hope you're not hurt.'

Still without any idea who he was, or where he'd sprung from – she had been so sure she was alone here – she nevertheless grasped the proffered hand and was hauled to her feet.

'You ought not to be in here, it's really not safe at all,' said the man.

Sarah looked up at him and saw him for the first time and what she saw made her shriek in alarm. She started back, staring at him wild eyed, putting both hands to her mouth to stop further screams escaping.

'Don't be afraid!' he begged. 'Please, don't be frightened of me. I was going to call out and let you know I was there but then I saw the old cupboard start to move.'

He was aged mid to late thirties and wore jeans and a leather jacket, both now covered in ash and grime. His suntanned features were framed with an untidy mop of dark hair. He was so like Matt that for a terrifying moment she thought she saw a ghost. But it wasn't Matt and far too solid for a ghost. She took her hands away from her mouth and whispered, 'Who are you?'

'I'm sorry if I scared you,' the man said. His voice was educated and he spoke quietly, sounding worried. 'My name is Gervase Crown. Please don't be frightened.' He lifted a hand to indicate their surroundings. 'This used to be my house.'

'Oh, Mr Crown,' Sarah whispered. 'Yes, they told me . . .'

He nodded towards the bouquet. The falling cupboard had just missed it. 'You're connected with the man who died here.' It was a statement rather than a question.

'Yes.' She pulled herself together. 'I'm Sarah Gresham. Matt was my partner.'

'I can't tell you how sorry I am,' he said and sounded sincere. 'I was horrified when I heard that someone had died here. It was always an unlucky place.'

Sarah heard herself say tightly, 'Luck didn't come into it. Someone killed him.'

'I know.'

Her eyes searched his face. 'You – you do look very like him, you know. That's why I screeched like that.'

'I've been told that, too.' He gave a wry smile. 'I'm not surprised that you screamed when a stranger manhandled you to the ground. Plus the sight of me, if I do look like . . .' He glanced at the flowers. 'The killer may have meant to strike at me,' he said briefly.

'Why would anyone want to do that?' she asked, bewildered.

'It's a long story and really, it wouldn't help if I started to tell you about it.'

Sarah said, 'Matt wanted to buy this house, you know.'

'I do know, that is to say, Reggie Foscott, the solicitor, did tell me there had been an enquiry about purchasing it. He'd told the enquirer that Key House wasn't on the market.'

Sarah sighed. 'Yes, he did, but Matt didn't want to give up. Key House was absolutely what he'd been looking for. He didn't bring me to see it because he wanted to be able to tell me we could buy it before he did that. In case I fell in love with it, as he'd done, and I'd be very disappointed if we couldn't buy. So he said it was

146

better to wait until he'd made another approach. But he never got to make it.'

Crown pushed his hands into the pockets of his leather jacket. 'You add to my guilt. I should have told Reggie long ago that any serious enquiry would be entertained. After all, I'd hung on to the place for years without living in it and I live abroad now, anyway. But I—' He broke off and shrugged. 'No excuse,' he said ruefully.

'But you don't need an excuse!' she told him. 'Of course you didn't want to part with it. It must have been a wonderful old place, full of history.'

He looked alarmed, took one hand from his pocket and waved it at her to silence her. 'No, no, you've got it wrong. I didn't keep it because I loved it. I kept it because I hated it. That sounds crazy, I know. I can't explain. It was my family home, but it wasn't wonderful to me. I don't have particularly good memories of being here, but I've never been able to bring myself to make the break. I'm afraid I specialise in making wrong decisions.'

'Whatever your reasons,' Sarah told him, 'you didn't want to sell and it was your decision. Anyway, it was only because it was empty and in need of attention that Matt thought we might be able to afford it. Perhaps if – if the fire hadn't happened, if Matt had been able to go back and talk to Foscott again . . . if Foscott had got in touch with you again and you'd changed your mind . . . But it's all "if", isn't it?'

'Yes,' he agreed soberly. 'It is all "if", as you say. If I hadn't done a number of stupid things in my life, and one in particular, this house wouldn't have been standing empty. It's a shame we can't go back and rewrite everything.' The silence lengthened until he said, 'I really think we ought to go outside before something else drops on our heads.'

'I'm trespassing,' Sarah said to him, as they picked their way over the rubble to the open air. 'Perhaps you're offended.'

'You can spend as much time here as you like, as far as I'm concerned. But the condition is rickety now, as was demonstrated.' He indicated the interior, and the fallen cupboard, behind them. 'The cops don't like people walking about in here because of it.'

'I realised it was risky.' Sarah didn't add that she now felt she had so little to lose, without Matt and their future together, that a lump of falling masonry would seem to offer nothing more than release. 'But I couldn't keep away,' she mumbled.

He studied her averted face briefly and then looked away himself, back at the house. 'No more can I, and I should, if anyone should. Only about an hour ago, I was talking to someone who knew me in the old days, when I lived here. She wishes I hadn't come back. As soon as she left, I got in the car and drove here. Crazy, really.'

Sarah looked at him curiously and opened her mouth to speak, but their conversation was interrupted.

Another voice, harsher and accusing, shattered the air.

'So, there you are! I heard you'd turned up like a bad penny – the same bad penny you always were!'

Gervase Crown spun round and Sarah moved to be able to see the newcomer more clearly. She saw a short, sturdy elderly woman with spectacles, wearing a strange bright yellow outfit of waterproof trousers and jacket.

Crown obviously recognised her. 'Well, well, Muriel, as I live and breathe! *You're* still living and breathing, obviously, and not a bit changed! Still your old jolly self, I see.'

'Don't you "well, Muriel" me!' snapped the woman. 'And spare me your twisted sense of humour. Who is that?' she pointed at Sarah.

'This is Miss Sarah Gresham, Muriel. Tragically, Sarah's partner lost his life here.'

'Oh,' Muriel looked discomfited. She dropped her stare and, addressing Sarah, said in a gruff voice, 'I'm sorry for your loss.'

'Thank you,' Sarah said.

'And this,' Gervase completed the introductions, indicating the yellow-clad woman for Sarah's benefit, 'is Muriel Pickering, a native of this parish. I dare say she's another one who wishes I hadn't returned.'

'Yes, I am a native of this part of the world and proud of it!' shouted Muriel at him. 'My family has lived here over one hundred and fifty years!' She turned to Sarah again. 'Time was,' she announced, 'when my family owned chunks of the land around here. Now we don't own any but my house and the garden.'

She nodded towards Gervase. 'His family turned up when his father came along and bought Key House, this house. They had no links with the area and he still doesn't.'

'I hesitate to correct you, Muriel,' Gervase told her quite mildly, 'but before he bought Key House, my father grew up and lived not twenty miles away. We were and are a Gloucestershire family.'

'Twenty miles away isn't here!' yelled Muriel. As if in reply to the sound of her voice, something else inside the house clattered to the ground.

Sarah was beginning to look alarmed again, and Gervase hastened to reassure her, 'Don't worry about Muriel. She can't help it. Her parents forgot to invite the wicked fairy to her christening, so it turned up and cursed her. Be glad that you and your partner didn't buy Key House and move in. Muriel would have been your nearest neighbour, and you will have gathered she doesn't like newcomers.'

'I don't dislike people,' said Muriel calmly. 'I just have no time for you. I don't know what you do with yourself over there in Portugal. I can't imagine it's anything worthwhile. And you're perfectly right in saying I regret your decision to return. However, in the circumstances, I suppose you had to.'

There was a movement and a small shape appeared, half hidden by Muriel's yellow legs.

Gervase peered past her. 'What on earth is that?'

Muriel's face, already red, turned an alarming shade of purple. 'You know perfectly well he's a dog. That's my dog, Hamlet!'

The dog in question confirmed this with a sharp bark.

'He's warning you,' said Muriel triumphantly. 'He's sussed you out. Knows you're a wrong 'un.' She turned to Sarah. 'Watch out for him, young Crown, I mean.' She pointed at Gervase. 'Rotten apple.'

'Muriel has never liked me,' Gervase told Sarah in a stage whisper, 'as you'll have realised by now. But, bless her cotton socks, she's never pretended otherwise. I, myself, am rather fond of her.'

Muriel gurgled alarmingly. Hamlet yelped.

'I think I'd better go,' said Sarah hurriedly. 'Nice to have met you both.' She crunched across the cinder-strewn ground, pausing only say, 'Hello, Hamlet.'

Muriel's expression softened. 'All my dogs have been named after characters in Shakespeare's plays.'

She and Gervase waited until the sound of Sarah's car had faded away.

'I hope,' said Muriel, 'that you are not now going to mess up that young woman's life, as you've messed up another's.'

'It seems by not selling Key House I may have helped to mess up Sarah's life already,' Gervase said quietly. 'You really are a dreadful old bat, Muriel. But there is something strangely reassuring about your not having mellowed with time.'

'I see you've learned nothing and forgotten nothing, like the Bourbons,' retorted Muriel.

'That's right, Muriel. I have forgotten nothing.' Gervase walked towards her. She stood her ground and, as he passed by, he stooped and whispered in her ear, 'I know where the body's buried, Muriel!'

Hamlet began a furious barking,

'Wretch!' spat Muriel at Gervase and struck out at him with the hand holding the coiled dog's lead.

He grinned down at her. Then he told Hamlet warningly, 'You keep your distance, pooch!'

He walked away, leaving Muriel in possession of the field and Hamlet bouncing up and down on the cinders in rage, raising clouds of ash dust. His hysterical yelps split the air.

Carter went alone to pick up Millie that evening. He fancied Millie looked a little disappointed at seeing him arrive without company. Monica made no reference to Jessica and although he found himself on the receiving end of several meaningful looks from his daughter, he suspected Monica had instructed her not to ask questions, either. That, of course, would make Millie all the more avid for information. As soon as he could, he got Monica on one side.

'You haven't seen anything of Gervase Crown, here in Weston St Ambrose, I suppose?' he asked. 'He's staying at The Royal Oak here.'

If he'd hoped to surprise Monica with the news, he failed. 'I heard he was back,' Monica said blandly.

Carter was the one who was startled. 'Who told you? You've seen him?'

'No. Stephen Layton told me, Dr Layton. I saw him last night, about nine in the evening. I went out for a stroll round the village

151

before turning in. I met Stephen in the street about three or four yards down the road from The Royal Oak. It's not the first time I've run into him on my evening strolls. I think he likes to have a whisky in the bar there before he turns in. But yesterday evening he was avoiding the place. He said he had run into Gervase, right outside, on the evening following the fire. Gervase had just got here from Portugal and taken a room there. That gave me a bit of a shock. I understand it had given Stephen Layton a shock, too. Stephen was Sebastian Crown's doctor, you know, and golf crony too, I fancy, but he didn't know Gervase very well. In fact, at first Stephen hadn't recognised him. Gervase had been standing in the street outside The Royal Oak, smoking a cigarette. Stephen thought he was just an out-of-season tourist, until Gervase called out to him and reminded him who he was. He told Stephen he'd just arrived back and meant to stay there at The Oak. Stephen took that as fair warning and has stayed away since.'

'Indeed?' murmured Carter.

'Well,' went on Monica complacently, 'I'm as curious as the next woman. I also thought you might like me to pick up any gossip, am I right?'

'You're right,' Carter said.

'And Stephen wanted to chat. Or that was the impression I got. He was intending to try the pub at the other end of the village and invited me along. We all know that's not much of a place. So I asked him if he wanted to come back here for a nightcap. I'm old enough to be able to ask a gentleman that without it sounding like a proposition!'

'And did he come?'

'Yes, he did. He stayed nearly an hour. We had a small whisky apiece – actually, I had one and he had two. I told him my ex-nephew-by-marriage – you – was investigating the case with Inspector Campbell asking all the questions. I thought I should tell him, in case he later told me anything he might not have told me, if he had known of my relationship to you. Do you follow me?'

'I follow. Very prudent of you, if quite the reverse of the police caution.'

'So then he told me he'd certified death at the scene of the crime and had met and chatted with young Jessica. We agreed it was a pity the old house had gone for good. Stephen said Gervase now looks like an actor in a film about pirates. He'd commiserated with him about the loss of Key House, but Gervase had been very ungracious about it all. Stephen said he'd no wish to hang around talking to him, so he left him there in the street outside the hotel. So, for all my effort to glean a vital nugget of information for you, I didn't, I'm afraid.'

'All the same,' Carter said thoughtfully. 'Thank you for telling me.'

'Where is Jess?' asked Millie as they were driving home. Her tone was suspiciously nonchalant.

'She had things to do,' he told her. He glanced up at the mirror, which reflected Millie sitting in the rear clutching MacTavish. Their eyes met and he looked away quickly, telling himself to concentrate on the road ahead. Not, of course, to avoid the accusing gleam in hers.

He reflected that perhaps it had not been such a good idea to take Jess along with him to Monica's last time. It had seemed fine when the idea sprang into his head. Moreover, Jess and Millie had appeared to hit it off. But that presented its own problem. If they hadn't got along, the question of inviting Jess to another meeting with his daughter wouldn't arise. Now Millie obviously expected to see Jess again and yet for Carter to invite her again made it look as if . . . well it was tricky.

'What things?' asked Millie, a touch of steel entering the nonchalance.

'How, what things?' asked Carter, playing for time.

'You said Jess had things to do. What things?'

'I don't know, Millie. She didn't tell me. Private matters to deal with.'

'Oh, private,' said Millie scornfully. 'That's what grown-ups always say when they want to shut you up.'

'I'm not trying to shut you up, love!' he protested. 'I honestly don't know what Jess is doing this evening.'

'Well, you should have asked her!' said Millie.

'That would be very rude of me,' said Carter virtuously.

Millie hissed in exasperation. After a moment she said with a carelessness that would have fooled no one, 'MacTavish liked her.'

'Good . . .' said her father unhappily.

Jess would not have described her evening as full of things to do. Not that the sight of her flat, when she let herself in that evening, did not suggest a list of useful chores. It was undeniably in need of a thorough dusting. There was a small stack of newspapers and magazines, some dating back a couple of months, that required putting out for the recycling collection or being taken to the nearest recycling centre, but somehow got overlooked every time. She was short of groceries, as she discovered on opening the fridge door. There was half a packet of sausages but they were already past their sell-by date. In the door of the fridge, however, was a bottle of Pinot Grigio with a glassful left in it. She retrieved it, poured out the wine and retreated to the sofa with the wine and Simon's latest letter.

She had already read her brother's letter at least twice but reading it again put him there in the tiny sitting room with her. He was in Africa working, as he had done for many years in various parts of the world, with a medical charity. His letters were rare and often written over a period of weeks. Thus he would begin to describe something and then there had obviously been an interruption so the writing broke off and the tale taken up at a much later date by which time something else had happened and the original account never really got finished. She kept all her twin's letters carefully in a folder because one day, when Simon got back home for good, he might want to write up his experiences. Or he might never come home, the correspondence cease, and all she and the family would have were these scribbled incomplete accounts scrawled by poor light late at night in a tent somewhere. It was not just the bugs and germs and unfriendly wildlife that threatened. The men with guns carried the danger. They did not like foreign medical workers any more than they welcomed foreign journalists observing the havoc and misery they wrought.

The street doorbell rang. Jess sighed and hauled herself off the sofa to put her ear to the intercom. 'Yes?'

'Tom,' squeaked a voice in her ear.

Tom? What on earth? In the days before Madison's arrival on the scene, Tom would do this, turn up unexpectedly from time to time wanting to go out for a drink or a meal. Since Madison had taken up a role in his life, these friendly outings had ceased. So what had brought him? 'Come up!' she called and pressed the button to release the door.

Tom had brought a fresh bottle of wine with him. Jess didn't know whether to interpret this as apology for having interrupted any plans she might have, or just that he meant to stay the evening.

'Busy?' asked Tom, collapsing on to the other end of the sofa and gazing at her like, she thought crossly, a puppy ejected into a cold garden.

'No,' she told him. 'But I am tired.'

'I won't stay late,' he promised. 'But you're a friend and you know how it is, sometimes you need to talk to a friend. I need your advice.'

'No, you don't,' said Jess firmly. 'I am a friend. But ask Madison for her advice.'

'It's about Madison.'

'Then you definitely shouldn't be discussing it with me, whatever it is. It's your business and hers. I don't come into it.'

Why is it, she wondered, people want to tell me about their problems? Millie wants to tell me about her mother and Rodney and how lonely her dad is. Ian himself, I suspect, wants propping up in his relationship with his daughter. Now Tom has a relationship problem. What am I? An agony aunt? No, I'm a copper. If only the villains were so keen to tell me all!

'Something unexpected has turned up,' Tom protested, rubbing his hand through his mop of thick black hair. 'Ten minutes, Jess, please. I haven't got anyone else I can ask about it.'

'Five minutes only – and I'll time you,' she promised.

'Fine!' He sat upright. 'Madison has had an offer of a year working in Australia.'

'Doing what? I don't know what her line is. You've never said.'

'Haven't I? Oh, well, she's microbiologist.'

'You two must have a lot to talk about.'

'It's not a job exactly; it's a year's funding to do research. She specialises in parasitic—'

'Tom!' Jess interrupted. 'I haven't eaten yet and I shall want to, later. So spare me the details of what Madison sees through her microscope.'

'She wants to go,' Tom said mournfully. 'It's a great opportunity.'

'I'm sure it is.'

'Should I try and talk her out of it? I know how selfish that sounds but I'd rather hoped we . . . Well, that things might progress. We seemed to be getting along so well.'

'And now some bug on a glass plate has come between you. Tom, if Madison wants to go, and it marks the end of your relationship, at least be graceful about it. You're a grown man not a schoolboy.'

'Ah!' exclaimed Tom, leaning forward. 'But does she want me to be graceful about it and just say, fine, off you go? Or does she want me to try and persuade her to stay?'

Jess groaned. 'How do I know?'

'If I don't try and persuade her to stay,' continued Tom, 'will she be insulted? Or, if I try and persuade her to hang about here, will she think I'm selfish? I don't want to be selfish. I wouldn't want her to think that I was giving her an ultimatum. You know, "It's me or the thing on the glass plate," or words to that effect. On the other hand, I'd hate to think I was being manoeuvred. Or am I being vain? I don't know what to think.'

Jess leaned forward so that their faces were inches apart. 'Tom, I can't tell you. Have this conversation or some version of it with Madison, will you? I absolutely refuse to continue. I cannot discuss this with you.'

'It's making me feel pretty fed up!' said Tom with more spirit.

'I sympathise but can't help. Your time is up.'

'I was relying on you,' he said resentfully.

157

'No, you were relying on Madison and you feel she's let you down.'

This caused Tom to look startled and then thoughtful.

'It's not easy finding a girlfriend when you've got a job like mine, you know. They ask what I do and I tell them I cut up dead bodies and they lose interest. Madison is interested in what I do,' he said finally.

'Men lose interest when they find out I'm police officer – except for the ones who've got a thing about women in uniform,' Jess retaliated.

'I'm beginning to think that it's what I do that interests Madison and not me. *I* don't interest her.' Tom had that puppy-out-in-the-cold look again.

'Oh, merry hell, if that's what you suspect, smile nicely and wish her well for her trip to Australia!' burst out Jess, goaded beyond discretion. 'If she wants to go, she'll go. If she doesn't really want to, I suppose she'll stay. But let the poor woman make up her own mind. And make up your own mind.'

Tom gazed into his empty wine glass. 'Am I allowed an extension of time to sit here and drink another?'

Chapter 12

'We have nothing on Katherine – otherwise called Kit – Stapleton on the police computer,' Phil Morton informed Jess early next morning. 'She has no criminal record, never been a witness to anything, never lodged a complaint. Dave Nugent's been busy delving into civil records of births, deaths and marriages. There's nothing much there of interest, either, just the usual stuff. She's thirty-five and divorced. She was married to a man named Davis, Hugh Davis, and lived in Wales at that time. She now lives in Cheltenham and works as a receptionist at a doctors' surgery. No children that Dave could trace.'

'What about Mr Davis?'

'No, nothing on him. On their marriage certificate his occupation is given as estate agent. A bit ironic that, I suppose, in the circumstances.'

'Right!' Jess drew a deep breath. 'Start again from the beginning, that's all we can do. I'll go and talk to Muriel Pickering.'

'I've done that,' observed Morton. 'You want to watch out for the dog. It's not very big but it's got a nasty look in its eye and a full set of teeth. Old Muriel's much the same and not the chatty sort. You won't get much out of her.'

'I know enough to be wary of both Muriel and her pet. But my feeling is the roots of this business go back a long way. Muriel appears to be a sort of oldest resident. She must have known Crown all his life, with gaps while he was backpacking or in jail, until he eventually settled in Portugal. We need to keep digging around, Phil.'

Jess set out for Mullions. She had driven a short way along the narrow road in which Key House stood and had almost reached the scorched ruins when she overtook Roger Trenton, marching along in parade-ground fashion, bolt upright, arms swinging. Jess drew into the side of the road and stopped. She got out of the car and waited for him to reach her.

Roger raised a hand in acknowledgement and was soon alongside. 'Recognised you as you went past,' he puffed.

'I thought you might have done.' Jess smiled at him. His face was wind reddened and shiny; and his halo of hair wilder than ever.

'You called at my house the other day and I was out,' Roger went on. 'Poppy told me. Sorry I missed you.'

'It was just a casual call, Mr Trenton.'

'Well, you've got me now. I was just walking up to Key House to check on it. I used to do that from time to time when it was still standing. Now the site will attract another set of undesirables, sightseers! It's all been on the local television news and in the local press. No doubt they will want to help themselves to lumps of charred wood as ghoulish souvenirs. How can I help?' He waited expectantly.

Already, thought Jess wryly, Roger had moved his sights from the dropouts who'd used the house to hypothetical sightseers to the ruins. Any question she asked would be answered with more of the predictable complaint. But Roger expected to be interviewed and Jess would oblige him, even if she didn't hope for much from the exercise, other than what she'd heard already.

'We've been wondering about the tramps and hippies you stated used Key House from time to time. You can't tell us anything more definite about any of them, I suppose?'

'They all looked pretty much the same,' said Roger, glowering at the wreck of the house a little further down the road. 'Although "pretty" is hardly the word for them! The younger men and women all wore grubby clothes and big boots. Nearly all had long hair, both sexes. Occasionally there would be some extraordinary appar- ition covered in tattoos and studded with metal rings and pins . . . and it wasn't always male. That was the other group, the drug-users. Some of the girls wore black make-up. They looked perfect frights.' Roger shook his head.

'I expect that was their intention,' said Jess.

'Really? What on earth for? There was one older man used to turn up from time to time on his own. You could hardly see his features for beard. He wore a filthy raincoat tied round the middle with string and had a little dog. The dog was his only companion that I ever saw. Otherwise he travelled alone, whereas the younger ones turned up in little groups. But I hadn't seen the old chap for a while before the house went up in flames. Perhaps he'd moved on or died or something. I couldn't tell you any of their names.'

'Did you ever approach them yourself? Not that we'd advise that,' Jess warned him.

'I told several lots of the younger ones that they were on private property. They laughed. One told me all property was theft, cheeky young blighter. He was a weedy individual with the usual metal in his ears and a shaven head. I never spoke to the old fellow in the raincoat except once, very briefly, when I met him limping along the road. He had a black eye. I wondered if any of the other louts had found him in the house and beaten him up. I – er – I gave him a fiver. He was touchingly grateful. I suppose it was spent on booze but I always felt . . .' Roger, who had already reddened when speaking of his own unexpected generosity, broke off altogether and shuffled about in embarrassment at having confessed it.

'Yes?' Jess prompted. She was surprised at his confession. But people often did surprise you.

'I always felt that he was the traditional type of vagabond, you see. What you might call a nomad by choice, not like the others. There have always been old chaps like that wandering around the countryside. I remember them from when I was a boy. Some were old soldiers. They were not quite right in the top storey, many of them, but harmless, quite harmless. They'd turn up at the back door and beg a crust of bread. My mother, who was a very charitable woman, once gave one of them an old coat of my father's. My father was mortified because the tramp wore it round the district for weeks and everyone recognised it. He – my father – got his leg pulled about it at the golf club.

'Of course, the old man with the dog was still trespassing on private property. But I felt he did no real harm, unlike the younger ones. I have wondered since the fire if the unfortunate young fellow who died there had encountered some of the other scruffs and they'd set about him. Things could have got out of hand and they took fright and decided to destroy evidence. That could have happened, couldn't it?' He waited for Jess's reply.

'It could have done, certainly. Had you seen anyone there earlier that day? Any of the drug addicts or hippies?'

Roger shook his head regretfully. 'One didn't always see them; one just saw the mess they left behind. They left needles lying about. I did persuade the council to send a special team out to collect the needles on a couple of occasions, although they were very reluctant to do it, again on the grounds it was private property and they weren't responsible. I thought it might prompt the council into contacting Crown and making him do something about the place, at least have it made secure. But nothing happened. They did bill Crown for the manpower and time taken for the collection, though. They sent the bill to his solicitor, who paid it.

'The young ones often had alcohol there, too, and left bottles. I collected those. Of course, in order to do that, I myself had to trespass. But I saw it as the lesser of evils. I took all the bottles I found to the bottle bank.'

'Very commendable, Mr Trenton. You are aware that simple trespass is a civil offence, not a criminal one? It's a tricky situation for the authorities, especially if, as in this case, the owner of the property has not himself requested the trespassers to leave, or instructed his representative to do so.'

'Of course I am. I must say I would have expected that solicitor to have done something on behalf of his client but if he wasn't specifically asked to, as you say . . . But he knew about it because I wrote to tell him often enough. If the trespassers do any damage, break in, that's different, isn't it? I realise it would be hard to prove they had broken in. They would always say they found a window forced and just climbed through.' Roger scowled. 'They have all the answers.'

'That's usually the defence they put forward,' Jess agreed. 'It's also complicated by the fact that these people using Key House for drink or drugs or just to sleep overnight did not, apparently, have any intention of staying there for a long time, taking up residence. By the time the police arrived, they'd have moved on.'

'No electricity,' said Roger, 'although that wouldn't have stopped them. More likely the remoteness of the house encouraged them to leave. On the rare occasions they tried to stay, they lasted about a week and then gave up and went off looking for somewhere nearer to the bright lights. They'd be too far away from all their chums at Key House – and from any pubs or clubs they frequent and where they probably pick up their supplies of whatever drugs they favour. The police have spoken to Crown, I suppose, now he's returned?'

'Yes, we have.'

'You don't happen to know what plans he has for the place now?' Roger looked at her hopefully. 'Surely he won't just bugger off back to Portugal – excuse my language – and just leave the ruins to fester? The whole business has been very upsetting. I don't only mean the fire. I mean living so near to a place that attracted so many undesirables. We have a number of elderly people round here and some of them live alone. Now there's been a murder there, too. The previous situation can't be allowed to continue. We would all of us, local residents, be under intolerable stress.'

'The ruins provide no shelter now, Mr Trenton, and I doubt will attract the sort of undesirables you were describing as being there before the fire. I am just on my way to see Muriel Pickering,' Jess added.

'There you are, then. Muriel lives alone!' said Roger triumphantly. 'That small dog she has won't protect her. Although Muriel can be quite fierce and would probably see off any intruder. But it's not right that people shouldn't feel safe in their homes!'

'We don't know Mr Crown's long-term plans,' Jess told him. 'But we are reasonably confident he means to make some decision about the property. It's been nice to talk to you, Mr Trenton. I must be on my way to Mullions.'

'Let me know if you need any more help from me,' Roger told her politely, ignoring the fact that he'd not had anything new to say.

He could be right, even so. Matthew Pietrangelo might just have walked in on a couple of drug addicts off their heads. They might have thought he was an undercover copper. Jess promised that she would get in touch if necessary, and Trenton seemed satisfied.

There was no sign of Muriel at the front of the house, but there was a strange smell filling the air. It suggested bran and seemed to come from the rear of the building. Jess walked down the side of the house and round the corner.

The cockerel and his harem were clustered around the back door. They seemed expectant. At first Jess was alarmed to see, through the kitchen window, what she took to be smoke filling the room, making it impossible to discern anything within. But Hamlet had begun to bark inside, signalling that he'd detected an intruder who had approached the house. The back door flew open and a great cloud of steam billowed out. The smell of bran became overpowering. The chickens fled, squawking, into the undergrowth smothering the back garden, as Hamlet erupted from the house and began a furious war dance around Jess's feet. An apocalyptic figure emerged in a haze of steam, appearing to brandish a weapon. It turned out to be Muriel, waving a wooden spoon.

'Don't mind the dog!' she yelled by way of greeting and reassurance. 'Shut up, Hamlet!'

Hamlet stopped darting at Jess's shins and stood glowering at her, growling softly in his throat.

'He's a good watchdog,' Jess observed.

'Doesn't miss a trick!' said Hamlet's proud owner. 'He can suss out friend from foe in a second or two. He's stopped barking, you see. That means he thinks you're probably OK. He might just keep a close eye on you, but don't worry about that. Come in.'

The invitation was hospitable but Jess accepted it with a certain reluctance. The kitchen air was still full of steam. Sinister glooping noises came from a large enamelled tub on the stove and the overpowering smell was frankly awful.

'Mash for the chickens,' explained Muriel, prodding at the tub's contents with the wooden spoon, 'old fashioned but cheap. I cook up all the peelings and odd leftovers with it. Chickens love it. It's about ready. I'll turn off the stove and leave it to cool. We can go into the sitting room. I'll leave the back door open. It lets in the cold but it lets out the steam. This way.'

Jess was led along a narrow, dingy hallway into the room she'd observed through the front window on her first visit. It was no tidier, although the plates of unfinished food had gone, the scraps no doubt fed into the mash. Books and newspapers still littered every surface. Muriel swept an assortment from a sofa.

'Sit down and I'll dig out the elderflower.'

'Thank you, but actually this is an official call.' Jess sat cautiously on the sofa. Shiny black strands protruding through holes in the cloth revealed the filling was of horsehair.

'Don't say you're on duty and can't have a drink,' said Muriel. 'Because it's only elderflower cordial, made by yours truly. It won't make you tiddly.'

A glass of some slightly muddy liquid was thrust into her hand. Jess thought apprehensively that it might as well be poteen, and she only had Muriel's word that it wasn't.

Her hostess plonked herself down on a sagging armchair against the opposite wall. Above her head hung one of the two oils Jess had seen through the window. She could now make out that they were seascapes, showing what looked like fishing smacks on an unquiet ocean. Hamlet had followed them and sat in the doorway, guarding the entrance and exit like Cerberus. Even if he only had one head, there was a distinct suggestion of the Underworld about him. Wisps of mash-scented steam escaping from the kitchen stood in for the smell of sulphur.

'What do you want, then?' asked Muriel. 'Cheers!' She raised her glass.

'Oh, er, cheers!' Jess waved her own glass feebly in reply and wondered if she would be given a chance to tip its contents into a plant pot nearby, the occupant of which had long since expired through lack of water. 'I'd like to talk about the past, Mrs Pickering.'

'I do wish,' Muriel burst out with a return to her habitual irritability, 'that you and that sergeant of yours would stop calling me *Mrs* Pickering! I'm *Miss* Pickering. I know it's the fashion for women nowadays, married or not, to style themselves *mizz*, but I'm *Miss*. I never married and I'm not ashamed of it.'

'I'm not married, either,' said Jess.

'Shacked up with someone?'

'No.'

'Sensible girl. I never married because Father wouldn't have it. My mother died when I was fifteen and after that, it was just Father and me here. He was a semi-invalid. I dare say he could have done more for himself, or to help me, if he'd had a mind to, but he didn't. "Semi-invalid" meant he could do the things he wanted to, like fishing. He was a keen fisherman. But he couldn't chop up wood or push a vacuum cleaner round. So I had to look after him, the house, garden, chickens . . . we even had a couple of goats back then and a donkey some gypsies left behind. So I never had time to get married. Not that Father would have allowed it.'

'He couldn't have stopped you,' Jess pointed out. 'Not once you were of age.'

'That just shows how much *you* know,' retorted Muriel. 'He told me if I didn't take care of him, he wouldn't leave me Mullions in his will. He'd leave it to some charity or other. Not that he was a charitable man, far from it, but he was a spiteful one. He meant it. My family has lived here for a hundred and fifty years and I wasn't going to be done out of my inheritance, or what was left of it.' She waved a hand in a circular motion indicating everything about them. 'We used to own all you can see out there. Bit by bit all sold to prop up our finances. The last lot of farmland was sold off in 1967. The Pearson family bought it and they're still there.'

'So you'll have lived here all your life,' Jess seized the opportunity to redirect the conversation to the subject that had brought her.

Muriel gave an unexpected laugh that sounded like an unoiled hinge creaking open. 'I bet you think I'm as old as the hills, eh? Well, I'm not. I just look it. I'm fifty-nine.' Observing Jess's face, she gave a satisfied nod. 'That shook you, eh? It's OK, I don't mind you sitting there with your mouth open.'

'I'm sorry,' Jess apologised, flushing.

'What for? You're not responsible. I ain't a beauty, never was. I started going grey when I was still in my thirties. Marriage was never on the cards for me. I never knew how to chatter away about pop music or films, or dance or flirt, or anything like that, never learned. So I dare say no one would have wanted me, anyway. I'm fit, mind you, and had plenty of time to learn other practical things. I have to do everything round here. Notice the gate as you came in?'

Jess recalled the chicken wire spread over a rough wooden frame. 'Yes.'

'I made that,' Muriel told her proudly. 'I've been up on the roof and replaced a couple of tiles several times. You name it, I can probably do it. You haven't drunk your cordial.'

'I'm savouring it,' said Jess firmly.

'Savour away. Let me know if you'd like a top-up.' Muriel topped up her own emptied glass.

'Miss Pickering!'

If she didn't insist now on asking Muriel the questions she'd come here to put, it was beginning to look as though Jess wouldn't get a chance. Muriel was showing distinct signs of settling in with the elderflower cordial. Jess suspected the contents had been pepped up with something stronger, like gin. She resolved to find a moment to tip hers into the plant pot, whatever else. Muriel's normally spiky attitude had mellowed and she'd relaxed in her chair beneath the storm-tossed fishing ketches. Even Hamlet had settled down in the doorway with his nose on his paws and his eyes shut. From time to time faint rumbling noises came from his direction. Muriel's eyelids were also drooping.

'Miss Pickering!' Jess repeated more loudly.

Muriel's eyes flickered open. 'What?' she asked, her hand groping for the bottle. 'Top-up now?'

'No, thank you very much. I came to ask you about Key House.'

'What about it?' enquired Muriel. 'It burned down and was empty for years before that, so what's to ask?'

'I'm interested in before that, when it was still lived in, years ago. Sebastian Crown, his wife and his child . . . do you remember those days?'

'Of course I do!' replied Muriel with a touch of her customary truculence. 'My brain's all right. I don't forget things. I have always . . .' She tipped up the bottle and peered at it critically. 'I have always had an excellent memory. This one's empty. I'll get us another.'

She began to struggle out of the chair.

'If we could talk about Sebastian Crown first,' Jess insisted.

'Oh, he's been dead years,' said Muriel, sinking back into the depths of the chair. 'I couldn't stand the fellow. They're a bad lot, the Crown men, in the blood – rotters. Like father, like son, as they say. I saw young Gervase yesterday. He was mooching round the house, visiting the scene of the crime.' Muriel added with a sinister curl of the lip. 'Hah!'

'In what way was Sebastian Crown a rotter?' Jess was not diverted as she sensed Muriel had intended.

'He's gone now,' Muriel told her with deep satisfaction, 'and I can say what I like about him. I can speak the truth. He was a millionaire, you know, and people are very careful what they say about you if you're rich, especially if you're a bully like Sebastian. All that money, all gone to that son of his,' she shook her head in sorrow. 'No fairness in life, is there? Sebastian wasn't nice, oh, no. Successful? Yes. Kept in with the right people? Yes. Decent man? Decidedly not. I liked his wife,' Muriel finished unexpectedly.

'No one talks about his wife,' Jess prompted.

'That's because she finally plucked up the courage to leave him. It was the big talking point and scandal hereabouts. Mind you, people talked about it behind closed doors because of Sebastian, who went about looking like Henry the Eighth on a bad day. I was sorry for Amanda,' Muriel continued. 'She was very lonely, poor girl. She used to walk along the lanes around here on her own.

"Getting my exercise", she used to call it. Getting out of the house and out of *his* way, more like it. I've always had a dog and walked it every day. You might say it got me out of Mullions and out from under Father's eye. He was always wanting something done, cup of tea, fetch something from upstairs, look for some book he reckoned he'd mislaid and probably never had in the first place! So Amanda and I had something in common if for different reasons.

'I used to bump into her somewhere along the way and, after a while, we got chatting and then we began walking together. We'd arrange a time and a spot to meet. Occasionally she'd go up to London for two or three days, shopping, or going to the theatre. She'd tell me what she'd seen, describe it all. I liked to listen to her. She asked me a couple of times to go with her, but Father would have decided to have one of his "turns" at the very mention, so I told her it wasn't possible. She was always happier when she'd been away from Key House for a day or two. Now, some people . . .' Muriel wagged a forefinger at Jess. 'Naming no names, you know. Some people might have thought she had a boyfriend in London. But I don't believe she did.'

Muriel jerked forward and hissed with such vehemence it made Jess jump, and Hamlet raise his head and give a little yelp. 'I don't suppose for a minute that she had a fancy man, because she was too damn scared of Sebastian!'

'Why was she afraid of him? You said he was a bully, I know.' The old scandals were coming out of the woodwork. It was what Jess had hoped.

'He was violent,' Muriel told her abruptly.

'She told you this?'

'No, I saw the bruises with my own eyes. She always wore long sleeves, even in warm weather, and silk scarves round her neck.

But she'd reach up to push back a spray of leaves drooping across the path from the hedgerow and the sleeve would ride up. She nearly always had bruises on her arms, like this . . .' Muriel gripped one forearm with the fingers of her other hand. 'Little round black bruises made by the pressure of his fingers. Or the scarf might slip. Once, when it did, I saw bruises round her neck. Ruddy maniac had tried to strangle her!'

There was a silence. Muriel stared past Jess, out of the window and back down the years. 'Every time she went up to London, I'd wonder if she'd come back. One day she didn't.'

'What about the child?'

'Oh, he was away at boarding school most of the time. They packed him off when he wasn't much more than a tot. My own theory about that was that both parents wanted him out of the way – but for different reasons. Amanda wanted to keep him away from his father. Sebastian, well, perhaps he just didn't like children or had no time for them. He couldn't be bothered or was too busy to spend time with his son.'

Jess asked quietly, 'Did you ever see bruises on the child, when he was home in the school holidays, for example?'

'No!' Muriel shook her head and spoke firmly. 'No. If he'd started to do that, I really believe Amanda wouldn't have stood for it. Maternal instinct, if you like. She wouldn't have allowed him to touch the child. But, you see . . .'

Muriel gave a strange, mirthless smile and, for the first time in their conversation, held Jess's gaze directly. 'She knew Sebastian wasn't interested in hitting the child, only in hitting *her*. Make what you like of that. I'm saying no more.'

Muriel heaved herself from her chair. 'And now, if you don't mind, I've got to feed the chickens. Come on, Hamlet!'

She stomped out of the room, Hamlet at her heels. Jess paused only to pour her elderflower cordial into the plant pot and followed her down the dark hallway and into the kitchen.

'Thank you for your time, Miss Pickering. If I could ask you just one more question?'

'Make it snappy!' ordered Muriel, scooping bran mash from the tub into a much-chipped enamel basin.

'How do *you* think Key House came to burn down?'

'Your guess is as good as mine. Roger Trenton's got a bee in his bonnet about yobbos using the place to enjoy their drugs and booze. Which they did – I saw them there myself several times over the years. Roger thinks they started the fire and probably killed the poor sod who died. Roger has all kinds of nutty theories about pretty well everything, but he might be right about that. Nobody's wrong all the time, are they?'

On this philosophical note, Muriel gave Jess a nod and set off down the garden with her pan of mash, Hamlet rolling along behind. From the bushes and long grass, chickens began to emerge, cackling excitedly and flocking behind her like hatchlings after their mother.

Carter had arranged to visit Dr Layton, doing him the courtesy of phoning ahead because doctors have patients and are busy men. He hadn't yet met Layton although he knew the doctor had been called to certify the death at the scene of the fire. He also knew from Jess that Layton had been well acquainted with Sebastian Crown and less well so with his son. Carter might have been content to leave it at that. But now Layton had popped up on the scene again, in Weston St Ambrose, sharing a drink and a gossip with Monica.

'Time for me to drop in on him,' he told Morton on his way out.

He knew Layton was in private practice and wasn't surprised to find the doctor lived in a large, comfortable Georgian former rectory. His consulting room was in what had probably once been the rector's study. An unsmiling, middle-aged woman, wearing a navy overall-style uniform with a nurse's watch pinned to it, showed him in. Layton got up to greet him, holding out his hand and thanking Carter for taking the trouble to phone. That their chat would take place in here, and not in any other room in the private part of the house, indicated the doctor saw this as a business visit.

Carter admired the room's elegant proportions and the original fireplace. Layton responded by pointing out that a tall bookcase fitting into a recess was also original to the room.

'Probably built by a local carpenter to the rector's specifications,' he said. 'It now has medical books in it, instead of theological ones.'

'Not all medicine!' remarked Carter, leaning forward to read the titles on the spines of a row of paperbacks. 'Someone likes detective novels.'

'Not mine!' Layton said immediately. 'My wife likes them and is a bit of a collector. Her collection has overflowed into here. Won't you sit down, Superintendent?'

Carter took the seat normally occupied by a patient and Layton retreated to his chair on the other side of the desk. They were set up like a regular consultation appointment, thought Carter with humour. I wonder, is that just habit or because, Doctor, you feel more comfortable on that side of the desk? Layton was waiting. Carter realised that, having requested this interview, he was expected to explain his symptoms, or place his cards on the table.

Aloud, he began, 'You have been here a little while yourself, Doctor, or so I understand. I've been speaking to Monica Farrell. She's my former wife's aunt. I thought I might like a quick word with you myself.'

'Ah, Monica,' said Layton sagely.

He crossed one leg over the other knee and actually put the tips of his fingers together, looking completely the part, thought Carter with amusement. So must the one-time rector have received parishioners who brought him their troubles. He could imagine Layton – or the bewigged black-clad rector – asking kindly, 'So what seems to be the problem?' Only the computer on Layton's desk and the overlying smell of antiseptic signalled real change in the use of the room.

'I understand you were Sebastian Crown's doctor,' Carter said. 'I already knew this from Inspector Campbell, by the way. But Gervase Crown was not your patient. Is that right?'

'He was not my patient once he grew older. As a young child he was.'

'You see,' Carter went on, 'we are beginning to think the man who was killed in the fire at Key House was the victim of mistaken identity. The intended target could have been Gervase Crown.'

'Really?' returned Layton, frowning.

'Monica tells me you have seen Crown since his return here from Portugal.'

'I ran into him briefly outside The Royal Oak in Weston on the evening of the day following the fire.' Layton's facial muscles twitched in what might have been meant as a dry smile. 'He had lost little time in returning.'

'You recognised him? You couldn't have seen him for years. I ask because of the possibility someone had mistaken the dead man – a Matthew Pietrangelo – for Crown. Crown had been abroad for some time. This might have been the cause of a mistake being made.'

'No, I didn't recognise him at first,' Layton said frankly. 'In fact, if he hadn't hailed me I'd have ignored him. It was late evening. He was standing in the shadows, smoking. Even so, when he stepped out into the light beaming from the pub behind him, I still wouldn't have known him if he hadn't said his name. He's older, of course, a mature male and not a youngster. He's very sunburned. I hadn't seen him since his father's funeral. He was dishevelled, no doubt from his long journey, and in need of a shave. Altogether he looked rather *louche*, I think the word is. I admit, when he emerged out of a dark corner and stopped me, I was alarmed for a moment.'

'But once he'd told you his identity, then you remembered him?' asked Carter.

'Oh, yes!' Layton nodded. 'I knew him then.'

'I sense you don't have a high opinion of him.' Carter smiled to take the edge off his comment.

Layton wasn't fooled. 'His father was my friend, not just my patient. I know what trouble Gervase caused the family as a boy. My opinion at the time of Sebastian's sudden death was that stress had hastened it. But that was, as you remarked, some time ago and Gervase has been living abroad. I've had nothing to do with him, and have nothing against him other than my sympathy for his father.'

'You can't suggest why someone might want to kill him?'

'No,' said Layton coolly.

'He was responsible for a car crash which left a young woman in a wheelchair.'

'I am well aware of that. But I think you may be haring off down the wrong road, Superintendent Carter, if you think someone hereabouts harbours a grudge that might turn violent. Of course, young Crown was not popular at the time of the car crash you mention. I dare say no one here would be delighted to see him return to live among us . . .'

'To the extent of burning down his house to keep him away? To make an attempt on his life when he does return?'

'No one around *here*,' Layton repeated. 'If you think Gervase Crown has an enemy somewhere who wants him dead, I suggest you look elsewhere. He has had ample time over the last few years to make such an enemy, even if he has been mostly in Portugal, as I understand. But I have lived here for a very long time and, as a medical man, I am the recipient of all kind of confidences and gossip. I know of no one and nothing that could explain what happened at Key House. Believe me, Superintendent, this remains at heart a very old-fashioned, traditional community, for all the apparent changes you see around you. Newcomers have arrived bringing some new ideas, but we have a way of absorbing them. Of course, we have crime here. Of course, we have our share of problem families. But we are not murderers. Of that I can assure you.'

Carter refrained from pointing out that someone had killed Pietrangelo. 'What about arsonists?' he asked.

Layton looked uncomfortable for the first time. 'It seems we do have at least one of those somewhere. Although I think it likely whoever started that fire came from outside the immediate locality. We have been plagued over recent years with some undesirable temporary visitors by way of tramps and hippies. We encourage them to move on.'

Layton smiled; unsteepled his hands and rested them on his desk. His fingers were long and the nails well kept. He made no attempt to add to his statement, just sat looking blandly at his visitor. Carter sensed that he was being told it was time *he* moved on.

Layton accompanied him to the front door. On the way, they passed a half-open door and Carter had a glimpse into a room that had been turned into an office. The middle-aged nurse-secretary was working there. Aware of his scrutiny, she looked up and returned him a stony stare.

'Mrs Layton . . .' murmured the doctor. 'The superintendent is just leaving, Miranda.'

'Goodbye, Superintendent,' said Miranda, still unsmiling.

She didn't add, 'and don't come back', but the look said it all. Mrs Layton liked her detectives on the page and not in her home. Well, she wasn't the only one, thought Carter ruefully.

'Goodbye, Mrs Layton, nice to meet you,' he said cheerfully.

'All right, what do you think, Jess?' Ian Carter asked, after they had exchanged details of the various conversations they had each had that day. 'That Gervase Crown arranged for the fire? Dr Layton, like Roger Trenton, wants to blame tramps or dropouts.'

'Why not Gervase? He must have hated the place,' Jess replied. 'If what Muriel Pickering told me is true, and I believe her, I'm not surprised he didn't want to live in it. He didn't want to sell it because he didn't want any other family living in it, either. He wanted it wiped off the face of the earth! He's been living abroad and he didn't need the money from a sale, so he put off doing anything about it. But it's always been on his mind and, in the end, he decided to get rid of it once and for all, and arranged a fire. I know it's only a theory but after listening to Muriel Pickering, I can easily imagine it.'

'If all Muriel had to say was true,' Carter reminded her. 'Layton was keen to stress Sebastian Crown was his friend. Muriel may have been imagining the cause of the bruises she says she saw on Amanda Crown. Wouldn't Layton – Amanda's doctor as well as Sebastian's – have known of it, if Sebastian were in the habit of beating up his wife? I can't believe he'd have condoned it.'

'Because Muriel knew – and found out by accident – it doesn't mean Layton knew,' argued Jess. 'He was their doctor, sure, but he also played golf with Sebastian. All the more reason for Sebastian to ensure Layton and others at the golf club never knew. I bet that when Sebastian Crown was in the bar of that club, he was the jolliest, most good-natured fellow there. Just like any other nasty little secret wife-beater. If anyone had suggested the contrary they would all have said it wasn't possible, he was a decent chap, and all the rest of it.'

Phil Morton, who'd been listening in silence with increasing impatience, now said, 'All that happened years ago, if it did. What about now? Where does Pietrangelo come into it? Was he just the wrong bloke in the wrong place at the wrong time? Mistaken identity, if you like, but I'm not satisfied why he was there in the first place. OK, his girlfriend says he was house-hunting, because that's what he told her he was doing driving round the countryside. He wouldn't have confessed to her that Crown had hired him for a spot of arson, would he?'

'Crown didn't crack Pietrangelo's skull,' Carter pointed out. 'He didn't arrive in the UK until nearly twenty-four hours later. Pietrangelo didn't set the fire and then crack his own skull. We're no nearer finding our murderer. And we've no evidence whatsoever that Crown arranged for the fire or that the unfortunate Pietrangelo was doing anything but checking out a property he'd taken a big fancy to. Muriel's information goes a long way to explaining why Crown didn't want to live there. It clears up one small mystery, if you like, and leaves us with the big one.'

'No further forward, then,' said Morton gloomily. 'Perhaps something will turn up tomorrow.'

Chapter 13

As Morton had hoped, something new did turn up the following morning. He and Jess were in her office, drawing up a plan of action for the day, when DC Bennison appeared in the doorway.

'Excuse me,' she said. 'But Mr Crown has been on the phone. He reckons he's been threatened.'

'Was he harmed?' asked Jess, startled.

'No, but he won't talk over the phone, just refused. He's pretty cross.'

'Cheeky blighter!' growled Morton.

Bennison smiled at Jess. 'He wants you to go out there and see him, ma'am, at The Royal Oak. He particularly asked for *you*.'

The road out to Weston St Ambrose was by now becoming very familiar to Jess. She turned her car into the wide entry beside The Royal Oak and parked it on the cobbles over which horse traffic had once clattered and the stagecoach had decanted its weary passengers. She got out and looked around. What had been stables had been turned into individual units for guests, mini-cottages. Large planters stood along the walls but now, in winter, were empty. A wooden sign indicated a rear entry to the main building and on the door was fixed a notice suggesting that customers might like to book now for the Christmas period.

Inside Jess took time to assess the general layout. The Royal Oak was a rambling old building. Over years alterations and additions had meant walls had been knocked down, new partitions erected, doorways blocked, others created, all turning it into a veritable rabbit warren of rooms, connecting passages and dead ends. The atmosphere was stuffy, warm, dark and smelled faintly of breakfast bacon. Presented with a choice of corridors, Jess was grateful for the arrow indicating Reception and Lounge.

She didn't know the nature of the threat received, or claimed, by Gervase Crown. He had not named the person who'd made it or how it had been done, despite Bennison's best efforts to obtain details. But one thing was already clear. An intruder, who didn't know The Royal Oak, could not slip in and out in a couple of minutes. You had to be familiar with its twists and turns or . . . or you had to be a resident. She set off, the ancient floorboards creaking beneath her foot. That was another thing. You'd find it hard to move about silently. She supposed the room plan upstairs to be similarly chaotic and the floors just as creaky. It would be well nigh impossible to carry out an amorous midnight tryst without alerting all the guests!

Gervase Crown was in the lounge, stretched out in a leather armchair. For someone who had been threatened and called the police about it, insisting on a senior officer's personal attendance, he appeared singularly relaxed. His elbows were propped on the stout leather arms of the chair and his hands dangled loosely. A beam of pale sunlight had angled through a nearby window and fell on him. He looked, thought Jess, rather like a streetwise tomcat, resting from the regular patrols of his territory.

On seeing Jess in the doorway, Gervase abandoned his slouched attitude, rose to his feet and greeted her. 'Glad to see you, Inspector Campbell. The coffee here isn't brilliant, you might do better with the hot chocolate or tea. Which would you like?'

'I really don't need either, thank you,' Jess told him. She'd been presented with the chippy Gervase at their last meeting, and now she was getting the charming one. Neither washes with me, Mr Crown!

'I've been told that you rang and reported a threat to your person.' She sat down and adopted a businesslike attitude. 'Was this a serious threat, Mr Crown? Who made it? You were unwilling to tell DC Bennison over the phone and I do have other matters to attend to. It has taken time out of my day to drive out here.'

'It was – is – serious enough,' Gervase replied sharply, 'to make me think I ought to tell the cops about it. In the circumstances, as you're already investigating the destruction of my house, I preferred to talk to you. I thought you would probably want to talk to me.' He retook his seat. 'I don't know who made it – wrote it. It came in the form of a note, pushed under my door.' He took a piece of paper from his pocket. This he put on the low table between them.

A waiter was hovering. Clearly the man itched to know what was written on the mysterious sheet but Gervase had been careful to put it down folded so that no glimpse of the message showed. The waiter looked peeved. 'Sir and madam?' he asked.

'If you don't order something,' Gervase told Jess, 'they get depressed.'

'Thank you!' Jess told the waiter crisply. 'We're fine.'

The waiter marched off.

'That's the way to do it!' Gervase's voice suddenly took on a Mr Punch squawk.

'Not serious enough, then,' Jess suggested, 'to stop you making jokes?'

'Never heard of gallows humour, Inspector? Aren't you going to look at it?' He pointed at the note.

Jess picked up two cardboard drinks' coasters on the table and used them to open the folded paper out flat, making no fingertip contact with it. She was aware Gervase was watching with amusement. 'Nice to watch an expert,' he said.

'You handled this,' she said. 'Has it been handled by anyone else?'

'The person who sent it, presumably,' Gervase said, sounding irritated.

'I mean, did anyone else to whom you showed it?'

'I didn't actually show it to anyone. It's not the sort of thing you shove under someone's nose, is it? I nearly screwed it up and chucked it into the wastepaper basket when I saw what it was. At first I didn't know whether to be angry or amused. Then I thought of that poor stiff burned to a crisp in my house, and it didn't seem so funny. There's a nutter running round out there.'

Gervase pointed towards the main street visible through the nearby window. The angle of the sunbeam had already changed a little and no longer fell directly on him. Instead it fell on the note on the table like a spotlight. Dust particles danced in it.

'Possibly.' Jess wasn't ready to commit herself to any theory.

Someone had been at work with glue and scissors. In characters clipped from newspapers, the message read, IM WATCHING NEXT TIME NO MISTAKE. But that wasn't what struck Jess.

'This isn't an original,' she said suspiciously, looking up at Gervase. 'It's been photocopied. Where's the original?'

'Ah, there you have me, Inspector. That is how it was when I found it. If there is an original, and I suppose at one point there must have been, I haven't seen it.' Gervase shrugged.

'So, exactly when and how did you find it?' Jess was mindful of her observations on entering the building.

'I told you, pushed under the door of my room. It wasn't there this morning when I got up. I came down to breakfast . . .' He pointed past Jess to some spot beyond the lounge. 'Breakfast room is through there.'

'What time was this?'

'About nine fifteen.'

'Any other person waiting about upstairs near your room?'

He shook his head. 'Some people had gone down earlier. I heard them walk past my door. The corridor itself was empty when I came out. But the cleaner was in the room next door, not the one I had to walk past, the other one, on the other side. I knew she was there because the door stood open wide and her little cart with cleaning materials was wedged in the doorway.'

Gervase paused, apparently reviewing his actions. 'I hung the little notice on my door handle, the one reading, "Please clean the room". I suppose I was about three-quarters of an hour at breakfast, after which I came in here to see if they'd put out a copy of any of today's papers. They had, but it was only a tabloid and it took me all of five minutes to glance through it. I went outside for a cigarette. I thought I'd give the woman time to clean my room.'

'Did you smoke your cigarette in the street or in the yard at the back?'

'In the street.'

'Did you just stand out there watching the world go by, or move about?'

'This,' Gervase told her, 'is turning into a regular interrogation. I am not the defendant. I'm the plaintiff.'

'We're not in a court of law yet,' Jess retorted. There was no denying Gervase Crown had a rare ability both to annoy and to be annoyed. 'But if I am to work out what happened here, I need to know what everyone did and where everyone was. This building is a maze of corridors. The timing, by your account, was pretty tight. You weren't away from your room for long. During part of that time, the cleaner was active along that corridor. Anything at all that you noticed – either upstairs or down here – is very important. You yourself might not yet realise how important it is. Witnesses often don't. It's not enough for you to report an incident and then loaf about in here waiting for me to work a miracle. I need your help! You've been pretty good so far,' she conceded. 'Don't clam up now deciding you've told me enough.'

'Oh, all right.' Gervase held up his hands in surrender. 'I stand corrected. What did I do next? I walked up the road as far as the church and back again. My father's ashes are under a stone in the churchyard, if you must know every little detail. I went to check it out. The inscription is overgrown and almost illegible. I shall have to give the church a donation and ask for it to be cleaned up. Not out of filial respect, you understand, more a sense of obligation. At the moment it's an eyesore. I don't suppose the whole exercise took me half an hour at the very outside. I reckoned the cleaner must have tidied up my room by then. So I returned, went back up, opened the door and all but stepped on that.' He pointed at the note.

'Had the cleaner been into your room?'

'Yes, all as neat as a new pin. She wasn't in that corridor any longer, but she was on the floor above. I went up and found her there. I asked if she'd seen a folded note lying on the carpet in my room and she insisted nothing was there when she was. She told me, rather snappily, if there had been anything on the carpet, she'd have picked it up. I apologised nicely and gave her a fiver. She very nearly smiled.'

If he'd hoped to make Jess smile, he was disappointed.

'Have you any idea who might have pushed it under the door?'

'No.'

'Did you enquire at Reception if any non-residents had come into the hotel?'

'There was no one at Reception. They don't man it all the time. There's a bell on the desk for anyone to ring for service. I did ring it. The manager came out of his office to see what I wanted. I told him that someone had left a note for me upstairs but I didn't know whom it was from. He gave me a funny look. Then he suggested I asked the housekeeper. That's the title they give the cleaners. I told him I'd already done that. He said he was very sorry but he couldn't help. They were always very busy in the mornings.'

'And you have no idea who might have done this?'

'If I knew,' Gervase Crown told her impatiently, 'I'd go and find them and ask them what the dickens they think they're playing at?'

'Do you think it might be meant as a poor-taste joke?'

'No!' Gervase snapped. 'I think it means I'm next in line to end up like the poor bloke who died at Key House!'

'So you think someone's out to kill you?' Jess asked him. 'That's rather extreme, isn't it? Even if you're not liked, to want to kill you . . .'

'*I* know I'm not liked,' Gervase said icily, '*you* know I'm not liked. My unpopularity doesn't bother me. I have no ambition to be Weston St Ambrose's Man of the Year. But I don't take kindly to being threatened. Moreover, seeing as someone was murdered at my house, I assumed the police would want to know.'

'Indeed, we do! You did absolutely the right thing to let us know at once, Mr Crown.' Jess opened her bag, took out an evidence envelope and, again using one of the coasters, slid the note inside, watched with interest by Crown. 'I'll take this with me. I wonder if you wouldn't mind waiting here while I go and ask a couple of questions of the hotel? I might not have much more luck than you did, but you never know.'

Gervase said nothing, but gestured expansively towards the door and the hotel beyond.

Jess went to the breakfast room, following the faint noises of movement within. She found the waiter who'd come to them in the lounge, now setting out the tables for the next meal. He gave her a jaundiced look. Jess produced her ID and his expression became even more distrustful.

'We're not accustomed to see the police at The Royal Oak,' he told her.

'Pleased to hear it,' said Jess. 'Have you noticed any non-residents in the hotel this morning?'

'Always a few,' he said. 'They come in for coffee in our lounge. It's a popular meeting place locally.'

'Do you remember any of them? Were they known to you? Were they strangers?'

'We always get strangers,' the man said, 'on account of this being a tourist area. We don't know them, naturally. But we're always pleased to see them. We depend on them, you might say. I can't say I've seen any strange faces this morning. We had a few regulars drop in for coffee, too. They'll be in later for tea.'

That would bring it down to staff and residents. On the other hand, outsiders did come into the hotel on a regular basis in the morning. Perhaps if one came a little earlier than normal, it wouldn't cause a stir.

'You saw no one appearing hesitant or acting furtively?'

'At The Royal Oak?' he exclaimed in horror. 'I should hope not!'

'I understand you're busy down here, in the lounge and in the dining room. Do you have any reason to go upstairs?'

'Only if someone wants room service, you know, breakfast in their own room, but no one did this morning. I don't have any call to go upstairs. If you have a query about anything that's happened upstairs,' concluded the waiter with dignity, 'you should address yourself to housekeeping.'

Jess left him and went to find the manager. On the way she passed by the lounge door and saw that Gervase Crown was still there, leaning back in the same chair and reading a well-thumbed copy of *Country Life*. Some other people had joined him in the lounge. It looked as though the locals had begun to drop in as the waiter had described. A couple of middle-aged women had deposited carrier bags of shopping around their feet, giving the impression they had camped out.

The manager reacted to Jess's ID much as the waiter had done. 'We don't expect trouble at The Royal Oak!' he said firmly.

'No trouble, sir,' she soothed him. 'Just a question. If someone – not a resident – came into the hotel and went upstairs, would it be noticed?'

He opened his mouth to deny indignantly that his hotel's security was anything but 100 per cent, but then recollected in time that this was a police officer asking. 'We do our very best,' he said cautiously. 'But the mornings are always very busy. Guests are checking out. The rooms are being cleaned. Deliveries are being made in the kitchen and for the bar. All the staff and myself included have a lot to occupy us. It is just possible but, I must stress, it is highly unlikely. Besides, non-residents come in all the time, local people, so there is a certain amount of traffic past this desk. They wouldn't go upstairs. They go into the lounge or the restaurant.'

'Do you have a lift? Even a service lift?'

He shook his head. 'This building dates from around 1600 and stands on mediaeval foundations. The cellars are original and considered to be fourteenth century. As you would expect, National Heritage have it listed. There is no room for a lift and because of the restrictions imposed by the listing, we can't alter it to install one. We have two bedrooms on the ground floor for guests with a disability preventing them using the stairs. May I ask, is this a complaint made by Mr Crown?'

'Why do you think this is connected with Mr Crown?' Jess asked.

'Because he came to see me earlier. He looked very put out and asked the same question. He said someone had left him a note, pushed it under his door. He said he didn't know who the note was from, which seemed very odd to me. Wasn't it signed?'

'There is some confusion,' Jess said vaguely. 'How about the cleaner who turns out the rooms on that floor?'

'The housekeeper,' he corrected her. 'You want Betty. Wait a minute.' He went back to his office and returned almost at once with a sturdy woman in an overall.

Jess put her question.

'It'll be Mr Crown, I suppose,' Betty sniffed. 'He came asking me about a note or a letter. I don't know nothing about a note.'

'Can you tell me if you saw anyone in the corridor, while you were cleaning the rooms, anyone who shouldn't have been there?'

'No,' said Betty. 'I was busy. I've got the whole floor and the one above to do. I can't be standing around watching who goes up and down the corridors. I tidy a room, make the bed, clean the en suite, empty the wastebasket, and so on down the corridor. Then I put the vacuum cleaner over the carpets in the whole lot and along the passage. After that I'm off up to the next floor and start all over again. It's no use asking me if I heard anything, either. The vacuum makes a racket. I need a new one . . .' She broke off to give the manager a meaningful glare. 'I don't hear anything and I don't see anything . . . and I don't know anything about a note.'

Jess thanked them both for their time and left them looking after her with equally dissatisfied expressions.

The lounge now had several people in it. The waiter had reappeared and was taking orders for snacks and drinks. Gervase Crown put down *Country Life* and raised his strongly marked black eyebrows.

'Any luck?'

She shook her head. 'I got pretty much the same answers you did. We'll get on to this, Mr Crown. In the meantime, take care. If there is anything else, if anyone contacts you in any way, or you remember something, let us know at once. Oh, and if you can think of anyone who might bear you a particular grudge . . .'

'I'm sure you've heard about the Stapleton family. Well, whatever you've heard, you can forget them as suspects. It wasn't either of the sisters!' Gervase said angrily. 'Petra couldn't and Kit wouldn't.'

You'd be surprised how out of character people can act, thought Jess, but didn't say it. 'You've seen both sisters since your return?'

'You obviously know that I have.'

'Actually, I only knew for certain that you'd seen Petra. I guessed you might also have seen Kit by now.'

'Indeed I have. She was round here like a shot to tell me off as soon as she heard I'd called on Petra. But that, Inspector Campbell, is Kit's style: right to your face. She wouldn't shove bits of paper under doors. And as for their mamma, she's a very proper sort of woman. She wouldn't send letters made of bits of newsprint. She'd write by hand on headed notepaper. What's more, she wouldn't send threats – and I haven't seen her since my return.'

Gervase had recovered his equanimity. He stood up and accompanied her courteously to the cobbled yard and her car.

'Thanks for coming so quickly, anyway,' he said. He smiled. 'I do appreciate it, and your taking my problems so seriously, because I don't suppose you've got much time for me, either.'

'Why do you say that?' Jess felt herself flush. 'Why on earth should I dislike you?'

'Why shouldn't you? Most people seem to. Anyway, I've done time, as they say. I've got "previous". Don't pretend you don't take that into consideration whenever you look at me, or discuss me with your boss.'

It was what she had thought when she had first met him. He knew it. He was using that knowledge now to rile her. It seemed an extraordinarily unwise thing for him to do and she wondered why he was doing it. She said angrily, 'I think, Mr Crown, that you are attempting to test me in some way. If you are, then I can tell you I don't have time to waste on that sort of mind game. As regards our dealings now over the matter of the threatening message you've received, and the arson attack on your house involving a fatality . . . I'm a police officer, a professional. That I am aware of your past history doesn't mean it influences any investigation I make. You've been out of the country until recent events. So far, you're the victim in all this. And Mr Crown, you *do* need me on your side.'

'Believe me,' Gervase said fervently, 'I'd *hate* to have you as an enemy!'

'I'm not your enemy. Don't treat me as one.'

'*Jess!*' yelled a childish voice. Feet clattered across the cobbles and Millie appeared unexpectedly, running beneath the arched entry into the yard. She came to a halt by them and stared long and hard at Gervase, who stared back saying nothing.

'Who is he?' asked Millie of Jess, pointing at the stranger.

'Don't be rude, Millie,' said Jess gently.

'I'm Gervase,' said Gervase. 'You are Millie, I gather.'

Millie greeted this coldly. 'Jess is my daddy's friend,' she told him in a stern voice.

'No!' gasped Jess, 'I mean, not like that . . .'

'Haven't you got some dolls to play with or something?' asked Gervase.

Millie's opinion of him, obviously already poor, now hit the floor. 'I don't play with dolls! MacTavish doesn't like them.'

Gervase looked enquiringly at Jess.

'He's a bear,' explained Jess. 'Millie, where's Monica?'

'Coming,' said Millie vaguely, waving towards the archway. She turned her attention to Gervase again. 'My daddy,' she said loudly and very clearly, 'is a—'

'Goodness, Jess!' Monica arrived, puffing, in the nick of time. 'Millie, you shouldn't run off like that. Gervase, it's you!' Monica realised that Crown stood by Jess. 'Monica Farrell, you remember me?'

'Indeed I do, Miss Farrell.' He shook the hand she held out. 'I passed by your old schoolhouse this morning. It seems to be a private residence now.'

'It is, everything's changed since you left here. I'm sorry such a tragedy brought you back, Gervase. But it's good to see you.'

Gervase glanced at Jess with a faint smile, as if to say, 'Not everyone dislikes me!' Then, soberly, he told Monica, 'I'm sorry about the dead guy, not sorry about the house.'

'Millie and I are about to treat ourselves to a hot chocolate in the lounge here,' Monica said. 'If either of you can join us?'

'Not me, thanks,' said Gervase. 'I've seen more than enough of The Royal Oak's lounge this morning. I'm just about to drive off seeking a spot of lunch somewhere else, well away.'

'I'll put my head round the door before I leave,' Jess promised Millie.

Monica and Millie departed, Millie casting a farewell warning glare at Gervase over her shoulder.

'You see?' Gervase smiled wryly at Jess. 'Miss Farrell aside, I'm cut out to be unpopular. She was the local schoolteacher. She's programmed to see something positive in the most unpromising subject. She's in the minority. Even your boyfriend's kid doesn't like me.'

'He's not my boyfriend!' insisted Jess. 'He's – he's a colleague.'

'Oho! A copper, eh? Well, whatever, no sweat.' Gervase waved a nonchalant hand in goodbye and strolled off towards his hired blue BMW, parked in a corner of the yard.

Millie and Monica were in the far corner of the lounge. Millie had obviously been waiting for Jess to join them and bounced up to wave vigorously. 'We're over here, Jess!'

'I'm glad I've seen Gervase,' said Monica placidly. 'I've been keeping an eye open for him, knowing he was staying locally. I didn't fancy actually calling round here to see him on purpose because he might think I was being inquisitive. You know he really does look like a— he does look as Stephen Layton described him to me. I told Ian about it. Stephen met Gervase outside the front door here, on the night he arrived from Portugal. Ask Ian how he described him.' Monica gave a slight nod of the head towards Millie, indicating she did not want to repeat it for youthful ears. She needn't have worried. Millie had already made up her own mind about Gervase.

'*I* think he looks like a murderer,' said Millie.

Gervase himself, having declared his intention to drive out and find a decent-looking place to lunch, had decided that he'd better do it. If the red-haired inspector came back to the yard and saw his car still parked there, she'd be looking for him again.

'Sod this,' said Gervase mildly to himself, 'I've had enough of the police.' He glanced around him. 'And enough of Weston St Ambrose.'

He got into the rented BMW as Jess went into the back entrance of the hotel, and pointed it towards the arched way out into the main road. The exit was blind, any car having to cross the pavement before it got to the street. Aware of pedestrians on the footpath, he looked carefully from side to side and, as a result, almost failed to spot a middle-aged woman on an old-fashioned bicycle in the road ahead of him. In the nick of time, he braked. The bicycle wobbled, a couple of books in the wicker basket on the front fell out; and its rider put a foot to the ground and glowered at him.

Gervase opened the car door, half got out and called, 'Sorry, you OK?'

'That is a very dangerous exit,' said the woman. 'You should take more care.'

'I was taking care,' returned Gervase unwisely.

'Not enough!' snapped the woman. She clambered from her bicycle. Under her quilted jacket she wore what looked like some sort of uniform.

Gervase realised she intended to retrieve the books on the ground and hurried to do it first, but she beat him to it. She stood there with the books – they had the look of library books about them – gripped in her hands. There was something vaguely familiar about her but he couldn't place her. She, too, was studying him.

'Gervase Crown,' she announced at last. 'My husband told me you were back.'

'Good grief,' Gervase said, 'Mrs Layton, if I'm not mistaken. Have you, er, been to the library?'

'Yes. Our local library is now staffed by volunteers. The cuts, you know.'

'Cuts?'

'Government cuts. It's disgraceful, of course, but we'll keep our library going as long as we can.' She peered at the books. 'Although it won't help if the books are damaged!'

'Are they?' asked Gervase. 'I'll replace the damn things if necessary.' They were, he noticed, both volumes of crime fiction.

'They're all right!' she said sharply. She dusted the jackets off before turning to replace the volumes in the wicker basket. 'How long do you intend to stay?' she asked.

'Until matters relating to my house are sorted out.'

'Can't Reggie Foscott handle that for you?'

Gervase said icily, 'I can handle my affairs myself, thank you.'

'Mm, I suppose you can.' Mrs Layton climbed aboard her aged metal steed. 'Don't pile yourself up in that car, too,' she said, nodding at the BMW, and pedalled away before he could retort.

'This,' Gervase informed a pair of late-season tourists emerging into the street from the hotel, 'is the village from hell.'

They looked understandably alarmed.

*   *   *

On leaving the lounge a little later Jess hesitated for a moment in the entrance lobby of the hotel. She had left Monica and Millie still sitting over their hot chocolate, and discussing the bar menu. She had excused herself from sharing their meal. The waiter, in any case, now appeared to have given up on ever persuading her to order anything, and had ignored Jess. Her car was in the courtyard car park at the back; but Jess turned to the front entrance and stepped out into the street. Three minutes earlier and she'd have seen Gervase drive away. As it was, all she saw were two tourists, husband and wife, peering cautiously around them.

What she was now doing, she told herself as she walked along, was checking out the story Gervase Crown had told her. But she knew in her heart it was blatant curiosity. She glanced at her wristwatch. Half an hour, so Gervase had said. That's what it took him to walk to the churchyard, find his father's gravestone, and walk back to The Royal Oak. He hadn't hung about.

The church loomed up ahead. It stood almost opposite Monica Farrell's cottage. Its churchyard was dark, shaded by ancient trees and overgrown with a thick tangle of vegetation. Only the very latest burials, few in number, were clustered together and an attempt made to keep the area tidy. As for the rest, it was a wildlife paradise, undisturbed and given over to nature. Sebastian Crown's ashes had been placed here some years ago. The spot would be marked not by an upright but by a flat stone and that, Jess stared around in despair, would be somewhere in this jungle.

But someone had been here before her and recently, treading down the grasses and making a narrow footpath twisting towards a far corner. Gervase? He would have known where to look. Jess followed this narrow trodden route. All around was a strong smell of earth and decay and a stillness as of time suspended. It was hard not to feel that the eyes of those who rested here were upon her. Birds flew up into the overhanging branches at her approach. A grey squirrel sitting atop a lichen-encrusted Victorian urn ran down it, dashed across the narrow track and up the nearest tree trunk. Small creatures scuttled about unseen in the long grass and insects buzzed around her. Even with prior knowledge of its location, she wondered that Gervase had found his father's memorial at all. But suddenly she came upon a flatter area in a far corner, where someone had chopped inefficiently at the grass in an attempt to keep it down and the area respectable. Here a plot had been set aside for the reception of ashes. Rows of small square stones in the grass marked the locations. A couple were quite recent, but dirt and moss had encrusted most of the stones rendering the words illegible. However, at one of them someone had recently scraped the grime away. Jess stared down. This was Sebastian Crown's last resting place. His stone was engraved simply with his name, his year of birth and that of his death.

This is it, then, thought Jess. Shelley's Ozymandias's broken statue emerging from the sand could not have said it better. Here was all that remained on earth of a wealthy, powerful, strong-willed and – towards his wife at least – violent man. Just this: one small square of stone, green with moss, the incised inscription filled with dirt. She glanced at her watch again and noted the time. Gervase would probably have spent a few minutes here, remembering his childhood, and then he would have set off back to the hotel. The timescale was about right. She had no reason to doubt his account.

Jess left the churchyard and began to walk back to The Royal Oak. But before she reached it any sober meditation on life and death she might be tempted to make was driven out of her head. Coming towards her she saw a vaguely familiar form. It defined itself as a young man, scrawny in build, narrow faced, and wearing only a thin short-sleeved T-shirt with his jeans, even in this chilly weather. The shirt had lettering on it, but Jess couldn't make it out at this distance.

The young man had seen her now, and recognised her too. He swung about to make off in the direction from which he'd come but Jess had remembered his name and called it loudly.

'Alfie! Alfie Darrow!'

Alfie stopped in his tracks at the sound of the law calling his name. When she reached him he was still standing there, head down, refusing to meet her eye.

'Hello, Alfie,' said Jess pleasantly. 'I thought I'd recognised you. Even though you've started to grow a beard since we last met.' She was being generous. Alfie's beard clung to his chin in ragged patches and resembled the lichen adorning the gravestones, rather than hair. She wondered why he'd decided to adopt a fashion that she would not have thought appealed to him. Was he trying to change his appearance? If he was, why?

'Yeah,' muttered Alfie, 'I know you an' all.' He raised his head. 'You ain't looking for me, are you? Because I haven't done anything.'

'No, I wasn't looking for you,' she reassured him.

Alfie required more reassurance than that. 'You got that sergeant with you?'

'Sergeant Morton? No, I'm here on my own. How are you getting on now, Alfie? Not got into any more trouble selling drugs around your mates, I hope?'

'You won't find nothing on me!' burst out Alfie with sudden passion. 'I'm clean. You can search me and you won't find *nothing*! Not unless you plant it there.'

'Why would I do that? Search you, I mean. I'm glad to hear

you're not dealing any more. Don't be tempted to go back to it.'

As if advice from me would make any difference! thought Jess ruefully.

'I haven't done anything!' Alfie howled. 'You coppers are all the same. Someone gets in your black book and you try and nail him for everything that happens. I haven't done anything, right?'

More starkly expressed, this echoed what Gervase had said in the yard of The Royal Oak. As for Alfie? No, Jess had already decided, you've done nothing I know about, but you are very jumpy. She could now make out the faded lettering on his shirt. *All Property is Theft*, it read. Did this go with the attempt to grow a beard? Had Alfie taken up politics? 'Have you got a job?' she asked.

'Naw.' Alfie scowled at her. 'I lost that and all, didn't I?'

'There can't be much going in Weston St Ambrose,' commiserated Jess. 'Perhaps you should try somewhere bigger, Cheltenham or Gloucester. You'd have to move out of here and live there.'

'I had a place to live in town, didn't I? Not a job, but I had a place to live. Only I had to leave it. So now I'm living back here with my mum. Only temporary,' Alfie finished.

'Well, good luck, anyway, Alfie,' she wished him.

Alfie took this as dismissal and scuttled away down the street.

Whatever it is he's into now, thought Jess, *the police will hear about it sooner or later. Hope it doesn't land on my desk.*

Chapter 14

'So, what do we make of this, Jess?' Carter asked.

The note, in its transparent envelope, lay on his desk. Morton, who had been called in for the discussion of this new piece of evidence, said mistrustfully, 'I don't buy it.'

'How about you?' Carter prompted her.

'It's certainly odd,' she admitted. 'Why not just use a computer? Who nowadays uses newsprint and glue for this sort of thing?'

'Someone who hasn't got access to a computer,' Carter said. 'Or wants us to think so.'

'Got access to a photocopier, though,' Morton growled.

'Coin-operated copiers are available all over the place,' Jess put in. 'Whoever composed this note knew that we'd test it for fingerprints and DNA. A newsprint and glue job would have provided masses of evidence pointing at whoever made it. So, having made it, the writer took it along to a copier and made a copy. The copy emerges untouched by human hand from the machine and the author, whoever it was, only handles it with gloves – or picks it up with tweezers, something like that. I didn't handle it. Gervase says he didn't show it to anyone at the hotel. The only fingerprints or DNA on that will turn out to belong to Gervase Crown.'

'So, is the author of the note being very clever?' Carter asked them.

'For my money,' Morton had made up his mind already, 'Crown

made that thing up himself. He's getting worried that we're going to finger him for being responsible for the fire. OK, he didn't go to the house himself with a can of petrol and a box of matches. But he organised someone else to do it. It wasn't Pietrangelo; I admit I went down the wrong road there. No, it's someone else and Pietrangelo turns up unexpectedly just as the fire-raiser is going to do the business. He gets bopped on the head. The fire-raiser strikes his match and leaves the house and the unconscious Pietrangelo to burn.'

'I'm sure Crown would find his way to a computer,' Jess objected. 'I just don't see him sitting there, painstakingly cutting up newspapers. Although the hotel puts out a daily paper in the lounge, generally a tabloid. Crown mentioned that himself. So he would have a source of old newsprint to hand. I still think it's strange the letter was composed that way. It's – it's old fashioned.'

'Not so old fashioned that the author is unaware of modern forensic procedures,' Carter pointed out.

'It's all part of Crown's game,' was Morton's opinion. 'He's smart. He hopes we won't think he did it, because it's an old-style threatening letter as would be composed by someone who doesn't have a computer; and either can't be bothered with punctuation or doesn't understand how to use it. Crown wants us to think this is someone without much education, not a public-school man like himself. But,' Morton raised a forefinger to mark his next point, 'he also realises we might just conclude that he's out to trick us like that. So, he photocopies the original as a hint to us that the composer isn't just a simple, old-fashioned nut. It leaves us not knowing what to make of it. Also, any traces leading back to him on it are put down to his handling it as it is now, not to his sticking the letters on to the paper. He's running rings round us, or trying to.'

'I think you're on to something there, Phil,' Carter agreed.

Morton looked startled at having one of his ideas approved at long last.

'Someone is certainly trying to put us off the scent. But is it Crown himself? You could say Crown's a manipulator. He's manipulating us, right now. Or he's on the level and he really did find the note in his room. What do you think, Jess?'

Jess took her time replying as the other two waited. At last, she said, 'I think Crown was a worried man when we spoke. He put up a good front, but he was genuinely rattled. At the end of the day, there was a dead man in the ruins of his house. Perhaps he thinks we aren't taking the threat to his personal safety seriously enough. So it is possible he created that note to make us do more than we are to protect him. But if it is real, then someone is using that to frighten him. Someone wants him to leave Weston St Ambrose. By the way, he was very keen I should understand that Kit Stapleton couldn't be responsible. He discounted Petra Stapleton and the sisters' mother, as well.

'I agree that Petra's in a wheelchair and couldn't have got upstairs at The Royal Oak. They don't run to a lift. Also, a wheelchair is noticeable. None of the hotel staff would have paid any heed to a local person who came in to the hotel this morning on their own two feet, but someone would have noticed a wheelchair – or a person using crutches as Petra does to move out of her chair. Kit Stapleton has already been there once to tell Gervase to stay away from her sister. Kit's a tough nut, very determined, in my judgement. If Gervase shows no sign of going, she might do something to encourage him.'

'Like this?' Carter indicated the note.

Jess looked unhappy, 'I wouldn't have thought it Kit's style. But who knows? She's tried direct confrontation with Crown. He's brushed that off. She could be trying something else.'

'Mother Stapleton?' he suggested.

'Too much of a lady, in Gervase's view.'

'It might be worth having a word with her, even so.'

'Send Stubbs,' suggested Morton. 'He's very good with old ladies. They make him tea and feed him biscuits and get out the family photo album.'

'DC Stubbs it is, then. Tell him to get along there. Also, we mustn't forget the Foscotts,' Carter murmured, looking down at the note again.

'Reggie?' Jess was astonished. 'He's Gervase Crown's solicitor, and his wife is Crown's cousin.'

Ian Carter had an answer for that. 'Families have been known to go to some extraordinary lengths to preserve a good name. A threatening letter isn't the worst. Crown caused a lot of grief when younger. His lifestyle suggests he might still be a loose cannon. It might suit the Foscotts to have cousin Gervase back in Portugal where he can't cause any trouble here.'

'Or they suspect he was behind the fire at the house,' Morton clung to his theory. 'Foscott's reputation as a solicitor might be clouded by an association with a fire-raiser.'

'There is another possibility, admittedly an outside one but it ought not to be overlooked.' Carter paused and they looked at him expectantly. 'Reggie Foscott is Gervase Crown's solicitor, as you reminded us, Inspector Campbell. That means he will almost certainly have drawn up Gervase's will. He must know what it contains. It does not appear to be an extensive family. Serena Foscott is Gervase's cousin. Gervase is a rich man.'

'He might have left it all to her?' Morton exclaimed.

'If not all, then why not at least a substantial sum?' Carter drew a deep breath. 'I'd say they need the money. It struck me when I called on Serena that the Foscotts might, well, not be living beyond their means exactly. But they are certainly living up to the limit of them. They have a large property on which, it wouldn't surprise me, there could still be a mortgage. Their daughter has a pony. No stable on the premises. The animal must be kept at a livery establishment, costing an arm and a leg. I'd put my money on young Charlie attending a private school. They will need to maintain and keep on the road two cars. The furniture in that house is good, but old and dilapidated and my guess is that much of it was inherited in the first place. No decorating has been done inside or out for some time. And they can't afford outside garden maintenance. The drive is full of weeds. It was the increased cost to maintain Key House that put Reggie Foscott off his wife's idea to buy it. It was buy the house or keep the pony, they couldn't do both.'

Jess said slowly, 'Gervase is safe from harm all the time he remains in Portugal, out of reach. When he comes back here, it's on flying visits. That gives anyone who wants to get at him a very limited window.'

Morton took up the hint. 'So, if anyone meant him any harm, they'd have to lure him back to this country for a stay of more than a couple of days. Burning down his family home could do that.'

'But surely the Foscotts wouldn't go to those lengths? Not if Serena really wanted to buy it!' argued Jess. 'The Foscotts would be the last people to want it in ruins.'

This interesting line of speculation was cut short. A knock on the door heralded the apologetic face of DC Bennison.

'Sorry to interrupt again, sir, but I thought you might like to know that there was an attempted raid on Briskett's bank this morning. Two guys rushed in, wearing stocking masks, and one brandishing a shotgun. A third, the getaway driver, waited outside.'

'Briskett's bank? Sarah Gresham works there!' Jess exclaimed.

Bennison's braids bobbed enthusiastically. 'Yes, ma'am.'

'What do you mean by "failed"?' asked Campbell tersely.

'Someone hit an alarm button, sir. The guy with the shotgun panicked and fired off the weapon but only hit one of those paying-in machines and blew a hole in that. Then the raiders fled empty-handed. Bit of a shambles, really.'

Campbell turned to Morton. 'You'd better get over there, Phil, and find out what's going on. What about the girl, Sarah Gresham?'

Bennison was informative about that, too. 'Apparently she'd broken down in hysterics by the time the uniformed officers got there, ma'am. Not because of the shock, although you wouldn't blame her. But it's because she got a glimpse of the getaway car. It was a Renault Clio and she swears it's the one belonging to her boyfriend, the missing Clio, even though the number plate was different. Something about a dent she recognised. A witness outside in the street did manage to jot down a partial number and it doesn't match Pietrangelo's. But Sarah Gresham is still insisting it's his!'

'She's going to think every Clio she sees is her boyfriend's car, poor kid,' said Carter with a sigh. 'That doesn't mean this bungled bank job one isn't his though. The number plates could've been changed. Robbers are well aware of new vehicle recognition tech-nology in the hands of the police. It's been made public we're looking for Pietrangelo's car. If they used it, they'd have given it different plates. OK, Phil, on your way. Take DC Bennison here with you.'

A little over half an hour later, Morton called in, all but crowing in triumph.

'We have the bank raider's car, sir. It was abandoned on the outskirts of Cheltenham. It is a Renault Clio. The number plates have been changed but not the identification marks, and it's the missing one, Matthew Pietrangelo's car! His girlfriend was right.'

'Good! exclaimed Carter with satisfaction. 'So now we have to find out how it got from Key House, where Pietrangelo had presumably parked it, to waiting with the engine running outside Briskett's bank in town.'

Morton suggested, 'Either the murderer drove it away from Key House, or someone else came along and found it. A joy-rider?'

Jess said slowly, 'It may mean nothing. But when I was in Weston St Ambrose this morning, I met Alfie Darrow in the street. You may remember him, sir? From the Balaclava House case?'

'I certainly do,' said Carter. 'Shifty little tyke, as I recall. I wonder if he's still peddling those pills.'

'He says he's not,' Jess told him. 'But he wasn't happy to see me. He's out of a job at the moment and, if he's really not pushing drugs now, he'll be short of cash. He used to work in a garage. He likes cars. He was definitely jumpy. He couldn't have been involved in the robbery; he just hasn't the nerve and the other members of the gang wouldn't be able to rely on him. Not that they could rely on each other, from the sounds of it! Anyway, Alfie was wandering along the street in Weston St Ambrose at a loose end not a couple of hours later, out in the open for anyone to see, even me. But I believe he isn't unacquainted with Key House. He's got a T-shirt with "All Property is Theft" written on it. Roger Trenton told me he spoke to one of the druggies using the house, and he was wearing a T-shirt like that. If Alfie had wandered up to Key House to stash some of his stock of pills, say, and he saw a nice car like the Clio parked with no one around . . .'

'Say no more, Jess,' said Carter. 'We'll invite Mr Darrow to come and have a chat with us. Alfie might not have been pleased to see you this morning, but he will be when he realises you could turn out to be his alibi.'

'I knew it!' declared Alfie passionately. 'I knew it, as soon as she,' he pointed at Jess, 'as soon as *she* clocked me in Weston St Ambrose this morning, that you lot would try and fit me up for something.'

'We're trying to trace a car, Alfie,' Phil Morton had rejoined them and, the getaway car safely in the skilled hands of forensics, he was now keen to piece together its recent history.

'Well, I can't help you, can I?' howled Darrow. His spindly frame heaved with emotion. 'I'm going to find myself a solicitor. I reckon I can sue you lot for harassment.' His manner changed to pathetic. 'When I think how I always try and help the cops . . . I helped you before, didn't I? Over that Balaclava House business? I'm a decent citizen.'

'Come off it, Alfie,' said Morton. 'You are a very small-time drugs pusher. But this time you may have got into something well out of your league. We're talking armed robbery.'

For a moment Alfie appeared about to faint. 'Armed robbery?' he gasped. Then he rallied. 'I don't know nothing about it. When was this robbery?'

'It took place this morning, a little after eleven.'

Alfie pointed at Jess. 'Ask her. I was in Weston all today, until he—' Alfie's finger moved to target Morton. 'He come and got me to bring me here. I didn't have to come here, you know. I've got rights! Anyway, she saw me about that time, eleven, in Weston, walking along the street, minding my own business. Would I be doing that if I'd been doing an armed robbery earlier? Course I wouldn't.'

'Actually, Alfie,' Jess took over the interview. 'We are not suggesting at the moment that you are involved in the robbery. But the getaway car, a Renault Clio, certainly was. It's the car we're interested in. You heard that a house near Weston St Ambrose, Key House, burned down and a body was found in the ruins?'

'Yeah, I heard.' Alfie shifted uneasily. 'Local news, that. Everyone's heard about it. Never much happens in Weston. Something like that, they talk nothing else for days. In the pub, most people reckon it was an insurance job.'

'Is that a fact, Alfie? Why would local people say that?'

'Those big fires usually are, aren't they?' Alfie shrugged. 'Don't see how it could catch fire all on its own.'

'And the body?'

Alfie considered the death of Matthew Pietrangelo. 'I don't know nothing about it. He shouldn't have been there, should he?' An idea struck him. 'Here, you're not going to try and stick me with that, and all, are you?'

'At the moment, Alfie, we're interested in the car and we're hoping you can tell us something about it. You see, the Clio used in the robbery was the car belonging to the man found dead at Key House.'

'What?' yelped Alfie. 'You *are* going to try and pin a murder on me! I never killed anyone. This is a fit-up!'

'The car, Alfie,' Morton repeated patiently. 'We're asking about the car. If the man who died in the fire drove it to Key House, it should have been parked nearby. But it wasn't at Key House when the fire brigade arrived that night, or anywhere to be seen in the morning when it got light. It should have been, shouldn't it? Don't pretend you weren't acquainted with Key House before the fire. It had become a hang-out for people just like you.'

Alfie opened his mouth to protest at the slur on his good name, but then thought better of it.

'Alfie, if you know anything about that vehicle, anything at all, if you saw it anywhere. We need to know what happened to that car after the fire started.'

Alfie's furrowed brow signalled he was thinking furiously. Eventually he said, 'Armed robbery, dead bodies, houses burning down . . . None of that's my scene, is it?'

'Not to our knowledge – yet. But you like cars, don't you? We do know that.'

Alfie drew a deep breath. 'I want a solicitor,' he said.

'I've discussed it with the client,' said the duty solicitor later. 'He has agreed to make a statement. He is anxious to make it clear he is not admitting to any illegal activity.'

Alfie, listening with his arms folded, nodded. 'Yes, I don't want you lot trying to fit me up for nothing heavy, right?'

The duty solicitor, an elderly man, had often wondered why he'd ended up, in his professional career, trying to protect the interests of a host of Alfie Darrows. Now he sighed. 'All right, Mr Darrow. We agreed, yes? You will make a statement. You don't have to say anything else.'

'Not at the present time,' said Morton.

'Go ahead, Mr Darrow,' urged the solicitor.

Alfie drew breath and launched into his prepared account. Both Jess and Phil Morton listened impassively. They doubted they were going to get the whole truth. But if they got something, it might help. Alfie's request for a solicitor indicated some sort of culpability, but for what?

'The day of the fire, I mean in the morning when it got light, when the fire brigade were still at Key House . . .'

'Yes,' Morton said wearily.

'Well, I'd gone out first thing to check my snares.'

'What snares are these? What were you trying to catch?'

'Rabbits. I know where there's a big old warren in the fields back of Long Lane.'

'Long Lane?' Jess asked. She hadn't meant to interrupt so early in Alfie's tale, but to leave things to Morton. However, the mention of Long Lane was a surprise. 'The turning just after Key House?'

Alfie stared at her. 'Yes, if you're coming from Weston St Ambrose. Well, that's where the rabbit warren is, in the fields back of there. There's some woods between the lane and the fields, but a track runs from the lane through the trees and comes out right by the warren. That's where I set my snares. I have done for years, since I was a kid. And before you try to get me for something, I don't use any illegal snares. I check them the next day and the farmer knows I'm on his land. You can ask him. It's old Pearson. I quite often get a big old rabbit. If I do, I take it home and my mum skins it and cooks it.'

Morton made a noise indicating distaste.

'Nothing wrong with wild rabbit,' Alfie told him. 'At least you know what it's been eating. Only grass, unless it's got into some-one's garden. There's no gardens along there, except the one behind the old mad woman's house. Only that's not what you might call a proper garden, it's just brambles.'

'Are we talking about Mullions, Miss Pickering's house?' Jess asked.

'I don't know what the place is called or what the old girl's name is. I only know she's crazy, bats in the belfry, Loony-Tunes . . .' Alfie touched his forehead, 'and bad tempered with it. I stay away from her. She's got a funny-looking dog and that's worth keeping clear of, as well. Do you want me to tell you how I found the car or not?'

They assured him that they did.

'Well,' said Alfie, relaxing now that he was in charge of the conversation. 'The track is a bit further on than her house, about a quarter of a mile, little bit more? Like I said, I intended to go along there but when I saw all the fire engines I got interested and hid up and watched for a while. But then the cops turned up and I thought, I won't hang around here. Fire crew was too busy to spot me. But the cops were different. They'd go poking about. If they saw me, they'd reckon I'd had something to do with the fire. That's how you coppers think. You'd think I'd started the fire and gone back to see how it had gone. Well, I didn't. But it was best for me to stay away so I went home and didn't check the snares that morning. I would've done, like I said, but the presence of the police prevented me,' Alfie concluded virtuously.

'My, you have been talking to your solicitor, haven't you?' Morton growled.

The duty solicitor shrugged.

Alfie continued. 'I went back the next morning. Fire brigade and cops had all cleared off. The house was still smouldering a bit. I didn't turn down Long Lane, I pushed through the hedge, where

I'd hidden the day before to watch the fire brigade, and cut across the fields.

'There were rabbits about, 'cause it was so early. But they went scattering all over the place when they saw me. There was nothing in any of the snares and one of them was missing. I went looking for it. They get knocked off the fence where I set it sometimes, especially if something bigger goes through, like a fox. I climbed over the fence. It's pretty near fallen down, so I just had to step over it, really. I went looking for the snare in the woods. And there, parked right under the trees, but on the track that leads off Long Lane, was a Renault Clio, not a wreck, one in first-class nick. I couldn't believe my eyes. First of all I thought someone was about in the woods. I stood really quiet and listened but there was no noise. It's not easy to move quiet over ground like that, twigs snapping and so on; and the birds go flapping about in the trees making a racket, specially the pigeons. But it was all real quiet.

'I took another look at the car. The roof was all covered in dew. It had been there all night, I reckoned. So I looked inside and what d'you think?' Alfie sat back and waited, savouring the dramatic moment.

'The keys were in it?' Morton suggested.

Alfie, cheated of his surprise, was disappointed. 'Yes, how did you know? Anyway, they was, so I thought someone must have pinched it, joy-riders or such, and they'd left it down the track, meaning to come back later for it and have another drive round. It seemed sort of meant. I'm only human. The doors weren't locked. I got in the driver's seat and thought, I'll take it for a bit of a spin.'

Alfie paused and glanced at his brief. 'I didn't steal the car. I reckoned it was abandoned.'

'Mr Darrow is somewhat confused about the law,' said the solicitor wearily.

'That's right. I thought, it's abandoned. It's OK for me to take it. So I took it and drove it round a bit.'

'And then?' asked Morton.

'I ran out of petrol, didn't I? There wasn't much in the tank to start with. But it ran out quicker than I thought it would, so I had to abandon it again. Well, I hadn't abandoned it the first time, whoever took it from the house did that. I mean, it got abandoned for a second time when I left it.'

'Just where did you leave it, Alfie?'

'By the side of the Cheltenham road, near The Fox pub,' said Alfie. 'I had a really long walk home from there.'

'And the car keys? What about those?'

'Left 'em in the car. They wasn't no good to me, was they?' He sat back. 'I can't tell you any more, because there isn't any more.'

'So, how much of that do we believe?' asked Carter.

'Funnily enough,' Jess said slowly, 'I believe most of it, at least up to the point when he found the car.'

'But he didn't drive it round until he ran out of fuel and was stranded,' Morton put in. 'We know Alfie's not very bright, but he's not that stupid. He'd keep an eye on the fuel gauge. What's more, he wouldn't drive it on a busy road because a stolen car would be more likely to be spotted. He'd stick to the back lanes. So we can forget about his leaving it at the side of the Cheltenham road. Crafty little sod mentioned The Fox pub because he hopes we'll think someone came out of the pub and nicked it, and whatever happened with that car afterwards, it's down to whoever drove it away from The Fox. That car was never near the Cheltenham road or The Fox, not while Alfie was driving it!

'Look, it was a nice little car, undamaged, clean, in good order. It was worth money, serious money as far as Alfie's concerned. So I reckon he drove it into the town to some backstreet garage and sold it to a dodgy dealer. Whoever that was passed it on to the gang. But we won't get Alfie admitting that. For a start, he probably didn't know what the dealer would do with it, and didn't care. But he cares now that he's found out it was used in an armed robbery. That doesn't mean he's going to tell us the name of the dealer. He's not going to tell us anything that will lead us to whoever was involved in the bank raid. Guys who charge into banks waving shotguns don't like grasses. Alfie will be far more scared of them than he is of us. He doesn't want his head blown off his shoulders.'

'On the other hand,' Jess pointed out, 'he knows we're examining the car and we'll find his prints if he was ever in it. So he admits he was in it, and gives us a plausible explanation. It could well be a true one.'

Carter heaved a sigh. 'And we don't even get him for trespass or using an illegal snare.'

Morton said gloomily. 'I hate it when a little lowlife like Alfie Darrow gives us all the runaround.'

When Morton had taken himself off amid encircling gloom, Jess said hesitantly, 'We were talking about Crown's will earlier, supposing he's made a will.'

'Yes?' Carter looked at her, curiosity in the hazel eyes that now made her think of Millie. She wondered what Millie and Monica were up to today; then ordered herself to keep her mind on matters in hand – and that meant Gervase.

'He is very wealthy,' she continued. 'You were suggesting he might have left a tidy sum to his cousin Serena Foscott. I'm just wondering if he might not have left a considerable sum to Petra Stapleton.'

Carter let out a low whistle. 'Blood money,' he said.

'Something along those lines. She did win substantial compensation in the courts at the time of the accident. But if his conscience is troubling him . . .'

'I understood, from what you told me of your conversation with her, that Katherine – Kit – Stapleton believes he doesn't have a conscience.'

'If she believes that, I think she's wrong,' said Jess. 'But does she? You know, and if this sounds strange I'm sorry, but I do sometimes feel, when I'm around the people involved in this business, that I'm being invited to watch a piece of theatre.'

Chapter 15

'I'll say this,' Kit Stapleton told her sister, 'you've managed to make the mutt almost attractive.' They were in the studio, examining several preliminary sketches of Hamlet made by Petra in preparation for his portrait.

'I'm hoping Muriel will like one of them well enough to decide she wants me to work it up into a proper portrait. I'm not trying to make Hamlet look a beauty, because he's not, poor old thing. But I have tried to bring out his personality, to look beyond physical features.'

'You must have X-ray vision because if Hamlet has a beautiful spirit, it's lost on me. All I see is his squashed mug. But I'm not an artist.'

Outside the swirl of wheels on gravel was audible. The muted growl of a car's engine was cut off abruptly, followed by the slam of a car door.

'It might be Muriel,' Petra said doubtfully. 'But it didn't sound like her old banger. The engine of her car sounds as if it's got a nasty cough.'

'He wouldn't—' Kit gasped, dropped the sketch of Hamlet in her hand and ran to the open barn doors. She erupted in a wail of fury. 'Would you believe it? The blighter has come back!'

From within, Petra heard the following short burst of conversation.

'What are you doing here? I told you to stay away! I thought that was understood. Just get back in that car and get out!'

'Glad to see you, Kit. I wanted to see you both. I thought there was a chance I'd find you here, guarding Petra.' The male voice caused Petra's heart to hop again in that ridiculous way. *Stop it!* she ordered herself.

'I have to guard her! I can't trust you, obviously. What's the matter with you, Gervase? Are you completely thick?'

Kit must be almost dancing in rage, Petra thought. I'd better do something before she biffs him. 'Gervase!' she called loudly. 'Come in! It's OK, Kit. Let him come in.'

Kit erupted back into the barn ahead of the visitor. 'No, it's not bally OK. Let me get rid of him.'

Gervase emerged from behind her and said, 'Too late, Kit. I'm here.'

Kit whirled round and glared at him, red faced and rendered speechless for the moment.

Petra took the opportunity to say, 'If you want to see us both, Gervase, let's go over to the cottage. We can have a cup of tea or something. It's all right, Kit, honestly.'

Kit stalked ahead of them to the cottage, Petra following in her chair and Gervase bringing up the rear. Once through the cottage door, Petra hauled herself out of the chair and grabbed the crutches propped against the wall. She knew Gervase was watching every move and avoided his gaze.

But she couldn't avoid it for ever and, once all three of them were established on the banquette by the window, she met his eye at last. He looked wretched.

Kit marched over to them with a tray and slammed it down on the little table. Tea slopped about in the cat mugs. Petra saw with amusement that Kit had given Gervase the mug with a black cat painted on it, back arched aggressively, big yellow eyes gleaming. The witch's cat, Petra had called that design.

'What do you want?' Kit asked sharply. 'If you're here, you're here. But at least don't hang around. Get on with it!'

This ungracious speech had the effect of wiping the wretchedness from Gervase's face. Now he looked at Kit and grinned briefly. Petra was pleased to see the misery fade but it struck her that Gervase's grin lacked its customary boldness.

'What's the matter, Gervase?' she asked quietly.

He turned to her. 'I'm sorry to disturb you, Petra. I really had not meant to come and bother you again. But I felt I should come and tell you – both – something.'

'You're going back to Portugal?' asked Kit hopefully.

'All in good time. That's not what I came to say, Kit. Sorry to disappoint you. The fact is, I've had a threatening letter.'

The sisters burst into speech together.

'What did it say?' asked Petra.

'Have you got it with you?' from suspicious-sounding Kit.

He chose to answer Kit's question first. 'Honestly, Kit, I have had a letter. The police have it now.'

'Yes, yes, so you say,' returned Kit with impatience. 'For all we know this is one of your spoof yarns, like the one you told me about the Key House ghost.'

'You're not going to nag me about that, are you?'

'Wasn't the ghost legend true?' asked Petra with interest. 'Kit told Inspector Campbell about it when she called.'

'No, it was an example of his misplaced sense of humour,' snapped Kit. 'As I know too late, now he's let me make a fool of myself to the police.'

'I didn't know you'd even remembered it!' Gervase protested. 'What did you tell the cops about it for, anyway?'

'I don't *know*. It's like that when you talk to the police, I suppose. You end up telling them things.' Once again, Gervase had wrong-footed her and she had to explain herself. Her frustration almost shimmered in the air around her.

'If you say so,' said Gervase politely.

Kit squawked.

Petra intervened again. 'Just tell us about the letter, Gervase. What on earth did it say?'

'Calling it a "letter" is, I admit, making it sound more elaborate than it was,' Gervase explained. 'It was more in the way of a note, pushed under my door at The Royal Oak. It's made of bits cut out of newspapers and glued on to a sheet of paper. Quite Agatha Christie stuff and, now that I think about it, a bit of an insult. The message is brief and what you might expect.' Gervase repeated the words. 'All in upper-case letters clipped from papers, as I said, and without any punctuation. Honestly, my first reaction on seeing it was to laugh. It was sort of childish.'

There was a silence.

'Just that?' asked Kit sceptically.

'Just that. I told you it was stark – and unoriginal.'

Petra's face had paled. 'It's horrible, and it's not funny. Whoever sent it means every word and the mind behind it is sick.'

'I do realise that. I only laughed once, probably more in surprise than amusement.' Gervase set down his mug. 'Now then, this is the really interesting part of it, the writer didn't deliver the original. It was a photocopy that came under the door.'

'Why?' asked Petra, bewildered.

'Were you in the room at the time?' from Kit, still suspicious. 'When this letter suddenly appeared from nowhere?'

'Of course I wasn't in the room, don't be daft, Kit. I'd have opened the door and grabbed whoever it was. I'd gone down to breakfast. There was nothing to be seen when I left the room. I went out for a walk after breakfast and came back mid-morning to my room, and there it was.'

'Chambermaid?' asked Kit tersely. 'Had she been in your room?'

'She had and she denies all knowledge. Likewise the manager. Hear, see and speak no evil, that's the motto of The Royal Oak.' Gervase turned to Petra. 'As to why I received a photocopied example, I assume it was because the original would have had the creator's dabs all over it, plus DNA. The photocopy would have been handled with kid gloves – or regular rubber washing-up mitts, as you please. Untouched by human hand, anyway. Except mine, of course. I picked it up to read it and carried it around with me in my pocket. My dabs and DNA all over it, as the cops will have discovered by now and be drawing the obvious conclusion.'

'And did you send it to yourself, Gervase?' asked Kit coolly.

'Don't be silly, Kit! Of course he didn't,' cried Petra.

'Thank you, Petra, for the vote of confidence. No, Kit, I didn't send it to myself. Did *you* send it?' He put the question in a casual tone, but his face was serious and his blue eyes fixed on Kit's face.

'Me?' howled Kit, bouncing up from the seat. 'Why would I muck about doing a stupid childish thing like that?'

'I did tell that lady cop with the red hair, Campbell, that you would never have done it. I said, you would come and tell me to my face. All the same, I'd be glad of your reassurance.'

'No, she didn't do it!' Petra burst out, losing her own temper. 'Honestly, Gervase, as if either of us—'

He interrupted her. 'I know *you* wouldn't, Petra. But Kit was cross with me about the ghost joke I told her donkey's years ago . . . you *do* bear a grudge, don't you, Kit, old thing?'

'I didn't know, years ago, it was a joke.' Kit appeared to have difficulty talking. Perhaps it was the effort to sound calm. The words were squeezed out of her throat. 'And I don't bear grudges. I – all my family has good reason to be "cross", as I suppose you'd call it, with you. That has nothing to do with jokes about ghosts.'

'Just stop it, the pair of you!' ordered Petra. 'And if you are going to talk about me, please don't.'

Kit, looking thoughtful, rubbed a hand through her mop of short hair so that it was left tousled as if she'd been out in a high wind. Something like a smile touched Gervase's face but it was so fleeting that even Petra, watching him closely, wasn't sure she'd seen it.

'How could someone come along and just push it under the door of your room, and none of the hotel staff notice?' Kit was still prepared to play devil's advocate. 'It's very fishy, Gervase, you've got to admit. I'm not accusing you, just pointing out the obvious.'

'You obviously aren't in the habit of dropping into The Royal Oak, other than to bite my head off,' Gervase told her. 'It's by way of being a local meeting spot. Non-residents are in and out of the place all the time and the staff have the knack of total concentration on what they are doing, oblivious of all else. A small army could tramp through there; and the only reaction might be from the lounge waiter, who would want them to order coffee.'

'I remember him,' said Kit and scowled. 'In this day and age you'd think security would be a priority.'

'It's not a top-notch London hotel with VIPs going in and out,' Petra said in The Royal Oak's defence. 'I can understand how someone might slip in and out. So, what happens now?'

'Yes, are the police taking it seriously?' asked Kit.

'I assume so. Once they decide I didn't send it to myself. I think the red-haired lady cop believed my account. Not that you can ever tell what the police are thinking.'

Gervase stretched out his legs and stared at the toecaps of his suede boots. 'I met the girlfriend of the poor guy who died at Key House, in the fire,' he said without warning.

Both sisters gasped.

'Where, how?' asked Petra.

'I was checking out Key House. It was after you came to see me at The Oak, Kit. I got in the car and drove out there. Talking about when we were kids made me unexpectedly nostalgic, not that what you see there now has the slightest resemblance to how the place was all those years ago. It's like a war zone. The fire brigade is still going back to dampen it down but I don't think they'll pay more than one more visit. Underfoot it's all very wet and mucky. All the same, I saw that someone was there ahead of me, this girl. She'd brought flowers. She left them on the floor in the kitchen area, where the body was found and the fire started. It was a dangerous thing to do because the house is so unstable and, while she was there, one of the old fitted kitchen cupboards fell off a wall and split apart. The wood was charred and fragile but it had some nasty-looking screws poking out of it. She told me the chap who died had been her partner. It was very touching. Yes, even me, Kit. I was moved.'

'It's so sad,' said Petra.

'I felt pretty useless,' Gervase went on. 'I didn't know what to say. Then, of all people, that old harridan Muriel Pickering turned up with a pop-eyed, bandy-legged dog in tow. The mutt looked rather like Muriel. She came to my rescue, although that wasn't her intention. She started berating me, which gave the girl a chance to make her excuses and leave. It was quite nice to see old Muriel and know she hasn't changed. But then, nothing much around here has, as I mentioned to you, Kit. The French have a saying for it, don't they? They've got a saying for most things. The more things change, the more they stay the same. Isn't that it?'

'*Plus ça change, plus c'est la même chose,*' Petra whispered. 'It might be true, but it shouldn't be, should it?'

Very slowly Kit said, 'I'm not speaking for Petra or myself now, about what we'd like you to do. I'm speaking as someone taking into consideration what's best for you, Gervase. Perhaps you *should* go back to Portugal. You'd be safe there from whoever means you harm here. Give the police a chance to find out what happened at Key House. Then come back to England and sort out what has to be done regarding the ruins.'

'Isn't that what the writer of the note wants me to do?' Gervase said sharply. 'I have a basic objection to being told to clear off out of my own property and my own country. You'll say that's what I did when I moved abroad. But it's one thing to do it because I decided to. It's another to run in panic from some murderous idiot. You agree, the whole business of the note is like a childish prank. Blowed if I'm going to run away from something like that!'

He paused and went on more calmly, 'Besides, I've been thinking. If I stay here, it might flush out the murderer-cum-arsonist. By sending me that note, he's put himself on the line. He's gone public threatening another attempt on my life. Now he's got to do it. So, I wait. He'll try something that will force him out into the open, but I'll be on my guard and either I or the police will nab him.'

'He might try and set fire to The Royal Oak!' cried Petra in dismay. 'He burned down Key House, why not the hotel?'

'No! He won't. It would be too hit or miss, Petra. I agree the place is old and would burn nicely. But it's also got smoke detectors in every ceiling and clearly marked fire exits. It wouldn't be at all like putting a match to an empty place like Key House,' Gervase assured her.

'Risky, all the same,' said Kit in clipped tones. 'Not to say, pretty damn stupid. You think you're smarter than he is, Gervase, but are you? After all, he knows you and you don't know him. He's knows what he's looking for – you – and you don't have a clue.'

'Thanks, Kit, for your usual gracious assessment of my ideas.'

'I'm not getting at you, Gervase, honestly.' Kit drew a deep breath. 'But he isn't going to give you a chance to see him first.'

'Oh, but he has,' Gervase returned gently. 'By sending the note in the first place, he's signalled his intention. That's tantamount to stepping out into the open.'

'Rubbish! He's still lurking in the jungle and you, by offering to play the role of tethered goat, won't help anyone, least of all the police.'

'And Kit and I will be worried sick, all the time, knowing someone is prowling round out there looking for you!' Petra said suddenly.

This unexpected statement was met with a silence in which Petra stared at Gervase and Gervase stared at Kit.

'We will naturally be very concerned,' said Kit, stony faced. 'I suggest you talk this over with Inspector Campbell and take her advice. I can't imagine she'd be very enthusiastic. We are dealing with a nutcase, Gervase, and neither you nor the cops have the slightest idea what he'll do next!'

'Yes, *please*, Gervase!' urged Petra. 'Ask for police protection.'

'If I've got police protection no one will be able to come near me and we'll be no further on,' he pointed out. 'OK, I will mention it to Campbell.' He rose to his feet. 'Thanks for the tea. I guess you painted all those moggies on the mugs, Petra. Thought of marketing the design commercially?'

Petra shook her head.

'You should. Well, cheerio, ladies. Sorry to have disturbed you. I'll be off.'

He walked out. They watched from the window as he went to his rented BMW. He opened the driver's door and turned to give a wave towards the faces behind the glass. Then he drove away.

'He's not going to tell the police about hoping to lure the – the killer – into trying again, is he?' Petra whispered.

'Probably not.' Kit's voice was bleak.

'Should we tell her? I mean Inspector Campbell.'

'I suppose I could give her a call.'

'Yes, Kit, you must. Please, call her and tell her. If you won't, I will!'

'No, you keep out of it, sweetie. I'll call Campbell and tell them Gervase is still being an out-and-out nuisance and intends to play at being Sherlock Holmes.'

Kit turned from the window and met her sister's anguished gaze.

'Oh, Kit,' said Petra in despair, 'what is to become of us all?'

Chapter 16

'Someone is downstairs asking to see you, ma'am,' said Bennison. 'Katherine Stapleton.'

Jess found Kit pacing up and down with her hands in her pockets. As Kit whirled to face her, Jess thought her visitor looked both truculent and worried.

'I need to have a word with you,' Kit said abruptly. 'I dare say you're busy, but it shouldn't take long.'

'Fair enough. I've got time to talk.'

Kit looked restless. 'Thanks – but do we have to talk here? I'm not making a statement or anything like that. I haven't come to confess to setting fire to Key House, which I didn't, by the way. It's just – personal.'

'We can talk elsewhere,' Jess said cheerfully. 'There's a café just down the road. The coffee there is better than it is here.'

The café was cramped and steamy but warm. They settled in a corner, with the buzz of chatter from other customers around them, and a large mug of latte apiece.

'This about Gervase Crown, I suppose?' Jess prompted Kit, as her companion sat and stared at the coffee with ferocious concentration but showed no sign of starting the ball rolling in the chat she'd requested.

Kit twitched and stopped staring at the coffee. 'Yes, it's about

Gervase and it's also about my sister – and I suppose you could say it's about me. I don't really know where to start.'

'The beginning is a good place, as someone or other said – or wrote.'

'Lewis Carroll,' said Kit absently. 'One of the characters in *Alice in Wonderland* says, "Begin at the beginning and go on till you get to the end." I know what the beginning is. I wish I knew what the end is going to be. In the beginning we were all three kids together. Gervase was away at school a lot but when he came home in the holidays we used to spend time with him. I saw more of him than Petra did, because he and I were of an age. Petra was two years younger. Gervase and I roamed around the countryside. He didn't like going home. He actually liked being away at school.'

'Any particular reason?'

'Well, his mother had bunked off and his father was pretty grim. But the atmosphere there was so tense that, even before his mother left, Gervase used to push off out of the house and only went home in the evening. He used to get whoever was employed to do the cooking at the time to make him a sandwich for his lunch. I'd ask my mother to make sandwiches for me. We spent all day out and about. Sometimes Petra tagged along but usually it was just Gervase and me. It was just kids' stuff, making camps, climbing trees, falling out of trees, swimming in the river. I pushed Gervase into a full drainage ditch once.'

'Why?'

'Don't ask me, I forget. We were arguing. I lost my temper and pushed him. I helped him out. He was soaking wet, smelled awful and was furious. I couldn't stop laughing, horrid brat that I was.'

'Nervous reaction,' said Jess firmly,

Kit looked at her in surprise. 'What was?'

'The laughter. You pushed him on impulse. You didn't really mean him to get soaked in ditchwater. You weren't laughing at him in a horrid way. You were probably a bit scared at what you'd done. I'm a twin,' Jess went on. 'My brother and I spent a lot of time together and most of it we spent arguing. It didn't mean we weren't very close – we still are.'

'Oh, I see.' Kit seemed to relax. When she took up her tale again she spoke more easily. 'Well, we grew up. At least, I did. I went off to college. Gervase, after some back-packing, hung round Key House doing nothing. I don't know why, as he didn't get on with his father, he didn't just leave and get a place of his own. But Gervase has always had his own reasons for his actions. Anyway, he'd got interested in cars. He went out drinking. He smashed up one car in a crash locally. The hoo-hah was all smoothed over and Gervase got another set of fast wheels.'

Kit paused, reddened, and said, 'Perhaps I ought not to say this, but I have sometimes wondered if Sebastian wasn't trying to placate his son somehow. I don't mean make it up to him because he'd had a rotten childhood. I mean that, in some peculiar way, Gervase had a sort of hold over him and enjoyed letting him know it.'

'If Gervase was his only child, then that would be a powerful hold on him,' Jess suggested.

'No, not that . . . I don't know. Perhaps I'm just being daft. Anyway, the next smash he had, my sister was in the car with him. I'd overlooked the fact that Petra had grown up too, and, well, I should have warned her about him, told her to stay away from him. He was going through a wild patch and Petra didn't need to be involved in that. But in the end, she was. They'd been to the same party and he was giving her a lift home. Only they never

229

got home. You've seen my sister. That's how Gervase left her, in a wheelchair. She was not quite eighteen when it happened. I don't forgive him. I never will.' Kit picked up her coffee and began to drink it slowly.

Jess waited. At last Kit put down her empty mug.

'Petra's forgiven him. Petra was always kind and sweet natured. I was always the unforgiving sort. I was livid when Gervase turned up here the other day, after the fire, and went to see Petra. How could he do that? Anyway, he came to see her again this morning. I was there. He said he was glad to see us both. He wanted to tell us he'd had a threatening letter. He said he'd given it to the police. Is that true?'

Kit paused to look questioningly at Jess. 'Only, sometimes, you know, Gervase teases. It's his warped sense of humour and he's being a pain. I've only just found out that the story I told you about the Key House ghost was one of his daft hoaxes. I don't mean I ever believed there was a ghost, but I did believe there was a legend of a ghost attached to the house. That's what I told you. Then, the other day when I went to The Royal Oak to see him, he told me he'd made it up.'

Jess smiled at her. 'It really doesn't matter about the ghost. I wasn't including that in our enquiries.'

'No, of course you weren't. Whoever bashed that poor young man over the head and left him to die in the fire wasn't a ghost. It matters to me because it was Gervase fooling me and I always hated that. So I need to know that he's really had an anonymous letter and it isn't just Gervase up to his tricks. Before he lets me make a fool of myself to you again.'

Jess said quietly, 'He has given us an anonymous letter.'

'So it's true.' Kit drew a deep breath. 'I told him he should go back to Portugal until the police have solved the business of the fire and the dead man. But Gervase intends to stay and loaf around openly. His plan, barmy of course, is that the murderer will be tempted out to try another go at him. Because he does believe the murderer meant to kill him at Key House, but got the wrong man.'

'Crown was in Portugal when the assailant attacked Matthew Pietrangelo at Key House,' Jess pointed out. 'Crown hadn't lived in Key House for some time. It was more or less abandoned. Why should the killer think it was Gervase at the house that night?'

'OK, yes, I know! But Gervase still believes the killer thought that he, Gervase, was back in this country and that it was him at the house that evening.' Kit drew a deep breath. 'Petra wanted me to tell you that Gervase is asking for trouble. She doesn't believe he'll let you know what he's doing. She wants you to protect him.'

'How?' asked Jess calmly.

'I don't know! At least, impress on him that he should leave detection to you, the cops.' She stared at Jess. 'Will you? Petra's worried.'

'And you? You're worried?' Jess asked.

'Yes, I am, because if anything happens to Gervase, Petra will be shattered. She's made a new life for herself, after he destroyed the life she might have had. If he gives some nutter out there a chance to attack him, even kill him, then what will that do to my sister?'

After Kit had left her, Jess took out her phone and tried the number Gervase Crown had given them for his mobile. But her call was only answered by a recorded voice asking her to leave a message after the bleep. She thought irritably that he was up to his old tricks, dropping out of contact.

'What's the matter with the wretched man?' she muttered. 'First he calls the police demanding I go immediately to The Royal Oak because he's been threatened. Next thing, no one can reach him.'

In her mind's ear, she caught the echo of Kit Stapleton's final words on their parting a few minutes earlier.

'Gervase is playing tethered goat.'

That was OK provided some backup was hiding in the bushes nearby, ready to save him from the tiger. Not so good when the goat and the tiger were left alone to sort it out for themselves. Jess left a message on his voicemail, asking that he call her back. It was hardly satisfactory. If Crown was right about being the target, his behaviour was the height of foolishness. Jess rang The Royal Oak and was told Mr Crown was not in the hotel. That wasn't a surprise. The Royal Oak wasn't the sort of place she'd expect Gervase to hang around. So, where might he be? After a moment's deliberation, she rang Foscott's Solicitors.

'I'm trying to get in touch with your client, Mr Crown,' she told Reggie Foscott. 'He's not answering his phone.'

Surprisingly, this turned up the desired information.

'I understand,' Foscott's dry tones said in her ear, 'that he was having tea with my wife this afternoon. She is his cousin. That will be why he's switched off his mobile.'

'Look here, Gerry,' said Serena, brandishing the sherry bottle at him. 'All this has got to stop.'

'I'd be delighted if it would stop, coz,' Gervase told her. 'I don't want a homicidal maniac roaming the land looking for me.'

'Then go back to Portugal.'

'You know, everyone seems very keen for me to do that,' he told her. 'No, I'm not ready to go back just yet.'

'Then at least come and stay here with us. It would be a damn sight safer than being at The Royal Oak where, from what you tell me, anyone can roam the corridors pushing threatening notes under doors. Next time it might be a bomb. Have you thought of that?'

'I'd rather not. But thanks for the offer, Serena. I won't take it up. It might put you and Reggie and young Charlie in danger.'

Serena topped up the sherry glasses and asked gloomily, 'Do you want any more cake?'

'Thank you, no. It was very nice.'

'I didn't make it,' said his cousin honestly. 'I'm no good at cakes, or pastry, or cookery in general, come to that. I can do a Sunday roast and tonight we're having lamb hotpot. I'm OK with that. Stay and eat with us, at least.'

'Will you have enough?'

'Oh, I should think so. I'll chuck a few more carrots in it. Reggie doesn't eat a lot, Charlie picks at her food like a sparrow. Yes, there will be plenty.'

'Then I'll stay.'

Serena threw herself back on to the chesterfield and pointed her sherry glass in his direction. 'You should have sold the ruddy house to Reggie and me when we asked you.'

'Probably,' he agreed. 'Although I didn't think, at the time, that Reggie was all that keen on it.'

'No, he wasn't. But I'd have talked him round. Reggie is ultra-cautious about everything. He gets courage up eventually.'

'Perhaps,' he told her ruefully, 'I should have married someone like you, Serena. Someone who'd have chivvied me along, kept me in line, made me achieve something.'

'Well,' said his cousin unsympathetically. 'You screwed up your chance of doing that, didn't you?'

'Yes, I did.'

After a brief silence, Serena heaved a sigh. 'Well, I'm sorry about all of it. But there's very little anyone can do, except leave it all to the coppers. The chap Carter who came here seemed reasonably competent and there's the woman inspector . . .'

'Campbell,' said Gervase.

'That's the one. She's got a good head on her shoulders.'

As she finished speaking the doorbell rang.

'Now,' said Serena, hauling herself from the chesterfield. 'Who's that at this time of day?' She peered from the window. 'Good grief, speak of the devil. It's Inspector Campbell.'

'I've been trying to get in touch with you, Mr Crown,' said Jess. 'Thank you, Mrs Foscott, it's a bit early for me to start on the sherry.'

'Sun's over the yardarm,' pointed out Serena.

It was indeed dusk outside the house. Serena had switched on a couple of table lamps that bathed the room in a muted glow and made it appear more orderly. It hid the dilapidated state of the furniture and the dust, thought Jess unkindly.

'Even so,' she said. 'I understand, Mr Crown, that you have expressed an intention of setting yourself up as a target for the killer.'

'It's daft,' said Serena briefly.

'Your cousin is right,' Jess informed Gervase. 'We are talking about someone who has already killed once. Whether or not that killing was premeditated or intentional in any way, a man died. It's a barrier broken. The killer will now feel there's nothing to lose. There may even be a redoubled determination to get the right man next time. That means you if, as I understand you believe, you are the target.'

'I don't doubt I'm the target, not for a moment,' Gervase said snappily. 'But I'm not talking about doing anything rash. It's more a case of what I'm not intending to do. I'm not going running back to Portugal and I'm not going into hiding.'

'I think he ought to come and stay here,' Serena told Jess.

Gervase shook his head. 'No, I've already told you. That could endanger you, Reggie and Charlie.'

As if on cue, a car drew up before the house and the sound of childish voices yelling farewells became audible. Serena went to the window where she waved at someone. The car roared away again.

'Charlie's home from school,' Serena said, turning back to them. 'Not my week for the school run, I'm pleased to say.'

There was further commotion at the rear of the house, a slamming of doors, clatter of feet. The drawing-room door opened and a girl of about Millie's age, with straggling fair hair and large pale blue eyes in a pointed face, appeared and surveyed the assembled company dispassionately.

'Hello, Charlie,' Gervase lifted a hand in salute. 'I see St Trinian's is out.'

The newcomer's school uniform was not the gymslip and black stockings associated with that famous educational establishment. It was a skirt with a drooping hem, a shirt escaping from the waistband and a blazer that had clearly been bought with a view that the wearer 'would grow into it'.

Charlie Foscott turned her gaze to him. 'Hi, Gerry.' Her voice lacked enthusiasm. She showed no interest in either of the visitors. Jess was ignored altogether. Instead, Charlie turned to her mother and asked, 'Is there any cake left?'

'You don't want any, do you, Inspector?' Serena asked Jess.

After an offer like that, there was little Jess could do but decline the cake. She did so without regret. It was of the sponge variety and there appeared little outward sign of any jam or other filling in it.

'Take it into the kitchen,' Serena ordered her daughter. 'Have a glass of milk with it.'

Charlie made off with the cake. Gervase caught Jess's eye and pulled a wry expression.

'She's starting to go through an awkward age,' explained Serena. 'Reggie says she spends too much time with horses and she's not learning to get on with people. He reckons she ought to have dancing lessons.'

Gervase uttered a strangled sound that ended in a cough.

'"We can't afford dancing lessons," I told him. "Sell the pony," he said. I told him, "Charlie dotes on that pony. Besides, better she's out in the fresh air than cooped up in some hall waving her arms around and bending her knees."'

'I admit I can't see it,' Gervase said, still in a muffled voice, and clearly able to visualise the scene only too well.

'Of course not. Besides, I've already spent a fortune on jodhpurs and boots and all the other kit. I can't start all over again buying leotards and tutus and ballet pumps. Reggie gets these potty notions from time to time. Anyhow, to get back to this threat you've had.'

It was time for Jess to step in again. 'Mrs Foscott has made a good point,' she said. 'You should consider moving from The Royal Oak. Actually, I wouldn't suggest this house.' Not least because Ian Carter had Reggie and Serena on his list of people with motives! Jess added silently.

'Plenty of room,' said Serena.

Jess tried to be tactful. 'But a little too shielded, such a big garden and so many trees. Also, as Mr Crown pointed out, it could expose your family to some degree of risk. I do advise you to change your hotel, Mr Crown. The Royal Oak has no security to speak of. Don't waste time. Go back there now, settle up your account and move elsewhere tonight. Let us know at once when you've done that. My advice is that you move into Cheltenham. We don't know where the assailant is based but it's likely it's locally around Weston St Ambrose.'

'And then what?' asked Gervase mulishly.

'It helps us. If we have to worry about your safety, even put a police guard on you, it uses up manpower and distracts us from finding out who and what is behind all this. We are particularly keen not to have any distractions at the moment. We've had a breakthrough. We have Matthew Pietrangelo's car.'

'Where was it?' demanded Gervase and his cousin together.

'It turned up in an unexpected place away from Weston St Ambrose, and there is an investigation underway. I do believe we are getting close and the killer may realise it, too. Time is not on the killer's side. Will you move out of The Royal Oak tonight?'

'Please, Gerry,' his cousin said firmly. 'For once in your life do the sensible thing.'

He threw up his hands. 'Oh, all right. I'll make my way back to The Royal Oak and phone round from there to find myself another room, preferably in Cheltenham itself. If I'm successful, I'll settle my bill and move out tonight. I'll let the cops know where I end up. I'll phone you, too, Serena.'

'Then I'll be off,' Jess said in relief. It was the end of a long, busy day and frankly she'd had enough of Gervase Crown and his problems. She'd go home, have a long soak in the tub and . . . and what? Fry the sausages that were lying around in the fridge?

Fall asleep in front of the TV watching fictional coppers perform miracles of detection? Talk about busman's holidays. This was the sort of evening when, before Tom Palmer met up with Madison and embarked on what appeared to be a rocky romance, she could have rung him and arranged to go out to eat, or even just for a drink. Now, if she did that, she'd have to listen to the latest on Madison and the proposed job in Australia.

But rescue was at hand. As she got back into her car, her mobile rang.

'Jess?' Carter's voice came in her ear. 'Millie is keen to go out for a pizza. Would you like to join us? If you can, I'm sure Millie would be pleased. I hope you'll come or I'll have to make conversation with MacTavish.'

'Yes, I would!' Jess told him, cheering as the image of the dubious sausages receded. 'That sounds like fun.'

'Good. I'll drive out to Weston St Ambrose to collect Millie and then call by your place and pick you up. Around six thirty? It has to be on the early side because Millie gets hungry. It doesn't give you much time to get ready. Where are you?'

'I'm at the Foscotts'. That's to say, I've just called on Serena Foscott and Gervase Crown who's there with her at the moment. If it's OK with you, I won't come back, I'll drive straight home from here. By the way, I've got Crown to agree to change hotels tonight. I'll explain later.'

Gervase left his cousin's house shortly after Jess Campbell. He'd apologised to Serena for changing his mind about the lamb hotpot, pointing out that he now had to get back to The Royal Oak, phone round for a different hotel, pack up and move and would very likely not be settled before late enough as it was. He was not regretting the lamb hotpot but he was regretting having agreed to change hotels. Throwing in the towel was how he thought of it. But he'd promised Serena and he'd told the lady cop with the red hair and he'd do it. Kit and Petra would be happy to learn what he'd done. He'd make everyone happy. That was a first.

His drive back to The Royal Oak took him within a quarter of a mile of Key House. It was getting really dark now, he had his change of lodgings to deal with, and it didn't make any sense to detour past the house. But nonetheless, that is what he did. The remains of his childhood home drew him as if with a magnetic pull. He drew in nearby, found the flashlight he kept in the car, got out and began to walk towards the building. The beam of the flashlight played over the blackened walls and fallen internal structure, the cracked beams poking up like the spars of a wrecked ship, the heaps of three-hundred-year-old stone tiles. The remaining walls would have to come down. The structural engineer had phoned through a preliminary report. The walls were not safe. They should be dismantled as soon as possible before they fell down on their own. No official body could possibly make any objections. To restore the whole thing would be a major undertaking, a rebuild, and would only be a pale copy. The most interesting features, the late Stuart wood carving and panelling, had gone for good and couldn't be replaced. 'You'll have to flatten the rest,' the expert had said.

'Flatten it,' murmured Gervase as he stepped carefully around a puddle of water and clambered over a fallen beam. Inside the building the walls provided only partial shelter. Cold night air blew in through the open roof and through the holes where windows and doors had been. It ricocheted around the walls and rustled the cinders, snatching up handfuls of ash and tossing them in the air. Gervase put his hand over his mouth and nose to avoid breathing in ash and grit. By treading through it all he was making it worse. His footsteps crunched the burnt debris to more powder. The wind had a voice, too. It whistled through narrow chinks and sighed around him. There was a constant background movement, odd bits falling and wood creaking and snapping. It was, he imagined, like being at sea in one of the great wooden sailing ships, the fabric a living thing, constantly calling for your attention. He was conscious of the cupboard that had fallen when Sarah Gresham had been here. He'd told her it wasn't safe here and he should take his own advice.

He directed the beam of the torch in his other hand around the floor area and the bright arrow of light targeted Sarah's flowers, sadly wilted amid the fragments of cupboard. The sight of them reproached him. He wasn't responsible for the actions of a maniac. But in some way, he was sure, those actions were linked to him, and he was linked to the house like a Victorian jailbird to his ball and chain.

'Why didn't I think of putting a match to the damn place years ago?' he asked himself aloud.

As if in reply, he heard a new sound, not like the others. He turned his head and swept the immediate area with light. The flickering beam picked up details of the wrecked surroundings but nothing more. Probably the sound had just been yet more debris settling, yet he had the curious feeling he was not alone.

He waited for a repetition that would help him pinpoint whence it came. The strange sound was not repeated. Instead there was a soft wheezing of moving air quite different from the earlier sighing of the wind. He could not immediately identify it; then he did. It was laboured breathing. Someone or something was in here with him. His heart leaped painfully and he fought the instinctive panic.

'Is somebody there?' he called sharply, his voice sounding louder than anticipated on the night air. 'I can hear you, and if you're trying to frighten me, you've failed,' he added with more confidence than justified. 'Just come over here and stop prowling around out there in the dark. It's bloody stupid. The place isn't safe.'

'*No . . .*' the word drifted through the night air towards him, little more than a moan.

It froze his blood. He shook his head to clear it. He didn't believe in ghosts. They were stories like the one he'd invented to scare Kit so long ago. But a man had died here very recently, practically on this spot: a nasty, a brutal, cruel death, and something moved out there, something shared this space with him.

'Stop playing silly buggers!' snapped Gervase. 'If you've got something to say, speak up!'

This time the voice, barely a whisper, asked, '*Gervase?*' The final sibilant trailed away.

It was still so faint, he couldn't be sure he was not imagining it. Perhaps it did emanate from somewhere inside his head. It was so difficult to tell from which direction the ghostly voice could have come. The darkness was disorientating. He flashed the beam around again to no avail. Where? And who?

He called again, 'I know someone's there! Kit? Is that you?' He held his breath. No response, not even the laboured breathing.

'Whoever you are,' he said more loudly, 'come out here!'

The darkness itself seemed to be moving, a kind of undulation of shadows. But the torch couldn't pick up any intruder and by using it, he signalled his exact location to the other person here. He switched the beam off, plunging the area back into darkness.

He was alert now, as alert as when taking on the rollers surging towards the shore at Guincho. Something was going to happen. Anything might. It had already begun. He had to judge the moment.

There was a movement at his shoulder. The breathing was close now, hoarse and animal-like. He felt the breath brush his cheek. He fumbled to switch on the torch again. He should not have switched it off. Keyed up to react as he was, so expected, yet so sudden was the attack when it came that he could no more than strike out with the still unlit torch. It made contact with something, someone, but he could be sure of no more than that, before intense pain sheared through his brain accompanied by an explosion of tiny glittering diamonds. He dropped the torch and staggered forward, sinking to his knees in the rubble and dirt.

Chapter 17

Roger Trenton stood at the window gazing into the gathering dusk.

'How long till dinner?' he asked.

'What?' called his wife from the kitchen. 'Can't hear you!'

'Dinner!' shouted Roger. 'What time?'

'Normal time, about seven, it's spaghetti Bolognese!' came back the information, followed by a clatter of something falling on to the tiled floor. 'Damn!'

'What was it?' he shouted again.

'What was what?'

'What fell down?'

'Saucepan lid.'

This conversation, thought Roger in irritation, was going nowhere as, increasingly, conversations with his wife of some five and thirty years were inclined to do. Roger was aware this was unsatisfactory, but had anyone ever suggested that his marriage was in any way imperfect he'd have denied it indignantly. They were a model couple, he reflected now. Possibly a trifle unadventurous? Roger would not have considered using the adjective 'boring'. Even 'unadventurous' was not, to his mind and in most circumstances, a bad thing.

Thus he was surprised to find himself wondering now whether his wife was happy. At once he dismissed the notion that she could be anything else. How could she? She had a nice home. He was a considerate husband. She appreciated his reliability, his even temper, his excellent gift for organisation, his financial acumen. *If I died tonight* . . . he thought and amended that immediately to *if I died tomorrow* . . . because he didn't feel like dying tonight. That is to say, he felt perfectly well. So, if he died the next day, due to some unforeseen and unforeseeable event like a meteor strike, Poppy would have no worries. She'd be financially secure, have a roof over her head. She'd miss *him*, of course.

Even so, he regretted the futility of any hope of a decent conversation with Poppy about things that mattered (to him): the government, the European Union, potholes in the road from last winter still unrepaired and, until recently, the condition of Key House. But Key House, even in ruins, remained a problem. He wouldn't put it past young Crown to take himself off back to Portugal and leave the place a ruin. Not, thought Roger grimly, if I have anything to do with it! All this led him to make a decision. There was time before dinner.

'I'm just going up the road to check on Key House,' he announced.

This was greeted by silence followed by footsteps and Poppy appeared in the doorway.

'Why?'

'Someone should. It's unsafe. What's more, it's a crime scene. It ought to be kept under surveillance in case it's disturbed, contaminated . . . or deteriorates.'

'Who's going to disturb it?'

'The same sort of people who got in there before.'

'They're not going back now with it in the state the fire's left it,' argued Poppy.

'We can't be certain. These are not people who think like you and me, Poppy.'

244

Poppy was looking at him in a way that could be described as exasperated. The old girl was clearly worried for his safety.

'If you go trampling over it, *you'll* be contaminating a crime scene,' she said. 'The police put tape round it. You can't go in. As you've just said, the walls look very rickety now. They might fall down.'

Roger was uncomfortably reminded of his earlier use of a meteor shower as an example of a fatal mishap.

'I won't go on the property, I'll just check the exterior,' he promised.

'It's dark,' she said crossly.

'I've got a torch.'

'Take the car, then,' advised Poppy, turning back kitchenwards.

As it happened, Roger's intention had been to take the car. Now he felt bound to declare, 'I'll walk!'

'Suit yourself!' floated from the kitchen.

Well wrapped up against the chills of a November evening and carrying the largest torch he could find, Roger set off. He had not gone far when a bend in the road cut him off from the supporting glow of light from his own house. It was not only very dark out here but it was cold and it was lonely. Just how lonely he had never appreciated before. The countryside at night was a black hole into which he might be sucked at any moment never to be seen again, or that's how it felt. Meteors, black holes: he had astronomy on the brain tonight. Perhaps he ought to take it up, buy a telescope, study the stars. Roger glanced up at the sky, trying to remember what he'd been taught as a boy about the Great Bear and Orion's Belt and all the rest of it. But the night was overcast. He couldn't see much in the way of stars and even the moon was obscured by scudding drifts of dark grey cloud.

His footsteps sounded unnaturally loud. He tried to walk more quietly but found himself tiptoeing along like a blasted ballet dancer. In an effort to counteract that, he began to march along with his feet striking the road surface with the precision of a regimental sergeant major. There ought to be a footpath along here so that he need not walk in the road. If some road hog, imagining that an isolated country road was a racetrack, came roaring along here, he wouldn't see Roger until far too late. There wasn't anywhere to jump to safety, only into a ditch or a hedge. Worse, he was passing by a traditional low stone wall edging a field. A footpath was needed. He'd write to the council about it. He'd write about the potholes again too. Roger flashed the torch ahead of him along the surface, seeking out any possible trap. He might put a foot in one of those and go flying, break his ankle. The list of possible calamities was endless.

The clouds moved away from the moon and in the silver gleam of light bathing his surroundings he saw, ahead of him, the stark shape of the walls of Key House, standing up against the night sky like some ruined castle. Relief flooded him. He'd got here. He'd take a quick look round the exterior and then set off home.

He had crossed the road and stepped over the police tape, despite assuring Poppy he wouldn't, and had begun to play his torch beam over the outer walls when he realised that the beam was shining back at him, like a reflection. That wasn't possible, surely? No, it wasn't. It was another torch beam, not his, flickering about over there inside the house.

Automatically Roger switched off his torch. He was sure whoever it was had no right to be there. Poppy was wrong. The druggies or tramps, whoever it might be, had come back. It was one thing to confront them in daylight, quite another to tackle them in the darkness. He couldn't see how many of them there were. He stood, rooted to the spot, and watched as the point of light within the house disappeared and then reappeared, moving around the internal area like some will-o-the-wisp. For a brief moment he wondered if it could be no more than some natural phenomenon. Marsh gas, it was called, wasn't it? But it was not marshy hereabouts.

Then he heard a sound. Someone was walking in there, feet crunching on the rubble. Now he heard a voice. He couldn't identify it, even to say if it had been male or female, but he was sure he'd heard one. The light flickered again and then was abruptly doused. There was a cry and a crash, then silence.

Roger waited. What to do? Go and investigate? He'd come here to check things over and something in there definitely deserved to be checked. He began to move cautiously forward, feeling his way in the darkness, holding the unlit torch on high as a weapon.

'Anyone there?' he called.

His voice on the night air quavered uncertainly. He tried again, more robustly.

'Is anyone in there? Are you all right?' It might be as well for whoever was there to believe Roger was not alone. He added, 'We are coming in!'

Something moved in the shadows, but not inside the house now. The shape stood beside an outer wall, blacker in the gloom and without clear definition. It – something, someone – moved.

'Who's that?' The annoying quaver was back in his voice. 'I – I'm armed . . .'

Oh Lord, he should have listened to Poppy. He should have stayed home. Why did he trouble himself over a house that didn't belong to him and now hardly existed at all? He didn't *care* who was in there. If a whole coven of witches had occupied the place to conduct satanic rites, they could carry on without interference from him.

He thought he heard footsteps, a series of muffled thuds, but further away, retreating from him. Someone was cutting across the field behind the house. First relief and then new courage flooded Roger's veins. He'd frightened off whoever it had been! Someone had almost certainly been up to no good. Wait until he told Poppy about this! Or perhaps, on second thoughts, he wouldn't tell Poppy. She'd fuss.

Buoyed by relief and the thought that the other person had fled, Roger switched on his torch again and moved confidently forward. 'I'm coming in there!' he announced.

To his horror his words, which he'd been sure would have fallen into silence, called up a response. Not a voice, but another movement. Now, within the house someone was stumbling about on the rubble, so noisily it couldn't be dismissed as mere wreckage settling. In the empty doorway, a figure appeared. Roger turned the full beam of torchlight on to it and gave a cry.

It was tall, appeared misshapen, black. It staggered forward with raised arms, making for him like an iconic Frankenstein's monster. Roger let out an involuntary squeal and stepped back. The creature lurched forward and crashed to the ground at his feet to lie still.

His heart beating wildly, Roger remained where he was for a few seconds – though it felt like much longer. At last he moved forward again and asked hoarsely, 'Who are you?'

The inert figure at his feet did not move. He shone the torch down on to it and saw a face, blackened with soot and unrecognisable. He stooped over and reluctantly stretched out his hand. It touched human hair. Roger snatched his hand away. His fingers were sticky. He shone the torch on them and it picked up dark fluid. 'Oh, my God, blood!' he whispered.

At that moment his ear caught the sound of an approaching vehicle. A car's headlights swept over him. He turned towards them and waved his arms above his head to attract attention and signal help was needed. The car stopped. A door slammed. Footsteps and another figure, tall and thin, coming briskly towards him.

'What's the trouble?' called a competent voice.

'S-someone's hurt,' Roger stammered. 'I don't know who he is.' Nor did he know who the newcomer was. Rescuer or the attacker returned? No, not the attacker who had run away. But someone in league with the attacker?'

'Badly hurt?' enquired the new man.

'B-blood,' Roger could only babble. 'There's a lot of blood.'

'Roger, is that you?' asked the voice unexpectedly.

'Yes. Who is that?'

'It's Stephen Layton. Let me take a look.'

No voice and no name could have been more welcome. 'Thank goodness!' cried Roger. 'We need a doctor here!'

Layton had reached him. He stretched out a hand and, wordlessly, Roger handed over his torch. Layton hunkered down over the fallen figure.

'It's Gervase Crown!' he exclaimed. 'Someone's hit him over the head.'

'What?' croaked Roger. 'How can it be him?' (In moments of stress, he afterwards told himself, one does say daft things. Why shouldn't it have been Crown? It was Crown's house.) '*Blood*,' he repeated. He wanted to say something else, more sensible, but the word came out of its own accord. 'Lots of blood . . .' Oh hell, he was sounding like Lady Macbeth.

'Steady on, old chap,' urged Layton. 'Nasty shock for you, but get a grip. Yes, quite a bit of blood but head wounds do bleed a lot. Have you phoned for an ambulance?'

'Er, no,' admitted Roger. 'I only just . . .'

'I'll do it.' Layton handed back the torch and took out a mobile phone. As a background to his thoughts, Roger heard the doctor organising the ambulance and requesting that the police be informed. All the things, in fact, that Roger should have been doing. But Roger's mind was on something else: that other shape, that amorphous shadow running away from the building. He, Roger, had been alone out here with a violent criminal, probably a murderer. The full horror of it all engulfed him. The apocalyptic figure reeling from the ruins, the mysterious shadow of an attacker flitting away through the night like some great bat, Gervase's blood on his hands, the humiliation of his own paralysis, uselessness . . .

'They're on their way,' said Layton. 'You all right now?'

'What? I, no, excuse me,' mumbled Roger.

He took a few uncertain steps away from the fallen man and threw up comprehensively, thereby, as he was miserably aware, contaminating a crime scene.

Jess, Carter and Millie had just about finished their pizzas when the news came through to Jess on her mobile. The ringtone caused both Carter and Millie to look up in interst. Even the shiny black eyes of MacTavish, whose head poked out of a pink tote bag hung on the back of Millie's chair, seemed to take on an added gleam.

Jess took the call, asked the other two to excuse her for a moment, and moved outside the restaurant to take the rest of it. When she came back, she said quietly to Carter, 'Gervase Crown has been taken to the General Hospital.'

She hadn't said it quietly enough to keep the news from Millie's sharp ears.

'Is that the man called Gervase you were talking to when Auntie Monica and I found you?'

She was not the sort of child whose questions could be ignored.

'Yes, I'm afraid he is,' said Jess. She said it in a way she hoped conveyed that the matter was not up for any more discussion, at least with contributions from Millie.

'Badly hurt?' asked Carter calmly.

'Conscious.'

'I thought he was the murderer,' observed Millie thoughtfully. She looked up with renewed alertness. 'Has someone tried to murder *him*?'

'I've asked for a guard to be put on his room,' Jess told Carter. 'They're still examining him at the moment.'

'You stay here, I'll check it out,' said Carter and disappeared into the street in his turn.

'I'm interested too,' complained Millie. 'You ought not to leave me out. That's bad manners.' She was watching her father through the plate-glass window as he walked up and down with his phone to his ear.

'I know you are, love, but it's police business and I'm sure you know that makes it private.' Jess tried to sweeten the rebuff with a smile.

Millie, and MacTavish from his tote bag, regarded her with disgust. 'According to you,' said Millie accusingly, 'everything interesting is private.'

Chapter 18

The police constable seated outside the room rose to his feet as Jess came down the hospital corridor towards him. 'Everything OK here, ma'am,' he said confidently.

'Good, have you spoken to the victim?'

'I stuck my head round the door earlier and asked how he felt,' admitted the constable. 'He answered me all right, said he was fine. Well, he don't look fine,' the constable qualified Gervase's claim. 'He's got his head all bandaged up and they've got him hooked up to a drip. So far no one's tried to see him. Nurses and a doctor were going in and out all morning, of course, but no visitors from outside and none have turned up so far this afternoon. But I dare say the word won't have got round yet, will it? That he's here?'

'You'd be surprised,' Jess told him.

'I was told I wasn't to let any visitors in.' The constable looked enquiringly at Jess.

'For the time being, that's right. I'd rather no one other than the police and hospital personnel see him. But make a note, would you, of anyone else who asks? Name and address. Examine any flowers, chocolates or grapes, anything like that, brought or sent in for him. Oh, and make a note of who they're from.'

Gervase had few friends so it would be interesting to see who might turn out a well-wisher.

As the constable had said, Gervase's head was indeed impressively swathed in bandages and a neck brace held his head immobile. He was propped up in bed with his eyes closed, but opened them as Jess came in. He raised a hand in salutation and said hoarsely, 'Hi! O guardian of the law.'

'Hi to you,' returned Jess. 'I'm sorry to see you here.'

'Better than seeing me on a trestle down at the morgue.'

'Yes, I won't argue with that. You sound compos mentis. Can you talk to me for a while?'

'The dreaded police interview.' Gervase sounded resigned.

'It's entirely your decision. The doctor wasn't very happy about my talking to you. They're concerned about concussion. He said it would be all right if you felt up to it.'

'Oh, my mind's all right or I think it is. My vision's fine. I'm not seeing two of you there. I've got a bloody big headache, or would have, if they didn't pump painkillers into me via that hatstand they've got me attached to.' Gervase gestured weakly at the drip line hanging from the dolly. 'That's probably affecting anything I say. The best way to describe how I feel today is as if I have a bad hangover. I can't turn my head because of this collar. That's a nuisance. I wrenched my neck somehow when I twisted trying to avoid my attacker.'

'The same doctor I spoke to on my way in,' she told him, 'said you'd been very lucky. Another blow would have resulted in much worse.'

'Like Pietrangelo? I realise that.' His fingers twitched as if he would make another hand gesture, but he decided against it. 'I really feel bad about that poor guy. I met his girlfriend, you know.'

'Sarah Gresham? Where? When?' Jess was startled. 'Last night?'

'No, not last night.' Gervase tried a negative movement of his head, but frowned and abandoned it. 'I have to try and remember not to do that . . . I was looking round the house, a couple of days ago, and she was there, leaving flowers on the spot where his body was found. The flowers are still there. I saw them last night, all withered already. She should have put them in a jam jar of water or something. Poor kid. I was so sorry for her and felt to blame because it does seem he got killed instead of me. I should have let Reggie sell him the house.'

Gervase's speech sounded disconnected but Jess persevered.

'You knew Pietrangelo wanted to buy?'

Gervase waved a hand in negation. 'Not specifically him, no. Reggie had emailed me to say *someone* had enquired. I emailed back to tell him, no chance. I really didn't know what to say to Sarah. It was my damn fault really, that's what I kept thinking while I was talking to her. I should have sold the house or told Reggie to tell anyone enquiring I'd be happy to sell. Perhaps I should have sold it to Serena when she was so keen to buy, or given her the damn place. Then that poor fellow wouldn't have been creeping round on the quiet. Poor girl, she looked so wretched and I could only blather nonsense and not say a damn thing to comfort her. She kept saying she understood why I hadn't wanted to sell, but she'd totally misunderstood. She thought I'd been attached to the place. Fortunately, Muriel turned up and saved the day for me.'

'Miss Pickering? What was she doing there?' asked Jess, surprised.

'Walking her dog. She's always had a dog. She's a feature of the lanes around here, stumping along with mutt in tow. This one looked pretty weird, like something a mediaeval mason might have carved for a gargoyle. But she started telling me what a waste of space I was, or words to that effect, and that gave Sarah an excuse to leave us and spared me having to try to make any more conversation with her. So Muriel, ghastly old bat, did me a good turn.' He smiled wryly.

'Why does Miss Pickering think you a waste of space, in your words?' Jess asked. It sounded, from Gervase's description of Muriel, as though the opinion might be mutual.

'She thinks that of everyone,' Gervase said. 'Men, in particular. She had a tyrannical father. She didn't like my father, either, as it happened. Don't blame her for that. Neither did I. But she did like my mother, funnily enough.'

'I have spoken to Miss Pickering,' Jess told him. 'She said she had been friendly with your mother.'

'I remember it. It was a strange sort of friendship.' Gervase became thoughtful, his eyes unfocused and apparently looking back down the years. 'I think my mother was sympathetic to Muriel, liked her, I suppose. On Muriel's side I fancy it was more in the nature of a schoolgirl crush. Only neither of them was a schoolgirl, of course. I tagged along occasionally on one of their shared walks. I could see the hero-worship in Muriel's phizzog. My mother was a good-looker. She used to go up to London sometimes, shops and theatre, that sort of thing. Then she'd tell Muriel about it all. Muriel never went anywhere; and always looked like one of her dogs. That's unkind. I shouldn't say that. But my mother must have seemed glamorous to her, like a film star – if Muriel had ever gone to the cinema. I suppose she had a TV.'

I didn't see one, thought Jess. When I visited Muriel there was no television in that sordid sitting room.

Gervase was continuing, 'She was upset when my mother left. Told everyone my father had murdered her and buried her in the countryside somewhere.'

'*What?*'

'He hadn't, of course. I can tell you that as a proven fact because I met my mother again just under a year ago and had lunch with her. She still looks good. Anyway, no one but Muriel suggested it at the time. My father got on to his lawyers and I presume they told her to shut up. So she did. I have teased her occasionally by telling her I know where the body's buried. I shouldn't do that. I think when my mother left, Muriel felt it like a bereavement.'

'Why did she hate your father? Just because your mother left the marriage and the area?' Jess asked carefully.

Not, apparently, carefully enough. Gervase's expression suddenly became unexpectedly shrewd. 'You've spoken to Muriel. She probably told you. Dad used to beat my mother up. I don't mean all day, every day. Only in the bedroom, after they'd gone to bed. I understand now it was a sex thing. He couldn't do it, I suppose, unless he beat her up first, to get himself going.'

'But you knew? As a child you knew that he used violence towards her?'

'Not *why*, but that he did it, yes.' Gervase's eyes narrowed to slits. 'He was clever enough not to hit her face. He just went for the rest of her. I could hear the thump of his fist landing and the muffled cries she gave, stifling her shrieks in case I heard. I heard, anyway. I used to sit on the stairs in my pyjamas, strangling my teddy bear and wishing I were brave enough to rush in and protect my mother. But I knew I couldn't.'

'Poor kid,' said Jess involuntarily. 'That was a terrible burden for you to bear all alone.'

'Oh, I don't think I was alone in knowing about it. Muriel knew, after all. The au pair – we always had one of them – had a flat up in the attic so she might not have heard them, but I dare say she did. Sounds, even small ones, travel in a house at night. Besides, there are other ways of knowing. People knew or suspected, but they didn't say anything. That's how it goes. None of our au pairs stayed very long.'

'I have dealt with a number of domestic violence cases,' Jess told him. 'Often other people do suspect. But they think it's private, between husband and wife.'

'There you go, then. I shall always believe that old devil Stephen Layton knew because he was their doctor. But he didn't do a damn thing. Anyhow, I have that prize bore, Roger Trenton, to thank for my not ending up stretched out dead last night, and to my great annoyance I have to be grateful to Stephen Layton, too.'

'Layton was there last night?'

'Came along in his car and found Trenton stooped over me, wringing his hands. Or so I gather.'

'Tell me about it,' Jess invited. 'Stop if your head hurts or you feel the painkillers are making you muzzy.' She took out her little tape recorder and placed it on the bed. 'I'll record if you don't mind. Start from when I left you with your cousin.'

'OK.' Gervase drew a deep breath. 'After you left I stayed chatting to Serena for a few minutes. Not longer because it had got dark and I had agreed to go back to The Royal Oak and settle my bill, move somewhere else. Only I never got back there to do that, so all my stuff is at The Royal Oak. Has anyone told them I'm in here?'

'I'll make sure they understand that you want to keep the room on,' she promised. 'I suppose you will have to, for the time being, if you've got your belongings there and you're in here.'

'Got everything including my passport there.'

'We still suggest you move elsewhere when you leave here.'

Gervase grimaced. 'Serena's been on the phone insisting I move in with them. Poppy Trenton rang her last night and told her what had happened. Both of them, Serena and Poppy, are threatening to visit me.' He closed his eyes briefly. 'Serena says I need nourishing fare to recuperate. Hospital food not good enough. I thought I'd escaped the lamb hotpot. I think my cousin learned to cook over a campfire when she was a Girl Guide, and hasn't progressed much since then. Don't let her hear me say that on your tape . . .' He gestured at the tape recorder and smiled weakly.

Jess smiled back and shook her head. There was a silence during which Gervase stared past her at the opposite wall. She said quietly, 'I will go and come back later if you want.'

'No, stay. Just don't rush me. I left Serena's place and set off back to Weston St Ambrose. The route took me within half a mile of Key House. Although I had things to do, I made a detour to see if everything was OK there. I didn't expect to stay more than ten minutes. I parked up under the hedge. I turned the car lights off and perhaps should have left them on. Then I'd have seen if anyone else was out there. I walked around a bit inside the house. Made a lot of noise because of the rubbish underfoot. If anyone else followed me in I wouldn't have heard. They would know exactly where I was from the racket I was making. I had a torch. I was shining it at the walls in what had been the kitchen. I personally don't regret the loss of the house, but the general poor state of what's left does have me worried. While that girl, Sarah, was there, what was left of a cupboard fell down. I was just able to pull her out of the way in time. We both fell to the ground. She screeched like a banshee. I thought it was because she believed I was the killer on the loose. But it turned out it was because she saw in me a resemblance to her boyfriend. It must have given her a heck of shock. Anyway, last night I was just thinking perhaps I ought to leave in case a chunk of stone fell down on my head . . .' Gervase's lips twisted wryly. 'Then I realised someone else was there. I couldn't see who it was. But I knew I wasn't on my own.'

'You heard someone?'

Gervase took a moment to consider his answer. 'Not at that moment. I just – you know how it is when you feel you're being watched? I can't tell you exactly what alerted me, if anything did. Yes, there was breathing. Someone breathing noisily.'

'Panting?' Jess asked. 'Out of breath?'

'No, more like, well, excited. I called out. Just asked if anyone was there.'

'No one answered?'

'No,' Gervase said perhaps a touch too firmly.

Jess asked quietly, 'You have just said that at first you didn't hear anything to alert you to another presence, other than a sound like heavy breathing. But you felt you were not alone and you called out to ask who was there. Are you quite sure no one else spoke?'

'Quite the Sherlock Holmes, aren't you?' said Gervase resentfully. 'Picking up every little word. I could be wrong about the breathing. The wind makes noises. I don't know I did hear anything human. It was very faint. It could have been ash settling, something falling down . . . But the whole place is like that, crackling and rustling. It was like being stuck in a forest at night. It might have been an animal strayed in there.'

'We know the presence was human because you were attacked.'

. 'All right, all right!' snapped Gervase and winced, putting a hand to his head. 'You can't expect me to have a very clear memory! Something moved – or seemed to be moving. I couldn't see anyone, or anything, but I did believe I had company. I switched the torch off because it occurred to me it was acting like a marker buoy, guiding whoever was there towards me. I'd got my bearings by then and thought I could manage without the help of the torch. I grew up in that house, for pity's sake! I didn't need a map. I thought – wrongly – I'd know if someone was about to jump me and I could deal with it. But then someone whacked me over the nut. All I saw was stars. I was stunned but I wasn't laid out. I've got a hard head. That's not a joke. Doctor here told me so. Some people have quite thin skulls. Mine's the heavy-duty sort.

'Anyway, I managed to scrabble to my hands and knees. I was expecting to be attacked again. I had it in my mind that I must get up on my feet. I was too vulnerable on the ground. But then I certainly did hear a voice. Someone was calling outside. Calling to know what was going on, I think. It must have frightened off whoever hit me. I heard someone moving across the rubbish on the floor, away from me. I'd got to my feet and I started off towards the sound of the new voice. I nearly reached him. I couldn't see who it was because he was shining his torch right at me. Then I passed out at his feet.'

'But you know now it was Roger Trenton.'

'That's right, operating his one-man neighbourhood watch. Then, as I've been told, old Layton turned up coming back from somewhere, and picked up the whole scene in his headlights. He organised the ambulance and followed it here to the hospital. He waited to see what they were going to do, last night. Good of him, I suppose, or just his doctor's training. Or his conscience. I came to in the ambulance. I saw him briefly before they wheeled me into X-ray. He said Trenton had found me.'

The door opened and a nurse came in. 'Everything all right?'

she enquired of Gervase, and gave Jess and the tape recorder a hard look.

'Fine,' Gervase assured her.

'You ought not to talk too much.'

'I'm nearly finished,' Jess said.

'Five more minutes!' warned the nurse and departed.

'If I've only got five minutes, I've got to ask you this now,' Jess said quickly. 'I've asked before but can you think of anyone who might be a particular enemy, bear a grudge? I know you said you weren't popular. That's not enough to make someone attack you. Mr Crown, this is no time to keep secrets.'

'They all keep secrets round here,' Gervase said drowsily. 'Sorry, head hurts. Can't talk any more. I'm going to have a little nap.'

Jess returned downstairs and found the doctor she'd spoken to earlier. 'When will you discharge him? The police need to know.'

'We'd like to keep him in another twenty-four hours and carry out a few more tests before we let him go. But he's been fortunate.'

'What about the injury itself?' Jess asked him. 'Is there anything in particular about it?'

'Caused by a blow with some hard object? I really can't tell you more. Perhaps a glancing blow?' The medical man stopped and looked embarrassed. 'I'd rather not speculate. It's not my field of expertise.'

'Anything that might help us?' Jess encouraged him.

'I understand the attack was made in darkness,' the doctor said reluctantly. 'I wonder if that's what saved Mr Crown from more serious injury? The attacker couldn't see what he was doing, mistimed the blow . . . It's only a theory. I really wouldn't like to say any more about it. I'm not a detective, am I? I just deal with the physical trauma. I leave the whys and wherefores to you lot, but it seems to me that the blow came down like this.' The doctor brushed his hand across the back of his skull where Gervase had been struck.

Jess thanked him and set off towards the main exit. Before she reached it she saw a familiar figure coming towards her: Poppy Trenton carrying a large paper bag.

'Hello, Mrs Trenton,' she said. 'Have you come to visit Gervase Crown?'

'If they'll let me, or you'll let me?' Poppy fixed her with an anxious look. 'Is he allowed any visitors? We don't know how badly he's hurt. I do hope it's not very serious.'

'It could've been worse. I've just been talking to him and he was about to drop off to sleep when I came away,' Jess told her. 'Perhaps if you left a message for him? We've got a police guard on the room at the moment.'

'Oh, dear,' Poppy looked distressed. 'I've been worrying about him since Roger came home last night and told me what had happened. To think that someone is roaming about the countryside waiting to attack . . . I didn't want Roger to go out last night. But he would visit Key House and check on it. I suppose it was a good thing he did.' Poppy paused. 'Roger's been very quiet today. I think it gave him a terrible shock.'

'What have you got there?' Jess indicated the paper bag and smiled.

'Oh, well, I know one usually takes an invalid a present of grapes. But I didn't have any grapes and these bananas look very nice, so I brought those. Do you think Gervase will be allowed bananas?'

'I should ask the nurse.' Jess casually reached out and opened the top of the bag. Four bananas nestled within. They did look nice. 'If the nurse says he can, then tell the constable on the door that you've spoken to me, Inspector Campbell, and he can deliver the fruit to Crown. I'd rather you just waved at Gervase from the doorway. I think he's still at risk of concussion.'

'All right,' said Poppy amenably.

A thought occurred to Jess. 'Could we sit down over there and have a short chat? There is something I'd like to ask you.'

They made their way to a nearby waiting area. Poppy sat down and held the bag of bananas on her knees rather as she might have held a small infant. 'Is it about Roger?' she asked. 'I know he shouldn't have gone poking around Key House last night. But he's had Key House on the brain for a long time, with it standing empty and all sorts of odd characters turning up there from time to time. He's most anxious that Gervase should make some decision about it before he goes back to Portugal. But perhaps Gervase won't be in a position to do that for a while. I know it's not really Roger's business. But he's made it his business and when Roger gets a notion in his head, you really can't talk him out of it.'

'I understand. His decision to walk up to Key House last night probably saved Mr Crown's life,' Jess said. 'So I wouldn't feel too badly about it. But please tell him from me that I really don't want him – or any other person – wandering around Key House again until we have found out what's going on. Apart from anything else, the remaining structure has now been declared unsafe.'

'I'll tell him he's got to keep his nose out of it, and it's official!' said Poppy with satisfaction.

'Mrs Trenton, we are still investigating the first attack at Key House, not that on Gervase Crown but on Matthew Pietrangelo. In the light of what's happened since, there is a strong possibility, even probability, that Gervase Crown was the intended target of the earlier attack. He wasn't in England at the time; we know that now. But someone might have thought he was.'

Poppy was beginning to look distressed. 'I told you I thought I saw him a while ago before all this happened, didn't I? But it wasn't him. I found that out right after the fire. I worried all night about it, while Roger stood at the bedroom window and kept up a running commentary. So, in the morning, I phoned Serena very early to ask her, because she's family and Reggie handles Gervase's business. Didn't I tell you this? It was the first she'd heard of the fire because, of course, where they live is too far away to see or hear any of the hullabaloo, and no one had contacted them. She said first of all that Gervase – she calls him "Gerry" – absolutely wasn't in the UK and couldn't have been at the house when it caught fire. I heard Reggie asking her whom she was talking to, and she told him. Then Reggie came on the phone. He was upset to hear about the fire. He said he was ninety-nine per cent sure it couldn't be Gervase, but naturally he would contact Portugal and make sure. He said I shouldn't worry. He would get in touch with the police and it would all be sorted out.'

'He did phone us, I took the call,' Jess told her. *But I didn't ask him where he'd heard the news. I should have done so.*

Poppy was talking again. 'Later Serena rang me back and said Gervase had contacted her husband, so Gervase couldn't have been caught up in the fire. It was silly of me to imagine I saw him several days earlier, as I told you. Obviously, it was someone a little like him and it wasn't good light at the time. I was wrong.' Poppy drew a deep breath. 'I didn't know about the other man, when I rang Serena. I didn't know, then, that they'd found a body.'

'Just so. My question is: when you thought you'd seen Gervase Crown at the house, did you mention it to anyone else *at that time*? I'm talking of the period between you believing you'd seen Gervase Crown and the fire, after which you called Serena Foscott. Did you tell anyone at all before the fire? Because a rumour might have got round, you know how a rumour does, that Crown was back. If you could think hard.' Jess waited.

Poppy stared down into the bag of bananas as if they might be an inspiration to memory. 'I might have done. Not to Roger, I definitely didn't tell Roger.'

'You've told me you didn't tell your husband.'

'Absolutely not! But anyone else?' Poppy frowned. 'I'm not the sort of person who spreads rumour or gossip, you know. I hadn't been sure it was Gervase and I wouldn't have gone telling a lot of people. Anyway, I don't think I went anywhere about that time, not into Weston St Ambrose or into Cheltenham. So whom would I have seen?' Poppy brightened. 'Oh, Muriel. I did see Muriel Pickering and mention it to her.'

'Miss Pickering? What did she say?' Jess thought she could make a guess.

'Oh, something about Gervase being a blot on the landscape. Muriel says potty things like that. She's a bit, well, curmudgeonly you could call it. She doesn't mean anything by it. She's had a difficult life.'

'Gervase told me Miss Pickering has no time for him, had no time for his father either.'

Poppy seemed to find the bananas very interesting. 'Sebastian? Well, he wasn't a very friendly man. One couldn't warm to him.'

'Tell me, Mrs Trenton, did you ever hear any rumour that Sebastian Crown mistreated his wife?' Jess asked. 'The man is long dead and you can speak freely.'

'Not about that I can't!' said Poppy immediately. 'There was a rumour, you're right. I won't deny it. I even repeated it to Roger and oh, my goodness! You should have heard him! He was furious. He said it was nonsense and slanderous and I must never repeat it again to anyone. Roger played golf with Sebastian and got on very well with him. He thought him an excellent chap. Well, I knew Sebastian when I was young. He was attractive and he could be a charmer. But he could turn the charm on and off, like a tap. I never felt easy around him. I can't say more than that.' Poppy's mouth closed in a determined line.

Gervase is right! thought Jess. Rumour of the way Sebastian Crown treated his wife had gone round the neighbourhood. But they didn't talk about it then and they're not willing to talk about it now. Only Muriel, Amanda's friend, still feels deeply enough about it to tell me.

She asked carefully, 'Is that the only reason Miss Pickering doesn't like Gervase? Because of his father? I understand she was friendly with Amanda Crown, his mother.'

'Oh, yes, she was! After Amanda left, Muriel was quite distraught for a while. She even made some wild—' Poppy broke off. 'Speculations,' she finished.

'She accused Sebastian of murdering his wife, I believe?' Poppy was looking at her as though Jess had second sight. 'Gervase told me,' Jess explained.

'Oh, did he? I hadn't realised he knew about it. He was only a child. Oh dear, that was bad. Of course Sebastian hadn't murdered her. But it's an example of how wildly Muriel can talk . . . and why you shouldn't pay too much heed to her.'

'I would have thought,' Jess suggested, 'that Muriel might have liked Gervase, when he was young, because of her affection for his mother.'

'It didn't work like that,' Poppy told her frankly. 'She looked at Gervase and she saw Sebastian. I think she decided Gervase would turn out like his father. When he got older, and got into trouble, it confirmed her worst suspicions. She decided he was a bad lot.'

Jess was still waiting, so Poppy took a deep breath and, apparently addressing the bananas, blurted, 'See here, the fact is, Muriel will never forgive Gervase for what happened in the accident.'

'Ah!' Jess thought she saw where this was leading. 'The accident that left Petra Stapleton in a wheelchair.'

But she was wrong. Poppy looked up and said, 'Oh, no, not *that* accident! The other one.'

'What other one?' Jess couldn't help but look and sound taken aback.

'The previous one, the first accident, if you like. Of course, Muriel was very upset, as we all were, about the later accident involving poor Petra. But there was an earlier one. Gervase caused a pile-up between his car and two others. Luckily, a miracle really, no one was seriously hurt in that one. At least, no human being was.'

Jess's brain was buzzing as she made a rapid review of what she knew of the earlier accident involving Gervase Crown. It was on record, of course. But she hadn't thought of it as having any bearing on this case and had put it out of her mind. Wrongly, it seemed. 'Could you explain, Mrs Trenton? How do you mean, no human being?'

'It was poor Warwick,' Poppy explained, 'Muriel's dog at the time. All Muriel's dogs have names from Shakespeare's plays. Moments before Gervase caused the pile-up – and I suppose about a mile or three-quarters of a mile further back down the road – he was driving so erratically that Muriel, who was walking Warwick, had to jump for her life into a hedge. There are no footpaths along our country roads hereabouts. Sadly, Warwick was hit. He had to be destroyed later. The vet couldn't do anything because he had so many injuries and he wasn't a young dog.'

Jess said slowly, 'There's no mention of this in the file on that accident. Muriel's name doesn't come up. She would have been a witness, surely, to his erratic driving just before the crash.'

Poppy looked embarrassed and miserable. 'I understand that Sebastian went to see Muriel. Look, you'll really need to talk to Muriel about this. Anything I tell you is just hearsay.' She got up, cradling the bag of bananas. 'If you don't mind, I'll pop along and leave these for Gervase. Roger will be wondering where I've got to. I'll tell the policeman on the door that you said I could wave a greeting if Gervase isn't asleep.'

'Yes, he might be – and thank you,' Jess said.

Outside the hospital, she sat in her car for a few minutes and reviewed her visit. She had to make allowances for Gervase having suffered a head injury and not perhaps being as consistent in his story as he might have been. On the whole, though, he'd been surprisingly coherent. One tiny thing still niggled at her brain. Gervase had denied hearing anyone, although he'd suddenly realised he wasn't alone in Key House the previous evening. He had called out, he'd said, but no one had replied. His insistence on that was suspicious. Had he, in fact, heard a voice he thought he'd recognised? Or had something else given him the impression he knew who was there? Someone whose name he did not want to give Jess.

She sighed. It wasn't much of a discrepancy and perhaps she was making too much of it. *Not at that moment* . . . It could be no more than a chance expression. After all, later, he had heard

Roger Trenton calling, so perhaps that was what he meant. By then Gervase had been struck on the head and must have been very woozy. It was unrealistic to expect him to be one hundred per cent accurate in his recollection of events.

But another annoying detail had cropped up as a result of Poppy's story. When Jess had called on Muriel, they'd had a long talk and Muriel had been very forthcoming about Sebastian Crown and his wife. But she hadn't said a word about the accident resulting in her dog, Warwick, having to be put down. And why hadn't she been a witness? Because, Poppy had said, Sebastian Crown went to see Muriel. Had he bought her silence?

On reflection, Jess was beginning to find Gervase's recent account far from the lucid tale she'd thought she was hearing. Muriel had apparently accused Sebastian of murdering his missing wife. 'I have teased her', Gervase had said, 'by saying I know where the body's buried.' That would be a literal meaning of his words. But 'knowing where the body's buried' had another meaning: that you are party to a scandalous or embarrassing secret. Such, for example, as Muriel accepting Sebastian's pay-off, despite Muriel's antagonism towards him? It now appeared that Muriel, too, had not been as frank during her conversation with Jess as Jess had thought her to be at the time.

And I won't find out all the missing bits, thought Jess, *unless I go and talk to Muriel Pickering again.*

She took out her phone and rang through to Ian Carter. 'I've seen Crown. He's not in too bad a shape. They're keeping him in for observation for a little longer and I understand Serena Foscott is anxious that he go and stay with them after he leaves the hospital. There are some discrepancies and omissions, both from Gervase's account and from what Muriel Pickering has been telling me. I'm just driving over to Mullions now. Muriel doesn't seem to go anywhere much and I'm pretty confident of finding her there. I think all this might have something to do with the earlier car crash Gervase was responsible for, not the one in which Petra Stapleton was injured. In the earlier one, Muriel's dog at the time was killed. Also, there's a possibility Sebastian Crown bought her silence.'

'You carry on,' Carter's voice said in her ear. 'I'll drive over there and join you.'

Chapter 19

Jess turned into Long Lane and pulled up on the verge. Mullions, behind its chicken-wire gate, loomed like a film set for a haunted house. The single sign of life was a spiral of smoke coming out of its chimney, but she noticed no other indication of human presence or activity.

She got out of the car, wondering if Muriel would hear the slam of the door. Jess let herself through the gate, careful to close it as requested on the notice, and walked up to the front door. Within the house she heard Hamlet bark, but no Muriel appeared. Jess pressed the rusty bell-push and, hearing no ring within, knocked loudly on the door for good measure. Hamlet's barks increased and became louder. He must now be in the entrance hall.

Jess risked pushing open the letter box flap and shouting through it. 'Muriel? It's Jess Campbell!'

In response Hamlet, on the other side, leaped up and threw himself, snarling, at what he could see of the trespasser who dared to demand entry. His teeth snapped within an inch of Jess's nose. She jumped back in alarm and let the flap fall. Hamlet, deprived of the sight of his quarry, threw himself in rage against the door panels. They shuddered beneath the force. His claws scraped at the woodwork.

Muriel wasn't there, Jess decided. But she seldom went out without Hamlet. Perhaps she'd taken the car? Jess walked round the side of the house to investigate the garage. Hamlet, tracking her from within, moved round to the side also. His furious face appeared at a window, working in rage, like an old-fashioned country squire bellowing an order at her to get off his land.

His cries followed her to where the car stood idle in the garage. Muriel couldn't have gone far. The last time Jess had called, Muriel had been busy cooking up bran mash in the kitchen but there was no smell of it now. Jess approached the kitchen windows. They were free of steam and nothing moved on the other side. She was reluctant to go right up to them and press her nose against the panes because of Hamlet who, rightly divining she was just outside, was hysterical. If her face appeared staring right at his with only the width of a glass pane between them, she wouldn't be surprised if he didn't have some sort of fit.

Jess was now beginning to be concerned. How long had Hamlet been alone? Had Muriel fallen somewhere on the property? Was she lying on the damp ground, unable to get up unaided? If so, the most likely area would be in the overgrown garden with its obstacle course of untrimmed bushes, discarded tools and wire netting. She decided to investigate. The hens were at the rear of the premises, pecking about. The cockerel rushed at Jess and flew up at her face. She clapped her hands and shouted at him. He retreated but took up position on a water butt and flapped his wings at her. Between Hamlet and the cockerel, Jess thought wryly, Muriel had no need of a burglar alarm.

But Muriel wasn't in the garden. Jess walked back towards the house and her eye fell on the garden shed. It was the only other place she could check. If Muriel wasn't in there, she would drive down to Ivy Lodge to see if by any chance Muriel had gone to visit Poppy Trenton.

The shed wasn't locked. Indeed the door was swollen and distorted and couldn't be properly shut. Jess hauled it open and peered inside. As before, she was struck by the motley collection of tools and junk. Muriel had claimed her family had lived here for a hundred and fifty years. It appeared that during that time, little had been thrown out. Curiosity led Jess to go inside and investigate. The fishing rods propped in the corner must have belonged to Muriel's father. When he'd died they'd stayed there, never moved again. Thick cobwebs swathed them. Jess's gaze moved from them to the back wall, above the workbench, covered in a cloth of ancient sawdust and dirt. Some tools she recognised: rusty spanners, hammers and chisels. But what was that?

Jess reached out her hand and took down a curious implement, a wooden stick thick enough to be grasped comfortably in the hand, culminating in a heavy metal head. She peered at it, trying to work out what might be its purpose. It was then she saw, smeared on the metal head, dark stains and tiny fragments of what appeared to be hair.

Careful not to touch the head, Jess took an evidence bag from her pocket with her free hand and slid the metal head into it.

'Put that down!' ordered a brusque voice behind her. 'It belonged to Father.'

Jess turned casually and saw Muriel in the doorway, glowering at her.

'What is it?' she asked.

Muriel blinked. 'It's a priest. Father was a fisherman. You hit a trout, or whatever you've caught, on the head with it, kill it quickly. Or if you've got a rabbit or something like that, you give it a whack to send it off into whatever next world awaits animals. You perform the last rites, you see? That's why it's called a priest.'

'I'd like to take it with me and examine it, Muriel.'

'Well, you can't!' Muriel retorted. 'Why are you poking about in here? You're trespassing.'

'Originally I was looking for you. I tried the house, but only Hamlet was there and he got very upset. So I looked in the garage and garden. This was the last place I checked. Where were you?'

'I walked over to the farm, across the fields. I don't take Hamlet with me. He doesn't get along with the farm dogs.' Muriel paused. 'I cut through the coppice. That little rotter, Alfie Darrow, has been setting his snares again on the edge of the rabbit warren. If I find one, I always unhook it and toss it in the nearest nettle bed.' She pointed at the priest in Jess's hand. 'It doesn't matter where I was. You still can't take the priest with you. It's an antique; and it's not yours. Put it back.' There was a wild glitter in her eyes behind the spectacle lenses.

'You know I'm not going to do that, don't you, Muriel?' Jess said as calmly as she could.

'Snooper!' yelled Muriel. 'I knew you for a snooper when I first clapped eyes on you!'

'It's what I do, Muriel, I told you that.' Muriel stood silent and sullen, so Jess continued, 'Muriel, did you strike Gervase Crown on the head with this?' She held up the priest.

'What if I say I didn't?' asked Muriel, still sullen.

'Then I take it with me for forensic examination and before you start telling me that I can't, let me assure you that I can. I'm a police officer, Muriel. I believe this priest, as you call it, to be evidence.'

Muriel's response was to dart to one side with surprising athleticism and grab an implement leaning against the wall just inside the shed by the door. She raised it threateningly and Jess saw, to her alarm, that it was an old-fashioned pitchfork. Its still-sharp tines were now pointed at her.

'Put it back!' Muriel's rage now mirrored Hamlet's back at the house earlier. Her complexion had turned purple, her eyes bulged, red veined, and her voice had risen to a shriek. 'You can't have it! It's mine! It was Father's and now it's mine!' She jabbed the tines in Jess's direction and Jess was forced to jump back out of the way.

'Just put that down, Muriel,' she suggested, trying not to show her alarm.

'No! I won't! Go away, go away! This is nothing to do with you. If you won't put down that priest, I'll stick this in you! Don't think I won't!' The tines threatened Jess again. Spittle flew from Muriel's lips.

'Won't attack me? As you attacked Crown and before him, Matthew Pietrangelo?'

'Got it all worked out, have you?' asked Muriel with a sneer and another jab of the pitchfork towards Jess. She had lowered her head like a defiant horned beast, ready both to charge and to repel a charge. She no longer shrieked but her voice was hoarse and had deepened to almost a male pitch. 'What do you know about anything, any of you? I told you just now what that priest is for. It's to dispatch your quarry humanely when you've got him. Thump, thump on the head and it's gone. Gervase Crown was my quarry. I cornered him and I was going to dispatch him, nice and quick. I would have done, too, if that interfering old duffer Roger Trenton hadn't come along. But I'll deny it if I'm asked in front of a witness or your little recording machine.' Muriel raised her face and smiled triumphantly. *And without that priest you can't prove it, so just put it back where you found it, go on!*

'And if you spear me with that pitchfork? What explanation are you going to give for that?'

'No problem at all,' retorted Muriel, hunching her shoulders in a shrug. 'I'm on my own here and I'm not young. I believed there was an intruder in my shed, and I was right because you were there. But I didn't *know* it was you, so I grabbed this pitchfork for self-protection and approached the shed. Then you threw open the door, ran out and speared yourself. Terrible accident, of course.' Muriel sighed. 'Just as that fellow with the Italian name was a terrible mistake. But accidents happen and sometimes they are fatal. So there,' finished Muriel. Unexpectedly she smiled in triumph. 'It would have served you right for being such a snooper.'

There was no denying she meant what she said. Crazy as it might seem to anyone else, to Muriel it appeared quite logical. What now? wondered Jess. She couldn't leave the priest behind. Muriel would dispose of it, or clean it up so thoroughly any DNA would be either eradicated or contaminated so severely as to be useless in a court of law. Why, wondered Jess, hadn't Muriel already got rid of the priest? But Jess knew the answer to that instinctively. Because it had belonged to Muriel's father and, like all the rest of this property, house, garden, ramshackle shed and its contents, it was part of Muriel's inheritance.

What to do next was settled for her.

'Come on, now, Miss Pickering,' said a calm male voice behind Muriel and, with immense relief, Jess saw Ian Carter loom into view.

'This is nonsense. You don't want to harm Inspector Campbell. Besides, that dog of yours is going frantic up at the house. You ought to go and calm him down.' Carter stretched out his hand towards the pitchfork. 'Why don't you just let me take care of that?'

Muriel turned slowly towards him still holding the pitchfork but now, Jess saw to her immense relief, the tines pointed downward. 'She was in my shed.'

'Yes, yes, but now you know who it was there.'

'I don't care. She was trespassing on my property. What's more, she's taken *Father's priest*.' Muriel appeared suddenly near to tears.

'Believe me, Miss Pickering,' Carter told her sympathetically. 'We'll take great care of it.'

'You're as bad a snooper as she is,' Muriel told him in the same morose tone. 'You've been there a while, listening to what I said to her. Did you hear it all?'

'Most of it. I don't think, by the way, that a jury would accept Inspector Campbell ran on to the pitchfork with such force that she speared herself. You've got to face up to it; all things come to an end, Muriel. This is the end of this very nasty business. Call it Fate, if you want.'

'Oh, all right, then,' said Muriel sullenly, throwing down the pitchfork. 'If you want the priest, then take the bally thing.'

She stalked past him and paused to stare towards the house. Hamlet's barks had turned to doleful howls that floated on the air towards them.

'Poor old fellow, he doesn't like being left. I'll have to go and calm him down,' said Muriel, her expression changing. 'You can come along too, if you want to keep me in sight.'

'How will Hamlet take that?' asked Carter. 'He's not going to attack either of us, is he?'

Muriel turned and treated him to a look of disgust. 'Of course he won't. Not when he sees you're with me.'

'I don't know about this,' whispered Carter as they set off after Muriel. 'You never know. It's moot point which of the two of them is the more unstable, dog or owner. Should I take the pitchfork in case we need to fend him off?'

'Don't joke about it,' Jess whispered back. 'But I don't think it will be necessary. He barked a lot the last time I called, but once Muriel said I was all right, he subsided. Muriel's not as potty as she sounds. She won't set him on us and I don't think he'd do anything but bark if she did.'

'He's full of sound and fury?' Carter met her gaze and smiled.

Jess smiled back uncertainly. 'Pretty well, I think. I'm prepared to risk it.' She raised the evidence bag with the priest in it. 'I think this may be our murder weapon.'

Hamlet greeted his mistress with ecstasy and his visitors with a ferocious growl. However, after Muriel had instructed him to 'shut up, old chap!' he appeared to grant them grudging acceptance.

Muriel's dingy sitting room had changed little since Jess's previous visit. The potted plant was a little more shrivelled and had dropped a couple of brown leaves on to the carpet where they remained, along with sundry other bits of debris. One of the seascapes had received a knock and had tilted to an angle. As a result the fishing smack on a mountainous sea that it depicted now appeared about to plunge with all hands down to Davy Jones's locker.

Carter sat in the worn Queen Anne style armchair, laconically indicated to him by their hostess with the words: 'Best chair – Father's.' Jess had retaken her former seat by the expired plant. Hamlet had taken up a position directly in front of Carter and fixed him with an unwavering stare of his pop eyes.

'Elderflower?' enquired Muriel politely.

Equally politely, they declined. Muriel sat down heavily beneath the slanted seascape and gazed at them thoughtfully. She had taken off the gumboots she'd worn for her walk to the farm. Her feet were now clad in purple woolly socks and thrust into an ancient pair of mules whose once-velvety finish of plush had rubbed almost completely bald over the years.

'Funny thing,' she said. 'When things start going wrong, they carry on going wrong, only more so, if you see what I mean? All the wrong things pile up . . .' Muriel waved at an untidy heap of newspapers by way of illustration. 'You start with one and you end up with dozens, all making one big heap; and all of 'em wrong, through and through.'

Carter asked, 'If we look in the pile of newsprint, Muriel, shall we find some lettering has been cut out?'

'I haven't got to that yet,' said Muriel resentfully. 'I haven't begun.'

'Before you do,' he told her, 'I feel I must caution you. You are not obliged to tell us anything now, but if you don't tell us something you may later rely on in court, it may harm your defence.'

'With a caution like that, you can't lose, can you?' Muriel retorted with her customary asperity.

Carter smiled at her.

She blinked. 'Good-looking fellow, aren't you?' she remarked, assessing him.

'You're too kind, Miss Pickering,' he told her.

'No, I ain't. I've never been kind. Are you married?'

'No, I once was.'

'Divorced, eh? That's it, people walk away from bad situations nowadays.' Muriel frowned. 'I never have. I should have done, perhaps, but I never did. That's why I'm sitting here and you're sitting there and everything's gone to hell in a handcart, as Father used to say.'

Jess had taken out her little tape recorder. Muriel made no comment on that other than a snort of derision.

'Take your time, Muriel,' Jess prompted her.

'Time? Time doesn't mean a thing. Nothing ever really changes. That's what makes it so difficult to say when things start. In a sense they've always been there. They just grow, like plants from seeds, do you understand what I'm saying?'

Jess found herself shifting in her seat beneath Muriel's sharp eyes. 'Yes, I think so,' she managed to say. She felt Carter look at her. 'Shall we say it all started with Sebastian Crown – or before that, with your father?'

Muriel scowled. 'Sebastian Crown? Yes, you're right there. An awful lot of what's happened is down to him.' Unexpectedly, her weather-beaten features lit up in a smile. 'I danced on his grave,' she said.

'I can understand you weren't sorry to hear he'd died.'

'No, no, you misunderstand me!' Muriel said crossly. 'I wasn't speaking metaphorically; I'm not that sort of fancy speaker. I was speaking literally. I did dance on his grave. I went down to the churchyard in Weston St Ambrose and jumped up and down on that stone they put over his ashes. I did it when no one else was around, of course.'

Carter passed a hand over his mouth. Hamlet stiffened and peered at him suspiciously.

'Muriel,' Jess invited her, 'Why don't you tell us about the day Warwick was injured?'

'Heard about that, have you?' Muriel nodded at her. 'I must say, you don't miss much. As snoops go, you're an expert, aren't you? It was that young blighter Gervase Crown's doing, of course. Wherever Crown men go, they cause trouble and grief. It's like sowing dragon's teeth. Gervase was about nineteen at the time, maybe twenty. He was young, but not innocent or harmless. He'd been at the bottle, too, I afterwards learned. I was out walking Warwick, my dog back then. He was quite an old dog and stiff in the joints, so we never walked far and always slowly. But he liked to be out and about, have a good sniff round.'

Muriel's voice and eyes were sad. 'The road was empty, everywhere peaceful, birds singing, all that sort of stuff. Then, like a bat out of hell, young Crown roared on to the scene, driving like a maniac all over the place. I leaped to safety and got tangled up in a mass of blackberry bushes. Poor old Warwick wasn't nimble enough. He was knocked clean off his feet, poor old chap, flew right up in the air. Gervase careered on down the road and a few minutes later caused a pile-up of cars. But I learned about that afterwards. I didn't see it and I couldn't now tell you whether I even heard it. I should have done, but I was concentrating on trying to free myself from the brambles and cussing Gervase fit to bust. Warwick was lying in the road. I thought he was dead. Then I saw he was breathing but blood was coming out of his nose. He never regained consciousness. I managed to pick him up and carry him home here. He weighed a ton. I thought my arms would drop off. I put him in my car and drove him to the vet. But there was nothing he could do. So it was curtains for poor Warwick.' She paused. 'I told the vet it was a hit and run. That bit was true. I didn't tell him whose car it was. Don't ask me why. I wasn't protecting young Gervase. I just wanted the vet to concentrate on Warwick.'

Muriel straightened up and spoke more briskly. Hamlet turned his head towards her. 'It was after that day that I took to wearing that yellow suit, trousers and jacket, that you've seen me in, whenever I walk my dog. Gervase probably hadn't even noticed me, and I wanted to be sure that another motorist would.'

Carter spoke. 'You say you didn't tell the vet it was Gervase Crown's car that struck your dog. You also think Gervase might not have seen you. But word got round even so, didn't it? That he was responsible?'

'Oh, yes, word got round,' Muriel nodded. 'Pretty damn quick!'

'Did you tell Mrs Trenton?' Jess asked.

'Poppy? Yes, I did, but later, and it wasn't Poppy who told Sebastian Crown about the whole business. She said she didn't and I believe her, because she always had a soft spot for Gervase on account he had a lonely childhood.' Muriel snorted. 'I could tell you something about lonely childhoods! But I've never made mine an excuse for anything. I fancy the way Sebastian got to hear about Warwick was that the vet told him. I think the vet heard about the smash Gervase had the same day, about the same time, and he put two and two together. Sebastian had made his fortune out of what he liked to call canine health products. That meant everything from conditioning shampoos to pills for bad breath. So he, Sebastian, was very thick with local vets and dog breeders, that sort of person. Sebastian was pally with anyone he thought might be of use to him.'

Muriel paused and Hamlet, having decided he'd maintained a state of alertness for long enough, uttered a gusty sigh and settled down with his nose on his paws. Carter and Jess waited.

'I'd never been of use to Sebastian. He didn't like me because I'd befriended his wife . . . and because he'd guessed I knew his nasty secret.'

'You mean by that, you knew that he beat his wife?' Jess asked for the benefit of the tape recorder.

Muriel jerked her head. 'Just so. But now Gervase was in trouble and Sebastian needed me on side. He came to see me here at Mullions. He sat there, where you're sitting.' Muriel pointed at Carter. 'There, in Father's chair. My father was dead and gone by then, had died about two years earlier.'

'Muriel,' Jess asked suddenly, as a thought occurred to her. 'How did your father die?'

The question did not appear to surprise Muriel. 'He fell in the river while out fishing. I found him floating face down. Silly old fool must have had a giddy turn. I told the coroner he used to get them. Accidental death, that's what he ruled. I took Father's ashes down to the river where he used to fish, and scattered them on the water, right there where he tumbled in.'

'That was a nice idea,' Carter told her. He glanced at Jess meaningfully as he said it. They had both had the same thought, but after all this time there would be no point in reopening the inquiry into the sudden death of an elderly fisherman, found floating by his devoted daughter.

'I didn't do it to be nice!' snapped Muriel. 'I did it because I couldn't afford a stone in the churchyard. And that's it, you see. I don't have any money, never had any and Sebastian knew it. He offered me a large sum in compensation for the loss of my pet. That's how he put it. He also offered a lifetime's supply of any canine health products produced by his company that I might need for any future pets. He then had the effrontery, the sheer brass neck, to remind me how fond I'd been of Amanda, and how it was Amanda's son who was in trouble now, charged with being drunk at the wheel of a motor vehicle and causing the crash. Gervase couldn't deny he was drunk; he'd been well over the limit. So the expensive legal team Sebastian had got on to it were trying to make a case that, even fuddled with booze, Gervase hadn't been driving recklessly; the other drivers had. They had a very slim chance of getting away with that! But they wouldn't get away with it at all if I stood up and told them about my being forced into a blackberry bush and poor Warwick. Plus, I might be able to sue Gervase for my loss and my injuries. I was a mass of scratches from those brambles. So what Sebastian really meant when he talked about compensation – what he proposed paying me for – wasn't the loss of my dog, it was my silence. He didn't want me to go to the police and report how wildly Gervase had been driving just before the crash. Plus he didn't want the whole business rehashed if I decided to sue.'

Muriel fell silent, her expression stony. 'Mullions is an old house. It needs a lot doing to it now and it needed a lot doing to it back then. At the time it was the roof that was leaking. I had buckets all over the place up there in the attics. So I took the money. Perhaps it was a little for Amanda's sake, too, making my silence a kind of gift to her, wherever she was by then. I never knew what became of her,' Muriel finished sadly.

'I understand that Gervase Crown saw his mother not long ago, and that she's well,' Jess told her impulsively.

Muriel brightened and looked at her with gratitude. 'Is she? I'm glad to hear it.' Her expression darkened again. 'But it was the wrong thing to do, wasn't it, to take the money? I should have told the police. It was blood money, poor Warwick's blood. And then, of course, that wretched young man went on to smash up another car, this time with poor young Petra Stapleton in it. I shall always feel it was partly my fault.'

'You weren't responsible for that crash!' Carter exclaimed.

Muriel contradicted him. 'You're wrong. I did my little bit to pave the way to it when I took that money and kept quiet. It encouraged Gervase to think he'd always get away with it, that he could drive round the countryside causing mayhem and that money would always talk. That's why I had to put things right, you see.'

'Perhaps, Miss Pickering,' Carter suggested, 'you'd like to continue this at a police station?'

'Are you arresting me?' asked Muriel with a sort of detached interest.

'Yes, I'm arresting you for threatening Inspector Campbell with a pitchfork and attempting to prevent her removing possible evidence. As for arresting you for anything else, you've made vague references but given me no details, so we'll talk about that in official surroundings.'

'I shouldn't have taken Sebastian's money, should I?' muttered Muriel.

Carter hesitated before he replied. 'Of course, you should have come forward as a witness at the time of the first crash when your dog was killed. But you were very shocked and distressed at the time, and it's hardly a criminal offence. I really don't think you should blame yourself for accepting the payment Sebastian Crown made you. You weren't thinking straight.'

'Good of you to say so,' Muriel told him, 'not that it makes any difference to how I feel. I'll tell you the rest, at a police station if you like. I'll have to sign a statement, won't I?'

They all got to their feet and Hamlet stood up too. Muriel nodded towards the dog. 'We'll have to stop by Ivy Lodge on the way so that I can leave Hamlet with Poppy. We'll have to take his bed and bowl and a bag of dog biscuit, if you don't mind. I have an understanding with Poppy about any dog I might have. If ever I'm ill, or drop off the twig, can't look after my animals, Poppy will take my dog. I walked over to the farm earlier to make a similar arragement with Ray Preston about the hens and the old cockerel. I told Ray I might be going away for a bit.' She glowered at Jess. 'I knew you'd come, sooner or later. Snooping around like you do, you were bound to ferret it all out.'

The image that had been haunting Alfie's subconscious mind was that of the rat, scuttling along the inner wall of the garage. He had dreamed of it the night before. In his dream, the rat had grown to monstrous size and reared up to stand on two legs. It had also worn a waistcoat and a bow tie. In the way of dreams, this had made perfect sense at the time. In this form, it had stood at the end of his bed, watching him with its beady eyes. He could glimpse its razor-sharp front teeth. It had not made any threatening move but it had been worse, somehow, to have it just stand there, clad in its waistcoat and tie, watching. He had not known – in his dream – what it intended and so could not make any countermove. All he could do was cower down between the pillow and duvet and keep his eyes fixed on the rat. He knew that if he ever took his eyes off it, then, and only then, would it make its move.

He had awoken sweating, his heart thumping in his thin chest. He'd reached out to switch on the bedside lamp and had succeeded in knocking it over. It had fallen to the floor. He'd rolled out of bed in a blind panic and found it, terrified it would be broken and he'd have to brave the darkness between his bed and the wall switch by the door. But when his searching fingers found the lamp and he pressed the switch, a dim light flooded the room and he gave a deep sigh of relief. The rat was gone. But he left the lamp on for the rest of the night.

It was not that Alfie was afraid of rats. He rather liked the type he encountered in the wild. They were feral creatures and he was himself something of a feral human. When setting his rabbit snares he often met a rat scuttling through the undergrowth. He always ignored it and it ignored him, because neither was interested in the other's business. In his experience, that type of rat was not aggressive unless cornered and Alfie took care never to corner one.

But city rats, they were another matter. Gaz was, in Alfie's judgement, a city rat and he, Alfie, was about to corner him. No wonder he was nervous.

He stood at the entry to the garage and peered into the dim interior. There was an old Volkswagen Beetle, stripped of its wheels and propped up on blocks, but he couldn't see anyone working at it. He moved cautiously into the gloom and as his eyes adjusted was able to see more clearly. Gaz was there, in his office, his head visible through the glass. He was talking on a mobile phone. Alfie waited until he'd finished before making his approach.

He had not seen the dog. The first he'd known of it was a low menacing growl over to his left. He froze in his steps and turned his head in the direction of the sound. Something stirred in the shadows. He could smell it now, a rank smell of an animal kept out of doors. It had scrambled to its feet from an improvised bed made, incongruously, of an old satin quilt thrown on the floor. It was of mixed breed, mostly of pit bull type, and its brindle coat had camouflaged it well against the wall. Alfie was relieved to see it was chained up; and his first reaction to that was to calculate how long the chain was, and whether he could reach the door of Gaz's office without moving into the dog's orbit.

'Hello, old chap,' he said placatingly. 'It's all right.'

As he had caught the dog's scent, so the dog had caught Alfie's. It hesitated. Alfie, too, had the smell of something that roamed outdoors in the wild. The dog was unsure for a moment or two. It didn't know quite how to place the intruder.

'I've come to see your boss,' Alfie informed the dog in as cheerful a tone as he could muster. He didn't smile because a suspicious dog could misinterpret a show of teeth. He didn't hold its eye, which would be a challenge, but allowed his gaze to wander vaguely around it without ever losing sight of it completely. He didn't move. He knew better than that. As long as he stayed absolutely still, the dog would remain uncertain. If he turned to flee, it would leap at him immediately. It might be chained, but the chain was fairly long. More than likely it would grab Alfie, if only by his jeans' leg, at best to cause him to stumble before the material ripped; in the worst-case scenario to bring him down. If that were to happen it would maul him and even if Gaz heard and came to the rescue – and Alfie couldn't be sure about that – he would be at least horribly scarred, possibly have whole chunks of his ears or face torn off.

But he couldn't just stand here. He was in the same situation here as he'd been in his dream, vis-à-vis the rat. He couldn't move but that meant he couldn't retreat.

The dog moved. It padded up to him. Alfie held his breath. The dog sniffed at him. Then it sat down on its haunches and waited. Stand-off.

But Gaz had observed the situation from within his glass-panelled office. He'd finished his mobile call. He opened the door of his sanctum and called out sharply, 'OK, Oscar! Stay!'

Then he turned to Alfie and asked curtly, 'What do you want?'

'Can I come in?' asked Alfie. Inside the office the dog wouldn't be able to reach him. It had settled down in response to its owner's order, but it still watched him with its evil little bronze-coloured eyes.

'Scared of the dog?' asked Gaz with an unlovely grin.

'Yes,' confessed Alfie.

Gaz assessed him. 'You done the right thing, anyway,' he said suddenly. 'If you'd done the wrong thing, Oscar would've had you by now.'

'He's a great dog,' said Alfie. Dog-owners, whoever they were, liked people to admire their pets. 'He's – er – in good nick.'

'Yeah . . .' agreed Gaz in suddenly sentimental tone. 'He's a good old brute. I brought him in because of the rats. He caught several of the blighters. The rest can smell him and they've cleared out for a while. They'll come back, like they always do. But not while Oscar's here. OK, come on in, then.'

With relief, Alfie entered the office and Gaz closed the door. Sanctuary. Except, of course, that in here Alfie was closeted with another type of beast of uncertain temperament. The expression 'out of the frying pan and into the fire' did not occur to him, but it would have described his situation well. Moreover, when he left, no matter how, he'd have to pass by Oscar again.

'Well?' asked Gaz impatiently. 'I'm a busy man. Get on with it.'

'It's about my – it's about the money for the car I brought in.'

'You little toad!' said Gaz, in a blaze of anger that made Alfie cower back. 'That motor wasn't just hot; that motor is part of a murder inquiry.'

'I didn't know that,' whimpered Alfie.

'Yeah, well, the raid went belly-up and now it's tied into a murder investigation and half the cops in the county are on it. They found the car, knew it for the murdered bloke's, and if that wasn't enough, the next thing to go wrong was they picked up the wheelman. I don't know who fingered him . . .'

'Not me!' yelped Alfie. 'I don't even know who he is! I didn't know what you wanted the car for. It was just a little bit of business for me.'

'Yeah, well, now we're all lying low – except you, you dead-brain. If you had any sense, what you haven't, you'd be keeping away from here. You'd be keeping away from *me*!' Gaz glowered at him. 'I oughta let Oscar have you.'

'Gaz, I'm really sorry if what you needed the car for didn't turn out. But I'm skint and you did say . . .'

'That was before everything went wrong, wasn't it?' Gaz accompanied the interruption with a wave of his hand. 'I can't pay you yet. You'll be flashing the cash around and attracting attention.'

'I *won't*, Gaz, I promise!' Alfie wailed.

'Yes, you bleedin' will! You come back in a couple of months' time.'

'Months!' howled Alfie. His anguished tone penetrated the glass screen and, outside, Oscar sat up and let out a single sharp bark. 'I'm stony-broke, Gaz. I gotta live with my mum out at Weston because I can't afford to move out anywhere else and the council won't help me find a place. It's not like I had a girlfriend and kids . . .'

'Spare me the sob story. All right.' Gaz moved a hand towards his lapel and Alfie's hopes soared. But the move suddenly changed direction and gathered momentum. Gaz's fist smashed into Alfie's nose and he was pitched backwards on to the floor to land in a sitting position with his back against the door. Warm salty liquid trickled down his cheek and into his mouth: blood.

On the other side of the fragile panel of thin wood, Oscar went into action. He leaped at the door like a battering ram, chain clanking. It shuddered beneath his weight. His hoarse breath sounded terrifying close to Alife's ear. His violence threatened to demolish the obstacle and gain him entry.

Alfie put a hand to his face and it came away coated in his blood. 'Whad did you do thad for?' he managed to say. 'You broge my dose . . .'

'I'll do more than break your nose. I'll break your bloody legs!' Gaz stooped over him and Alfie cowered back. On the other side of the door, Oscar gave vent to his frustration at not being able to reach his quarry by giving a howl that would not have disgraced the hound of the Baskervilles. 'Now then, I'll let you out of here and you go back to that dump of a village and your mum. In two months' time you come back, right? Just like I said. And if – *if*, mind you! If everything's quietened down and the cops aren't sniffing around here, I'll pay you a hundred quid.'

'A hundred?' Alfie gasped. He didn't know whether to be grateful at the offer or appalled at the thought that a car in such good condition was going to be worth so little to him.

'Don't like the sound of a hundred?' enquired Gaz.

'Well, I did think it was worth—' Alfie was unwise enough to begin.

'Worth *less*? You're right. OK, when you come back, I'll give you seventy quid.'

Alfie got the message. He scrambled to his feet. 'You gonna call that dog off first?' he asked sulkily. He had no handkerchief and was dabbing his sleeve at his smashed nose.

'I'll call him off.' Gaz surveyed Alfie and possibly the youngster's abject misery suggested some humane gesture. Gaz was not a charitable man, but he did pick up a soiled rag and offer it to his victim. Alfie accepted it.

Gaz opened the door and spoke once more to the dog, ordering it to stay. Alfie hurried past Oscar whose battle-scarred face expressed as much disappointment as a dog's face could. His bronze eyes promised Alfie, 'Next time!'

Alfie made his way home, the rag pressed to his face. Passers-by avoided him. Only one elderly woman enquired if he needed help. But after he'd sworn roundly at her, she waved her umbrella threateningly at him and told him he was a disgrace.

The bus service to Weston St Ambrose was notional. A bus made the round trip there, through several other smaller places, twice a day. Alfie had to huddle in a corner of the bus shelter until it came. It had begun to rain. He was hungry, wet, frightened, disappointed and in pain. The driver didn't want to let him on at first. 'I live at Weston!' protested Alfie. 'How am I going to get home? I've had an accident.'

'You'll bleed all over the seats,' said the driver unsympathetically.

'For Pete's sake, Darren, you know me!' Alfie pleaded. 'And I'm not bleeding much now. It's stopped.'

'Yeah, I know you. I let you on my bus one time when you'd had a skinful and you threw up all over the floor. It stank the place out, even after the cleaners got in, for a week.'

'I'm not drunk, Darren, I had a fall.'

Clearly Darren didn't believe that, but he did allow him on the bus at last, with instructions to sit right at the back. All the other passengers squeezed themselves into the front seats.

His mother was not at home when he let himself into the house. He had no idea when she might return. It could be late, or even the next day. When he was a school kid she'd done the same. He'd come home in the late afternoon and there would be no one there. Occasionally, if she remembered, she'd leave a note and something in the fridge for his tea. More often than not, there had been no note and no food. He would scavenge around for anything to eat: biscuits, cornflakes if there was any milk or even eaten in dry handfuls, peanuts. Once he'd retrieved some dry old bread from the back garden, thrown out for the birds.

When she eventually reappeared she would atone by bringing home fish and chips or pizza, hamburgers and cola, and he'd gorge himself. She had not been so much a neglectful mother as an absent-minded one. When she'd been enjoying herself, wherever she was, she'd simply forgotten about him. But she'd never turned him away, not after he'd started getting into trouble, nor after the police started turning up regularly at the house to look for him, or started searching the place for his hidden stash of grass or other drugs. 'It's your home, ain't it?' she'd said once.

Now he was glad of her absence. He went upstairs, pulled off his bloodstained upper clothing and stowed it in a supermarket carrier bag to be disposed of later. Then he ran the taps in the washbasin and sluiced away the blood. He peered into the mirror and groaned. His nose had swollen to clown-like proportions and appeared to veer to one side. His upper lip was split. He waggled a front tooth. It was loose.

Behind him, the bathroom door swung open. Against the noise of running water he'd not heard her return.

'Now what have you done, you stupid little bugger?' she asked in maternal concern. 'And don't think I'm going to clean that washbasin after you. Look at the mess!'

Chapter 20

Jess came into the interview room where Muriel sat facing Carter across the table and Phil Morton lurked in the background. Carter looked up and raised his eyebrows in question. Jess nodded.

For the benefit of the tape recorder, Carter said, 'Inspector Campbell has just come into the room.'

Jess took a seat beside him. 'Miss Pickering,' she said, 'the implement called a priest that I removed from your garden shed has been sent to the forensics laboratory.'

'Do what you like with it!' Muriel shrugged and gazed past her towards Morton, stationed by the opposite wall. 'I recognise you,' she informed him. 'You're the policeman who first came to talk to me at Mullions.'

'Miss Pickering has indicated Sergeant Morton,' said Carter to the tape recorder.

This had the effect of attracting Muriel's attention to the recorder. 'It's like a person,' she mused, 'just sitting there, listening to us.'

'Would you like to tell us about the fire at Key House?' Carter invited.

'Fire?' Muriel was still staring thoughtfully at the tape recorder.

Carter glanced briefly at Jess. It had been obvious, during the journey here from Ivy Lodge, where a protesting Hamlet had been left with Poppy Trenton, that Muriel's previous loquaciousness was giving way to an introspective taciturnity. Was she now going to refuse to admit to anything? Perhaps it had been a tactical mistake to stop off at the Trentons'. Roger, thank goodness, hadn't been there, but Poppy had been so dismayed at the situation and Hamlet made such desperate efforts to follow his mistress that it was possible the reality of what she faced had come home to Muriel for the first time.

'Miss Pickering,' she asked, 'did you set fire to Key House?'

Muriel stopped studying the tape recorder to look at her. 'The problem with you people,' she said, 'is that you go about things in the wrong order. You always want to know what happened last, when you haven't heard what happened first. How can you understand what happened later, if you don't know what happened before?'

'You've told us what happened before,' Carter pointed out. 'You told us about the drunk-driving incident involving Gervase Crown, as a result of which your dog, Warwick, died.'

'You also mentioned the later accident in which Petra Stapleton was badly injured,' Jess added. 'You said you felt a moral responsibility for that. Would you like to go on from there?'

'All right,' said Muriel, amenable now that things were progressing in what she felt was the right order. 'After that second accident, when that poor young girl's life was ruined, Gervase went to jail. He didn't go for nearly long enough in my book; they let him out halfway through his sentence. Sebastian took it badly. His precious family name was damaged and, with it, his social standing in the community. That meant a lot to him. He didn't like other chaps at the golf club looking embarrassed when he hove into view. He even gave up playing for a while; Poppy told me that. He'd also been put under an obligation to me and that must really have bugged him. He didn't trust me to keep my side of the bargain.

I wouldn't have welched, mind you. I'd given him my word and I'd have kept it. He'd lost his wife (through his own fault, mind you!). Now, in a sense, he'd lost his son. One would have felt sorry for anyone else in his situation. But I didn't feel sorry for him because he carried the major share of the responsibility. He'd brought every darn thing on himself. He shouldn't have kept buying Gervase those fast cars. Then Sebastian upped and died while Gervase was still doing time. He had a heart attack. You'll have to ask Trenton if you want the detailed description of that.'

'Roger Trenton?' Carter and Jess spoke together.

'That's the one. Fate has a way of having the last word. Sebastian had finally got up enough courage to reappear at the golf club. Roger Trenton, Dr Layton and Sebastian Crown were playing a threesome together. They'd finished and walked back to the clubhouse, and went to the bar. There, without any warning, Sebastian fell forward into his gin and tonic and that was that. Layton, who was his doctor, was right there on hand but couldn't help.' Muriel paused. 'That's pretty well how Poppy told me about it. You can check with her. Does it matter? He died.

'Gervase came out of jail early because his father had died. Compassionate grounds, they call it. He didn't get any sympathy around here and soon found he wasn't welcome back in the area. It couldn't have surprised him. The sight of young Petra in a wheelchair must have been uncomfortable for him, too. So he went travelling again. He'd done a bit of that when he was younger, before he started driving fast cars. This time he ended up in Portugal where, we heard, he'd bought a home and settled. Key House was emptied out and we all expected it to be sold. But it wasn't. It stayed there, an attraction for every ne'er-do-well in the area.' Muriel's expression sharpened. 'Roger Trenton would have you

299

believe he kept an eye on Key House. How could he? He can't even see it from where he lives. But I could. If anyone kept an eye on Key House, it was me!'

'How did you do that? Your house, Mullions, is in Long Lane,' Jess pointed out. 'Mullions isn't visible from Key House. I couldn't see it when I was there. I was surprised to come on Mullions when I turned into Long Lane. So, like Roger, you couldn't see Key House from your home either. Do you mean you checked out Key House when you walked your dog?'

'Jumping the gun again!' Muriel told her. 'No, you couldn't see Mullions from ground level at Key House. I can't see Key House from my front gate or garden. But I haven't been keeping an eye on it from *ground level*. You remember that Mullions has a pigeon loft up on the roof? It looks like a tower.'

'Yes, I do,' Jess admitted.

'Well, then, that's my observation post. I've been climbing up there pretty well every day, partly to see how the roof is holding up because it's going to need some more repairs soon, but also to take a look round the countryside. I've got a good view of Key House from up there.' Muriel gave her a triumphant smile, sat back and folded her arms. 'So I watched out for activity at Key House. I saw 'em come and go, drug users, hippies, odds and sods of all kinds. It was in my interest to know who was sleeping there or using the place. I had to be on my guard. I'm on my own at Mullions. I was afraid some of them might wander up Long Lane and see Mullions and try and break in. They might think it empty, just like Key House.'

Carter was growing restless. 'Why did you set fire to Key House?'

'You're as bad as she is,' Muriel told him. 'I haven't got that far, nor have I admitted to setting fire to the place.'

'Did you?' prompted Jess.

'Later, I did. Hang on a bit. I'll have to explain how it came about. If I'd just wanted to set fire to it, I could have done it any time. Perhaps I should have done.' Muriel frowned. 'That would have taken care of it. I wish I had thought of burning it down. But I didn't do anything. I thought that eventually it would be sold, although as it began to deteriorate it was a problem as to who would want to take it on! Trenton kept writing to the council, a waste of time. I just watched the house crumble. But I kept up my observation because from time to time all kinds of undesirables continued to turn up there, drinking and doing drugs too, as I told you. I kept waiting for the "for sale" notice to go up, and it never did. Then, one day not all that long ago, I met Poppy and she told me something really strange. She said she thought she'd seen Gervase Crown at the house. She wasn't sure because the light hadn't been good and she hadn't seen Gervase for a long time. But she was eighty per cent sure.

'I went back to Mullions and camped out in the pigeon loft. Sure enough, a couple of days later, I saw him with my own eyes, or I thought it was Gervase. I saw him again a few days after that. I said to myself, the blighter is looking the place over with a view to moving back in again! He's keeping a low profile because he knows he's not Mr Popular. But he's coming back. I was so angry. After all the trouble he'd caused, to even think of returning to live among us!'

Muriel paused but this time they didn't make the mistake of trying to hurry her. 'After that, I didn't see him for a week or two. I thought, good: he's gone back to Portugal. Then we had some rain, quite heavy. I was worried about the roof. I took to going up to the attics and the pigeon loft at all hours to check for leaks if it was raining again, middle of the night sometimes. One evening I saw a light flickering in Key House. Usually, that's meant another bunch of dropouts, often Alfie Darrow and his pals, has taken over for a few hours to have one of their parties. I'd had enough. I went down to the shed and got the priest. It was the best thing I could think of for a weapon. I wasn't going to attack anyone!' Muriel glared at them. 'I took it for self-defence. If they were doing drugs, or drunk, or both, they could turn very nasty. But I was going to tell them to clear out, even so, or I'd phone the police.'

'Perhaps,' Carter couldn't resist telling her, 'you should have phoned the police straight away and not gone yourself.'

'And how long would it have taken your lot to come out?' enquired Muriel sarcastically. 'Key House is private property and trespass isn't something you coppers worry about. You probably wouldn't have turned up before the morning, if you'd turned up at all!'

There was, regrettably, an element of truth in that. If more serious incidents had been reported that night, a break-in to a vacant and unfurnished house would have been given low priority.

'So I went,' said Muriel. 'If I'd seen Alfie, I'd have faced him. He knows me. Even with his mates to back him up, he'd have been careful of me. If I hadn't been able to see Alfie, I would probably have just turned tail and gone back home again. I wouldn't have faced complete strangers. But, when I got down there to the house, I saw a car parked up under the hedge, a Clio. I crept up to the house and peeped in through a window. Whoever it was, it was just one person. He was walking around from room to room, flashing a torch about. When he turned, the beam fell across his face and I saw him. I thought it was Gervase, back again, just as Poppy had told me she thought he was. I decided to give him a piece of my mind. I knew how to get in. There's a window catch broken at the rear of the building. I believe Roger Trenton reported it to Reggie Foscott and he sent someone over to board the window up. But the boards were pulled out again, probably by Alfie and his crew. So I clambered through there and went to look for Gervase.'

Muriel paused. 'I still only meant to tell him to clear off, tell him he wasn't wanted and ask why the hell he didn't put the house up for sale. He was in the kitchen. He seemed to be taking a lot of interest in the fitted cabinets in there. Going to have a new kitchen put in, are you? I thought – and I just saw red. All of it, Warwick's death, Petra being left in a wheelchair, the way he'd left the house empty to be used by any old miscreant. Even the things that had happened before that . . . Sebastian's appalling treatment of Amanda. That was not Gervase's fault, but the Bible says the sins of the fathers are visited on the children. All in all, I thought to myself, you are bad news, Gervase Crown, and if you come back here, there will be more mischief, more sorrow, more lives ruined. You are not going to live here again! I'll stop you. I marched up behind him and hit him with the priest and down he went. I hit him again for good measure. He lay still.'

Muriel frowned. 'I sobered up a bit after that. I don't mean I was drunk. I'd only had a couple of glasses of elderflower that evening. I meant, my head cleared and I realised what I'd done. I'd killed him.'

'What made you think you'd killed him?' asked Carter.

'I shone the torch on him. He was absolutely still, eyes shut, mouth open a bit. I hoped he was only unconscious, so I put my face close to his but I couldn't feel any breath. I shook him and slapped his face to bring him round, but his head fell back like a rag doll's. I even had a go at the kiss of life!' Muriel leaned forward to make sure they got the point of how much she'd tried. Then she sat back and heaved a sigh. 'I'd never tried it before and only read about it, and might have seen pictures on First Aid posters. I'd never seen a demonstration or had a go, even on a dummy, and these things aren't as easy as they try to tell you. So next I tried finding his pulse and couldn't. He looked and appeared in every way as dead as a doornail to me. I thought, he's a goner, so now what, Muriel? I decided that as I'd got rid of Gervase – I still believed it was Gervase – I'd finish the job and get rid of the house as well. I went back out through the window at the rear and I saw the car parked there again. The keys were in it. I drove it back to Long Lane, past Mullions and parked it in the coppice further down the lane. Nobody goes down there so I thought it wouldn't be seen and I'd have time to get rid of it somewhere later. Then I went to my garage, put some petrol in a plastic bottle and took it back to Key House with me. I sprinkled it all round the kitchen and put a match to it – and that was that.'

She paused. 'I didn't think the whole place would go up quite so quickly, but it did – whoosh! I must say that, at the time, it was very satisfying. Later on, I found out I killed the wrong fellow. It wasn't Gervase in the house that night; it was some other man. Poppy had been wrong about seeing him as she told me,' finished Muriel resentfully. 'She got me all worked up about Gervase returning, and he hadn't!'

'Nor had you killed the intruder at Key House with the priest,' Carter told her. 'He wasn't dead, Muriel, even though you thought so. In the circumstances, in the dark, and lacking first-aid skills, it's hardly surprising you didn't find a pulse. But if you'd called an ambulance, they'd have taken care of him. However, you left him there and the fire killed him.'

'I'm sorry about that,' said Muriel. 'I really am. I did my best at the time. It's like I was telling you. When things start going wrong, they carry on going wrong, just piling up, one on top of another. But they begin long before they appear to happen. You say I left that man to die in the house. But I was there in the house – and he, the Italian, was there in the house that night – because Gervase Crown had left the house empty for so long, giving us all such worry. So why don't you blame *him*?'

She leaned forward suddenly and declared, 'Not even my plan for getting rid of the Clio went right, you know? I meant to drive it out into the countryside somewhere the next day and abandon it, perhaps set fire to that, too. But the fire crews arrived very quickly and they stayed for nearly the whole of the day immediately following. The police turned up too because the body hadn't burned away to nothing, as I hoped it might. So I couldn't move the Clio.' She gazed sorrowfully at Jess. 'I did hope the fire would have burned the body completely, you know. It was so fierce! They cremate dead bodies and it all goes away, or nearly all of it except for a few bits of bone. They put those through a crusher because there's nothing more they can do with them. I thought that's what would happen with any fragments left at the house. When I walked down there with Hamlet, and saw you and that idiot Trenton, I learned that the body was more or less intact! Badly charred but still a proper body. That was a nasty shock.

'The next morning, after that, the fire crew came back and damped down, so I still had to wait. It wasn't until they'd finally left, around lunchtime, that I walked along the lane to the coppice where I'd left the Clio and, would you believe it? Someone had pinched it! Who on earth would have found it there? I couldn't believe my eyes. I saw some tyre marks. There were two lots. One lot had been caused when I drove it in there to hide it, and the other lot must have been when it was driven out again. The countryside used to be such a peaceful spot and now you can't even park a car for forty-eight hours in a lonely patch of woodland, but someone comes along and steals it.' Muriel glowered at them.

'We have recovered the car,' Carter said.

Muriel's mouth dropped open. 'That was good going. Where was it?'

'Just outside Cheltenham.'

'How did it get there?' She looked amazed.

'We're working on that,' Carter said evasively.

'So, Muriel,' Jess pointed out, 'your actions resulted in Gervase Crown returning from Portugal to see what was left of his house.'

Distracted from her surprise over the car, Muriel turned back to Jess. 'Yes, Gervase turned up and he started wandering around the house. I found him there with that poor young woman, the girlfriend of the fellow who died. They were both inside the burntout shell. I warned her about him.'

'How about the anonymous letter?' Jess asked. 'Did you write or make up that?'

'Yes, I tried to frighten him off back to Portugal,' said Muriel simply. 'I made up a letter and then I thought, just a minute, the police will trace this because of fingerprints and DNA and all the rest of it. You read about it in the newspapers. Then I remembered that in the library at Weston St Ambrose they've got a copier machine. The library is only open two days a week now and mostly it's run by volunteers. It gets pretty crowded on the two days it is open, so I wasn't afraid anyone would take any notice of what I was doing. I went down there, as it was a day it was working, and sure enough, there were plenty of people there chattering and looking at the books. Miranda Layton was there but she's not a chatty woman. She had her nose in a book. No one took any notice of me at the copier and it did it very quickly. I pressed a button and out came a copy. I picked it up wearing my winter gloves. No fingerprints, see?' Muriel nodded at them, pleased with her cleverness. 'I stuck the original in my pocket and when I got back home later, I burned it. The other one, the copy, I'd folded up very nicely, gone along to The Royal Oak and slid it under Gervase's door. I knew it was his room, because I saw him come out of it.'

'He didn't see you,' Jess objected. 'He said the corridor was empty. The only person around was the cleaner and she was in the next room.'

'It wasn't the cleaner in the next room,' said Muriel in triumph. 'It was me! I was looking up and down the corridor, trying to work out which was his room, when a door started to open. So I nipped into the next room. The door of that was standing open because the cleaner was about somewhere, but she'd gone for a moment. I heard Gervase come out and just stuck my head out of the door in time to see him at the head of the stairs, going down to his breakfast. So now I knew which was his room, but I heard the cleaner coming back. She must have gone to fetch the vacuum cleaner because she was dragging it along and muttering at it. There's a lavatory on that corridor. It's an old Victorian one. It dates from before the rooms had their own facilities, what they call "en suite". Before that, people queued up for use of the bathroom and didn't worry about it. Anyway, I nipped into the old lavatory and bolted the door. If the cleaner came and tried to open it, she would think someone from downstairs had come up to use it. I did hear her come back. She went into his room and then she wheeled her trolley full of cleaning stuff away. It had squeaky wheels. She put the vacuum round as well. In case you're thinking I must have been lurking in that lavatory for a long time, you're wrong. That cleaner must be the fastest worker in Weston St Ambrose. Bump, bump, splash of tap running, door slam, room clean. Buzz-buzz and the vacuuming finished.

'So I came out, slipped the note under his door and left. That will give you a nasty surprise! I thought. No one took any notice of me as I walked through downstairs and out into the street. Nobody does. It's only when I wear my yellow suit that people see me at all. Otherwise, I'm just old Muriel. I'm practically invisible.' Her smile was unexpected and wistful.

'What about the attack on the real Mr Crown at the house?' asked Carter, quelling a momentary feeling of sympathy. He couldn't afford that. He replaced it with an image of Muriel painstakingly shaking petrol around the prone body of Matthew Pietrangelo, standing back and tossing a lighted match . . .

'It was late, after dark, and he was struck down by a blow from the rear. It was practically a copycat attack to the one on Matthew Pietrangelo.'

'Yes, I got a second chance, but that went wrong, too,' Muriel grumbled. 'It was his fault. I warned him to leave. He took no notice of my note. But at least I *tried*. He came out to Key House again. I saw the moving light from my pigeon loft, so I went down there again – carrying the priest. This time I meant to make sure of him. I didn't want to get the wrong man again, as I'd done the first time. So I waited until I was positive he was the person poking about in there. I think he must have realised someone was there.

I even called out his name, Gervase. I was nervous and it didn't come out very loudly, more a hoarse whisper, so I don't know if he heard me or not. But he called back, and I heard his voice so knew it was him. I didn't get in the perfect blow because he struck out with his torch and deflected the priest just enough to make it glance off his head. It was good enough to make him fall down on the floor. I was getting ready to hit him again when that prize booby, Roger Trenton, turned up!'

Muriel's voice quivered in outrage. 'Would you credit it? I'd never known Trenton go there after dark. I had to slip out of there and scuttle off home by a roundabout route. It just wasn't meant to be. Twice I tried to kill Crown. The first time I got the wrong man and the second time I was foiled by someone turning up. The devil looks after his own, they say, and certainly something has looked after Gervase Crown!'

'Well,' said Carter to Jess as they returned back upstairs later. 'If either Pietrangelo's DNA or that of Gervase Crown is on that priest, that will pretty well sew up a case against Muriel Pickering.'

'Her story does explain how Alfie Darrow came to find the Clio in the coppice near Mullions,' Jess pointed out. 'So it does look as if Alfie was telling the truth – as far as that part of his story goes. I still don't believe he drove it around and then just abandoned it.'

'And I don't think he'll ever confess to anything else, unless we find the person to whom he sold it. But you never know with police work,' Carter added more optimistically. 'Perhaps something will happen to make Mr Darrow change his mind and supply us with the truth.'

Chapter 21

Carter's optimism was unexpectedly rewarded. They found themselves facing Alfie Darrow rather more quickly than they'd anticipated. The following morning a message was relayed to Jess that Mrs Sandra Darrow, accompanied by her son, wished to speak to her.

'This I gotta see,' muttered Morton.

'Be my guest, Phil.'

The interview room was not very big and with the two police officers, Alfie and Sandra Darrow in it, it appeared an awful lot smaller. Sandra was built on generous lines. Her bulk, startlingly clad in a baggy black top festooned with sequins and a sagging purple skirt, was majestically, if precariously, enthroned on a very small chair. Masses of improbably black hair cascaded over her meaty shoulders and large hoop earrings swung from her ears.

Beside her, her son looked a mere wisp of a human being. He also looked one of the most miserable and his face was a mess, much of it bruised purple and yellow. His nose was bulbous, he had two black eyes and his upper lip was split and puffy. He was hardly recognisable.

'Hello, Alfie,' remarked Morton, inspecting the damage. 'What happened to you? Were you in a fight or did someone beat you up? You look as though you've walked into a wall.'

Alfie clearly intended to give a colourful reply but was cut short by his mother, who dug a well-directed elbow into his ribs, so that whatever he'd been going to say, all he let out was a gasp of pain.

'Are you that Inspector Campbell?' enquired Mrs Darrow of Jess, after studying her minutely, top to toe. 'Are you the one my boy is always talking about?'

'I'm Inspector Campbell,' Jess agreed. 'I wasn't aware Alfie talks about me a lot.'

'Well, he does,' said Mrs Darrow. She transferred the sharp gaze of her dark, beady eyes, sunk in her doughy face like currants in a hot cross bun, to Morton. ''Oo is he?' she asked. She didn't ask it of Jess, she asked it of her son.

'He's a sergeant, name of Morton,' muttered Alfie. 'He's another one always on at me.'

Jess and Morton exchanged glances. Were they about to be accused by Mrs Darrow of harassing her blameless boy?

Jess decided it was time she took control of the interview. 'Well, Mrs Darrow, I'm leading the team looking into the attempted robbery at Briskett's bank.'

But Mrs Darrow had her own agenda. 'I'm a woman on my own,' she announced. 'My husband left.'

Both officers looked nonplussed.

'I'm sorry,' said Jess, not sure what else could be said.

'I wasn't,' said Mrs Darrow. 'I was glad to see him go. He was useless. Now my Alfie here . . .' She threw out a hand and struck her son in the chest to indicate she meant that Alfie and not any other Alfie lurking in the room. Alfie winced and gurgled. 'My Alfie was never a bad boy. I don't say he was ever a saint, but what kid is a saint, especially these days?'

Jess and Morton made vague noises of agreement. Morton followed it with a sigh of exasperation and a muttered, 'Here we go!'

'Of course, he's been in trouble from time to time, but he's never meant any harm by any of it,' Mrs Darrow informed them in tones suddenly confidential. Her ample bosom tilted forward but the rolls of fat at the level of her waist did not allow of bending. 'His problem is he don't think. He's never been what you'd call very quick on the uptake. He was never no good at school. But I blame the teachers he had. They said he couldn't keep up in the class he was in. I said to them, that's what they were there for, to help him keep up. Then they put him in one of those classes for slow learners but he never learned anything there, either, so they might just as well have left him where he was.' She frowned. 'One of them people what come to the school and assess the kids said he'd got a deficiency. He'd got no attention.'

'Attention deficiency disorder?' Morton was getting into the swing of Alfie's educational problems.

'That's it,' she said, nodding at Morton. 'And he has. I know that for a fact because for years I've talked to him until I'm blue in the face and he never has listened.'

'Mrs Darrow,' Jess asked, seeing that the discussion of Alfie's failure at school, and resulting failure at life in general, might take over the interview, 'may I ask—'

She got no further.

'I'm just coming to that!' snapped the lady. 'If you'd hang on a minute.'

Wildly, Jess wondered if the Darrows were in any way related to Muriel Pickering, who had a similar linear approach to any narrative. But Muriel had expressed such a poor opinion of 'that little rotter, Alfie Darrow' that it seemed unlikely.

'He told me,' said Mrs Darrow, 'how the police had pulled him in, because of that car he found abandoned.'

'Yes, we're very interested in—' began Morton in a new attempt to introduce his questions regarding the getaway car.

Mrs Darrow rolled over his words inexorably, like the tide. 'And then you told him it had bin used in a bank raid. That right?' She was still addressing Jess.

'That's certainly correct, Mrs Darrow,' Jess told her. 'Your son has admitted taking the car from—'

Mrs Darrow was impervious to attempts to wrest control of the interview. 'I heard about that bank raid on the local news on telly. The robbers never got any money, I heard. Then he comes home looking like that.' She pointed at her son's damaged face. 'Blood all over my bathroom. So I said to him, you listen to me, my boy. You tell the cops all you know because otherwise . . .' Mrs Darrow drew a deep breath and declared, 'you'll be an accessory.' The little black eyes fixed Jess. 'That right?'

'Er, yes, Mrs Darrow, Alfie could be an accessory if he's not told us all he knows.'

'See?' said Mrs Darrow to her son. 'That's what I said, isn't it?'

'Yes, Mum,' said Alfie miserably.

Morton passed a hand over his brow.

'"What did you do with that car?" I asked him. Didn't I, Alfie?'

'Yes, Mum.' Alfie, who was in reality almost nineteen years old, now seemed to have regressed to the age of six.

'He said first of all he'd left it by the road somewhere. But I didn't bring him up all these years not to know when he's holding out on me. That right?' she demanded of the hapless Alfie again.

'No, yes, Mum,' said Alfie, sinking further down beside his imposing mama.

Mrs Darrow retrieved her capacious handbag from the floor beside her. It was made of black shiny plastic and was decorated with appliqué pink plastic daisies. From it she took a bloodstained, oily rag and threw it on the table between them.

'He come home with that,' she said. 'He come from Cheltenham on the bus with it. I know that because my neighbour, Leanne Somerton, she was on the bus and saw him. She told me later, in the pub. That rag,' Mrs Darrow pointed at the object as a barrister might have indicated Exhibit A. 'That rag's been in a garage.'

'Ah!' exclaimed Morton, seizing what he feared might be his last chance to get to the information he wanted. 'Sold it on somewhere, did you, Alfie? Who was the dealer you took it to?'

'I never,' said Alfie obstinately.

His parent turned a gimlet eye on him and he sank down even further in his chair. If he'd tried to go any lower, he'd have rolled off on to the floor.

'So, if he tells you what he really done with it,' continued Mrs Darrow, turning back to Jess, 'will that go in his favour? I reckon it should. Because he's come in here voluntarily.'

At that even Alfie looked as though, for a split second, he might disagree, but then obviously realising the futility of arguing with his parent, just sniffed.

'He didn't tell you right off first time you asked him about the car,' explained Mrs Darrow, 'because he was scared. He knew he *should* tell you, because he knows right from wrong.'

Now it was Phil Morton who looked as if he longed to disagree with her.

'So,' concluded Sandra Darrow, 'he's come in here now to do the right thing and tell you what he really done with it.'

There was a silence in which Alfie found himself the target of three pairs of eyes. He made a last attempt to avoid the inevitable.

'If I tell you,' he said pathetically, 'I'll get well done over.' He pointed at his face. 'This'll be nothing to it. He'll set the dog on me.'

'Who is "he", Alfie?'

'I can't tell you, can I?' Alfie again pointed at his disfigured features. 'You blind or something?'

'It could go in your favour, as your mother says,' countered Morton.

'That won't help me if I've got two broken legs, will it?' cried Alfie in despair.

'You tell them right now!' ordered his mother. 'And if anyone comes threatening you afterwards, you tell them they'll have to deal with *me*!' She straightened up, folded her hands over her patent handbag, and stared serenely at the police officers. 'I weigh just a smidgeon under eighteen stone and I like a fight,' she said.

For a moment, it seemed to Jess she could hear the clash of weaponry and the cries of battle. Perhaps there was something in reincarnation, after all. Beneath that black sequinned top did there beat the heart of Boadicea?

'Go on, then,' urged Mrs Darrow of Alfie. 'Tell them.'

So Alfie, after a pause to allow Morton to caution him, told them.

'There's this bloke called Gaz, and honest, he ain't going to like this one bit. But he buys old cars, so I sold him that one, the Clio. I never knew what he was going to do with it. What's more,' and now real tears welled up in Alfie's eyes, 'he's never paid me for it. Nuffin', not a lousy penny.'

'So I reckon,' interposed his mother, 'that my son didn't *sell* the car, if he didn't get paid. He might have *wanted* to sell the car, but he didn't get any money so you can't say he did *sell* it, did he?

All he did was find it, abandoned like he said, and drive it around a bit. Any youngster would do that,' concluded Mrs Darrow. 'It don't make him a criminal.'

Under continuing protest, Alfie had made his statement and been warned that charges would be made once it had all been checked out. He departed forlornly in the company of his mother.

The oily rag from Gaz's premises had been carefully bagged up and sent to forensics. They had already found the wheelman for the bungled bank job ('where would we be without informers?' Carter had remarked). Pretty soon they would have the other members of the gang.

'And everything, murder, arson and attempted robbery, will be neatly tied up . . . in due course,' Carter observed.

'He means,' Morton grumbled to Jess, 'now for all the paperwork.'

Chapter 22

Petra was again at work in her barn studio when Gervase came. She heard him call her name faintly from beyond the closed barn doors, and twisted to face them. They slid apart with a groan of wood and a teeth-grinding scrape along the gravel.

'Gervase!' she exclaimed when his dark outline filled the newly opened entrance. 'We've been so worried about you! How are you? How did you get here?'

Gervase tugged at the doors to exclude the fresh breeze that swept across the yard today. He crossed to where she sat and took his former seat on the wobbly chair, uninvited. 'I drove here. I'm quite all right, just got a sore head. Old Muriel's aim wasn't so good. I'm quite tall and she's on the short side so she had to reach up; and it was dark. She still fetched me a heck of wallop.'

'She could have killed you!' Petra said fiercely. 'She meant to kill you. Just as she killed that other poor man.'

'She didn't mean to kill *him*: she meant to kill *me*. She'd got it into her head I was the one wandering around the house in semi-darkness that night. Poppy Trenton gave her the idea. She thought she'd seen me around, earlier. But it was that unlucky chap, Pietrangelo, who apparently looked like me. He'd been investigating Key House in the hope of buying it.' Gervase swept out his arm in a gesture that might have been exasperation. 'Now Poppy is racked with guilt! She shouldn't have told Muriel she'd seen me

319

when she wasn't sure it was me, and so on . . . I've told her, if we got blamed for crimes because of some passing remark we'd made, or a genuine mistake, we'd all, at some stage of our lives, find ourselves in the dock! But she's in full *mea culpa* mood and won't be persuaded out of it. Pity, because she's such a nice woman. Anyway, I told her not to brood on it. Her husband, on the other hand, isn't brooding but he is in a dither. Poor old Roger, having saved my life by his intervention, now can't decide whether to lecture me – as his instincts tell him to – or treat me as an unexpected boost to his ego.'

Gervase gave a wry smile. 'I always knew Muriel didn't like me much. I hadn't realised she harboured murderous intentions. Poor old girl, I ran over her dog, years ago. Or ran into it, one or the other, and nearly ran her down into the bargain. I have to confess, my memory of the exact events is hazy.' His smile faded. 'I should remember, of course. I shouldn't have been fuddled with booze. I should have learned my lesson from that episode and not—' He broke off and waved a hand vaguely towards Petra. 'Not done it all again.'

'Can't be changed now,' said Petra simply. 'Don't start telling me you're sorry, Gervase. I know you are. It's OK, right?'

'No, not OK, but thank you. Dad bought her off, apparently, that first time. I didn't know about that then. He didn't tell me, but he wasn't in the habit of telling me anything, so it was par for the course. It was Reggie who told me, quite a few years later, long after Dad had died. Reggie is another one who keeps shtum about things. But one Christmas, when I was over here and called in to wish them seasonal good cheer, we had a few whiskies and he got loquacious.

'Dad meant well, I suppose, but even so. Muriel hated him for it. When people have taken the high ground, as she'd always done vis-à-vis my father, it was humiliating for her to be shown to be as mercenary as anyone else. She wanted someone to blame, not just for the loss of her dog and her brush with injury, but for having Dad there in her living room, holding out a bunch of notes and her acceptance of the bribe. When she's gone out of her way to be rude to me, I've usually found a way of reminding her about that little episode. Not wise of me, you'd say. It added to the little pile of grievances she harboured towards me. But I'm not wise and one way and another I've caused a lot of heartache, haven't I?'

There was an awkward silence. Petra said at last, 'There's no excuse for what she did at Key House the night of the fire. It was barbaric. Trying to do the same to you the other evening was just as unspeakable. But in spite of it all, I feel a little sorry for Muriel. As for her taking your father's money so long ago, well, she was poor, Gervase. You've never been hard up. Your father knew she wouldn't refuse. After the way she'd bad mouthed him for so long, he probably got a kick out of it, just as you say.'

'You bet he did!' said Gervase fiercely. 'I can just imagine him sitting there, crackling the notes under her nose. But she did accuse him of murder after my mother left. So you can't altogether blame the old blighter for enjoying the moment.'

He caught Petra's eye. 'And you're right. I have never been poor and I didn't behave well when I reminded her. Perhaps there's something of the old man in me, after all. I shall have to watch out for that!'

Petra pointed at the easel. 'I've made a start on my portrait of Hamlet. I'll finish it, whether she ever pays me or not. It will be waiting for her when she gets out of prison. She will go to prison, won't she?'

Gervase nodded. 'Probably. It will be hard on her. It bloody scared me out of my skin when I got banged up all those years ago. But Muriel's tough; and I'll make sure she's got a good defence barrister to argue her case, don't worry about that. Reggie's making sure she'll get bail until the trial comes up. I'll underwrite it. She has commitments – her chickens – and she isn't going to flee the country . . . but I am. That is to say, I shall be returning to Portugal in a few days' time. I'll come back for the trial.' He paused. 'She's not going to attack anyone else, not once I'm out of the way.'

'I'm glad you're making sure she has a good brief,' Petra said. 'That's generous of you, in the circumstances.'

He shrugged. 'It's the least I can do.' He looked past her at the easel. 'Is that it? You're making the mutt look almost attractive.'

'I don't pretty up my subjects,' Petra said, affronted. 'I just concentrate on their best aspects. Hamlet's got lots of character.'

'If you say so.' He looked down at the floor and, when he looked up again, asked unexpectedly, 'Why don't you come out to Portugal for a holiday?'

Petra blinked. 'Visit you, you mean?'

'Why not? I've got a big house, plenty of room, and I could accommodate you on the ground floor. I'll book the flight and make all the necessary special arrangements, pick you up at the airport in Lisbon.'

'I couldn't, Gervase, really.' Petra gazed at him, stupefied. 'I've – I've got work here.'

'You could work there. You could paint a portrait of my horse. I mean to sell him but it would be nice to have a souvenir of him.'

Petra shook her head. 'No, thank you all the same for the kind offer.'

He became argumentative. 'Why not? It would do you good,

sea air and sunshine. If you didn't want to travel alone I could come over and collect you. Or Kit could come with you.'

'I really *couldn't* . . .'

'At least think about it. Promise me.'

'I promise. I'll think it over.' Petra spoke the words hastily since there appeared to be no getting out of it.

He seized on her haste. 'You say that in the way people do when they mean they won't give it another moment's consideration.'

'I will consider it, Gervase, truly. But I really can't see it happening.'

'Anything can happen,' Gervase said suddenly. There was a silence and he got to his feet. 'I'm staying with my cousin, Serena. She's made it a project to look after me until I leave.' He pulled a face. 'She means well. I should be grateful. I am grateful. But it was more comfortable at The Royal Oak. I'll look in again before I leave.'

'Oh, yes, please do!' Petra said impulsively.

He studied her for a moment until she felt herself blush.

'I wish I could turn the clock back, Petra. I wish . . . No bloody use wishing, is it?'

'Then stop, please.' Petra reached out and touched his arm. 'It's past now. It's gone. I don't look back. I don't want you to.'

He took her hand and raised it to kiss her fingers lightly. 'Think about coming out to Portugal.'

'You're not thinking of going!' Kit cried out in horror, when Petra recounted all this later on that day.

'No, I'm not. I told him I'd think about it and I have thought about it. I couldn't go, but you could.'

'Me?' Kit gaped. 'Have you gone nuts or something?'

323

'No,' Petra said calmly. 'I've come to my senses and it's time you came to yours, Kit darling.'

'You have gone nuts,' said Kit flatly.

Petra put down her coffee mug and said with surprising sharpness, 'This has got to stop, Kit!'

Surprised at her gentle sister's unusually abrasive tone, Kit asked, 'What?'

'All this blaming Gervase and letting it ruin all our lives. I couldn't go out to Portugal because all the time I was there, Gervase would be running round trying to do things for me and make it up to me somehow for – for everything that happened. He'd keep on saying he was sorry and I couldn't stick it. He's sorry, I'm sorry, you're sorry, Mum is sorry . . . we all are. But it doesn't change what happened. To let it ruin what's left of our lives is madness. In any case, he doesn't want *me*. He wants *you*. He always wanted you. When we were kids, he only ever wanted to hang out with you. I used to tag along, but I was in the way. I knew it then, and I still do. I've always been in the way, coming between you. Just like I am now.'

'I thought,' Kit said in a small voice, 'that later on, not when we were kids but when you got into your teens, you fancied him.'

'Yes, I did – then. Not now. Back then one of the reasons I wanted him so badly was because I knew in my heart I could never have him. I was jealous of you, Kit. I hopped into his car that night, when he offered me a lift home, because I thought, wonderful! I'll have Gervase to myself for a little while. I could see he wasn't fit to drive. If I hadn't been such a blind little idiot I'd have reached out and grabbed the car keys – and refused to hand them back to him. Think how much trouble that would have saved all of us! But no, I just thought I'd be with him. You weren't there that night. It was my chance. I was being selfish and incredibly naïve, obstinate and stupid,' Petra finished fiercely. 'So there!'

'You were seventeen, you can't blame yourself.'

'Don't patronise me, Kit, please don't do that. I've faced the truth. Do, please, face it, too.'

'All right, then, even if you were being all the things you've just said,' said Kit bleakly, 'and I'm not agreeing with you that you were . . . You've paid a high price.'

'And so have you!' Petra leaned forward. 'I wrecked the future I might have had. I've been lucky and made another decent one. But I wrecked yours, too, and you haven't. I've watched you try to make a life without Gervase in it. I watched you make that hopeless marriage to Hugh. I've watched you grow bitter and unhappy. It won't do, Kit. You've got to forgive him. You've got to give yourself a chance.'

'I can't do it,' Kit said quietly.

'Do what, forgive? You're as bad as he is. He won't forgive himself.'

'Gervase is OK. Even when Muriel took a swipe at him in the dark with that priest, she more or less missed. He's got a charmed existence. Don't feel sorry for him, Petra!' Kit burst out.

'What do you mean, charmed existence?' Petra shook her fist in frustration. 'Don't you see that Gervase can't come to terms with the past? What kind of life does he lead, stuck out there in Portugal with nothing to do? Afraid to come home, afraid to come back here and face *us*. Buying a horse – good grief! When was Gervase ever interested in horses? He's been doing anything that's come his way to fill his time. Living without the woman he's always wanted. You say I've paid a high price, but so has he!'

'What about Mum and Dad?' Kit asked suddenly, steering her

argument in a new direction. 'What about Dad dying full of bitterness, or Mum struggling to come to terms with it all? When I had to tell her Gervase was coming home, following the fire, she was terribly upset.'

'Yes, she was upset and one of the reasons for that was because she was worried what effect his return would have on *you*, not just on me. Have you really ever tried to talk to her about it, about how she feels deep down? Have you?' Petra challenged.

'I know how she feels!' her sister retorted.

'No, you don't, because you've never asked her, not recently. You've been so determined to think that everyone has been of a mind with *you* . . . and you've closed your mind completely to anything but brooding over the past.' Petra fell silent. 'If I'd spent all my time after the accident brooding over what had happened, I'd never have made a future for myself. I've said what I needed to say, that's it,' she finished.

Kit stood up. 'I refuse,' she said stiffly, 'to be cast as the villain of the piece.'

'I'm not casting you as a villain! Honestly, Kit . . .' Petra tailed off in exasperation. 'Just try, can't you? Can't you see, we've all got to move on?'

'And forgive? No, I won't.' Kit set down her mug and grabbed for her bag. 'I've got to go. I'll call by again tomorrow, or the day after.'

Kit didn't drive far from her sister's before she drew into the side of the road and did something she hadn't done in years – she gave way to tears. She was angry with herself for her weakness but the tears kept coming until in the end there just weren't any more, leaving her exhausted. She leaned across to the passenger side and pulled down the sun visor to peer into the mirror on the reverse.

'What a mess,' she muttered. Her face was blotchy, eyes reddened, nose glowing like Rudolph's. After a moment she drove off to a nearby pub that boasted a beer garden, and so had an additional ladies' powder room outside the main building, in a converted stable. Fortunately at this time of the afternoon it was free of customers fixing their make-up. Kit washed her face in the basin, dried it on paper towels and did her best with the lipstick and eyebrow pencil she found after a hunt through her bag. The result wouldn't have passed muster on one of those TV programmes where the presenter guarantees to make this week's guinea pig turn from frump to icon of chic with some eyeshadow and a new haircut, but it would have to do. She snapped the handbag shut, slung it over her shoulder and marched outside to her car.

She drove to her mother's house. There was no sign of Mrs Stapleton but the back door was unlocked and she walked in.

'Mum?' called Kit.

'In the conservatory!' came a faint reply.

Kit made her way towards the sound and came upon her mother surrounded by a motley collection of potted plants. All appeared to have suffered some disaster. Some had leaves that had withered and turned brown; others were reduced to mere stubs of branches and bare twigs. Kit thought privately that the plants looked the way she felt.

'Hi, Mum!' She kissed her mother's cheek. 'They don't look very lively.'

'They're all things I've brought in from the garden to overwinter in here. They wouldn't survive outside. They don't look much now but they've bloomed all summer and autumn, and done sterling service. These fuchsias, for instance, aren't a hardy variety so have to be brought under cover. Now I've cut them back I'm fairly certain they'll sprout new growth in the spring, and do well next year when I put them outside again.'

'Why not chuck them out and buy a new lot next year?'

Her mother looked at her reproachfully. 'I've got to know them. They're individuals. I've taken care of them. They've given such pleasure to the eye all summer. It would be churlish to abandon them now. Besides, I've told you, they'll come back.'

Kit drew a deep breath. 'Things do come back, don't they? People, too?'

'You want to talk about Gervase,' said Mary Stapleton, straightening up and dusting her hands together. 'I meant to ring you. A young police detective came to see me. Let me wash my hands. Just put the kettle on while I do, will you, dear?'

A little later, as they sat either side of the kitchen table, she asked Kit, 'Have you heard how Gervase is? I considered ringing the hospital, but I'm not a relative so I thought they wouldn't tell me.'

'Oh, he's OK. He's been let out of the hospital and he's been to see Petra this morning,' Kit told her with a note of exasperation in her voice. 'Gervase always survives. He's indestructible, like some sort of plague they can't wipe out. He's moved out of the hotel and gone to Serena's place, to be looked after by her. You see? Fallen on his feet!'

'Oh, Kit, dear . . .' said her mother with a sigh. 'I wish you didn't hate him the way you do.'

'Don't you hate him?' asked Kit, surprised. 'After what happened to Petra?'

'I'm very angry about what happened to Petra. I'll always be that. No, I don't hate Gervase. If he'd been a stranger – at the time of the crash – it might have been different. But I knew him as a little boy. I saw him grow up. You and he were such good pals. What happened was terrible. But Gervase has suffered, too.'

'How can you say that?' Kit gasped. 'And please don't tell me he had a rotten childhood. It doesn't mean you have to grow up to drink and drive.'

'He didn't have a good childhood,' agreed her mother. 'But you're right, having an unhappy childhood doesn't excuse what you do later. Gervase went wrong when he was about nineteen. But he hasn't been in any trouble I've heard about since he left here, and went to live in Portugal. On the other hand, I've not heard that he's done anything positive. It saddens me that he's wasting his life. He's harmed himself by his actions.' She broke off and smiled at her daughter's outraged expression.

'I'm not defending him, Kit. I'm not making excuses for him. To see Petra as she is now breaks my heart; even though I admire the way she's fought back. I'll never feel differently about the accident. But I also feel sorry for Gervase in so many ways. I certainly don't let myself hate him. Hatred harms the people who hate, far more than the one who is hated. Do try and remember that, Kit. Hatred eats you up. Sometimes, when I look at you or listen to you talk, I'm afraid you've become bitter. I know you aren't happy. That failed marriage to Hugh didn't help matters, either. All of that has to sadden me. But Petra hasn't let it eat her up. It hasn't made her bitter. Don't let it do that to you, please, Kit.'

'Petra's forgiven him,' Kit said bleakly.

'I know.'

'She told you?' Kit stared at her.

'No, she doesn't have to tell me. I know my child.' Mary Stapleton sipped her coffee. 'Will you have a piece of my fruitcake? I must say it turned out rather well. Sometimes they sink in the middle, but this one didn't.'

'Is all this,' Kit asked in a low, tight voice, ignoring the invitation, 'what you told the copper who came to see you?'

'I was going to tell you about that, wasn't I?' Her mother had got up to fetch the battered old cake tin that Kit remembered so well. It had a Victorian Christmas scene on the lid, much scraped and faded now. It showed carol singers standing knee-deep in snow. How long ago childhood seemed and how carefree.

'His name was Stubbs,' her mother continued, returning with the tin. 'Detective Constable Stubbs, like the artist. You know, the one who painted all those horses. He was plain-clothes, the detective, I mean. He was a very nice young man and, by a stroke of luck, I'd not long taken this cake out of the oven. He ate two pieces, even though it was still a bit warm. I hope it didn't give him indigestion.'

'And you told him you had nothing but kind thoughts about Gervase, and didn't make up any nasty notes threatening him harm,' Kit said crossly. 'Sorry, Mum, but really, I'm beginning to wonder if I'm the only person left who sees Gervase for the waste of space he is!'

'If you'd spoken like that to the police, they would have thought you'd concocted that note!' her mother said crisply. 'Although I like to think that neither I, nor you, would ever have done anything so pretty and vicious. We know now it was Muriel Pickering responsible for all of it. That did shock me. But if you thought Gervase had a bad childhood, well, you never knew old Major Pickering. He was a tyrant. But for Muriel to behave as she did . . . I can't bear to think of her striking down that young man and lighting the fire.' She sighed and shook her head. 'She was always an unhappy woman and she let it eat into her, with what terrible results!'

'All right, all right,' said Kit, 'I do get the message.'

Her mother smiled. 'How is the cake?'

'Very good, one of the best you've done in a long time.'

'Yes, I thought so.'

After a pause Kit said sadly, 'I wish Muriel had let well alone and not done the horrible things she did. I wish the fire hadn't brought Gervase back; and now I wish he'd just go back to Portugal.'

Her mother looked at her downcast eyes and miserable face. 'I dare say he will, if he has no reason to stay here. But before he does, do think about making your peace with him, Kit, won't you?'

Chapter 23

For a brief time Gervase had the Foscott house to himself. Serena had collected Charlie from school and taken her into Cheltenham to keep a dental appointment. Reggie was at work. Gervase had switched on the fake log fire in the hearth to boost the inadequate central heating and draped himself over the chesterfield to tackle the *Daily Telegraph* crossword. When he heard a car draw up outside he thought that, now Serena had come back unexpectedly early, her first action on entering the room would be to turn off the fake logs, just when the additional heating was beginning to make some impression on the atmosphere. He folded the *Daily Telegraph* with a sigh, slid off the chesterfield and went to the window.

When he saw Kit getting out of her car he blinked, at first unable to credit his eyes. Then he went to pull open the front door as she approached.

'Hi,' he said.

'Hello,' said Kit, standing rigidly some four feet away as if at the barrier marking an exclusion zone. 'I came to see how you are.'

'I'm fine and I'm not contagious. Won't you come in?'

Kit sidled past him into the hall and halted there.

He stood back and gestured towards the room he'd quitted. 'I've managed to get one spot in this fridge of a house just about warm enough for human existence.'

'OK,' said Kit, and followed him to the dusty drawing room. She sat down awkwardly on a chair and it twanged under her.

'All Serena's furniture is like that,' said Gervase. 'Would you like a drop of Reggie's whisky? It's decent malt. One of his clients must have given it to him.'

'I'm driving. Well, all right. Just a small one, lots of water,' Kit said. 'Thank you.'

As she accepted the tumbler he handed her, she repeated her enquiry after his health.

'I'm all right,' he told her, retaking his seat on the chesterfield and slouching back. 'My head's still sore but there's no damage to anything that matters, no brain damage. I suppose you'll tell me there's not a lot of brain there to harm.'

'I wasn't going to say that,' Kit said crossly. 'And don't make me angry because I've come here to be *pleasant*!'

'I look forward to it,' said Gervase with a smile.

But his eyes were sad, and Kit saw it. She thought ruefully that she probably wouldn't have seen it, before her talk with her mother. She would just have thought he was being flippant again. Whereas he was protecting himself in the only way he could. Mum is right and he's wretched. *Well, he should be!* Damn! cursed Kit silently. Damn, damn, damn it all!

Then she thought, *but so am I wretched, and it's getting us nowhere. Mum and Petra are right about that, too.*

Aloud she said, 'Petra and my mother both think I should bury the hatchet – and no jokes about that, please, either.' She sipped her whisky and water.

'Suits me,' Gervase said. 'But it's no use saying you forgive me if you don't . . . because it won't work, Kit. You were always the most honest of beings and lying doesn't become you.'

'I didn't say I forgave you. And I've got a question for you before we can discuss this any further.'

'Go ahead,' he urged when she fell silent again and stared into her glass.

'Did you really ever think I set fire to Key House?' Kit raised her eyes to his surprised face. 'You did ask at The Royal Oak if I knew who did it. Then, when we were at Petra's cottage, you asked if I'd pushed that stupid note under your door.'

Gervase had the grace to look embarrassed. 'Yes, I did. That upset Petra, didn't it.'

'It upset *me*, you idiot!' Kit burst out, leaning forward. 'Did you really imagine me concocting anonymous letters or, even worse, creeping round with a box of matches? Perhaps you thought I'd killed that poor man, too?'

'No, no! Of course I didn't. Look.' Gervase put down his glass to hold up both hands, palms outwards, in a gesture of appeasement. 'I asked you to be honest with me and I'll be honest with you. When Reggie first informed me of the fire – when I was still in Portugal – I did, just for a mad minute or two, wonder if you'd finally taken revenge. I never thought you'd *killed* anyone. I was never crazy enough even to imagine you might kill *me*! If Pietrangelo had been attacked by someone else earlier, you could have lit the fire without realising he was lying unconcious in the building. The place was used by dropouts. Perhaps you hadn't seen him . . .' Gervase let the sentence trail away as it was obvious every word made things worse.

'Great!' returned Kit through gritted teeth.

'But as soon as I saw you again, when you walked into the lounge at The Royal Oak to tell me off for calling on Petra, I knew you were the same Kit as ever was, and you hadn't done it.'

'You still asked if I'd written the letter, in front of my sister!' she accused him.

'Well, all right, I still asked about that although of course I knew it wouldn't be your style. I told Campbell you wouldn't have done it.'

'Oh? Discussed it with her? Was I top of her list?'

'No – how do I know? I just said to her she could count out the Stapleton family.'

'Mum too?' Kit's face had turned an alarming shade of red.

Gervase held up his hands placatingly. 'Do calm down, you look as if you're going to throw some sort of fit. I agree it was stupid of me to ask you about the letter in front of Petra. As you are fond of reminding me, I do stupid things. But I'm not going to be like Poppy Trenton, apologising to anyone who will listen for a careless remark to Muriel Pickering. I shouldn't have asked you but I still, somehow, wanted to hear you say you hadn't done it. Call it a desire for reassurance. Call it whatever you like. I'm not going to go on apologising for that.'

There was a silence. 'And the crash that put my sister in a wheelchair or forces her to creep round on crutches? Is that also to be written off as another piece of stupidity?'

'No!' Gervase said savagely. 'Don't be a bloody idiot, Kit! That's entirely different. There isn't a day of my life—' He broke off.

After a moment Kit said quietly, 'I do realise that. I'm sorry. I shouldn't have said what I said just then.'

'I should have said this, you shouldn't have said that – are we going to continue this conversation on those lines indefinitely?' Gervase asked crisply. 'Because if so, it will be extremely boring, get us nowhere, and you are going to have to manage it by yourself, one sided.'

'No. But any other conversation will have to mean both of us trying to understand.'

'Put your cards on the table, Kit,' Gervase invited. 'Let's see what I'm supposed to try about.'

'Fine. It isn't just about realising how you feel or my forgiving you. My problem is that I can't *forget*, Gervase!' Kit burst out wildly. 'How is that possible when I see my sister every other day, and even if *she* has forgiven you? I suppose you might say, if she is the injured party and she's found it in her heart . . . then I, as a mere bystander, ought to find it in mine. But it's somehow easier to forgive than to forget.'

'Neither can I forget,' Gervase told her. 'So what do we do?'

'I don't know,' whispered Kit miserably. 'I want everything to be as it was once, but one can't go back, can one?'

'One can go forward,' Gervase said, after a moment.

'That's what my mother and Petra keep telling me. It's not that I don't want to do that. I will try. Truly, Gervase, I will. But I find it very hard. It's like crawling up an icy rock face and slipping back down all the time.'

After a moment he asked quietly, 'Do you hate me?'

'No, I don't hate you.' Kit sounded tired. 'I thought I did once, because I was so furious. But I don't. I don't want us to be enemies, or go on fighting. If that's burying the hatchet, then consider it buried. But to be friends again as we were . . . Much as I want that, how can we get there?' She raised a sorrowful face to his.

'I'm glad at least you don't hate me. I've never wanted us to be enemies, Kit, God knows, quite the reverse. Can we call a truce, start again from there?' Gervase raised his eyebrows in question and, a couple of seconds later, his whisky tumbler.

'We can start from there,' said Kit after a moment, and joined in raising her tumbler in salutation to whatever future lay ahead.

Of all places to eat, thought Carter, those located in motorway service stations, though no doubt offering an excellent opportunity to rest and refresh oneself, remained probably the least inviting to the eye. The arrangement for returning Millie to her mother was that he would bring his daughter here, a convenient halfway point between their places of residence, and Sophie would collect her in a ceremonial handover. He and Millie had arrived early and Mille had demanded a burger. So now Carter sat gazing over a sea of plastic table tops, with a cup of tea in front of him, while Millie ate her burger and chips. From time to time she offered him a chip. But then, she'd also offered MacTavish a chip. MacTavish was propped against a menu card and gazed at the scene in his usual critical fashion. You and I, MacTavish, Carter mentally addressed the bear, are probably in agreement for the first and only time. Make the most of it.

He ought to be making the most of the last fifteen or twenty minutes he was able, if lucky, to spend with Millie until her next visit. But as usual he was stuck for something to say to her. It wasn't that there was nothing he wanted to say, but he couldn't find the way. At a nearby table sat a family of five, all of whom looked as if they had eaten nothing but burger and chips for their entire lives, and who were managing to tuck into yet more, while conducting a lively discussion at the same time. It was more of an argument than a discussion, perhaps, but they were communicating.

'I hope you haven't been bored, Millie,' he said now, avoiding MacTavish's beady gaze. 'I'm sorry I had to go to work and leave you with Auntie Monica. But you like her, don't you?'

'Yes,' said Millie. She stopped eating to suck at the straw sticking out of her milkshake. 'Did the old woman really kill that man?'

'You've been watching it all on local television news, I suppose?'

Millie nodded enthusiastically. 'I thought that man, Gervase, had done it. But then the old woman tried to kill him as well. Are you sure that man Gervase didn't kill anyone?'

'I'm sure, Millie.'

Gervase left someone in a wheelchair for life, thought Carter. His actions as a young man probably set Muriel on the path to murder. But he hadn't killed anyone. He'd messed up lives, including his own. Perhaps the best you could say was that he hadn't killed outright.

Muriel might have taken the path to murder anyway. One couldn't overlook the sudden demise of the tyrannical Major Pickering, found floating in the river with his fishing rod beside him. Not difficult to creep up behind him and give him a good shove. But that was the secret of a successful murder: no one ever suspects it. Or not until thirty years later when there's no evidence and speculation is all it can remain. Perhaps it planted a seed of confidence in Muriel's mind. You can do it and get away with it. If she did, of course, push her old dad into the river. He must put that idea out of his head. No evidence, Superintendent Carter! he told himself sternly. No hard evidence, no investigation. Only in books do detectives have the time and funds to chase down hunches.

'There's Mummy's car!' announced Millie, pointing past him towards the plate-glass window.

Carter turned round and saw a blue Mazda easing its way into a parking slot.

'Eat up,' he said. 'We'd better go out and meet her.'

'I've finished,' said Millie. She scrambled to her feet, collected

MacTavish and her pink tote bag and trotted beside him out into the car park.

Carter was carrying her suitcase. He saw Sophie getting out of her car and at the same time felt Millie's small hand slip into his free one. He looked down at her and they exchanged smiles.

'Hello, darling,' exclaimed Sophie, swooping on Millie and hugging her. 'Hi, Ian, everything OK?' They exchanged chaste pecks on cheeks.

'Everything's fine,' he told his ex-wife.

'Daddy's been investigating a murder!' Millie announced gleefully.

'Oh, really?' That twitch of Sophie's right eyebrow that Carter remembered so well.

'Always something happening in the world of crime!' he said cheerfully.

'So I discovered.' Sophie's voice was icy now.

'But Millie had great fun with Aunt Monica, didn't you?' he asked his daughter.

'Oh yes. I thought I knew who the murderer was. He was staying at a hotel near Auntie Monica's cottage. But it wasn't him, after all, it was an old woman. She tried to kill the man I thought was the murderer. He looked like a murderer.' Millie paused and added regretfully, 'I met him; but I didn't meet the real one.'

'Let's be thankful for small mercies,' Sophie said.

'She learned all about it on the local television news,' Carter explained. 'I didn't talk about it with her.'

'I'm sure. Well, we must be off. Thank you for taking care of her at such short notice.'

'Any time. She is my daughter.' He heard his voice harden and added hurriedly, 'My good wishes to Rodney. Was New York fun?'

'Oh, yes, thanks. It was well worth it. Rodney had lots of meetings. Come along, Millie.'

Carter kissed his child goodbye and watched her led to her mother's car. As she was scrambling into the back seat, he heard her voice clearly floating towards him.

'And Daddy's got a girlfriend. Her name is Jess.'

Sophie straightened up and turned to look at him.

He waved a hand from side to side signalling, he hoped, that this wasn't so. All he got was another twitch of that right eyebrow.

'And she's a police inspector . . .' were the last words he heard from Millie as the car door was closed smartly on her.

It was Tom at the door of her flat again.

'Now what?' asked Jess unkindly. 'You can come in provided you're not going to ask me to solve all the problems of your love life.'

'Haven't got one any more,' said Tom simply, taking her words as an invitation to enter. 'Madison has dumped me. Well, she's made up her mind to take the research post in Australia and until she's leaves, she's going to be far too busy to make time for me.'

'I'm sorry, Tom,' Jess said contritely. 'I shouldn't have been so unkind to you. I'm really sorry, too, that things didn't work out between you and Madison.'

'I've got over it,' said Tom. 'It's been a learning curve. I am not indispensable in Madison's life, or in any other female's, but I do hope I still have you as a friend.' He looked at her hopefully.

'Of course you do.'

'Good,' said Tom, 'then let's go out for a curry.'